THE ROMANCE OF A MILLION DOLLARS

By
ELIZABETH DEJEANS

Author of
THE TIGER'S COAT, NOBODY'S CHILD,
THE MORETON MYSTERY, Etc.

INDIANAPOLIS
THE BOBBS-MERRILL COMPANY
PUBLISHERS

THE ROMANCE OF A MILLION DOLLARS

THE ROMANCE OF
A MILLION DOLLARS

CHAPTER I

MARIE ANGOULEME shoved her modest suit-case beneath the seat with a sense of satisfaction. She was going to have the section to herself. *Bon!*

They were leaving Buffalo in the murky darkness of a March evening. Wind-driven sleet peppered the windows of the car and melted quickly into zigzag rivulets that blurred the lights of the city; the car was oppressively hot. The passengers were settling themselves in the usual fashion, disposing of their luggage and preparing for the dining- or the smoking-car, with the porter much in evidence.

Marie Angouleme, though a young person, was an experienced and an economical traveler: she had dined at a lunch-counter near the station and intended to retire as soon as possible; the journey across from Canada had been wet, cold and wearisome. So she asked the porter to make up her berth at once and she went to the dressing-room; at so early an hour, she was less likely to be disturbed; she had noticed that there were many women passengers in the car and only a few men.

When Marie returned, the car had cleared somewhat. Her berth was shrouded in green, and the porter was busied making up other berths. Marie noticed that the berth across from hers was unoccupied and, as the berths on either side of it had been made up, she had a nook in which to open her suit-case and take out night-dress and kimono and boudoir-cap. She gathered her curly black hair into a wad on the top of her head, put on the much befrilled cap which left little else than her nose and mouth visible, disposed of her suit-case, then crept into her berth for a more complete undressing.

There was not much of length or breadth to Marie Angouleme, but stretched at her length, such as it was, she meditated upon her adventure. In a soft leather belt about her small waist was her entire fortune, one hundred dollars, and several papers which she valued highly. She was going to New York, which she had never seen, not to make her fortune she had decided modestly, but to earn a competence. With her qualifications that should be possible. Canada was so sad since the war, and quite unbearable with both her good aunt and her dear father dead. And to work as a servant in a place where she was known was too mortifying. Far better to work in a strange place. There were, of course, numberless intelligence offices in the city of New York, but what she must do, even before leaving the train in the morning, was to buy newspapers and study the advertisements; it might result in much saving of time. Thus ran Marie's thoughts, anxious yet determined—until the cradling of the train lulled her to sleep.

It was the cessation of motion that waked Marie, and subdued voices. Passengers must have entered, Marie thought, possibly some one for the upper berth? She raised the blind a little and saw the lights of what must be a considerable city. Then she peeped into the isle, for some one was speaking to the porter. It was a tall woman muffled in furs and elegantly gowned. Marie knew about furs: merely by touch she could tell the denomination and the quality of a pelt. These were sables, the real Siberian, not American marten, and must be very valuable. They framed a striking face, a woman of indeterminate age but not old; strong, very regular features, and lashes and brows as black as jet; her eyes were light, however, which made her face the more striking. Her hair was night-black and very abundant, and her lips were red and her color high,—a vivid brunette and with an air of great distinction. She was taking the unoccupied berth opposite.

Marie studied the woman's face with interest and, being an opportunist, she wondered if in the morning she might be able to win the favor of so wealthy a person. It might be of great assistance to her in New York, to make such a friend. The woman told the porter to call her at seven in the morning, then disappeared behind the curtains of her berth and the light overhead grew dim. Marie twisted about, seeking slumber; and, finally, curled up and with her hand under her cheek, she lost consciousness.

How long afterward, she did not know, Marie waked with a sense of discomfort. Her limbs were cramped and her left hand numb. She was rubbing sensation into it when startled into consciousness of a loss: her wrist-watch was not on her wrist. Stolen? . . . Marie's hands went frantically to her waist. The good Lord was kind! The money and papers and the address of the New York boarding-house were there! But the beautiful wrist-watch which had been a gift from her dear father!

Then Marie remembered. Imbecile! She had taken it off when she had washed in the dressing-room. She had put it on the rack for towels—almost certainly it was gone forever! The tears came in her eyes. But she would go instantly and see. Marie pulled on her shoes, gathered her kimono about her, and sped down the car. When half-way down, she realized that she was going in the wrong direction, her berth was fourth from the vestibule in which was the ladies' room. She hurried back. In the dressing-room was a row of newly arranged towels, and Marie's heart sank to such an extent that the rebound was upsetting—under one of the towels was her watch, unharmed.

After kissing it with French fervor, Marie returned to her berth and crept in . . . but upon a terrific surprise, a blanketed body which started convulsively. For an instant, Marie was conscious of that only, a

body that leapt up and away from her. The next instant, she was seized and flung backward in the berth,
hot powerful hands gripped her throat, a body knelt
on her chest pinioning her arms, and a face panted into
her own; she was choked and smothered into an intolerable agony against which she writhed and struggled
in a blind animal frenzy. . . . Then suddenly the
grip on her throat loosened, the weight on her chest
lifted, and she was thrust into the aisle and fell to the
floor. Her congested eyes could not see and the roar-
ing in her ears deafened her, but, with the instinct to
flee, she crawled for a distance, then staggered to her
feet, plunged into the vestibule, still strangling and
eyes bursting. The movement of the train threw her
back and forth, thrust her finally against a door.

When Marie returned to a consciousness that was
not merely mad terror and a desperate struggle for
breath, she found herself inside the dressing-room
which she had left a few minutes before; she was
braced against the door. Her throat within and without burned as if seared by a hot iron and there were
shooting pains in her chest. Though she could see,
black spots swam before her eyes, springing up and
down in queer time to the violent throbbing pains in
her chest. Her gasps were audible to herself now.

But no one tried to thrust the door in; there was
no outcry, only the noises of the train. She remained
unmolested and the pains in her chest lessened and
connected thoughts began to form in her aching head.
She felt weak and sick, but, with much effort, she

thought it out, the thing she had done: it was the fur, that woman's sables lying in the berth and against which Marie's head and neck had been pressed, which made it all clear.

It was so natural and dangerous a mistake: when she had started for the dressing-room to look for her watch, she had gone in the wrong direction and then had turned about and that in itself was confusing; then she had been excited at finding her watch, which was confusing also. Most certainly when she had hastened back to the berth she knew that hers was fourth from the vestibule, but it was the *left-hand*, not the *right-hand* berth into which she had crept; it was the berth of the woman with the beautiful furs; when flung back, her neck had felt the furs. That woman was terribly strong; her hands had gripped like steel. The creature had first leaped away from her as if afraid of being seized herself, then she had gripped her with the intention of choking her to death. It was some second thought that had made the woman cast her forth.

But why no outcry? Why not the porter called? It was utterly unlike most women, not to notify the porter. Most women would scream, not silently and violently attack an intruder, and attack to kill, with a vicious determination and a consciousness of strength; then, as if having decided that the intruder was not dangerous, cast her out and keep silently within her berth. A thief who feared capture would behave in that way, but not the woman who had nothing to fear;

a murderess fleeing from a crime might be ready to murder again rather than be taken prisoner, but no woman innocent of guilt would act as that creature had.

Marie was well acquainted with danger and ghastly wounds and sudden death. The whine of shot and bursting of shells were customary things; she had been in France throughout the war. It was experience in danger that helped her to rally so soon, then act with caution.

So she examined her bruised and swollen throat in the mirror, wrapped a towel soaked in ice-water about it, and sat down then to think, and her decision was this: to the porter, to her fellow passengers, not a word. The woman had boarded the train long after every one was abed and could have no idea who was in the berth opposite. She could not have known even to what berth the intruder belonged, for Marie was certain that when she had crept into the woman's berth she had been sound asleep, for she had started so convulsively and had gasped. If she hid the bruises on her throat, the woman would not be likely to recognize her, for it had been dark in the berth, and when she had crawled away the woman could not have seen her features, for the light was dim and her frilled cap must have concealed her face almost entirely.

Marie decided to stay where she was until daylight; that was not far off, for it was now five o'clock. Then she would ring for the porter and ask him to bring her suit-case and her clothes, then there would be no chance of the woman's recognizing her cap and kimono. Marie was terrified at the possibility of being recognized; she wished that she could leave the train without having to return to her berth. She hoped intensely that the woman would leave the train before daylight; if she was a criminal afraid of detection, she would be likely to leave before any one was stirring. Marie's flesh crawled when she thought of the creature's proximity; she felt a sick terror. Ugh! That hot panting breath in her face! The terror of those murderous hands at her throat! Never in her life had she felt such a horror of a human being.

CHAPTER II

THOUGH fully dressed, Marie lingered in the dressing-room until two women entered with their bags and crowded her out. When they pushed the door open, Marie's heart stopped for an instant, for it might be her assailant; her dread of the woman had increased rather than lessened; the more she thought of her experience, the more certain she was that the woman was a criminal of some sort. When the porter had accepted a generous fee and had brought her things to Marie, he had shown no signs of knowing anything about what had occurred, and the two women who filled the dressing-room elbowed her in the usual fashion, without curiosity or interest. Certainly the woman had said nothing to any one; she wanted secrecy.

Marie took her suit-case and went cautiously to her section. Probably in recognition of her generous fee, the porter had put up her berth; the berth opposite was shrouded still, so were all the others. Marie had hoped intensely that the woman had gone; evidently she was still there. It was nearly seven o'clock, the hour at which the woman had told the porter to call her, and Marie braced herself for the time when she would emerge from her berth. Marie had wound a scarf

9

about her swollen and aching throat and, in addition, she put her fur about her shoulders; she sat looking out at the sleet encrusted landscape, but vividly conscious of the close drawn curtains of the woman's berth.

Marie breathed quickly when, at seven o'clock, the porter appeared and said to the closed curtains, "It's seven o'clock, Madame." Marie heard no answer, but the porter departed as if satisfied with having done his duty.

"She is there," Marie said to herself, and continued to look at the landscape. She decided that just as soon as she could escape to the dining-car she would do so and that she would remain there as long as possible.

But in a few minutes the porter returned and repeated his call: "It's after seven, Madame." This time he parted the curtains and looked in, then drew them aside: there was no one in the berth. He looked puzzled. "I ain't seen her get out," he said more to himself than to Marie, and looked under the berth. Then he looked the berth over and pulled the tumbled covers apart and, finally, went forward, Marie guessed, to the ladies' dressing-room.

In a few minutes he returned. "Has you seen the lady what was in that berth?" he inquired. "She ain't in the dressin'-room nor waitin' for the diner."

Marie was more determined than ever not to confide her experience to any one. If she should tell of it now, she would be suspected of strange conduct. Evidently the woman was a criminal of some sort and she had left the train as quickly and as secretly as possible.

"I have seen no one leave the berth since I came here," she said. It was the first time she had spoken aloud since she had been attacked; forming the words hurt her; her voice was husky.

"It's queer," the porter muttered. "I'd like to know where she got off at—we ain't had a stop and only one slow-up since midnight. She were bound for New York too." And he left the car, probably to consult with the conductor.

Marie welcomed the first call to breakfast; if the passengers were questioned, she might escape. Food was an impossibility, but she managed to swallow some coffee and spent as much time as she could over it. She returned to her car with trepidation, but everything was just as usual there; the porter, his black face inscrutable, sat in the rear of the car.

Muffled to the chin, Marie sat waiting for the morning papers. She reflected that it was a very good thing that she was inured to hardships, else she would be ill, for her throat was so painful. She felt much worse than she had ever felt after a hard day of ambulance driving in France. The night's experience was the worst she had ever known; she had come nearer to death than she had when a piece of shell had torn her shoulder.

Such persons as took notice of Marie Angouleme thought her a small person to be traveling alone, very young and velvety-eyed and innocent-faced—she looked a young nineteen. She looked foreign, as if her accent would be piquant and her little hands given to gestures. In traveling there is almost always some woman, either motherly, or curious, or ill-intentioned, who takes an interest in pretty girls who are traveling alone. It was a somewhat flamboyant woman who came to Marie's seat and asked, "Have you any friends in New York?"

Marie's velvety eyes lost their softness. She looked the woman up and down, then turned her back on her; Marie Angouleme was not an inexperienced country child.

CHAPTER III

TWO days later, at Kent House, on the north shore of Long Island, the Dunbarton-Kent family had just adjourned to the library for after-luncheon coffee. The conversation had been desultory, which may be the case either when a family group is at ease or at swords' points. Mrs. Dunbarton-Kent had settled her girth in a powerful armchair and her deceased husband's two nephews and niece, the children respectively of his three brothers, had chosen their positions.

West Dunbarton-Kent was seated in a rocker and cupped in his hand was his gold cachou-case. Yet West was by no means an exquisite. Though very blond and regular featured, only a little over medium height and gracefully slender, he looked an athletic and capable young man. He had a clear eye and a frank and exceedingly charming manner and, despite his almost flaxen fairness, he was very good-looking. He was so alertly alive and his expression was so pleasant; there was a laughter-loving air about him which the gravity of Kent House could not subdue; he seemed to find amusement even in his after-his-meal cachou, as if good-naturedly bent upon introducing a touch of frivolity to the ceremonious monotony of the Kent House family luncheon.

Breck Dunbarton-Kent, his cousin, who stood with his back to the mantelpiece and facing his aunt and cousins, was broader and taller than West and was as markedly dark as his cousin West was light. But his features were much the same, the straight Dunbarton-Kent nose, the same light blue eyes and well-chiseled mouth and chin. It was his very black hair and brows and lashes and the difference in his expression which made him such a contrast to his cousin West. There was a shadowed look about his dark-lashed eyes, and his face was so immobile as to be remarkable. His was not exactly a sullen personality, unapproachable rather, distinguished but too unsmiling. He was thirty, the same age as West, and three years older than his cousin Bella.

Of Bella it might be said, that one of the beautiful long icicles which hung from the eves of Kent House had draped itself in artistic garments, had haloed its regular-featured face with cornsilk hair and had invaded the family circle. She was a superbly built woman, wide-shouldered and small-hipped and with extraordinarily long fair lashes and surprisingly light blue eyes. She sat at a distance, by the window, but with her back to the lovely view of the sound. Her fingers knitted a pale blue sweater for her own wearing and her cold eyes were on the group by the fire.

Apparently all was as it should be in a well-bred family of millions and social prominence, but there was an ominous undercurrent of which every one present was keenly aware, even Buckingham Gibbs, the butler.

He had served them in his usual impeccable fashion and
now was standing aside awaiting the proper moment
for removing the coffee service.   Seemingly he was
wrapt in the contemplation of his Roman nose, nevertheless he had an exact knowledge of the attitude and
the expression of every one present.   Then his alert
ear caught the sound of a bell and he withdrew noiselessly.

In a few moments he returned and announced,
"There is a young girl to see you, Madame—for the
position of chauffeur."

Mrs. Dunbarton-Kent held her coffee-cup suspended.
"A girl! . . . For chauffeur?"   She tipped the scales
at three hundred, a tall big-framed woman grown fat,
and her voice had kept pace with her body, for it was
an astonishing baritone and volumed just now by secret
irritation.   The entire family looked at Gibbs as if he
had ruffled frayed nerves.

"Yes, Madame.   She states that she is an accomplished chauffeur."

"Haslett would hardly play a joke on me—it's a he,
not a she-chauffeur I want," Mrs. Dunbarton-Kent remarked forcibly.

"Yes, Madame.   But I thought you would want
the matter brought to you."

Mrs. Dunbarton-Kent's lips parted, then closed, and,
for a moment, she sat motionless.   Then she heaved
her chair about so she could see every one in the room.
"Bring her in," she said.

Gibbs withdrew and left a waiting silence behind

him. When he returned, he announced with unabated dignity, "Marie Angora Lamb, Madame."

The expected thing would have been at least a smile, even from Bella, and certainly a chuckle from Mrs. Dunbarton-Kent, for she possessed a sort of grim humor; that was why, ordinarily, she appreciated Gibbs, who had no sense of humor whatever. But, as it was, the girl who emerged from behind Gibbs' portly form was subjected on every hand to an intent and silent scrutiny.

They saw a small girl enveloped from cheek to heels in an arctic-looking coat of rough fur and wearing a tannish-brown service cap. Nestled in the collar of the coat was a rounded chin and a mouth with an upward turn at the corners. The nose was of no particular moment, and the remainder of the face was principally eyes, large and black and velvety and softened still more by a tangle of black lashes. It was a warmly tanned and appealingly smiling little face, piquant rather than pretty. They all noticed that she was smiling and that she glanced swiftly about the room, then that her eyes widened suddenly when they rested on Breck and that she lost her smile in a caught breath. Her eyes were startled when she looked at Mrs. Dunbarton-Kent and her color rose.

"Well? What do you want of me?" Hulked in her chair and with a red light in her small brown eyes, Mrs. Dunbarton-Kent resembled a suspicious bear.

"You—you wished a chauffeur—Madame?" Marie faltered.

"Yes. Were *you* proposing to drive me about?"

"But—yes, Madame."

"Who sent you here?"

"I was not sent, Madame—I came because of hearing that a chauffeur was wanted at this place," Marie said confusedly. "It was also because of an advertisement."

"Indeed!"

Marie conquered her embarrassment. She had committed no crime in coming here, though they all looked at her as if she had. "It happened in this way, Madame," she said resolutely. "I must seek employment, so I looked in the papers for advertisements. There I saw an advertisement for a chauffeur who was accomplished and could give only the best of references. He was asked to go to a room with the number 906, in the Franck Building upon Wall Street, to present his references. I went to that place. I was met first by a boy,"—the color deepened in Marie's tanned cheeks, for the experience had been an unpleasant one— "then, he took me to a stenographer to whom I explained and who said finally that the gentleman who was to decide upon me was not there for that day. Then I left the room, but at the elevator was standing a lady waiting like myself to go down, and she asked me what I was doing in the office of 'the great Mr. Haslett,' for so she called the gentleman whose name was upon the door of the room to which the advertisement had directed me.

"I do not usually speak with strangers, Madame,

but she had a pleasant face and a humorous manner. I liked her, so I told her and showed her the advertisement. She drew me aside then and asked me about myself and my qualifications, then told me to write down the address of your home, and your name, and directed me just how to come here. Her name she would not tell me; she laughed only and said, 'You go talk to Mrs. Dunbarton-Kent—I know she'll take you.' So, Madame, I came at once," Marie concluded resolutely.

There was perfect silence until Mrs. Dunbarton-Kent asked, "What did the woman look like?"

"She was not tall, Madame, though taller than I, and I think a little large, though I could not tell so well because she wore a very beautiful long fur coat. Her face is round and she has small black eyes that twinkle. All her features are small but very full of fun."

"How old a woman?" Mrs. Dunbarton-Kent demanded.

Marie hesitated. "It is a little difficult to tell, Madame, for she is made to look quite a young woman."

From any but so grave a company, Marie's earnest desire to render a truthful account would have elicited a smile. But Mrs. Dunbarton-Kent persisted grimly, "Uses bad grammar?"

Marie was anxious not to be disparaging. "A little bad perhaps, Madame, but my own English is so uncertain that I should not criticize."

There was another moment of silence, then Mrs.

Dunbarton-Kent asked curtly, "What's your correct name? Where did you come from?"

There had been something breathless and uncomfortable about that moment's silence that oppressed Marie, but she answered bravely, "Marie Angouleme is my name, Madame. You see, Madame, I am twenty-three, quite more grown up than I look. Since years I drove for my father. He was a trader in skins, in Canada, and to get them we must go distances. When we could we went by automobile. When quite in the North Country, we went by sleighs. The roads were difficult and about the insides of cars and their troubles I know everything. Though I appear little and without much strength, I can place a tire upon any car, and the batteries of them I understand perfectly. A car should be kept clean within and shining without like a beautiful house—like this one. I love a car that shines. . . . Then, Madame, came the war. My father was a French Canadian and a patriot, and he said all the time, 'Eh, Marie, if you were a boy, you must go, but the good Lord did not give me a son, only a little girl.' I wished also that I was a boy. Then, in a little while,"—her softly accented voice thickened—"my father—he died. There was nothing in money for me, but that did not matter, for I went to France to drive ambulances."

She paused to sigh. "But that is all over! . . . I remained in France after the war, yet I wept sometimes for Canada, so I came back. But without my father I could not bear it there. I must work for my living and this country is very wonderful for those who must work, so I came to New York. It seemed to me quite as possible for me to be a chauffeur as for a man, so I gave attention to such advertisements. I brought my papers of service in France and came as that lady directed, inquiring my way to Kent House. But first I went to quite the wrong house, the large old house which is nearest to this. There is a man there who was —unpleasant—but now I am safely here."

Her recital was followed by another pronounced silence. Finally Mrs. Dunbarton-Kent said, "Let me see those papers."

Marie saluted, then took from her bosom a packet. She courtesied when she presented it. The military salute and the feminine courtesy were a quaint combination, but no one smiled and no one spoke, though Mrs. Dunbarton-Kent spent some moments over the papers. Then she looked up and asked abruptly, "What did that drunken beast at whose house you inquired say to you?"

Among other unrepeatable things derogatory to the mistress of Kent House, the man had said, "So, you pretty little chicken, you're proposing to chauffeur that old hippopotamus about, are you?" Then he had put his arm around Marie.

"He was impertinent, Madame," she said in confusion.

"Did you go into his house?" Mrs. Dunbarton-Kent demanded.

"I knocked upon the knocker, Madame, and he

opened the door a little way and asked what I wished.
Then, when I said I wished Mrs. Dunbarton-Kent, he
said, 'Come in.' We talked in the hall and from what
he said I knew instantly it was not Kent House in
which I was, and I went quickly."

"Um! Allen Colfax gave me a bad name, did he?"

"He is quite too despicable to be noticed by any one,
Madame!" Marie declared warmly.

"Is that so. What did he do?"

Marie's eyes lost their softness. "I struck him in
the face—it was necessary," she returned succinctly.

This flash of speech elicited a sudden chuckle from
Mrs. Dunbarton-Kent, but she made no comment.
"What do you look like under that coat?" she asked.
"Take it off."

Marie had caught the gaze of both young men, West,
who was smiling encouragingly at her now, and Breck,
who was regarding her stonily; when she drew off her
coat she was crimson. She stood revealed, blushing
vividly, slender and petite and uniformed in tannish
brown, a mannish jacket and breeches and tan boots
laced to the knee, a picturesque ensemble to which was
given a touch of color, a red silk scarf wound about her
throat and the ends thrown over her shoulder. Her
throat was discolored still from her experience on the
train and she had muffled it well to hide the bruises.

She eyed Mrs. Dunbarton-Kent confusedly and
anxiously: "I designed this for being chauffeur to my
father—I hope it does not displease you, Madame?"
Marie felt that her case was hopeless. She was op-

pressed. She felt a curious discomfort, as if she were being accused of wrong-doing; with the exception of the blond young man with the pleasant face, they all stared at her so intently and coldly.

"I'll pay you sixty dollars a month and board and room," Mrs. Dunbarton-Kent said abruptly. "Your room is above the garage."

Marie was astounded and vastly pleased. "Thank you, Madame," she said quickly and courtesied.

"You have a trunk, I suppose?"

"Yes, Madame—at the boarding-house in the city."

"Very well—I'll send for it. Give her a pencil and paper, West. . . . Write your name and the address and your instructions if you have any."

When West supplied her, Marie dropped on one knee and, using the other for an improvised desk, complied with Mrs. Dunbarton-Kent's request. Hers was the attitude of an officer in the field penning a despatch, entirely without self-consciousness and gravely earnest. She was a pleasing picture as well; the bend of her head revealed the little feminine curls at the nape of her neck. West smiled down on her, watching her appreciatively.

Mrs. Dunbarton-Kent took possession of the paper, then turned to Breck. "Take her out to the garage, Breck, and show her the cars and her room. . . . You can bring the car around at four o'clock, Angouleme." She pronounced the name correctly, for, despite her remarkable bulk and rough speech, Mrs. Dunbarton-Kent was lettered. She wore a very apparent red wig,

her small eyes looked pugnaciously out of a huge countenance, and her chins were treble. Nevertheless there
was an air of culture as well as an amount of impres-
sive force about the big woman; one could not stand
in her presence and not feel that she was a personage,
and more because of her individuality than because of
her wealth.

Breck stood motionless for a moment. Then he went
to Marie and took her coat from her arm. "It's only
a short distance," he said in an expressionless way.
"You won't need it."

He spoke without looking at her; it was West who
smiled at her in the same encouraging way in which
he had when she had been anxious and confused, and
the ever rebellious corners of Marie's mouth lifted in
a hesitant yet grateful smile. Then she followed the
grim-looking young man who walked before her
through the back hall and straight out to the garage
without even turning his head to see whether she followed him.

CHAPTER IV

WHEN Marie and Breck left the library, Gibbs preceded them to the back door which he held open for them, his eyes lowered and without even a stolen glance at them as they passed. He did not look at Marie when she said softly, "Thank you;" he bowed only.

But on entering the kitchen immediately afterward, Gibbs whispered in the cook's ear and, with a startled air, she went with him to the rear window where together they watched Marie's progress to the garage. Breck had opened the big garage doors wide, so Gibbs and the cook could see them, Breck taking Marie up to show her the chauffeur's room, then coming down again and pointing out the cars to her. They watched the two with absorbed interest, taking care that they themselves were not seen.

And from an upper back window they were also being observed, for when Marie and Breck had gone out the family party in the library had instantly dissolved. Mrs. Dunbarton-Kent had risen without a word and gone up to her room where, with door locked and in lowered tones, she had called a New York number. "Is that you, Haslett?" she asked. "Yes? . . . Well, this is Mrs. D. K. Something queer has happened—a

girl appeared this afternoon and applied for the chauffeur's place."

"A girl!" came the answer. Then after a pause,
"That is strange. . . . There was a girl here in answer
to our advertisement, my stenographer told me about
it, but no one here gave her the address—who could
have done so?"

"Mrs. Brant-Olwin."

"That can't be—Mrs. Brant-Olwin is in Florida."

"She says she doesn't know the woman's name who
sent her to me, but she described her and the description fits exactly. She says she met the woman just
outside your office door." And Mrs. Dunbarton-Kent
gave the history Marie had given her and related
Marie's experience with the woman at the elevator.
"If the woman wasn't Mrs. Brant-Olwin, it was some
one very like her, Haslett," she concluded. "The girl
looks an honest sort and she's pretty. The papers she
showed me are straight, she must have served in
France. She looks and talks like a French girl, the
better educated sort—the thing is, who has put her up
to this and why? It's reported Mrs. Brant-Olwin is
in Florida, but is she?"

"I know positively that she is in Florida," the man
reiterated. "Somebody may be impersonating her
though. And the girl may be either the gullible sort or
deep, used by them or acting for them. She did come
here to the office, for I had a description of her from
my stenographer. No one here in the office knows that
the advertisement was inserted by me for you, all

they know is that I advertised for a chauffeur for myself. They were amused at a girl's having answered it,
and I think they laughed at the girl when she appeared.
My stenographer told me about it as a great joke, so
she certainly didn't get your address from either the
boy or the stenographer. And she didn't get it from
Mrs. Brant-Olwin. The thing's ridiculous anyway, a
girl proposing to take charge of a garage like yours.
But they're raising heaven and earth—" He caught
himself up, then went on. "The right sort of person
ought to talk to her, draw her out, I believe. You've
kept her, of course?"

"Yes—it seemed the only thing to do. You see,
Haslett, I'm certain she knows Breck. I received her
in the library—we were all there—and she recognized
Breck the moment she came in. He looked like stone—
as usual — but she looked queer, taken aback, I
thought."

"That's curious," he returned thoughtfully. "It was
certainly the wise thing to keep her, though."

"I was afraid not to. I've sent her out to the garage
with Breck—Willetts is there."

"That's just right. . . . I think I had better come
out this evening. You needn't send to the station for
me, I'll walk over and back. Oh, I want the address of
that boarding-house too—I'll make a few inquiries."

"I was going to give it to you. Her trunk is there
and I told her I would send for it."

"I'll attend to it. It'll be easy enough for us to go
through it too. And, whatever you do, don't show her

in any way that you're afraid of her. You need a chauffeur, you'll give her a trial, and she must prove that she is capable. If she is not, she will get her walking papers—let her understand that. And, Mrs. D. K., try not to worry over this occurrence. If it leads to trouble, we'll do our best to meet it—we'll talk it over to-night. Remember that suspecting and proving are two very different things."

"Maybe they are," Mrs. Dunbarton-Kent returned bitterly. "At present Kent House is hell—that I know." And she rang off abruptly. She rose and walked about her room restlessly. Then she sat down heavily and closed her eyes, her expression pained and troubled.

When Mrs. Dunbarton-Kent had left the library, West had taken up the afternoon paper and had gone into the morning-room; and as soon as she was alone, Bella had dropped her knitting and had gone lightly and swiftly up to her room. It was a corner room, two of its windows looked into the park, one of the big oaks grew almost against her window, but from the other two windows she could see the garage and the windows of the chauffeur's room. With the aid of the field-glasses which she took from a locked drawer, she watched Breck and Marie disappear in the direction of the stairway leading up to the chauffeur's room, saw Marie come into the room and lay her coat on the bed, stand and look about her for a moment, and disappear again.

When, almost immediately, the two came into view

in the garage below, Bella watched them intently. They stood so plainly in view and the glasses were so powerful that she could almost see their expressions. When Breck and the girl disappeared behind one of the cars, she continued to watch, and when they appeared again and Breck left the garage hurriedly and walked off rapidly in the direction of Kent House farm, she watched his going until the trees of the park hid him. Then she watched Marie until she closed the garage doors.

When Breck took Marie up to her room, he had not entered it, and when they came down he had stood in plain view from the house while he pointed out the cars.

"That roadster is West Dunbarton-Kent's, the young man you saw in the library, and the other three cars are Mrs. Dunbarton-Kent's," he said perfunctorily.

"Which one will she wish to drive to-day?" Marie asked.

"Ordinarily she would take the limousine, but to-day she's likely to telephone you that she wants the roadster—it's better adapted for conversation," he answered dryly.

Marie felt that this showing her about was a great nuisance to him. She stole glances at his profile: he was very handsome, but he looked most stern and unhappy, she thought. Frequently Marie had disarmed unapproachableness by a genuinely pretty speech and smile. And she had discovered that the American man likes to be called, "Monsieur." So she said, "It is a most beautiful place, this Kent House, Monsieur, and the garage is more elegant than are most houses. I shall take great care with the cars and try to please your mother."

He was giving her the keys and she was looking up at him, smiling, but with the finished air of respect which is rarely achieved by an American. But he gave her no answering smile. "Mrs. Dunbarton-Kent is not my mother," he said coldly. "West and Bella, the two you saw there in the house, and I, are only her step-relations, her nephews and niece. We three are cousins." He raised his voice slightly. "Mrs. Dunbarton-Kent has a number of millions which were left her by my uncle, West has a good income which was left him by his father, Bella is entirely dependent on Mrs. Dunbarton-Kent, and I have nothing, so I am earning my bread by managing the Kent House farm —for the present. The Allen Colfax whom you chastised is a distant cousin of the Dunbarton-Kent family and is a much disliked neighbor. His place is called Colfax Hall." He studied her face in his shadowed way. "But perhaps I'm telling you things you already know?"

Marie's soft wide eyes had assimilated his information. "No, Monsieur, I did not know. Thank you that you tell me—it is kind."

Then Breck went to one of the cars and stood close beside it. "This car is new—it's been used only once or twice," he said, but when Marie followed him, expecting further instructions, he came close to her and asked very low and swiftly, "Why did you look at me

as you did when you came into the library?" His
black brows had lowered suddenly into a straight line
and beneath it his eyes were cuttingly keen.

Marie caught her breath. Not for anything would
she have explained why for a brief moment she had
stared at him. It was his eyes that had startled her,
they were such a light blue and the lashes black, like
that woman's on the train. It was a mere resemblance,
but anything that reminded her of her terrifying experience was sufficient to startle her, and for an instant
she had felt a sort of panic. She flushed warmly and
took refuge in a half-truth:

"You—you stood so like a soldier, Monsieur. I
looked, then I thought most certainly you had been in
France. . . . Were you not?"

He scrutinized her intently. "Yes," he said finally,
"but most of the time in a German prison-camp." He
spoke now without lowering his voice.

There was something in his manner as well as his
words that touched her; his eyes were keen yet so som-
ber. "Ah, Monsieur!" she exclaimed with genuinely
profound pity. "Now I know why you look so sad!"

A curious expression crossed his face; he flushed
suddenly and painfully, stood for an uncertain moment, then turned on his heel and hurried out of the
garage.

Marie looked after him, wide-eyed and perplexed;
he was a very strange man. . . . Then soberly she
began to inspect her domain, the steam-heated and
luxurious garage, and her own pleasant and well-

lighted bedroom, but with thoughts only half given to what she was doing. She was still warmed by her good fortune, yet she was puzzled and troubled.

"Most certainly there is a strangeness about this entire family," she confided to herself. "I do not understand it."

CHAPTER V

A S Breck had predicted, Mrs. Dunbarton-Kent telephoned to the garage shortly before four o'clock that she wanted the roadster. "Put in a foot-warmer and one of the fur robes, Angouleme," she commanded. "I don't propose to freeze myself, but I do want a breath of fresh air."

Marie was having her garage troubles: outwardly the place looked well cared for, but a close inspection of cupboards, mops, sponges and the like had wrought Marie to a pitch of indignation. The seats of the cars covered evidences of long continued neglect, but worst of all there was a puzzling absence of necessary tools; not one of Mrs. Dunbarton-Kent's cars was properly equipped. West Dunbarton-Kent's car was in perfect condition, a high-powered roadster, shin-ingly clean within and without and equipped with every device for long travel: extra tires, a locked con-trivance in the rear which was large enough to carry a small wardrobe and blankets, every imaginable auto-mobile tool, and gasoline tank and oiler well filled— an object lesson to any chauffeur of what a car should be.

"It is quite certain that the same abominably neglect-ful person who has not cared for the cars of Mrs. Dunbarton-Kent has had nothing to do with this car of Mr. West!" Marie commented to herself indignantly.

When Marie brought Mrs. Dunbarton-Kent's roadster to the porte-cochère, the glow of haste and irritation warmed her cheeks; the roadster had needed all sorts of things done to it, a regular house-cleaning, and Marie had been able to give it only a hasty brushing up. Besides, a rear tire was in a very bad condition.

She had kept Mrs. Dunbarton-Kent waiting for fifteen minutes and she was reprimanded for it. "When I say four o'clock, I mean *four o'clock!*" she said sharply. "That is one objection I have to women —they're always either fussing around before time, or forgetting that there is such a thing as a clock. . . . Go down the driveway, then turn on the road to the left—I want to go to the farm first."

Marie's color deepened, but she said in soft accents, "When everything is new to a person, it is a little difficult. I shall not again be late, Madame. There was very much to be done to this car. I did the best I could in a short time."

But Mrs. Dunbarton-Kent was not appeased. "What was the matter with the car? Glidden was a perfect chauffeur—when he didn't drink."

Marie had not meant to tell at once of conditions in the garage, to do so gradually, for Mrs. Dunbarton-Kent had impressed her as being in a state of continual irritation. But Marie possessed a lively temper and she was seething. "He must then have drunk often, Madame. I think that that chauffeur was a two-face. It is evident that he polished your cars upon the outside, out within they are abominable. You yourself are now sitting above such a condition within the seat as is disgusting and which I have not had time to clean. Besides, I do not understand certain things about this garage—nothing is there that should be."

Mrs. Dunbarton-Kent flushed crimson; the young person was asserting herself early. "Indeed! My garage doesn't please you, eh? Well, that's quickly remedied," she returned grimly. "There are several trains into town to-morrow, for as your things have been sent for, you'll be wise to wait till they come."

The big woman's anger set Marie afire: she had done only her duty in telling of conditions in the garage; why should she be spoken to in this way, as if accused of wrong-doing? She turned hot eyes on Mrs. Dunbarton-Kent. "I think your garage beautiful, Madame. It is because of deception to you that I am angry. I think you do not know that in your garage, aside from neglect of cleanliness, I have found not one full set of tools and not one new tire. The extra tires upon the backs of your cars, so carefuly covered, are all worn-out tires, put there to deceive you, I think. That same perfect chauffeur! I call him a two-face— I do not like to apply the word 'thief' to any one!"

Mrs. Dunbarton-Kent's bulk stiffened suddenly and curiously, and her expression changed to a bleakly gray look, blank and troubled; so much so that Marie's anger vanished. Mrs. Dunbarton-Kent looked so terribly distressed.

Marie's eyes became sympathetic. "I am sorry that you should suffer such annoyance, Madame," she said softly. "It was thinking of it that made me so angry."

"I haven't thought much about the cars lately. It's possible Glidden exchanged the tires for whisky, but I doubt it," Mrs. Dunbarton-Kent returned dully.

"I am sorry that I should worry you," Marie apologized. "I spoke only because it did not seem possible that in that beautiful garage everything should be wanting. It is not so with the roadster which belongs to Mr. West Dunbarton-Kent. It is in most perfect condition."

"Yes—West takes care of his own car—he's a mechanical genius," Mrs. Dunbarton-Kent answered absently. Then she roused somewhat. "That is the road to the farm, Angouleme. Turn there."

The porte-cochère was at the side of the wide-fronted house, off the library wing, and they had come down the driveway which circled the slope of lawn and into the park. Marie had come up through the park when she came to Kent House, so she knew the road and the big stone-pillared gateway at the entrance to the park. Just this side of the gateway there was a road that ran close to the park wall, and this was the road into which Mrs. Dunbarton-Kent ordered Marie to turn. The farm-house was hidden from Kent House by the semicircle of woodland against which Kent House backed; the only view Kent House possessed was its fine view of the sound. From the front of the house to the water's edge was a long and widely undulating slope, a vivid lawn and a green meadow in summer, a dun and snow-streaked slope in March.

Some distance beyond the entrance to Kent House park, was another entrance with a winding and unkept driveway through neglected-looking trees to a huge old brick house which Marie, on her way from the station, had mistaken for Kent House and where she had encountered Allen Colfax. Colfax Hall could not be seen from Kent House, but from the lower end of the park the brick pile was distinguishable. Marie had thought it the nearest house to Kent House, but now, as they drove along beside the park wall, she saw that there was a small house between the two places, a modern-looking and very artistic house that had been built so close to the Kent House park wall, that its windows topped the wall. It was built just above the park cottage, a little vine-covered stone cottage that backed against the park wall, and on a terrace reared against the park wall, as if its owner was determined to overlook both wall and cottage and gain a view of Kent House park. The pretty little house had an impertinent air, like a head lifted above a wall and prying into the dignity of a neighboring estate.

It was a surprise to Marie, and she said involuntarily, "Ah, I did not notice that house. I thought the house of Mr. Colfax was nearest to yours. . . . It is very close to the wall of your park."

"It is indeed—fairly sitting on my cottage roof!" Mrs. Dunbarton-Kent answered grimly. "Some of Allen Colfax's work. He sold the narrowest possible

strip a house could be built on to that Smith woman,
purposely to spoil our privacy. He has ruined the
cottage which my husband built for a quiet retiring
place. The men about the place use the cottage now
for a sort of workshop—West has his tools and work
bench in one of the rooms. That's what my dear husband's little cottage has become. He loved the little
place."

Marie discovered that the big woman's voice could
be low and soft; it was so when she spoke of her husband. "She loved her husband very dearly," was
Marie's instant conclusion. "In spite of much money,
I think she is lonely and distressed."

Marie felt that though irascible and severe, Mrs.
Dunbarton-Kent was a very upright and honest woman. "It is difficult for a woman with much money
to be without a husband," Marie reflected wisely.
"There are always those who wish to take advantage of
such alone women. She looked so shocked and distressed when I told her the truth about the garage, as
if there was no one whom she could trust. And as yet
she does not trust me, but I shall lead her to do so."

Marie's wiles consisted mostly of a certain sympathetic cheer, tinctured by native shrewdness; of softly
bright glances and pretty smiles. "I do not think well
of a woman who would build a house disagreeable to a
neighbor such as yourself," Marie said to Mrs. Dunbarton-Kent with genuine sympathy. "She must be a
person who considers only herself."

"She lives to herself, certainly," Mrs. Dunbarton-

Kent said grimly. "There are reasons why no one here has anything to do with her. Happily she's not here very much. . . . She's a handsome woman of the high-colored sort and a good musician though," she added as if willing to give the woman her due. "They say she is a Russian."

Marie welcomed her first view of Kent House farm as a better subject. It stood a pasture's width beyond the park, was snowy-white and green-roofed and deep-eaved, with tall elms about it and its white and green barn. Even the barnyard, in which were several horses and cows, suggested spotless neatness. "Ah, Madame! This now is most charming!" she exclaimed with genuine pleasure. "It is a little like my pretty Canada, the green and white and the cattle! It seems so peaceful and plentiful, even more lovely than a great house, I think."

Mrs. Dunbarton-Kent glanced down at her and her face softened. Then she asked with astonishing abruptness, "Was it in France you met my nephew, Breck?"

Marie's eyes widened, then the color swept into her face. Mrs. Dunbarton-Kent had noticed then how she had stared at her nephew and she had thought it strange, just as Breck himself had thought. But she could not explain to Mrs. Dunbarton-Kent any more than she could to her nephew. Was she going to be reminded forever of that hateful experience on the train?

Marie's annoyance and embarrassment made her

denial very positive. "I never saw or heard of your nephew, Madame, until I saw him in your house to-day."

"You looked as if you knew him. You looked as if you'd seen a ghost," Mrs. Dunbarton-Kent asserted vigorously.

"He looks like a soldier," Marie returned firmly. "I looked at him, but in one minute I knew that I had never seen him before."

"The ghost of a soldier, perhaps," Mrs. Dunbarton-Kent remarked with bitter sarcasm, "come back to haunt his family."

Marie caught her breath and crossed herself hastily. "Madame! You have not seen them die as I have! Do not say such things!"

Mrs. Dunbarton-Kent eyed her in a puzzled and interested way, but all she said was, "Don't drive in at the gate—keep to the right. You know the way to the farm now, if ever I have to send you over here. Keep on up this road. It comes out on the High Road which runs behind all these places on the sound."

They went on in silence up the road that skirted the pasture and passed close to the barnyard. The house and barn had hidden what Marie saw now was a considerable chicken farm, numbers of runs each with its white and green roofed house. It was feeding-time and two men, Breck and an elderly man, were feeding the chickens. They were all white, not a black fowl among them, a pretty sight.

Marie wished that Mrs. Dunbarton-Kent would

order her to stop, but she did not. "Anderson!" she
called to the elderly man who had paused to smile at
her. "Come down to the house this evening—I want
to see you."

And he answered, "I will, Mrs. Dunbarton-Kent."

To Breck she said nothing, she did not appear to see
him, though he looked at them in his shadowed way
and lifted his cap.

They went on, passing a vegetable garden, an
orchard, and berry patches covered with straw, all in
perfect winter order, then came out upon a broad road
from which there were far views of the sound. But
the sight of her well-ordered estate seemed to have
afforded Mrs. Dunbarton-Kent no pleasure. Her look
was grim and, presently, she began to question Marie,
about her birthplace, upbringing and connections, just
where she had been and what she had done in France,
and particularly about the last few months, studying
Marie keenly meantime.

Marie answered her questions exactly, trying not to
be irritated, and succeeded in emerging from the ordeal
with her liking for Mrs. Dunbarton-Kent intact, for
it seemed that there was a restless distress behind all
this questioning; something which puzzled Marie.

"But she intends to keep me," Marie consoled herself, for when they passed the Country Club, a palatial
place it seemed to Marie, Mrs. Dunbarton-Kent said,
"There's not much doing there now, but you'll drive
over here often in the warm weather." And when they
turned homeward on the Lower Road which passed

the station and led on past the entrances to several
estates, the road Marie had taken when going to Kent
House, Mrs. Dunbarton-Kent said, "You'll come this
way to the station half a dozen times a day, for I'm
always having guests out from town, or some one of
us is taking the train in. You'll—"

Mrs. Dunbarton-Kent stopped abruptly, for they
were approaching the entrance to Colfax Hall and a
man stood there, aimlessly tapping his boots with his
cane, while a big mastiff circled about him. Marie
recognized the man instantly, Allen Colfax. She felt
Mrs. Dunbarton-Kent stiffen and she herself held her
head high and looked straight ahead, though she was
conscious that he was grinning at her and also that
Mrs. Dunbarton-Kent was staring at him and through
him in no pleasant fashion. In the dimness of Colfax
Hall, Marie had not seen his features distinctly, but
she noticed now how dissipated he looked, a reckless-
looking man. He was young, as young as the two
Dunbarton-Kents, and he showed his Dunbarton-Kent
blood plainly; save for his mustache, he looked very
like Breck, for he was dark. He twirled his cane between his fingers derisively and grinned broadly at
Marie as they passed, then said something to his dog
which made it bark.

"He is making fun of us, the despicable man!" Marie
thought indignantly. " 'A sparrow driving a hippopotamus,' he says to himself."

"Drunk, of course," Mrs. Dunbarton-Kent muttered
with vivid contempt. Then she sighed heavily and

said to herself so low that Marie barely caught it, "This generation of Dunbarton-Kents! The Lord help us!"

Marie brought the car to a stop beneath the porte-cochère, her heart warmed by a feeling of sympathy for her huge mistress. "There is here some great family trouble," she thought. "It is a pity it should be so in the midst of so much wealth and beauty."

Then Mrs. Dunbarton-Kent heaved herself out of the car. "Make a list of the things that are needed for the garage, Angouleme, and give it to me to-morrow. I've given Gibbs orders—you will take your meals in the servants' dining-room. Gibbs will telephone you half an hour before each meal, so you'll have time to get ready." And she went slowly into the house.

In the hall she met West. She looked at the satchel he was carrying. "Where now?" she asked.

"To Washington—to see about my patent. I told you I was going, didn't I?"

"I don't remember—I suppose you did. . . . West, you went through the supplies in the garage after Glidden left, didn't you, and found everything all right?"

"Yes—why?"

"That girl tells me there isn't a new tire in the place and the tools are gone too." She had lowered her voice.

They looked at each other, West's pleasant face grown as anxious as hers. "That's something new," he said slowly. "A bit of defiance, I suppose. . . . You're worried over this girl too, aren't you?"

"You heard what she said."

His eyes grew merry. "A quaint little feminist!"
He mimicked her softly, " 'It seemed to me quite as possible for me to be a chauffeur as for a man.' She's a
charming little thing—keep her for a day or two and if
by that time she hasn't had enough of it and doesn't go
of her own accord, pay her well and persuade her to go
back to Canada—New York's no place for her. I'll
wager anything she's as straight as a die. Mrs. Brant-
Olwin had nothing to do with her coming here, she's in
Florida, I had a letter from her this morning. Some
plump black-eyed acquaintance of yours in town is playing a joke on you, that's all. You've probably remarked
at some tea that you'd a deal rather be chauffeured by
a baby than by such a whisky soak as the magnificent-
looking Glidden. I've heard you say something of the
kind myself. Some one has taken you at your word."

Mrs. Dunbarton-Kent did not relax. "Possibly.
Did you see how she looked at Breck?"

West's face grew grave. "Yes, Breck's a striking-
looking man."

"She told me she had never seen him or heard of
him before."

"I'd believe her, I think. He made an impression
on her—another good reason for not keeping her."

"She wasn't telling me the truth," Mrs. Dunbarton-
Kent said decidedly. "I know an open countenance
when I see one."

"A still better reason for assisting her back to
Canada," West persisted. "I'd be willing to swear
that she's just a sweet honest little thing. If she

knows anything about him, it will be far better to have her out of the country."

"I shall take Haslett's advice," Mrs. Dunbarton-Kent said firmly. "A misstep may have tragic results."

West shrugged. "Haslett's apt to be overly suspicious—in some ways. I fancy it'll be too much for her, poor child, and she'll pack her small belongings and depart within the week. . . . Wish me good luck, Aunt Bulah, and a speedy return."

Mrs. Dunbarton-Kent's face softened. "I do, West. I wish you every success."

"Success may come later," he said cheerfully. "There's one member of your family who may amount to something after all."

A spasm of pain crossed her face. "God grant it! We seem to have reached a pretty low ebb!"

"It's bad, of course," he said sympathetically, "but try not to worry over it so much. And, Aunt Bulah, take my advice: don't keep that child here."

"I shall take Haslett's advice," she reiterated.

West shrugged again. "So be it! . . . I'm going to take the roadster, Aunt Bulah. It's at the cottage now—I'm going there to pack my model. If the weather's good, I may motor to Washington."

"Very well," Mrs. Dunbarton-Kent said indifferently, and went on toward the stairway.

West paused a moment, watching her ascend. He smiled slightly, his aunt climbing the stairs did resemble the ascent of an elephant. Then, with shoulders squared, he went out to meet the March chill.

CHAPTER VI

HER dinner that evening and her breakfast the next morning in the servants' dining-room proved a puzzling experience to Marie. Gibbs seemed to have ordained that she should eat alone, for which Marie was thankful until it became evident that she was treated strangely. To her pleasant, "Good evening, Mr. Gibbs," she had received a bow and an intensely reserved, "Good evening, Miss." He had deposited his tray of viands and had hastened away as if to escape conversation. Then, at breakfast time, Marie had encountered the cook in the passageway and to her smiling, "Good morning," she received a flurried murmur followed by a hurried retreat into the kitchen. The cook looked back at her in such a peculiar way, then quickly averted her gaze.

"There is a strangeness in the kitchen as well as in the rest of the house," Marie said to herself, puzzled.

It troubled her, and her experience with the man whom Mrs. Dunbarton-Kent sent her to the station to meet after breakfast increased her bewilderment. It was all well enough on the way to the house from the station, the man chatted pleasantly with her about the weather and complimented her on her skilful management of the car, but, afterward, when Marie was or-

45

dered by Mrs. Dunbarton-Kent to wait and take, "this gentleman" to the farm and afterward to the Country Club and bring him back to Kent House, it was quite different.

Marie had decided that the man was a smoothly spoken person who wished to make himself very pleasant to her. He was a young man, very well groomed and he evidently considered himself very charming, he was so keen-eyed, smiling and facile-tongued. He was not quite a gentleman, Marie decided, not a friend of Mrs. Dunbarton-Kent's, but perhaps of considerable business importance to her, so he must be treated with extreme politeness and a definite reserve.

After half an hour in Kent House, the man came out to Marie as smilingly pleasant as before and his first remark was a compliment: "You look like a pretty Canadian snow-bird, perched on the seat there. Mrs. Dunbarton-Kent was telling me you came from Canada. It's a splendid thing for a girl to do, fill a man's position, and do it so well too."

Marie said, "Thank you, Monsieur," and swept him down the driveway.

He talked about Canada then, a country of which he knew nothing, Marie decided, and interspersed his remarks with questions: By what route had she traveled from Canada? What train had she taken out of Buffalo? On what day had she arrived in New York? He talked then about New York, mentioning various restaurants and streets as if she must be acquainted with them. He seemed to think that she must have

met some gallant man in New York who had shown
her the city. "A pretty girl like you in New York and
no beau?" he said teasingly. "I can't believe that!"

"I was in New York but a few days," Marie answered calmly, though she was angry. What right
had he to question in this way? It was natural that
Mrs. Dunbarton-Kent should wish to know all about
her, she was her employer. But for a strange man to
question and be so familiar! Evidently he thought that
all girls were silly and easily impressed by smiling
looks. She did not like him.

Then, looking full in her eyes, he asked abruptly,
"But what of the little adventure you had on the train?"

Marie's heart gave a leap; she was terribly startled.
Was it possible that he was in search of that fearful
creature on the train?

He scrutinized her confusion. "He told you Kent
House was a good place to come, didn't he, little girl?"

Marie was swept by relief, and anger as well. The
conceited, impertinent imbecile! Did he think she was
some ignorant servant girl? The density of some men
was remarkable! They may be very keen and sensible
in conversation with men, but with girls they had no
judgment whatever, if the girls looked little and pretty,
they considered them as brainless!

Marie flamed at him. "I do not make friends with
strange men, Monsieur, nor do I speak with persons
on trains! I have no use whatever for the kind of man
who thinks by smiles and talk to make an impression
on me! I am in the employ of Mrs. Dunbarton-Kent

and will drive you where she has ordered me, but you will kindly restrain yourself from questions which would make me seem a silly fool!"

The man looked as if he had suddenly encountered a hornet's nest, vastly taken aback, then driven into a lively retreat. "I beg your pardon—it never occurred to me to be impertinent," he apologized hastily. "You see, you have no idea how charming and unusual you look. I was interested in you the moment I saw you, and what Mrs. Dunbarton-Kent told me about you interested me still more, so I seemed to be impertinent when I hadn't the least intention of being so."

"Perhaps that is so," Marie returned severely, "but I think rather that you formed a wrong impression of me. It is necessary only for you to correct your manner, then I have nothing further to say."

She paused abruptly, for they had emerged from the park and had come suddenly upon Breck, who was standing beside the road. Evidently he was on his way to Kent House and had stopped out of the road to let them pass. He looked at them fixedly and he lifted his cap, but his face was like granite and his eyes like steel. Marie saw how he looked at the man beside her, a cutting stare that traveled over him.

Marie smiled hurriedly at Breck, fearing that he might wonder at her flushed and angry appearance. Perhaps he had heard what she had said. It was most unfortunate that she lost her temper so easily; he might think that she had been rude to a guest of Kent House. She felt anxious and miserable.

The young man beside her studied her drooping lips and her wistful expression. Then he said without a trace of his previous facetiousness, "That's Breck Dunbarton-Kent, poor fellow! He had a dreadful experience during the war. It's made a lonely sort of him. What he needs is sympathy—some one to talk to. He's standoffish, even with his family, but there are few men who won't melt if a woman's really kind to them. It's a pity about him."

Marie was so interested by this information that she forgot to be severe. "Do you wish to stop at the farm?" she asked.

"No, thanks—just drive slowly by. . . . I'm thinking of buying property out here, and Mrs. Dunbarton-Kent offered to have me driven about. I want to take a look at the Country Club too."

They passed the farm in silence, apparently the man engrossed in looking about him, and Marie thinking of what he had told her. She wished he would tell her more, but not for anything would she have asked a single question.

Until they reached the High Road, her companion was silent, but when they could see the roof and tall chimneys of Colfax Hall, he spoke again. "That's Allen Colfax's place," he remarked. "He's let it run down, still it's a very valuable piece of property. His land runs from this road clear through to the sound and he owns half the field that's between Kent House and the sound too. There's been trouble between Mrs. Dunbarton-Kent and Colfax over that field—Colfax

could build on his part of it or sell it to some one who'd
build and shut off all the view Kent House has. Still,
Allen's not such a bad sort, though the Dunbarton-
Kents and society in general are down on him. What
he needs is a sensible wife to keep him straight. A
nice girl, if she took him in hand, could do wonders
with him and with Colfax Hall. The Colfax family is
one of the oldest on the North Shore."

Marie received this information in expressionless
silence. She had her own opinion of Mr. Allen Colfax,
and her shrewdness wondered why this man was recom-
mending him. Everybody she had met here acted
strangely; it was unaccountable. It was interesting
though to learn just why the Dunbarton-Kents disliked
Allen Colfax so much. Evidently there was a family
quarrel over property and it caused Mrs. Dunbarton-
Kent great anxiety.

The man continued to talk, his observant eyes on
Marie. "It's too bad Allen sold off that strip next to
Kent House park to Mrs. Smith. She's a queer woman. They say not a single woman out here has called
on her, but she seems to be satisfied with only her
piano for company. She's gay enough when she's
away from here though."

This information also Marie treated with silence.
"This person is a gossip," she said to herself with firm
disapproval.

As they went on, he commented on the places that
they passed, wealthy owners who were absent for the
winter, or families who lived the year round in their

North Shore houses. He talked for some time of a
Mrs. Brant-Olwin whose imposing house was near the
Country Club. She had grown up in a mining camp,
he told Marie, but, because she had immense wealth,
she had worked her way into society; she was noted
for her wonderful jewels and her lavish entertainment.
When they left the Country Club, he told of the parties
given there in the summer. "It's a millionaire's play-
ground!" he declared.

Though she looked as expressionless as possible,
Marie was interested; it was entertaining to hear about
these people. But why should he care to tell her about
them? He looked at her too much, and paused too
often as if expecting answers. She maintained a determined silence.

But he puzzled her most by what he said when she
brought the car to a stop at Kent House. "I've enjoyed my ride immensely," he declared, "and now I'm
going to tell you something, Miss Angouleme: I liked
best of all the way you sat down on my joshing. You
have plenty of good sense, and if I can ever be of any
assistance to you just let me know. This is my card,
my name is Walter J. Greene, and I can always be
reached at that address. There's trouble waiting
around the corner for almost everybody and, in case
you run up against it, please remember you have a
friend in me and make use of me."

Marie looked at the card. "It is most kind," she
said reservedly.

"And shake hands?" he asked.

"With pleasure, Monsieur," she returned politely.

Her unsmiling aspect did not seem to lessen his cordiality: he gave her hand a close clasp and lifted his hat a second time when she drove off to the garage. As she circled to the back of the house, she saw him still standing in the porte-cochère, looking after her.

Marie's cheeks grew hot. "If I did not think him a two-face, talking and acting for a purpose, I should call him an imbecile!" she said to herself with decision. Then she sighed. "Each person I meet here is more strange than the last—I do not understand it."

CHAPTER VII

IN the days that followed, Marie sighed often to herself. She did her very best, but things were not at all as they should be. She was certain that Mr. Walter J. Greene had complained of her, for the next time she saw Mrs. Dunbarton-Kent she behaved so strangely. Marie drove her about every day, but Mrs. Dunbarton-Kent would not talk to her and she gave her orders so curtly. When the garage supplies arrived, Marie asked her what disposition she should make of them and she answered impatiently:

"I don't want to be bothered about the garage, Angouleme. Breck will look after the garage. He'll give you my orders and you can report to him, so don't come to me about anything—I have too many other things to attend to." Then she relapsed into a grim silence.

So Breck appeared in the garage and inspected the cars. Marie explained the shortage of tires and tools and showed him the supplies she had unpacked. Hoping for a word of praise, she told him, "The condition within these cars was abominable, but now every inch is clean—as you see."

Breck looked but said nothing. Without a word, he carried the useless tires into the store-room and helped

Marie put the new tires into their cases. Then he jacked up the roadster and took off the worn tire which had worried Marie on her first drive with Mrs. Dunbarton-Kent. He declined her help: "No—it's not work for a girl."

He did not look at her, he seemed to be looking at her hands, and Marie flushed: why did he not speak more kindly? It pained her, his looking at her hands; it was impossible to keep them looking well. "It is the black oil that has stained the nails," she said involuntarily. "Now that the cars are clean, my hands will be different."

Breck had glanced up at her then, a swift keen look into her troubled eyes, and she had flushed still more deeply. She wished that she had not spoken, and she felt terribly hurt when he finished his work deftly and departed with the brief order: "When there is a heavy piece of work like this, I'll do it. You can tidy up now." She was shivering with cold too, for he seemed determined to work with the garage doors wide open.

And so it had continued. He was a very strange man, Marie thought. She puzzled over him. Every morning, and sometimes at noon, he came to the garage door and delivered Mrs. Dunbarton-Kent's orders for the day, apparently determined not to enter the garage unless it was absolutely necessary. Evidently he hated having anything to do with the cars; Marie felt that he thought it beneath him. Then he would tramp off to the farm. Usually he would stop at the garage on his way back in the evening, after dark, and

ask in an even voice, "Are the cars all right?" receive
her answer and stride on to the back entrance of the
house, then up to his room.

Marie knew which was his room, for, very often, he
did not draw down his blinds. To change his clothes,
he went into another room which Marie thought must
be his bathroom. He would reappear in evening dress,
then go down to dinner and return in about an hour,
wrap himself in a dressing-gown and sit at the desk
near his window and read and write late into the night.
Often Gibbs brought his dinner up to him on a tray;
that was when there was company for dinner, either
people from the neighborhood or guests whom Marie
was sent to the station to meet.

Marie could see all this from her bedroom window,
for she was given her dinner early, before the family
or the servants were served. If she brought guests
from the station, she must wait for Gibbs to telephone
whether she was to take them back that night or not.
When people came in their cars, either they themselves
or their chauffeurs, if the night was at all inclement,
ran their cars into the garage. The chauffeurs were
most troublesome, Marie thought, for they tried to talk
to her and even presumed to make love. She found
that, having seen the cars properly placed, the best
thing was for her to go up to her room and lock herself in. They soon tired of the garage then and went
off to the house where they were cared for by Gibbs.
There were sleeping apartments there for such servants
as Mrs. Dunbarton-Kent's guests happened to bring.

But it was not pleasant to discover that she was
regarded as a joke by every chauffeur in the neighborhood and of course by their masters and mistresses.
Marie was aware of the covert smiles of the people who
passed them when she drove Mrs. Dunbarton-Kent.
Often they passed Allen Colfax riding a big gray horse
and followed by his mastiff, and always he grinned
widely; Marie driving Mrs. Dunbarton-Kent seemed
to afford him immense amusement. The guests whom
she brought from the station to Kent House asked her
all sorts of amused questions. When she parked her
car among others while waiting for Mrs. Dunbarton-
Kent or Bella to emerge from some entertainment, she
understood perfectly the smiles and nods of the other
chauffeurs. Sometimes they persisted in surrounding
her car and talking to her facetiously. Occasionally a
chauffeur tried to be really friendly, for "Mrs. D. K.'s
French Baby," as they called her, with fire in her
eyes and her black curls escaping from her service cap,
was a tempting vision. But Marie proved adamant;
she reared the huge collar of her fur coat against friend
and foe and turned a contemptuous back upon them.

During nine days' time, Marie was literally a nine
days' wonder and discussed in every household within
miles. Mrs. Dunbarton-Kent had defied custom; she
was trying to establish a precedent. And she had put
that little feminine tot of hers into trousers! Of course
their daughters rode astride and wore breeches, they
had done that for some time, but think of turning over
one's garage to a girl, and such a baby as that! And

this at Kent House which was a byword for conservatism!

Then what Mrs. Dunbarton-Kent said on the subject was passed about. "Whose business is it whether it's masculine or feminine, big or small!" she had roared at an afternoon tea. "It doesn't drink and go joy-riding, which is more than most of you can say of your six-foot nuisances. Advertise for a respectable girl ambulance driver and consider yourselves fortunate if you get her—I'm tired of all this fool talk!"

Bella Dunbarton-Kent, though she made no comments herself, was open to either amused or derogatory remarks concerning her aunt's remarkable choice of a chauffeur, but, after the above incident, no one ventured any comments in Mrs. Dunbarton-Kent's hearing. Mrs. Dunbarton-Kent was a much respected and, sometimes, a much feared person; when she struck it was usually a well-directed and a forcible blow.

And whatever were their private councils, the Kent House servants also maintained a complete silence regarding the new chauffeur. But there was one occasion when Gibbs administered to a lively young chauffeur a mysterious reproof which traveled. The man had asked Gibbs for court-plaster for his scratched face.

"Where did you get that?" Gibbs had demanded in a startled way.

"The little tiger-cat in the garage," the chauffeur confessed disgustedly. "I picked her up, in fun, mind you, and she clawed me up like this! The little she-devil!"

Ordinarily Buckingham Gibbs was a most lenient father confessor to any man-servant, but on this occasion he looked horrified. "You mend your own face, you—chump!" he said aghast. Then solemnly, "Remember that angels are sometimes entertained unawares."

But when questioned by the next visiting chauffeur, Gibbs denied any knowledge of the occurrence and the other servants were equally reticent; there was one subject upon which they were dumb, and that was Marie Angora Lamb.

Marie knew nothing about Mrs. Dunbarton-Kent's championship of her, or of Gibbs' mysterious reproof. She knew only that she seemed to be ostracized, that Mrs. Dunbarton-Kent would not talk to her, that Breck avoided her, that Bella never even nodded to her and looked at her as if she hated her; that she was regarded with curiosity and amusement by every one in the neighborhood, and that the Kent House servants shunned her.

Those servants! What was the matter with them? One day Marie, driven by loneliness, had approached in friendly fashion Mrs. Dunbarton-Kent's personal maid, a bright-faced intelligent-looking girl who had ventured upon the grass-plot between the house and the garage. The girl had started convulsively and had almost run back to the house; she had looked frightened out of her wits. Marie had been cut to the quick; she had retreated to the garage with the tears burning her eyes. It was so utterly unaccountable! The attempts at rough love-making on the part of the chauffeurs troubled Marie far less than the conduct of the Kent House servants, for she had met with that sort of thing before and felt quite able to defend herself. But to be feared and avoided when she had done nothing to deserve it!

She was utterly lonely and miserable. What did it all mean? It had never been so in any other place where she had been; always her smile had been answered by smiles. "Were it not for the good pay I would leave to-morrow," Marie confided to herself. "It is as if I had committed a crime!"

But she was compelled by necessity. She had been horrified by the high cost of living in New York. Her hundred dollars would last her only a very short time in that place. And her experience with the Kent House servants gave her a terror of working in any household capacity; the other servants might make life unbearable. No, she must cling to her present position until she had saved enough to feel independent. Then, when not utterly miserable, she was stubbornly determined to behave as if she was indifferent to the slights shown her.

Fortunately, during the day, Marie had little time for repining; there was so much to do. But when night came it was very hard. Then she sat in her room and thought. In the darkness, she could sit close to the window and could see Breck sitting in his window and studying. Marie felt certain that he was studying. Even when his window-shades were down, she could see his silhouette cast upon the shade. In a way, it was comforting to feel that some one besides herself was lonely; he seemed quite apart from his family.

She wondered endlessly about him. What was the dreadful experience during the war which had "made a lonely sort" of him? Such a war experience should have made his family sympathetic. It was strange with this family: they were highly respected, that was evident, and their servants were devoted to them, yet no member of the family seemed to have any love for any other member. Bella spent days at a time in the city,—Marie knew because she was constantly driving her to and from the station, a duty which she dreaded, for, though muffled to the eyes in a fur coat which concealed all but her unusual height, Bella's eyes looked cold contempt at her, and her icy commands were little better than an insult, Marie thought. Why Bella hated her she could not imagine, unless it was Bella's nature to hate most people, yet Bella must have friends, for she spent so much time in the city.

Certainly it was a strange family: between Bella and Mrs. Dunbarton-Kent there was almost no conversation, and certainly Breck was entirely apart from his family. West Dunbarton-Kent was the only one who seemed to have a smile in his eyes, but Marie had not seen him since the first day and thought he must live in the city as his roadster had disappeared from the garage at the same time that he had from Kent House. Perhaps the reason he was able to smile was because he did not have to live in Kent House?

Marie decided that there was some bitter family quarrel over property; it was so often the case in families where there was much money to quarrel over. Certainly there was a quarrel with Allen Colfax over property, and very likely Breck had taken some part in it which displeased his family so much that he was in deep disgrace with them; perhaps at some time he had been a spendthrift. At any rate, this was an unhappy family, so very different from the way it had been with her father and herself; they had been like two loving comrades.

Marie's throat ached when she thought of her father. Then she would try to console herself by thinking of the three years of the war when she had been a favorite in her ambulance corps, and beloved by many a soldier, by more than one officer too, and respected always. It was that made her heart ache and burn with indignation; to be treated with avoidance by these people; to be compelled to loneliness and silence; not one word of kindness or human interest. It was cruel.

The result of Marie's puzzled and indignant meditations was a desperate eagerness to prove her worth to these people. She scrubbed and cleaned, oiled and polished. She was proud of all her cars, but she loved best the splendid new seven passenger car that was not used much now the weather was bad. As one must love something, Marie fixed her affections upon the big car; its running-board was her favorite seat; she patted it sometimes and talked to it. When the rain spattered on the garage windows or the March wind whistled under the big doors, her favorite car was a comfort. Being a young twenty-three and aching for amusement, she tried to regard her cars as people. She gave them names: West-Dunbarton-Kent's roadster which he had taken away with him, she called "The Unknown"; Mrs. Dunbarton-Kent's roadster she called "Bella"; it was such a cold gray. The limousine was "My Lady"; it was a fashionable equipage and did not interest her particularly. Her big car she called, "Breck"; it interested her greatly, in spite of its immobile and severely dignified appearance.

One evening, when darkness had settled without, Marie amused herself by lying on her back and chalking on the under side of the running-board of each car its name. When she had returned from the station that evening she had found West's roadster in the garage, so all the cars were there. She was unconscious of being observed, though a man was watching her intently through one of the narrow windows up near the ceiling of the garage. These windows were used as ventilators in the summer; now they were closed, but through any one of them the entire floor of the garage could be seen. They were just above the sloping roof of the store-room, and by climbing to the roof and crawling up to the windows, one could lie flat and look down into the garage. By sliding the windows back a little, one could hear as well as see.

It was Breck who was watching her. He had taken

a roundabout way through the park that had brought
him to the back of the garage. He had used caution
in coming, he had even crawled on his hands and knees
across the shrub-dotted space behind the garage and
had crept beneath the cedar-tree which grew against
the corner of the store-room. Here the roof sloped
to about twelve feet from the ground and, after listening intently for a few minutes, he had removed his
boots and had climbed up the corner as nimbly as a
cat. When his hands gripped the eaves, he had lifted
himself clear of the wall and had swung himself up on
the roof with the skill of an acrobat; he was a tall and
broad-shouldered man, but he did it with an ease that
suggested practise. Then he had crawled up the roof
to the row of windows and had lain prone; he had
opened one of the windows slightly so he could both
hear and see.

He saw Marie, chalk in hand, crawl under each car,
then saw her get to her feet and bow deeply to each car
in turn, calling it by name. With each bow, her loosened curls fell over her face, then were flung back for
another effort. But for her half a yard of hair, she
might have been taken for a boy-soldier doing a stage
turn. A Cossack dance taught Marie by a Russian
soldier, a great clicking of heels and leaps into the air
and rapid whirls, completed the ceremony. She looked
a live, lithe little thing, brim full of fun, grace and
energy.

Flushed and smiling, Marie sat down then on the
running-board of the big car. Then, gradually, flush

and smile faded; her lips began to quiver and her eyes filled and, suddenly, she flung herself down on the running-board and began to sob, a perfect passion of weeping. Of what good were cars as companions!

Breck had watched her throughout, but also with his attention given to the garage doors. When they parted, he drew back, but still watching and listening; some one was coming into the garage.

CHAPTER VIII

IT was West Dunbarton-Kent who came into the garage. Evidently from the door he had seen Marie doubled up on the running-board of the car, for he tiptoed over and stood looking down at her. She was a woebegone figure, given over to grief; for three weeks she had been holding back her tears, now they were a deluge.

West waited for some time, until she quieted, then he said with concern, "What's the matter, Little Chauffeuress?"

Marie came upright with a start and thrust back her hair. When she saw who it was, she was utterly confused. "Monsieur—" she gasped.

"What is it? What has happened?"

"It is not a—happening," Marie returned with an attempt at dignity. "It—it is—continuous, and I do not understand." She set her teeth on a quivering lip and gathered up her hair. Her hair-pins being scattered over the garage, she twisted it up in a knot. Then, finding her handkerchief, she rubbed the tears from her face, terribly ashamed at having been caught weeping.

"Everything all wrong, of course. I was afraid it would be so. It's a shame!" he declared.

They were the first kindly words Marie had heard since she came to Kent House and her heart overflowed. "I do not understand the strangeness of your people, that is my trouble, Monsieur!" she said passionately. "Am I a criminal that your people speak to me with eyes turned away and even the servants run from me? . . . Monsieur, you have been away, so you have not seen, but indeed I have done my work well—I have tried in every way to please—yet I am treated as if I were in deep disgrace. If only I knew the reason. If only I could understand what it is about myself that displeases, I would try to be different, but it is to me a mystery and no one will talk to me to explain. You are the first person here to speak kindly. On the first day you were the only one to smile at me. Be kind still, Monsieur, and tell me what it can possibly be." Marie had begun hotly and had ended in pleading.

"You've upset a few old-fashioned ideas, for one thing, Little Lady," West answered gravely but kindly.

Marie looked as puzzled as she felt. "I think I am stupid, Monsieur, I do not understand." The tears still hung on her lashes, but her eyes were wide and questioning.

West smiled at her. Then his expression changed. "Oh, Kent House and the Dunbarton-Kents!" he said scornfully. "Their troubles and their family pride! . . . Mrs. Brant-Olwin, who came out of the West and turned some of her deceased husband's gold nuggets into strings of pearls and then invaded the North Shore,

once asked Bella how long she had lived on Long
Island. Bella looked over her head and said, 'For four
hundred years.' Mrs. Brant-Olwin, whose original
name was Kelly, returned sweetly, 'Good gracious! I
wouldn't confess to being that old, if I was you!' "
West laughed and sat down beside Marie, clasped his
knee in his hands and swung his foot. "You see, we
are a conventional lot. Aunt Bulah, that's Mrs. Dunbarton-Kent, occasionally tilts at tradition—that's one
reason why she took you. I think you're a bit too
modern for Kent House. You believe in doing as you
please, being a little chauffeur in trousers, if you want
to. And why shouldn't you! But some people can't
see it that way—it's a bit of a shock to them. . . .
It's the only explanation I can give you for what you
call the 'strangeness,' little Marie. I'm a Dunbarton-
Kent, so I don't like to say too much about my family's
troubles."

At first Marie looked blank with amazement. Then
her dark little face flamed: Bella's frozen stare and
Breck's avoidance and Mrs. Dunbarton-Kent's manner
to her were explained. "But I do nothing wrong!" she
declared hotly.

West looked at her appreciatively. "Of course you
don't! I think you are a brave little woman—I thought
so that first day—but to them just the fact that you
spend the nights here in the garage unchaperoned is—
reprehensible."

"But I have slept in dugouts or shell holes, anywhere, so did American girls, and with men all about

me and not one word of censure! The war has made
changes in the independence of girls! We are proud
to have worked like men, together with men."

"I know it. But families like mine can't see broad,
Marie. The conventional man or woman is the greatest evil thinker in the world!" His manner was very
earnest; he released his knee and pointed in the direction of the house. "I stifle over there, so I get away
as often as I can. Happily, business takes me away—
I have just been to Washington about one of my inventions. . . . You know, it was some time before I
learned that, if surrounded by conventions, it never
pays to kick them over. Better to seek a different at-
mosphere. Unfortunately, my family is double-dyed
conventional—there is no such thing as changing their
prejudices."

Marie's eyes had grown brilliant. "You think it
would be best for me to leave this place? That always
I will be treated in this manner?"

"I would go, if I were you—at once. Ours is not a
cheerful family—it hasn't been for some time, and
there is likely to be still more gloom. I know a dozen
families in the city and several in Washington and elsewhere who would be glad to have such help as you can
give them. And there are office positions, too, for a
girl as capable as you are."

Marie looked full at him. "I thank you for all you
have told me, Monsieur, and for your kind interest.
I think now I understand better, and I have decided:
because of this same narrow-mindedness of which you

tell me, I shall remain *here*. Perhaps to such prejudices
I can teach something." She nodded her head decidedly.
"Yes, those who will come no farther than the garage
door and talk at me with eyes fixed on everything else
than myself—they will do differently before I leave
Kent House. That is my decision."

West looked somewhat blank; then he laughed out.
"Well, I never!" He added admiringly, "You are a
plucky little person! I like it." His eyes were merry.
"Go straight ahead, my little friend, and remember
this: I like you and I'll do anything I can to help you."
Then his look sobered. "I can't change conditions
though, and there will be many things I shall not be
able to explain—my black-a-browed cousin, for one
thing. . . . Every family has its black . . . black-
sheep, I suppose—" he said slowly, and sighed.

"Monsieur," Marie ventured timidly, "he seems to
me a man in trouble and depression. Is it not so?"

West said nothing; he looked down, for the moment
his expression as stern as his cousin's. His features
were more mobile than Breck's and more clear-cut, his
fair-lashed, light blue eyes, merry one moment, keen
the next, then, again, as cold as Bella's or Breck's.
Marie did not venture another question, only noted his
extreme fairness, so unlike his cousin. Yet he looked
strong, trim and straight and with slim pointed-fin-
gered hands, suggestive of an infinite delicacy of touch.
He had strength as well as grace and charm.

"Without doubt he invents wonderfully," Marie
thought admiringly and, to lift the cloud from his face,

she said, "Mrs. Dunbarton-Kent told me that you invent. It has seemed to me always so wonderfully impossible a thing to invent. Look, for instance, at the mechanism of an aeroplane. I think I could drive one through the air, but to build such a thing out of one's brain, that is to me a miracle."

His face cleared. "You're a charming little person. Where did you learn to speak such pleasant English? Not in the North Country where 'we went by sleighs?'" He mimicked her playfully. "I've never heard a prettier accent than yours."

"Monsieur!" Marie smiled. "That same troublesome accent of mine! It was in the convent they taught me English and endeavored to teach me manners."

"They succeeded," West said decidedly. "I know a hundred girls whom I have met socially who ought to go to your convent—they don't know what manners are."

Under such appreciation, Marie expanded. "It was my dear father who wished for me a good education. You see, Monsieur, I had no mother since a baby and I was with my aunt in the little village of St. Felix where all are French. She taught me neatness and system and cooking, but no learning at all. My father would come often to visit us and always he said, 'Eh, my little Marie, the thing for a woman is the training in a house, then there should be learning and polish.' So, by and by, he took me to the nuns in Quebec.

"Never had I been in a city before and always my eyes were wide open to learn everything I could. It

seemed to me a great world without limitations to those
who are not ignorant. But, Monsieur, the years I
loved best were those when I traveled with my father.
I loved the long snows of winter and the frozen lakes.
Then the beautiful flowers of spring and the brief heat
of summer! I love the country. And I enjoyed sell-
ing the skins. All over Canada we went, and often my
English was helpful. I talked with the American trad-
ers and my father would say, 'Eh, little Marie, you
drive a better bargain than your old father—you have
business sense.' He praised me, and in France they
praised me for competence and fearlessness, so to be
treated as I have been here is—painful." Her lips
quivered, then set, and she flung back her head. "But
it shall not be so always!"

West had watched her absorbedly, his eyes now keen,
now smiling. "And in all that time, no lover who
begged to be a husband, little Marie?" he asked softly.

She lost her belligerent air. Her mouth lifted at
the corners and laughter glanced between her lashes.
"None who spoke the language I wished to hear,
Monsieur. The trees of your park are tall, but my
heart sits upon the topmost branch. A kiss flung
upward does not reach me, nor does he who climbs up
roughly. I think some day a little bird with red wings
will bring me a message from another tree-top, and
we will bend together—so,"—she lifted her arms and
brought her finger-tips together— "then we will come
down to earth together, but never forgetful of the tree-
tops seen against the sky." She looked at him through

the arch of her arms. "Is it not so, that love should
be, Monsieur?"

West made a quickly restrained movement, hands
raised to touch her, then withheld. "So you are quite
heart-free then, little Marie?"

The gleam of mischief fled from her eyes; she
dropped her lifted arms and sat with head bent, oddly
motionless, and West moved close to her. "You're
not?"

She shrugged suddenly, then sighed, then sprang up.
"Who knows, Monsieur! . . . Please look now at your
car. When I returned this afternoon it was here and
muddy. See now how it shines! I worked upon it."

West followed her over to his roadster. "That was
very kind of you," he said appreciatively. "I've been
thinking—some day would you like to see my workshop, in the park cottage?"

"Would it not be entirely against these family conventions of which you speak?" Marie asked demurely.

He laughed. "I think it could be managed. The
best way to treat conventions is to walk around them."

"Perhaps, Monsieur—I shall have to give the matter
a most careful consideration."

West held out his hand. "Shake hands with me,
please? You know now that you have one friend at
Kent House, don't you?"

"I hope so indeed, Monsieur—that is why I am
happy. I thank you very much," she said with genuine
gratitude.

There was a caress in West's eyes; he bent over her

hand, then straightened abruptly, for a sound at the door startled them both. Breck was standing there, looking at them from beneath bent brows. "I am sorry to interrupt," he said in level tones, "but I have a message from Mrs. Dunbarton-Kent: she wants the limousine ready to take her into town directly after breakfast to-morrow."

"Yes, Monsieur," Marie answered unsteadily and drew her hand from West's hold. She was frightened, for, though Breck had spoken to her, he was looking at West as a man does who levels a pistol with deadly intent.

West eyed him calmly. "She gave me the message, Breck, but I forgot to deliver it. Evidently you forgot to deliver it at noon as you were told to."

Breck made no answer, but he looked his cousin up and down in a way that made Marie catch her breath. Then he turned and went out.

"I am sorry, Marie," West said with concern. "I didn't know that thunder-cloud was going to burst in on us."

"It does not matter, except that he seems to misunderstand," Marie said distressedly. "I have been so long without pleasant conversation with anybody that I smile more than I should."

"He frightened you. Don't pay any attention to his queer ways. I can't explain, but what he thinks or says doesn't matter to anybody."

"I am not frightened because of myself, Mr. West, but tell me please why he is so strange?" Marie begged.

"I can't tell you, Marie. Just remember that we are friends and forget about him. . . . I'm going now, but I shall see you to-morrow." And he lifted her hand and kissed it. "My homage to a brave little woman and a very charming one," he said.

He went with a backward look at her.

CHAPTER IX

LEFT alone, Marie went up to her room and sat in the dark. Her thoughts were not happy ones. She did not ask herself why Breck's thinking ill of her mattered so much more to her than West's thinking well of her. "If he has thought me unwomanly, what must he have thought when he saw me standing together with his cousin and my hand in his?" Marie asked herself in flushed misery. "I should not have been so friendly, only I was so terribly lonesome. Mrs. Dunbarton-Kent too—she would not understand. I have not begun well in trying to make this family respect me."

Marie had known very few ultra-conventional people, but she knew the world and its judgments as well as the average girl. She could well imagine that the Dunbarton-Kent family and their servants regarded her as West had said they did. It explained everything. But Breck ought to know that the soldier-girl of the war was as straight as the girl who had remained at home. Marie burned to prove to the entire Dunbarton-Kent household that they were wrong. It hurt her terribly to feel that Breck was furious with his cousin for what he considered a flirtation with his inferior. That was why he had glared so at West.

75

"It would seem so to one who had not heard all Mr. West said to me and had not observed his manner," she confessed to herself.

Marie was well aware of her attractiveness; in France she had experienced any amount of love-making. She had given many smiles and pretty speeches and had listened to all sorts of things. It was quite a matter of course, feeling that men were attracted by her. West's manner to her had not flattered or flustered her in the least, but she had been intensely pleased that a Dunbarton-Kent liked her, in friendly fashion and, as it seemed to Marie, with a touch of genuinely charming gallantry. Marie felt that West was a great social favorite, rich and of a proud family, and all he had intended to convey to her was a kindly and friendly spirit; he was sorry for the way in which his family had treated her. She attached no importance to his gallantry; undoubtedly it was his manner to all women.

But to be so misunderstood by the man by whom she wished most intensely to be understood! It was useless to tell herself that he was "strange" and apparently set apart from his family, that there was something, she could not imagine what, wrong with Breck. It simply hurt her all over, the way he had looked and had spoken. It made her feel quite ill.

Marie looked at Breck's windows and her throat ached. There was a light in his room, the shades were drawn and his silhouette was distinctly outlined against the window-shade near his desk. The darkness was yielding to the rising moon, the outline of the house grew distinct and the tops of the trees began to show against the sky, and Marie thought of what she had said to West, that her heart sat upon the topmost branch. It was quite true. Almost ever since she could remember, she had cherished a dream, and it had kept her out of trouble. Some day there would be the man of firm character, a man of worth and distinction, who would love her profoundly. Marrying any one of the men she had known had seemed so impossible; no one of them had been in any way the man of her dreams. It was for him she had taken such pains to speak French and English correctly and had noted so carefully what were ladylike manners. And how wonderfully she would love him, when he appeared! How carefully she would educate herself to be just what he wished her to be! He would be a man to whom small social prejudices did not matter, he would be above all such trifling things—they would simply love each other and help each other. Sometimes when wrapped in thoughts of her dream-lover, Marie turned quite pale with emotion; she thought of her dream-lover now and grew tense. Then she thought of Breck's frowning brows and was utterly depressed; he seemed to regard her almost with aversion.

The garage stifled her; she could not sit still. She opened her window to the night, felt the relief of the cool air, and longed to get away from the garage and out of sight of the house. She had never left the garage, night or day, except for her meals or under

Mrs. Dunbarton-Kent's orders. But she had not been
told that she must stay in the garage all the time.
There was no reason why she should not walk in the
park; there were no guests this evening and Mrs. Dunbarton-Kent had given no order for the car.

Marie put on her coat and went down into the moonlight, crossed the grass-plot behind the house and went
into the park. It was clear and cold, the brisk air was
delicious; Marie felt better. After all, time was the
best test. She would go quietly on, doing her very
best, be polite to every one and very careful of her
manner to West; he must not talk much to her in the
garage. In time she would win the respect of the
entire Dunbarton-Kent household; to honesty and determination were not all things possible?

It was very still under the trees, only the noise of
the dead leaves. Marie looked up through the bare
branches at the fleece of clouds whitened by the moon.
Her spirits rose and she began to amuse herself by
making a great rustling among the dead leaves, seeking out the hollows where they lay thick. She skipped
and danced about among them, gathering up armfuls
and throwing them up to the moon, then dodging the
descending shower. Then she stopped and listened,
for there was music somewhere, a piano touched
lightly. Then there followed brilliant chords and
thrills, then a thunder of bass notes.

At first, Marie could not determine just where she
was, for she had wandered aimlessly. Then she saw
that she had followed the slope of the park and that

she was near the park wall, some distance from the park cottage, and that the piano must be in the house just above the cottage, the pretty house that belonged to the ostracized Mrs. Smith. Some one was playing brilliantly.

Marie followed the wall along until she reached the park cottage. It was shuttered and dark, but Mrs. Smith's house was brightly lighted and the shades undrawn, for, even with the view cut off by the wall which was a foot taller than she was, Marie could see the ceiling of a room and pictures on the wall. Evidently the piano was in that room, but she was not tall enough to see who was playing.

It was tantalizing, and Marie looked for something that would raise her high enough to look over the wall. In the corner made by the joining of the wall and the cottage, she found it, a stump on which she could stand. She mounted it and looked full into the brightly lighted room.

It was a lovely room, low-ceilinged and long, with a big fireplace, a shining floor on which were soft rugs and luxurious chairs and couches. There were a number of lamps of curious design and many paintings on the walls and in the near end of the room was a grand piano. Before it sat a woman who looked a fit tenant for all this artistic luxury. Marie could see only her back and her moving arms, but even so she impressed Marie as supremely rich and graceful, her ink-black hair was so abundant and banded with red, her shoulders were so regal and her waist and hips so slim. She was wearing a clinging gown of some shimmering material, there were gold and red lights in it, and the sleeves were a wrinkled sheath over long arms. Her head was thrown back as if enraptured by her own playing and she swayed from side to side as her fingers swept the keys. It was a magnificent, thunderous thing she was playing, and Marie looked and listened with parted lips, unconscious at first that there was some one else in the room. Then she saw that a negro woman in serving-maid's cap and apron and carrying a coat and furs had come up to the piano and appeared to be waiting; evidently her mistress was going somewhere.

The music came to an end with final thunderous notes, the woman sat for a moment with hands lifted from the keys, then whirled about and stood up. The queer crane-necked lamp suspended above the piano cast its light full on the woman's face, features and coloring were distinct, and Marie stood rooted to the stump on which she stood, paralyzed, except for the chills which crept from the roots of her hair and ran down her spine, held motionless during the moments while the maid helped her mistress with her coat and adjusted the sables about her shoulders: the woman's rich-hued face was unforgettable; the tickle of those furs against her flesh a well-remembered horror.

Then the woman moved out of sight. Into the hall? To the front door? Quite able to see a face staring at her over the wall? . . . Marie sprang from the stump and fled blindly, but for only a few steps, for she col-

lided violently with a man who must have been standing just behind her—Marie knew it was a man even
before powerful arms gripped her—and when he
pressed his hand on her mouth, stifling her scream and
said, "Hush!" she knew who it was. . . . The next moment, the man was jerked aside and loosed his hold,
and Marie staggered and fell, striking something hard
which jarred her body and sent a sharp pain through
her head. She heard voices and sounds of a struggle
and a dog barking, all of which seemed to fade into the
distance. . . . The last thing of which she was conscious was the pain in her head.

CHAPTER X

WHEN Marie waked to consciousness after her fall in the park, it was at first only to a confused realization that she had been wounded, a pricking, smarting pain in the left side of her head. Then she knew that it was a cut being bound up; there had been the same sensation when they had dressed the cut in her arm made by a piece of shell. She had the same feeling of deafness and numbness all over, all but the place that ached. She wondered vaguely whether her ambulance had escaped. . . .

It came to her by degrees. She was not deaf; she heard a cloth being torn and water dripping into a basin. And she was in bed, her fingers felt a sheet. Then she heard distinctly a voice she knew well and which did not belong to France: "She is coming to now. . . . Lie still, Angouleme! I want to fix this thing."

It was Mrs. Dunbarton-Kent's booming command, and Marie's confused visions of the past fled before an onrush of recollections: the garage, the park, the terrible woman coming out to her front door, the man who had gripped her until he had been flung aside. She had struck her head when she fell, now she must be in her own room and it was Mrs. Dunbarton-Kent

who pressed her head back on the pillow. She was
bandaging it, and it was her black satin bulk bent over
Marie which prevented her from seeing just where she
was.

Marie lay perfectly still, but thinking clearly now:
had Breck been hurt too, she wondered? It was he
who had been behind her while she looked over the wall
and had gripped her when she ran and had kept her
from screaming; he had put his hand over her mouth.
Then some one had struck him, there had been a struggle and another voice which had sounded familiar and
a third voice which she did not know and the barking
of a dog. It had been a terrifying experience.

But the thing that frightened her now, even when
safe with Mrs. Dunbarton-Kent, was that woman.
That fearful creature at the very entrance to Kent
House! Marie never thought of her experience on the
train without a shiver of horror: there had been something so relentlessly murderous in the way the woman
had throttled her; nothing had ever frightened her as
had the steel-like grip of those fingers. There was
something secret and evil and desperate about that
woman; Marie was as certain of it as that her head
ached and as that she was still shaking with fright.
The woman must have seen her often; Marie had to
steady her breathing by reminding herself that on the
train the woman had not seen her and that she would
never connect her with the girl she had so nearly
killed.

Mrs. Dunbarton-Kent heard Marie's caught breath,

for she said, "It must hurt, but it's not a bad cut, child. You struck your head against a stone when you fell— it stunned you, that's all. I know something about first aid, and I've sent for a doctor, so don't be frightened."

They were the kindest tones Marie had ever heard from Mrs. Dunbarton-Kent, as if she was feeling regretful and sympathetic. "I am sorry to give you such trouble," Marie said faintly. She began to wonder what she would say when Mrs. Dunbarton-Kent questioned her.

"Lie still on your right side and don't talk," was Mrs. Dunbarton-Kent's next order. "I have the bandage fastened now." And she stood up. "Gibbs, take these things away, but not to the house. There's no need of frightening the girls by saying anything about it."

"Certainly not, Madame."

Marie could see the room now, her room as she had thought, brightly lighted and Gibbs standing with a towel over his arm and looking at his Roman nose, quite as usual. He took the basin from the chair beside the bed, gathered up sponges and strips of cloth and vanished in the direction of the stairway without even a glance at Marie; quite as if he were merely removing the coffee-service from the Kent House library.

Marie thought that now Mrs. Dunbarton-Kent would question her, but she did not. She switched off all but the light on the landing, then sat down by the window. There was silence for a time, then Mrs. Dunbarton-Kent sighed heavily. Marie had been cherishing hurt feelings against Mrs. Dunbarton-Kent and West's explanation had stirred her pride, but if Marie liked any one, and she did like Mrs. Dunbarton-Kent, her resentment was not proof against kindness; Marie's grievance had melted under the word, "child," as Mrs. Dunbarton-Kent had spoken it; it had expressed so much anxiety and regret and sympathy. If Mrs. Dunbarton-Kent felt in that way toward her, it would be best to tell her everything, all about the woman on the train and why she had stared at Breck that first day and how miserable she had been since she came to Kent House, everything.

"It is kind of you to sit with me, Madame," she began.

"I'm waiting for the doctor—West went for him," Mrs. Dunbarton-Kent said impatiently. Then anxiously, "What I'm afraid of is fever." She heaved herself up and came to the bed, touched Marie's cheek, then her hand. "Do you feel feverish, child?"

The note of kindness again. Marie's hot little hand closed about Mrs. Dunbarton-Kent's fingers. "No, Madame—only the wish to tell you something."

"About Breck?" swiftly. Then, with mingled eagerness, irritation and compunction, "But it's criminal to let you talk now! Keep quiet, child, until the doctor has seen you, then tell me. Tell me everything then. I've known all along that you did have something to tell. I couldn't help believing in you, all along." The big woman was shaken; she sat down on the edge of the bed and held Marie's hand tightly.

Marie was startled by the grimly eager way in which Mrs. Dunbarton-Kent said, "About Breck?" It had not occurred to Marie before, but it occurred to her now that perhaps Mrs. Dunbarton-Kent had not believed her when she had declared that she had never seen or heard of Breck before she came to Kent House. His family seemed to regard Breck with anxiety and stern disapproval, perhaps at one time he had been a spendthrift and had lived a fast life, so there was no telling what wrong things they had been thinking about him and about her, and that had had something to do with their treatment of her. Perhaps that was the reason Breck had acted so queerly? If he had been pleasant to her, they might have thought wrong things? Whatever had been his fault, Breck was certainly trying to do right now, for no man could live more quietly than he, work hard all day and study for most of the night. It would be justice to him to tell Mrs. Dunbarton-Kent the truth.

"I do not feel too ill to talk, Madame—only the burning of the cut," she returned earnestly. "I feel that your family must have thought wrongly about me, because I seemed to have known Mr. Breck before I came here. I wish to explain: it is all because of that strange woman who lives in the pretty house next to your park, and that comes about in this way." And Marie told shudderingly of her experience on the train.

"I was so certain that the creature was an escaping criminal," Marie said vividly. "And it would seem so, for she left the train, as I have told you, quickly and

with no word to any one. She wished to be unnoticed.
. . . Let me explain further, Madame: the reason I
stared at Mr. Breck that first day was because I looked
first into his eyes and they looked to me like hers because of their lightness and the heavy black lashes.
Then in one moment I knew the features were not hers
at all nor the body. I had never seen this man before,
never, and I was confused. . . . Then, Madame, when
we rode together that day and you asked me where I
had met your nephew, I felt I could not explain and I
told you only half the truth. But I thought that,
though you were severe, you were going to like me, and
all I wished was to please you." Marie's voice
quivered. "I—I have wished so much that all your
family should like me, and I worked so hard to be
worthy, but on all sides I met with avoidance, a
strangeness all about me which I could not understand.
Then, this evening, Mr. West talked with me in the
garage kindly. My heart was broken, so I asked him
what it was in me that displeased everybody, and he
told me that to a family like yours my filling a man's
position was shocking. I could see that it might be
so, and I was glad that at last I understood. I thought,
'In time I will prove to them that, though I wear
trousers, I am womanly.'

"Still, I was distressed and lonely, so I walked in the
park to forget. Then, while walking without aim, I
heard music from the pretty house and went to the
cottage to listen and see who played. I stood up upon
a stump. Then I saw at the piano a magnificent wom-

an with abundant black hair. She played wonderfully, with passion, but her back was toward me. Then came a maid carrying furs, and the woman turned about and stood and I saw every feature.

"Madame," Marie said dramatically, "it was the very same creature of the train! Anywhere in the world I would know that woman and the expensive sables she wore. Madame, I was like the wife of Lot! I could not move, but from terror. Then she went as if to the front door and my feet were suddenly loosed. I was quite mad with terror and I ran, striking against a man whom I did not know was there behind me. I would have fallen, only he held me up, and he put his hand over my mouth to keep me from shrieking and startling everybody. He said, 'Hush!' Then I knew it was Mr. Breck. But no sooner did I know than he seemed to be struck by a blow and I fell headlong, striking my head and knowing nothing until I waked here. But first I heard a dog bark and the voice of Mr. Colfax and another voice I did not know. . . . I have told you everything now, and I beg you to understand." Then when Mrs. Dunbarton-Kent neither spoke nor moved, "Madame, do you not believe me?"

"Yes—" Mrs. Dunbarton-Kent said slowly and thickly, "I do. . . . I told Has—I've felt all along that you had no—that you were honest." She rose suddenly and walked the floor, a big dark object, passing back and forth before the bed. Then she walked to the window and stood there motionless.

From the bed, Marie stared at her. It was strange

that she should be so moved. In her surprise, Marie
forgot to rejoice that she had won Mrs. Dunbarton-
Kent's good opinion. But joy swept her when Mrs.
Dunbarton-Kent came and stood over her.

"I can't change the peculiarities of my family or of
my servants," she said steadily, "but, Marie Angouleme, just remember that I'm not a bit shocked over
your doing a man's job well, and that you have a friend
in me. West meant well when he told you what he
did, and he'll always have a pleasant word for you.
West has always been keen in reading character—he
liked you from the beginning. And I want you to
stay with me. I like you and respect you."

"Ah, Madame! You make me happy!" Marie said,
almost weeping.

"Oh, don't cry over it!" Mrs. Dunbarton-Kent exclaimed with a touch of her usual roughness. "Quiet
down now and try to sleep. I'll stay here, so you
needn't get shivers over that wearer of sables who tried
to choke the life out of you. She'll get her deserts—
I'm afraid." Her voice dropped on the last words, and
she drew a quick breath. "It's true—unfortunately:
'What's bred in the bone will come out in the flesh.' "

"I hope she may flee from this neighborhood as she
did from the train," Marie said earnestly.

Mrs. Dunbarton-Kent said nothing.

There was another matter which had troubled Marie
throughout, but she approached it obliquely. "Why
did they fight in the park, Madame, and who brought
me here? I have wondered, for I know nothing."

Mrs. Dunbarton-Kent hesitated. "Why—as nearly as I can gather, Allen Colfax, who happened to be trespassing on our property—he and his dog were in our park—thought that Breck was taking his turn at choking the life out of you, or something of the sort, so he came to the rescue. Then the night-watchman fell on the two of them. It was the night-watchman who brought you up here and called me."

Marie had not known that Kent House possessed a night-watchman. This information did not assuage her anxiety however. "It was all my fault—all Mr. Breck did was to keep me from falling when I ran against him and from screaming aloud," Marie said distressed. "I think he must have been walking in the park and came to see who it was who was looking over the wall. Then suddenly I ran against him." Then when Mrs. Dunbarton-Kent said nothing, she ventured politely, "I hope Mr. Breck was not hurt, Madame?"

"No. He probably had his reasons for being where he was, but I think he'll keep to his room in the evenings, after this."

Mrs. Dunbarton-Kent answered so sternly that Marie asked no more questions.

But she was troubled. Beneath all her abruptness and severity, Mrs. Dunbarton-Kent had a kind heart; why then was she so unforgiving of her nephew? Even if he had done something wrong once, she ought to be more kind. He had been for months and months in a German prison-camp! *Mon Dieu!* Was that not enough to make the whole world sorry for him!

CHAPTER XI

THE doctor made light of Marie's injury. "You've raised a considerable bump," he said cheerfully, "but no harm done. There is no occasion to feel anxious, Mrs. Dunbarton-Kent—a day or two and she will be about again."

He was a narrow-faced, effeminate-looking man who smiled a good deal and spoke to Mrs. Dunbarton-Kent with great deference. He gave Marie the impression of wanting to please the rich, and whether her wound was a serious one or not made very little difference to him, except as it affected Mrs. Dunbarton-Kent. From his remarks Marie learned that he lived at Huntington and this was the first time he had been called to Kent House. West must have driven his roadster at top speed to have brought him so soon.

He was a voluble man. "That dog of Colfax's," he said with disgust. "I certainly wouldn't want the brute leaping at me out of the dark—I don't wonder your little chauffeur was knocked down. Mrs. Brant-Olwin was speaking to me of Colfax just before she went to Florida—saying a good word for him—but I disagreed with her, entirely. Colfax goes too far—much too far." And he shook his head in disapproval.

If he expected to please Mrs. Dunbarton-Kent by his

remarks, he was not successful, for Marie thought that she had never seen her look more severe. It was surprising how regal the big unwieldly woman could look; her presence filled the chauffeur's room, a grimly restrained contempt for the doctor and his efforts. It was also evident to Marie that the doctor had been given an erroneous account of her mishap. But that was quite right, Marie reflected; it was best that no one but the family should know that Breck and Allen Colfax had fought; families who had pride in themselves should keep their troubles to themselves; the night-watchman, if he was as devoted to Mrs. Dunbarton-Kent as were the other servants, would say nothing, so there would be no neighborhood gossip, only blame on the dog, to whom it would not matter.

But Marie could not help looking at West, who had brought the doctor up and had stood aside while he was examining her wound. While he watched, he looked as immobile as his cousin Breck, but at the doctor's verdict his face lighted and he smiled at Marie, a reassuring congratulatory smile, and Marie smiled also: they were her friends now, Mrs. Dunbarton-Kent and West; the ache in her head did not matter. When, in addition, she won Breck's friendship, then it would be a smiling world.

Mrs. Dunbarton-Kent cut short the doctor's remarks. "Are you going to give her something to make her sleep? There's been more or less excitement, of course."

"Oh, surely. I intend to give her something—if I

may have a glass and a little water? Just a few drops
of something soothing. She ought to sleep well on into
the morning then, without any trouble to you, Mrs.
Dunbarton-Kent, and I'll come over before noon."

Glasses and water were at hand, and Marie swallowed a sweetish draught. "There, we'll get on very
nicely now," the doctor assured Mrs. Dunbarton-Kent,
and went on talking. "We have never forgotten the
lovely baskets of fruit from your garden, Mrs. Dunbarton-Kent. Delicious. I've always said that Kent
House was the most beautiful place on the sound. Mrs.
Brant-Olwin has a palace, of course, but it's too modern, money sticking out all over it, not the dignity of
Kent House. No wonder it's been the mark for
thieves. They say—"

"I hope your wife's in better health?" Mrs. Dunbarton-Kent interrupted with an ill-concealed note of
exasperation.

"Oh, very much better, thank you, Mrs. Dunbarton-
Kent. She wanted me to—"

"I'll expect you at about eleven to-morrow," Mrs.
Dunbarton-Kent interrupted again, and with an air of
finality. "West, take the doctor down now and see
him safely home. Just telephone to Gibbs from down-
stairs, will you, that he may go to bed, that everything's
all right here."

West covered her dismissal as well as he could by an
air of cordiality. "Come on, Doctor, we'll beat it for
wife and home now. We're all tremendously obliged
to you—you for mine, if I ever get a broken head!"

But as soon as the doctor had embarked on the stairs, West came back. He bent and stroke Marie's hand. "I'm so sorry, Little Chauffeuress," he said, his eyes and voice tender. "I know it hurts like the deuce, but it will be all right in a few days. There isn't a better nurse on earth than Aunt Bulah, and I'll do my best too, so don't worry."

Marie's eyes were misty with sleep and gratitude. "I do not mind the hurt, Monsieur—by and by I shall be altogether happy, so I am contented."

"That's right," he said with feeling. He straightened, looked down at her in a grave absorbed way, then turned to his aunt. "You'll stay with her to-night, won't you?" he asked with a touch of appeal.

Mrs. Dunbarton-Kent was looking from him to Marie in a curiously blank way, brows suddenly lifted and jaw dropped; for a second she seemed to be searching for her voice. "Yes—" Then she gained fuller command of it. "Of course I'm going to stay."

"Oh, Madame!" Marie objected, trying to rouse from drowsiness. "You must not. I can not be of such trouble."

"I shall stay here," Mrs. Dunbarton-Kent returned briefly.

West looked relieved. "You're a brick, Aunt Bulah! I'll get back as soon as I can. I can make myself comfortable in the garage till morning."

"It's after midnight. Take that idiot back to Huntington, then go to your room and your bed, and I'd advise you to do some thinking before morning," Mrs.

Dunbarton-Kent said sternly. "The Lord knows I have enough to think of to keep *me* awake."

"Madame—" Marie began, but her voice trailed off; her eyes were closing.

West bent to her again. "Don't try to talk," he begged anxiously. "I want you to get well, Marie. It means a great deal to me—your getting well."

But Marie did not hear him; she was asleep. When he straightened, Mrs. Dunbarton-Kent was eying him even more sternly. "Have you lost your senses?" she demanded.

"Oh, I don't know!" he retorted with an air of suppressed excitement. "Why not? She's the sweetest, most attractive thing I've ever known. It was too much for me, Breck's performance—he's insane, I think. . . . I don't know, Aunt Bulah—I won't sleep to-night, that I know. Why, she might have been killed." And he turned hastily and went down-stairs.

Mrs. Dunbarton-Kent stared after him. Then she walked about the room, her brows knitted; she looked as if an additional anxiety had been thrust upon her. Several times she paused to listen, as if impatiently waiting for West's and the doctor's departure. Then, when Marie sighed in her sleep, she stopped and looked at the little face framed in bandages, the sweet lips parted slightly, dark brows and long lashes distinct in a white tired face. On the counterpane, Marie's hand lay relaxed; it was red and work-hardened, nevertheless a shapely little hand. Mrs. Dunbarton-Kent moved it gently, put it beneath the covers.

CHAPTER XII

MRS. DUNBARTON-KENT had told West that she was going to stay with Marie, but, as soon as there was quiet below, she went down and locked the garage doors, then went into the store-room and switched on the light.

In the store-room, Marie had evolved neatness out of what had been dusty confusion: she had cleared the shelves and had sorted out the rubbish that had littered the place. When Mrs. Dunbarton-Kent turned on the light, a man who had been sitting on the pile of old tires rose and removed his cap. He was a stockily built, powerful man with a heavy but by no means an unintelligent face; it was the thick wool sweater and his baggy corduroy trousers that gave him the appearance of a pugilistic day-laborer.

"I couldn't come before, Willetts," Mrs. Dunbarton-Kent said hurriedly. "If only I'd had my wits about me, I'd have told you to go straight back and watch Mrs. Smith's house, but I was too worried over that child. I want you to go at once and keep watch on her house—see whether any one goes into it and whether she leaves it. I haven't time to explain, but it's important."

The man nodded. "I got the same idea, so I went

back the minute I'd handed the girl over to you. Then
I put Jones on the watch and came back here. You
said for me to wait here, but I thought it best to go
back. And it's a good thing I did, for—"

"Has she gone?" Mrs. Dunbarton-Kent interrupted.

"No, I think she's there still, but, Mrs. Dunbarton-
Kent, something I hardly expected happened: Breck
went to the Smith house."

"Willetts!" she said with a note of despair. "Since
talking with Angouleme I have been hoping against
hope that there was no connection between those two!"
Her flushed face grew alarmingly white.

"Don't stand, Mrs. Dunbarton-Kent," the man said
quickly and took her arm. "I'm sorry I told you suddenly. Sit here on these tires—there may be nothing in
it after all, you know."

Mrs. Dunbarton-Kent seated herself mechanically.
"I thought Breck went to his room, Willetts. When
you and he were carrying Angouleme into the garage,
I told him to go to his room and I saw him go into the
house." She was terribly shaken and distressed.

"He must have gone straight through the house and
out by the front way, for he beat me to the Smith house
by about ten minutes only, just the time it took me to
carry the girl up-stairs and then get Jones and take
him with me to the Smith house."

"And he actually went into that woman's house?"

"Jones and I got there in time to see him come out
of it. He came out of the front door and slipped along

the porch and went around the house and then struck off up to the High Road. It was plain enough he didn't want to be seen. But he came back to Kent House though, for he came into the garage and spoke to the doctor when the doctor came down from above. He asked the doctor how the girl was. 'Only stunned —the cut won't amount to anything,' the doctor said, and then Breck asked, 'Can she talk?' The doctor said, 'Yes, of course—she's quite all right,' and Breck went out quick as he came in. He left before West came down. I had the door there a crack open, so I heard and saw."

"It's an entirely new devolpment, his connection with that woman, but, if it's so, particularly after what Angouleme has told me, it would explain a good deal that's been puzzling," Mrs. Dunbarton-Kent said more collectedly. "Perhaps he and the Smith woman will leave, Willetts?"

"I don't think so, Mrs. Dunbarton-Kent. He wanted a word with her quick, no doubt of that, he'd want to tell her just what the racket was about if nothing else —he may have warned her to clear out, but, if both of them went, it would be a dead give-away. He's too cool a hand and too clever to do a thing like that. It was a mistake on his part to go back to speak to her, but he must have thought that she might be frightened and do something rash. He knows perfectly well why I'm here, he didn't expect me to be so quick, that's all. . . . What did the girl tell you, Mrs. Dunbarton-Kent?"

"It's a curious story, but I believe her," Mrs. Dun-barton-Kent said decidedly, and she told him of Marie's experience on the train. "I know fear when I see it, Willetts, and that child was still trembling at the mere sight of that woman—she told me the truth, I'm certain of it."

Willetts said thoughtfully, "It was a perfectly possible thing to happen, that on the train, and I should say that she drew the right conclusions. It's interesting. But about the resemblance to Breck, that sounds pretty far-fetched to me."

"Have you seen Mrs. Smith near by, Willetts?"

"No—only at a distance."

"I've passed her once or twice driving her runabout, but she's always veiled, and, anyway, I always avoided looking at her. I have just the general impression of a handsome dark woman with a good deal of high color, showy, like the gold eagle on the nose of her car. She always drives with the top down, affecting a racing air, it seemed to me. I didn't care to look at the woman, I wish now I had."

"She may be some one Breck used to know," Willetts suggested.

"It's possible. I've thought of that," Mrs. Dunbarton-Kent said heavily.

"Mr. Haslett ought to look into it for you."

"I'm going to get Haslett first thing in the morning. He'll have to come out here. . . . Tell me just what happened to-night, Willetts?"

"Why, some of it's guesswork, but it was like this:

I saw the girl come out of the garage and go into the
park and I trailed her. I thought surely we were on to
something. Breck was in his room, for I saw his
shadow on his window-shade. Perhaps she did simply
go for a walk, for she scuttled about in the leaves like
a squirrel and led me a dodging chase. Then, when
Mrs. Smith began to play, she made for the cottage.
I'm certain now that Breck was trailing her too, but,
as I've often told you, when it comes to light foot and
keen ears, I'm not in his class. I'm no dub in my profession, but Breck can out-sleuth me every time.

"Well, I saw the girl looking over the wall, for her
head came into the moonlight then, and I stopped back
under the trees to watch. I saw Colfax coming up
from Kent House entrance, and then it struck me that
it might be him she'd come to see. He came up to the
cottage, then everything happened at once. The girl's
head suddenly disappeared and out of the black shadow
of the cottage, where I couldn't see anything, she let
out that choked scream and I ran. But Colfax was
nearest, and it wasn't until I was on them that I saw it
was Breck he was fighting. Breck had used the
shadow to hide himself. The girl was lying on the
ground, and Breck had kicked the dog into next week
and had already given Colfax one in the eye—they
were at it hard."

There was the enjoyment of a fight and more than
a touch of admiration in Willetts' voice. "Your
nephew's a good puncher, Mrs. Dunbarton-Kent, I'll
say that much for him. . . . And a cool hand," he

added gravely. "He picked up the girl. 'She's hurt,' he said. 'We must get her up to the house.' He didn't bother about Colfax who was nursing his eye and talking to his howling dog, but started off carrying the girl, after I made sure Colfax was able to limp off home—he may be a crazy loon, but he's got pluck too, Colfax has—I caught up to Breck and we carried her between us."

"What did he say to you on the way?"

"Just what he said to you when we carried her into the garage, that he was 'on the road to the farm,' and when he reached the cottage the girl ran into him almost knocking him down and the next thing Colfax and his dog attacked him. He said he thought something must have frightened the girl and, as for Colfax, his intentions were all right, Colfax must have thought he was attacking the girl—'Just a concatenation of mistakes,' he said to me. The dog tore his coat into shreds and Colfax must have bruised him up some. Though he talked quietly enough, he was white as paper and excited, and when you sent him off he must have gone the straightest road down to the Smith house. He beat me to it, all right." The fact evidently rankled, for Willetts shook his shoulders impatiently. "I'd like to have seen them together."

"She must have heard the noise," Mrs. Dunbarton-Kent said.

"Sure she heard it. She came out on her porch to see what it was. I was busy separating Breck and Colfax, but I saw her. Then she went back in. The house was still lighted up when I went back with Jones and saw Breck coming out of the house, Then, in a little while, we saw the darky couple who work for Mrs. Smith turn off the lights and then go off to their quarters above the garage. If she left, it was Breck who gave her the tip and she got out just before Jones and I reached the house, for I'll guarantee she didn't go while we were there—unless she made an astral body of herself."

"I don't know that it makes any difference whether she goes or stays!" Mrs. Dunbarton-Kent burst out suddenly in a sort of passionate depression. "Every day seems to bring new complications and dangers!"

"I know, Mrs. Dunbarton-Kent, and Jones and I are doing our very best. In spite of the servants knowing, I don't think a word has leaked. You have friends about you who'd give a good deal to see this thing cleared up in the right way."

"That's good of you, Willetts," Mrs. Dunbarton-Kent said more calmly. "This miserable night has brought me one comfort, and that's confidence in that child up-stairs. I'm glad I was right about her."

"Maybe," he returned doubtfully. "It's certainly interesting, what she told you."

"It's the truth, every word of it, I think, Willetts. I must see Haslett and consult with him. Meantime keep watch on the Smith house and Kent House—that is all we can do to-night. I must go back to her now. I'll let West in when he comes and send him to the house, then lock up again. You have your keys, if you need to speak to me knock on the garage wall—I'll hear you."

There was that something about Mrs. Dunbarton-Kent which had won Marie, which attached her servants to her, which, in spite of her almost laughable exterior, compelled deference, more than mere respect, a genuine liking. There was real sympathy in Willetts' answer. "I will, Mrs. Dunbarton-Kent. Things look bad, but I hope it'll come out all right."

"God grant it, Willetts!" she said deeply. "I thought I had problems enough on my hands, but tonight has developed an entirely new one—love springs up sometimes where it's least expected. . . . But that has nothing to do with what we've been discussing. Go now and do the best you can with one problem, and I'll try to think out the other."

CHAPTER XIII

IT was noon of the next day when Marie waked from a vivid dream that it was spring and she was gathering sweet-scented flowers in a meadow where the birds sang. She opened her eyes to a room which was not too much shaded to keep out the sun and, on the table beside her bed, was a bowl of roses; they scented her room, while on the window-sill a bird chirped and ruffled its feathers. There had been a truly American change in the weather, the third of April had dawned mildly and the sun had risen vigorously warm; the window where the bird preened itself was open.

Marie's eyes rested first on the roses, then on the open window and the bird. Then she saw Mrs. Dunbarton-Kent sitting only a few feet away, her head laid back and her eyes closed. But she was not asleep, for Marie noticed that her fingers played a noiseless tattoo on the arm of her chair. She was pale, she looked as if she had not slept at all; she looked very tired, yet her lips were set firmly.

Marie felt that she had waked to an entirely new world, April sunshine, flowers and a friendly spirit. Cautiously she drew herself up in bed. Her head felt muffled and sore, but there was no real pain. She felt very hungry.

Then Mrs. Dunbarton-Kent opened her eyes and turned. "So you're awake! How do you feel?"

Marie had hoped that there would be the note of kindness in Mrs. Dunbarton-Kent's voice. It was there, and Marie's smile was sunny. "I am so well that I am hungry, Madame. I am afraid I slept without any regard for you who have watched so kindly."

"Hungry, are you? Well, you've waked just in time for lunch." And Mrs. Dunbarton-Kent heaved herself out of her chair and felt Marie's pulse and touched her cheek. "Your skin's cool and your eyes are clear."

"But, Madame, it can not be noon!" Marie exclaimed aghast.

"It's one o'clock."

"And you sat with me through the night and all the morning! Oh, Madame, it is no wonder you should be tired!"

"I had plenty to keep me awake," Mrs. Dunbarton-Kent said grimly. "At any rate, we're rid of the doctor's palaver, he's come and gone. I wouldn't let him wake you. . . . Now, what are you going to eat?"

"Almost anything, please, Madame."

Mrs. Dunbarton-Kent chuckled. "Well, you're going to be disappointed, for that gassing idiot ordered spoon-food for to-day. And you're to keep to your bed till to-morrow. It's all very well, I suppose, but a little soap and water won't do you any harm while I go and call up Gibbs."

"But your luncheon, Madame? I am quite able to

be left. I must not continue to be a trouble to you," Marie protested.

Mrs. Dunbarton-Kent brought a basin and towels to the bed. "I shall have my lunch here," she said in a tone that disposed of argument. "Stop bothering and wash as well as you can, most of you is bandages." And she went off down-stairs.

While Marie washed, she thought with grateful appreciation, "She is without false pride. She has nursed me herself and now she eats with me in the chauffeur's room. It is the mark of a true lady." Marie felt a huge devotion growing within her.

Gibbs, with eyes for nothing but the tray he carried, appeared promptly, and Marie said softly, "Good afternoon, Mr. Gibbs."

Gibbs bowed in her direction. "Good afternoon, Miss."

His manner was exactly the same as it had been ever since she came to Kent House, a scrupulous politeness and as few words as possible. But it did not matter to Marie now; if Breck became friendly, all would be well. Bella might continue to scorn her, Marie felt that Bella actually hated her, why she could not imagine; but Bella spent so much of her time in the city that it did not matter greatly, a silent cold-eyed creature wearing a long fur coat that concealed all but her unusual height. Marie disliked her—an arrogant frozen sort of woman. She could not imagine her loving anybody or being beloved by any one; what man would want to caress such a woman or send her flowers?

Marie had wondered about the roses on her table, but she said nothing about them until Gibbs had gone and, bolstered on the bed, she shared the table with Mrs. Dunbarton-Kent. Then she reached and touched them. "They are so very beautiful and so sweet—I waked thinking it was spring."

"West got them for you," Mrs. Dunbarton-Kent announced, and watched closely Marie's flush of pleasure.

"Did he, Madame! That was most kind."

"West has a way of being kind to girls. He's been a much sought-after young man, Angouleme."

Marie partook pleasurably of her milk-toast. "That is quite natural, Madame, for he is both handsome and of a distinguished family, and his manners are most charming."

Mrs. Dunbarton-Kent suppressed a chuckle. She wished, somewhat grimly, that her nephew could have heard the speech, accompanied as it was by an enjoyment of milk-toast. It bespoke so complete a heart-wholeness and so entire a lack of self-consciousness. But Mrs. Dunbarton-Kent knew that, despite a certain volatile quality, West was both a persistent and a skilful person. He was an odd combination of worldliness and its opposite, of secretiveness and frankness, of coldness and of kindliness, quick-witted to a degree, but rarely sharp-spoken. He had great self-control, for only those who knew him well detected a restless spirit beneath his charm of manner; he seemed to be craving something, Mrs. Dunbarton-Kent could never determine what; that he was not a happy man, she was certain. He lived well; the temptations offered to money and good looks did not seem to stir him; women either amused him or bored him, and if he had ever had a love-affair deeper than a passing flirtation Mrs. Dunbarton-Kent did not know .of it; he had seemed immune.

She had been utterly astounded by his manner to Marie. And yet, when she considered the thing, was it so astonishing? West was thirty, he had a considerable fortune, he was beholden to no one, and he was ennuied. They were a highly conventional lot, perhaps what he craved was the unusual. There was a queer streak in those three Dunbarton-Kents, Breck and Bella and West; West was showing his peculiarity for the first time. This little Canadian girl had caught his fancy, but it would take very little to disgust a man as fastidious as West. He had announced his intentions plainly enough: by that gift of flowers he had notified her that he meant to court Marie. It might or it might not be a short-lived courtship, West required careful handling. For that matter, every Dunbarton-Kent did,—that was why she had not been successful with the children of her husband's brothers, she was too downright and they were subtle. West and this child! What an utterly impossible combination!

"How old did you say you were?" she asked abruptly.

"Twenty-three, Madame—but I am very little."

"Well, never let yourself get fat. It's a curse. . . . You've never had much illness, have you?"

"In my recollection I have had the mumps only. They were most disagreeable," Marie said with conviction.

"You told me you were at a convent—you've never been taught to keep a house, though, have you?"

Marie was pleased by Mrs. Dunbarton-Kent's interest. "Oh, yes, Madame! To keep a house was the first thing that I learned. It was my father's wish, and my good aunt in St. Felix taught me strictly how a house should be managed. Afterward, with my father, I cared for his house and he praised me as neat and thrifty. And my aunt taught me how to sew beautifully. If you will permit me, I will make for you some of the lace which she taught me."

"Very well. Did you make that lace on your nightdress?" In spite of her anxiety the night before, Mrs. Dunbarton-Kent had noticed the lace-trimmed nightdress. It was a beautifully formed little body she had divested of its mannish clothes, a soft-skinned, well-cared-for body.

Marie smiled at Mrs. Dunbarton-Kent through her tangled lashes. "Yes, Madame. There is some of it upon most of my lingerie. I like very much soft and pretty things."

"A man's job hasn't made you dislike housekeeping then?"

"Oh, no, Madame! I want very much to earn enough that I may have a home. I should much prefer to do a woman's work than a man's work, only the pay is not so great."

"Men seem to enjoy facing the world alone, but there's never been a woman who did, whatever she may say about it," Mrs. Dunbarton-Kent said with conviction. "Why haven't you married?" she demanded.

Though Mrs. Dunbarton-Kent had hurled her questions, Marie was not in the least discomposed; she was so certain that Mrs. Dunbarton-Kent was prompted by kindness. "I think, Madame, because no man has made me love him sufficiently. I think I do not love very easily," she confessed.

"Um! I should say you could love intensely."

"Ah, Madame! The man who altogether pleased me, yes. I could love *him* with great passion and tenderness." The fire lifted in Marie's eyes. "There is nothing I would not do and bear for *him!* . . . But those who smile and make soft speeches because of their conceit, or those who do not mean well, or those who are rough—poof!"

"You must have had some experience. I think you'll be able to take care of yourself," Mrs. Dunbarton-Kent remarked. "Are you ambitious, Angouleme?"

"I think I am more ambitious than almost anything else," Marie answered promptly.

"Oh, you are! You'd marry money, would you— if you had the chance?"

Marie flushed. "You may not understand, Madame, and will think me presumptuous, but I have always desired to marry a man of *worth*, a character that has strength, and that he should come of good ancestry. Money I should enjoy, but it is his character I would

love. . . . It is a dream I confess to you, Madame,"
Marie added apologetically, "but even to the chauffeur
of your car is permitted a dream."

Mrs. Dunbarton-Kent nodded. "Surely." Then
she surprised Marie by getting up and walking the
floor, her look thoughtful.

She continued to walk until there was the sound of
some one on the stairs. She stopped abruptly. "Gibbs,
I suppose?" she said.

Marie knew it was not Gibbs, not that light step. It
was West who called, "May I come up?"

Mrs. Dunbarton-Kent went out hurriedly to the
landing and closed the door behind her. On the stairway she confronted West, and her look was of the
sternest. "You mustn't come up here, West."

His smile vanished. "It's Marie should decide that,
isn't it, Aunt Bulah?"

"It happens to be my garage, West."

"I am determined, Aunt Bulah—do you mean you're
going to make it hard for me?"

"I don't approve of it. I think you've taken leave
of your senses."

"I haven't. She's different from everybody. It's
like finding a gem. I'm in earnest, Aunt Bulah."

"I'm thinking of the family, West."

He flung back his head. "The family! A little
honest blood would do it good! . . . See here, Aunt
Bulah," he added more calmly, "I'm in dead earnest,
but it rests somewhat with you. If you give your countenance, it will be a romance, the social ground won't

be cut from under her. If you object, play the family
against her, send her away, you'll as good as end it, for
I wouldn't ask a girl to subject herself to the treatment
she would receive. Don't make it impossible, Aunt
Bulah."

"Choose some one in your own class, West."

"Mrs. Brant-Olwin possibly?" he retorted with sarcasm.

"You've been attentive to her."

"Because she's amusing. But I couldn't *love* Mrs.
Brant-Olwin. But this little girl!"

"I don't approve of it," Mrs. Dunbarton-Kent maintained stubbornly. "Leave her alone, West, or I shall
have to send her away."

"I won't!" he returned hotly. "I can't! I shall see
her and talk to her the very first opportunity I get."
And he turned and went down the stairs, his shoulders
squared.

But at the foot of the stairs he stopped; then he came
back. "Jones tells that he had a chance to talk with the
colored servants at the Smith house and they told him
that Mrs. Smith left the house just after the commotion
in the park last night. They don't seem to know anything about her, except that she comes and goes in her
runabout, and usually without any notice to them.
They told Jones that occasionally she telephones out
to them from town that she is coming, but her orders
are that the house shall always be ready, fires kept
going and food in the pantry, and so on. They said
she must be wealthy, that she never stinted in anything.

Jones says they are good enough servants, but particularly stupid. Mrs. Smith hired them in New Orleans and brought them up here. They didn't seem to know anything about her reputation for gambling, which queered her with every one here. The men about town all know that she's a confirmed gambler, though, Aunt Bulah. Haslett told you that, didn't he?" West had lost his flush of anger; he looked as anxious as Mrs. Dunbarton-Kent looked as soon as Mrs. Smith was mentioned.

"Willetts told Haslett and me this morning about Jones' talk with the servants," Mrs. Dunbarton-Kent said in lowered tones. "Haslett and I talked things over. He went back to town and a messenger brought me a letter from Haslett at noon. He found out at once that the woman has been gambling heavily the last month, losing big sums, winning too sometimes. Every gambling resort knows her. But so far she has put up nothing but ready money. He's trying to trace her, find out just who she is, but that will take time. If only she doesn't stake a diamond or two sometime," Mrs. Dunbarton-Kent added heavily.

"I think she'd be too shrewd to do that, Aunt Bulah," West said reassuringly. "Discovering her may be a way out for us all. I'd try to look at it that way."

"Possibly. It's what Haslett said," Mrs. Dunbarton-Kent returned drearily. "I'm glad of one thing though, Haslett has changed his mind about that child."

West's eyes flashed. "I should think so! I never heard of anything so ridiculous! Any one with an atom of sense would know that she's nothing but sweetness! Haslett couldn't risk talking to her himself of course, but he might have chosen something better than a jackass like Walter Greene to interview her. I want to get her away from all this."

"Not as you propose to do it though, West," Mrs. Dunbarton-Kent said with an instant return to sternness. "I won't have it—leave her alone."

West looked his defiance only. He went down the stairs with his shoulders squared and his head high.

Mrs. Dunbarton-Kent looked after him. "Um!" she said to herself.

When she went back to Marie, she said gravely, "They say that the Smith woman has gone. She cleared out last night."

"Madame!" Marie exclaimed. "I think she has gone forever! I think there is something secret and very wrong about that woman. I am glad she has gone."

"Well, I fancy you can walk about the park now without fear of death. I'd do my strolling in the daytime, though. . . . Have you any girl's clothes, Angouleme?"

Marie was surprised by the sudden change of subject. "But—yes, Madame. . . . In my trunk."

"Good-looking ones?"

"A very neat suit, Madame, and furs that are really handsome and a little hat which is pretty, I think. Also some gowns for the house," Marie answered with a touch of pride.

"Well, as soon as you're fit, put them on and walk about. Walking will be good for you and, when you sit down, set to work on that lace you said you'd make for me."

"But, Madame, the cars?" Marie said wide-eyed.

"Oh, Anderson or somebody can do the heavy work and run the errands and you can drive me. You turn into a girl for a while."

"Yes, Madame," Marie said, submissive but amazed.

CHAPTER XIV

CLAD in feminine garments, Marie found herself a person of leisure. Even the lace-making was forbidden for a few days, besides the materials had to be ordered from town which necessitated a delay. "Consider that you're having a holiday. Walk about," Mrs. Dunbarton-Kent commanded. "Get that head of yours well as soon as possible."

Willetts, Marie discovered, was the man who had carried her up to the house when she was hurt. On the first morning that Marie was able to go down into the garage, Mrs. Dunbarton-Kent brought him in and introduced him. "Angouleme, this is Willetts," she announced with her usual abruptness. "He's the night-watchman, so if anything scares you again just remember that he's about and call him."

Marie liked Willetts instantly; though he looked rough, he had a nice smile. "It is a pleasure to meet you, Mr. Willetts," she told him. "I wish to thank you that you bore me to the garage the other night. From experience I know that an unconscious person is very heavy." And, to Willetts' evident surprise, she held out her hand for him to clasp. Her big eyes looked more than ever the larger part of her face, for her accident had told on her.

"Oh, that was all right," he said with some embarrassment. "You're no weight at all—besides Breck
and I had you between us." His observant eyes softened pleasantly; few men would be proof against such
a glance as Marie bestowed on him, for when Breck's
name was mentioned the light in Marie's eyes became
a positive glow. So Breck had helped carry her!
Mrs. Dunbarton-Kent had not told her that.

Mrs. Dunbarton-Kent was not pleased by the admission; it was so unlike the cautious Willetts. Then she
relaxed into amusement: it was Willetts, as well as
Mr. Walter J. Greene, who had regarded the little
chauffeur with suspicion, and now he was only too evidently distracted by a smile. Such was man! Marie in
her chauffeur's uniform was highly picturesque, but,
in the little blue dress with lace at throat and wrists
and curly hair bound with a red ribbon, she was remarkably pretty. With color in her cheeks she would
be beautiful, a purple-pansy sort of beauty that in a
picture-hat and furs would be ravishing, Mrs. Dunbarton-Kent decided.

She removed Willetts promptly with the parting in-
junction to Marie to, "Walk in the park."

Marie said, "Thank you, Madame, I will," but she
said nothing about a vague intention of hers which
took definite form as soon as Willetts had made his
admission; Marie had spent two days thinking of how
to win over Breck Dunbarton-Kent; that was the next
most important thing to be accomplished.

Her morning walk was down the driveway and designed to prove to Mrs. Dunbarton-Kent that she was obeying her; Mrs. Dunbarton-Kent sat in her room in the mornings and would see her. If she could keep up her courage, she would take a longer walk in the afternoon about which she would tell no one.

So in suit and furs and a little toque, Marie circled the house and started down the driveway and was captured at once by the breath of spring; it was both chilly and warm, invigorating. The birds had migrated from somewhere and were announcing their arrival. Marie stopped at the edge of the park and watched them; they were greatly enjoying themselves among the trees, Marie thought, but it would be much pleasanter for them when the leaves came out; then they would begin to build nests. And she would be there to see, for Mrs. Dunbarton-Kent liked her now and would keep her at Kent House; it was delightful to feel that she had a home.

"Are you conjuring the birds, Marie?" a voice behind her asked.

She turned quickly; it was West. He had come from the house and had crossed the lawn, so she had not heard him. He had gone straight to Marie, determination in every line of his body, a backward glance having told him that Mrs. Dunbarton-Kent sat in her window.

Marie smiled brightly. "No, Monsieur—still I do not know the meaning of the word 'conjuring.' I was thinking that soon in the trees there would be nests."

"It's the nature of birds—and men—to build nests,

if we can persuade a woman to help us." He held out
his hand, his eyes intent yet smiling, and when Marie
gave him her hand he held it. "Are you feeling as
well as you look, little Marie?" From the entire front
of the house they could be seen, Mrs. Dunbarton-Kent
from her sitting-room, Bella from the library, and
Gibbs from the dining-room were witnesses of the
meeting. West knew that they were.

It did not occur to Marie that they were being observed, it was West's manner that embarrassed her.
She drew her hand away and substituted a pretty
speech. "I think I am altogether well, Monsieur, and
partly because of the beautiful roses. I think they
brought the spring, and who could be ill in so lovely
weather?"

West's gaze swept her admiringly. "Are you going
for a walk?" he asked.

"A little—in the park, Monsieur."

"May I come with you?"

Marie was more surprised now than she was embarrassed. Most men either looked or made pretty
speeches, but there was something determined about
the way in which West looked and spoke, quite different from his manner when he had talked with her in
the garage. Suddenly there was about him the air of
the determined lover. It was astounding; men like
West Dunbarton-Kent did not look and speak in this
way unless they were in earnest; not unless they were
openly and honestly courting a woman. Marie's color
rose and, with the feminine instinct to withdraw when

approached with unexpected determination, her air
was reluctant: "But I shall walk such a little way
only."

"Very well, just to the park entrance then?"

"Perhaps, Monsieur—but you are without your
overcoat. I am afraid you will take cold."

"I'm not in the least afraid of taking cold—I'm
warm from head to heels. It's a delight to see you
again. Come!"

Having shown the proper degree of reluctance,
Marie had no objections to offer. However, she
looked at the trees and the road, at any object rather
than at West; she gave him her eyelashes to read and
answered his eager questions, meanwhile puzzling over
him. It was so utterly surprising; he was paying court
to her. But such an impossibility! He was doing it
quite openly, with Mrs. Dunbarton-Kent looking on.
The night she was hurt, he had seemed very anxious
and she had thought it was merely because he was kind.
But this way of looking and speaking?

"You really feel all right again?" West asked.

"Altogether well, Monsieur—only a little lazy."

"You feel weak. I've worried terribly about you.
The other night, I didn't know you were hurt until
Gibbs began fussing around the house trying to find
lint and things for Aunt Bulah. When I went out to
the garage and saw you laid out on your bed unconscious, I had a shock. You looked ghastly, Marie."

He spoke with such feeling that in sheer gratitude
Marie looked at him. "I will never forget your kind-

ness, Monsieur. You and Mrs. Dunbarton-Kent, you have made me happy so I begin to love Kent House."

West looked at her in a way that made her eyes fall. "I hope you will love Kent House still better, or rather, that you will love—a Dunbarton-Kent better. . . . As I told you, I am thoroughly sick of this life—there is no satisfaction in a merely social existence. I want to settle down and work. I have several inventions to which I'd like to give my time. I can't work here, family troubles cast a pall of gloom over everything. I want a home of my own. . . . I'd like to go to Canada—what do you think of that, Marie? Some beautiful place on the St. Lawrence?"

"There are such places, Monsieur, where you could work most peacefully," Marie answered with determined steadiness, though her heart was beating uncomfortably. She felt bewildered. She wished intensely that she could escape to her room and think. Happily they had reached the entrance to Kent House park; in going back she would walk more quickly.

West looked at her lowered lashes and crimson cheek. "You are utterly *sweet*, Marie," he said with sudden passion. "In all my life, I've never met any one like you!" They had paused at the entrance and he had come close. He slipped his hands into her muff and held hers, drew the muff up against his breast. "Listen, dear, I want to tell you something."

Marie caught her breath. "Monsieur—please—"

West bent to kiss her and Marie recaptured her usual elusiveness. She left the muff in his hands and put the road between them. "I prefer that we walk more apart," she said, poised for flight, her manner half grave, half mischievous. "I think I love this Kent House greatly, but whether I love—a Dunbarton-Kent—of that I am most uncertain. And I do not kiss when I am asked—unless I wish to."

"I am in earnest, Marie," West said decidedly.

"But you are in earnest too suddenly, Monsieur."

"I'm usually sudden—when there's something I really want."

"And I am most unsudden. . . . The thing I wish for at this moment is my muff—my hands grow cold." And she shivered with a mock chill, her small feet patting the ground, about as tantalizing an object as man could look upon.

West eyed her unsmilingly; then, suddenly, he relaxed. "Well, be 'unsudden,' if you want to—it'll be all the same in the end—you'll go with me wherever I want you to go. You were a quaint thing when you were a little chauffeuress—I thought about you all the time I was in Washington, and the other night in the garage, when you were crying, I didn't know whether I was in love with you or not. But when you were hurt, I knew. . . . In skirts, you're a formidably lovable person and the prettiest thing on earth. . . . Now, here's your muff—will you come for it?"

"I think not, Monsieur."

The half-serious laughter in her eyes had lodged in his. "May I bring it across the road to you?"

"I think it will be best for you to throw it to me."

"Oh, very well—catch!"

Marie secured her muff. "Now we walk to the house, but, please, you on your side of the road and I on mine." And she walked off resolutely, but with the corners of her mouth rebellious.

West looked both exasperated and amused. "You're pretending," he asserted. "At this moment, you're thinking about as hard as you ever did in your life."

It was true. Marie was walking jauntily, but in her muff her hands were tightly gripped. "Indeed, Monsieur! Of what is it I think so profoundly?" she asked with determined lightness.

"Mostly of the great mystery, my black-a-browed cousin, Breck."

It was so correct a guess that Marie caught her breath. She was embarrassed beyond words, and they walked in silence up the driveway to where the lawn touched the park and again they were in sight of the house. Then West came determinedly to her side. "Wait a moment, Marie," he said earnestly. "You must listen to me. I'm not dependent in any way on my aunt, I can marry any one I please and whenever I please, and I love you. I think you are the 'unsudden' sort—I'm glad you are. I'm going to make you love me. . . . As for Breck—Marie, don't wonder too much about him. There are things I can't tell you, but the girl who lets him take hold on her imagination is in for serious trouble. Don't misunderstand me, Marie—I'm not saying this because I'm jealous, I'm not in the least jealous of your interest in him, for if

you knew the truth about Breck, and you will in time,
you couldn't even pity him. I understand perfectly
why Breck is a tantalizing mystery to you,—it's because you are tender-hearted. It's a quality I love—
you're sweet clear through. But, Marie, if Aunt
Bulah suspected for a minute that you have any particular interest in Breck, she would be ruthless. I'm
telling you because I love you. I want you to stay
here and win out with everybody. I want you to feel
that you have a home and such a woman as my aunt
devoted to you; Aunt Bulah is a power, in a way—
she can do a great deal, either for you or against you.
. . . You know that I'm speaking for your own good,
don't you, dear?" There was forceful earnestness in
every word he had uttered.

Marie had grown white. "I must believe that you
speak for my good, Monsieur."

"I do, Marie. I'm a Dunbarton-Kent, it hurts to
have to say what I have about a member of my family,
but I love you too much not to warn you. . . . Will
you try to love me, Marie?"

Marie looked at the hand he laid on her arm, then
up into his earnest face. "I like you very much, and
I am very grateful, but to love you—I do not know.
. . . I—I must think," she said unsteadily.

His brows came together, then, suddenly, he smiled.
"That's somewhat doubtful encouragement, little
Marie, but I must abide by it, I suppose. You 'think'
and I'll try to help you to 'think.' We'll leave it that
way for the present, but, *Marie*, I never give up any-

thing I've sent my heart on, so 'think' hard, sweet-heart."

There was no coquetry in Marie's answer, and she withdrew from his touch gently. "I will, Monsieur. At the same time I am proud that you care for me, for I am so unimportant a person. . . . I wish now, please, to go to the garage alone."

"Very well, we'll say *au revoir* here. But you'll find fresh roses in your room—they'll help you to 'think' kindly, I hope." And raising his cap gravely, he went off across the lawn to the house.

"*Mon Dieu!*" Marie whispered to herself as she went on up the driveway. "*Mon Dieu!* Now I do not know at all what to do."

CHAPTER XV

FREQUENTLY a warning proves a stimulus to desire; more often than not "the other man" paves the way to his rival.

"*Mon Dieu!* Now I do not know at all what to do," Marie had said to herself. She was far more distressed than elated over her conquest, for, in the recesses of her being, was the longing to hear another voice, the unacknowledged ache to feel the touch of another hand.

Marie was so excited and troubled by her thoughts that even so odd a thing as Mrs. Dunbarton-Kent's sending to the garage for the little dress Marie had worn that morning scarcely stirred her into surprise. She gave Gibbs the dress and went on with her thoughts, or, more correctly, her longings. After lunch, Willetts came to the garage and took out the limousine; he said he was going to drive Mrs. Dunbarton-Kent, but he did not say where she was going.

"How are you feeling?" he asked, evidently desirous of lingering as long as possible; Marie looked flushed and vivid, a tempting vision.

"I feel quite tired," Marie answered. "This afternoon, I think I shall lie down because of my head."

"That's right," Willetts said approvingly. "I'll tell

Mrs. Dunbarton-Kent you're being sensible. You want to take good care of yourself."

Then West came to take out his roadster, and Marie fled to her room; she was thankful that he did not try to talk to her. She lay down and told herself that she would remain lying down until dinner-time, that it was the right thing to do.

But when the sun began to slant through her window the urge was too much for her. She got up and began to dress hurriedly. Why should she not do as she had planned in the morning? What harm could it do? She would be so much happier if she knew.

With nervous haste, she arranged her hair so that it fluffed out becomingly beneath her toque, and her furs she left open in front so as to show her pretty blouse. She pinned one of West's roses on her blouse, then quickly removed it; the red color was very becoming, but wearing it made her uncomfortable. She compromised by wearing a string of red beads that a French soldier had given her and when she remembered what he had said, her face quivered into a smile and, suddenly, she kissed the beads:

"It is the color that draws love, Mademoiselle."

Then Marie went down into the garage, but not out by the front way; she went through the store-room and rapidly across the shrub-dotted space behind the garage and into the far end of the park. To reach the road to the farm-house, she must either semicircle through the park, or go straight through the park and walk along its outer edge until she came to the road, a considerabl. walk and two fences to climb. She chose the latter way.

She felt burning hot. It was the first time since coming to Kent House, it was one of the few times in her life, when she had sneaked to accomplish a purpose. "They all speak ill of him, not one person to be his friend, he is not allowed any longer even to come to the garage!" she breathed passionately. "I do not care if I try to discover for myself! I can not bear it any longer!" And she mastered barbed-wire fences without any great difficulty.

First there was a plowed field, then the farm-house pasture. Marie kept close to the edge of the park where there was undergrowth until she came to where the road to the farm-house emerged from the park. Then she chose the stump of a felled tree and sat down. From her position she could see the farm-house and barn, but she was well hidden from the park by the undergrowth behind her and by the big oak tree; there had been twin trees and one of them had been cut down. Marie knew that feeding-time was over; she sat very still and waited.

She did not have to wait long: Breck came out of the barn and started down the road to the park. He walked slowly and with observant eyes on the semicircular sweep of park; when half-way down the road, he bent as if taking something from the ground and his backward glance swept the farm-house and what could be seen of the High Road. Then he came on deliberately as before. It was not until he came quite near that Marie noticed that he was carrying something white in the bend of his arm. She saw it only vaguely, for in her excitement everything but his face looked blurred; his face she saw with peculiar distinctness, its almost carved immobility and the shadowed eyes.

From the first moment Marie had seen Breck Dunbarton-Kent, she had thought him the handsomest and the strongest-looking man she had ever seen and, even now, when throbbing with excitement and scarlet from embarrassment, she felt rather than saw his splendid physical perfection, his well-carried head and wide shoulders. She felt a quiver of delight oddly commingled with the fear that he would simply lift his cap and pass her by without a word or the slightest change of expression; his eyes were fixed on her, but a marble face would have shown as little recognition. When he came to within a few feet of her, without knowing in the least what she was doing, Marie stood up. She was quite speechless; she had no conception of the appeal in her eyes. He lifted his cap then, without a smile, and, for an agonizing moment, Marie felt that he meant to go straight on.

He stopped close beside her. "I saw you coming," he said. "I brought you something."

Marie changed from red to white with alarming suddenness, for she was swept by the discovery that he did not smile simply because the muscles of his face were unaccustomed to smiles and that his eyes were shadowed and watchful because of habit. His voice was gentle; he was meaning to tell her not to be frightened.

"Yes—Monsieur—" she said with difficulty. She did not know why, but she wanted to cry.

"See?" he said.

Marie's misty eyes followed his glance downward to the curve of his arm in which was cuddled a spaniel pup, a fluff of white with black splotches; from between its long silky ears, it was staring roundly at Marie. "She's a cocker spaniel," Breck explained, his voice soft, his expression changeless. "They're affectionate and very little trouble."

"Oh—" Marie said unsteadily. She was trying to wink the tears out of her eyes; the result was that they hung on her lashes, and she crimsoned with confusion.

Breck looked down at the foreshortened view of wet lashes and quivering lips and the muscles in his cheeks twitched, whether with a desire to smile or from some other emotion it would be difficult to tell. "Suppose you sit down and take her in your lap," he suggested quietly. "She'll soon make friends with you."

Marie was glad of the chance to hide her face. "It is a most *beautiful* dog," she said with greater composure.

"This baby's weaned, you can feed her almost anything now. She'll be amusement for you."

Marie lifted wide eyes. "You mean you give her to me?"

"Yes—to take with you when you go away, if you want to." After a keen survey of the park, Breck had backed against the twin tree. Its trunk hid him from

any one who might be in the park and he could see
any one who might be about the farm-house or on the
High Road. He looked down at Marie. "I've named
her, but perhaps you won't like her name."

Marie's mouth began to curl upward at the corners.
He spoke so quietly and gently; there was a circle of
warmth about her heart; if she could make him smile,
she would feel like dancing because of joy. "I think
I guess the name," she said, eyes laughing.

"Well?"

"Miss Angora Lamb."

Marie saw the smile dawn in his eyes then creep
slowly over his face, as if struggling with stiff muscles.
"Poor Gibbs! . . . No—guess again."

"I think I shall call her Dorothy, which means a
gift of God."

"I called her the Little Detective." His face had
become immobile again.

"But why such a name, Monsieur?"

"What do you think the most vicious crime in the
calender?" he demanded abruptly.

"But, Monsieur? . . . Why, to murder intentionally—or intentionally to injure a helpless creature—"

"And next?" he asked in the same even way.

"I think—to steal and lie." Marie felt chilled, for
his face was like stone; again she felt like crying.

"There is a sin which is like unto it;" he said with
even bitterness, "to give a child a bad inheritance." He
touched her shoulder. "Marie Angouleme, go away
from here!" he said low and yet emphatically. "Go

back to Canada. Go at once and forget Kent House and every one in it."

"Monsieur—?" In her surprise and distress, Marie stood up, the dog clutched close.

"I beg you to go," he said profoundly.

West was right: Breck had taken hold on Marie's imagination and, except to the mere animal, that is the beginning of love. Mrs. Dunbarton-Kent's stern disapproval of her nephew and West's warning had merely deepened her sympathy and interest. It was entirely aside from her reason, the ache which had lain in Marie ever since she had first seen Breck; he was the person of whom she had thought constantly, whom she had both pitied and admired, whose good opinion she had longed for most, whose presence she had desired most.

It was love and sympathy which had brought her to him; the urge in her was too strong to be governed by warnings or fears. She wanted to see him and talk to him; she wanted to win him; she wanted his explanation of why he was treated as he was. It was the longing for oneness which is the kernel of love. His plea was simply a part of the mystery which surrounded him, he *must* explain. But to question him was not easy; she held the dog closer. "Monsieur—why do you make of me so strange a request?"

"Because you are in danger."

Her eyes dilated. "In danger? . . . What do you mean?"

"Will you please believe me and go? I can't explain.

There are those who do not mean well by you. There is real trouble in this family, Marie Angouleme. The storm will break one of these days—don't let it catch you. You walked into it knowing nothing about it— go, and try to forget us."

Marie took her resolution in both hands. "I do not know who could wish me harm, yet I am not afraid. I do not wish to go, for I have learned to care for— for members of your family. I could not forget. I do not know what this trouble is that distresses your family. . . . Monsieur, I wish to be honest, so do not be hurt with me, because I came to-day purposely to talk with you. Perhaps I am wrong, but it has seemed to me that this family trouble circles about you. But, in my heart, I have felt a great sympathy with you—I, lonely and misunderstood, as it seemed to me, by every one in your family, have felt that you also were very unhappy. Is it not so, Monsieur?"

The color surged into Breck's face. He looked down, but he said nothing.

In her earnestness, Marie put her hand on his arm. "Monsieur, tell me what this trouble is? Why do they treat you as they do? . . . I ask not at all from curiosity—indeed I do not—but—but because I have such sympathy. Tell me and, if you wish it, I will lock it in my heart—no one shall know."

Breck looked down steadily at the ground. He was silent a very long time it seemed to Marie, until the color slowly left his face and the muscles in his cheeks began to twitch, as if he was setting his teeth tightly.

He continued to stand with head hung, until Marie began to feel ill; a guilty man would look like that.

Then the little spaniel began to squirm; she was holding it too tightly. Marie drew back from Breck and put the spaniel down. Her throat ached; why did he hang his head like that?

Then, suddenly, he straightened and looked at her in the immobile shadowed way that set her miles apart from him. "It's best to leave things as they are for the present. Tell me—do you love my cousin, West?"

It was an abrupt question shot at her from beneath keenly observant eyes, and Marie flamed scarlet. Out of her confusion of feelings, a sickness at heart, pain and surprise, she answered swiftly. "He at least is kind. I think I shall not leave Kent House immediately, Monsieur."

"I judged as much, from what I have observed," he returned as coldly as Marie had ever heard him speak. "I'll wait a little and see." He lifted his cap. "Thank you for coming, Marie Angouleme, and I am sorry you think I'm not 'kind.' I hope you may never think anything worse of me than that." And he replaced his cap and strode off.

Marie looked after him until the welling tears dimmed everything. "I should not have told him that he was not kind," she said in sorrowful regret. "I should not have questioned. It is worse than if I had not come—nothing is plainer to me than it was before."

But Marie was not telling herself the exact truth. What hurt her most was the way in which Breck had hung his head.

CHAPTER XVI

IT was some time before Marie thought of the spaniel. She was feeling wretched enough, the ache in her had become a tormenting pain, she did not know which hurt her the more, the determined way in which Breck had urged her to leave Kent House, or the way in which he had hung his head when she questioned him; when she thought that possibly the neglected dog was following Breck, she felt desperate; Breck would think that she cared nothing for his present.

She looked everywhere for the animal. It had not gone up the road to the farm-house nor down the road into the park; Marie searched the park for quite a radius. The high park wall ended at the edge of the park, then there was a fence which ran along the road to the farm and up to the High Road. It divided the Kent House property from the neglected grounds of Colfax Hall, and, finally, it occurred to Marie that the spaniel might have wandered off beyond the fence.

She thrust through the undergrowth which made a hedge row of the fence and anxiously scanned the field behind Colfax Hall. At the rear of the house were tall trees and a tangle of shrubbery, but the field was fairly open, patched here and there by weeds. To Marie's relief, half-way between her and Colfax Hall, she saw the spaniel. The little animal was nosing the ground and going in the direction of Colfax Hall.

Marie climbed the fence and started down the field in pursuit before it occurred to her that the spaniel was in danger: Colfax's fierce huge dog would with one snap end the life of anything so tiny and helpless as the spaniel; it was probably the scent of Colfax's dog that the spaniel was nosing. And there was danger to herself too; both she and her little dog were trespassing.

Terror gave speed to Marie's pursuit, but the spaniel was in search of its own kind and, having reached a well worn path, it was running toward the house. Marie did not think of stopping—it was Breck who had given her the dog. For his sake she would have faced both Colfax and his mastiff. When the spaniel disappeared in the tangle of shrubbery, she plunged after it, praying fervently that Colfax and his dog might not be at home. She tore through the shrubbery just in time to see the spaniel maneuvering with difficulty the steps of a side porch. There was a blanket beneath one of the windows on the porch and the dog hastened to it and nosed it eagerly; evidently it was the resting-place of the mastiff—when the animal was at home.

Marie thanked the Good Father for immunity so far, and tiptoed up the steps and across the porch. She seized the spaniel, intent on getting away as rapidly as possible, and she did not think about the window, but as she lifted the dog she glanced in apprehensively and what she saw held her fast for a brief space of dumb astonishment: she looked into a large and very high-ceilinged room carpeted in red and furnished in heavy old mahogany; the evening sun streamed into it, so she saw distinctly the two people in the room, Allen Colfax, standing and facing the window, and, with arms about his neck, a woman, the long lines of whose body were terrifyingly familiar to Marie; the woman of the train, Mrs. Smith?

For a paralyzing instant, Marie was certain of it, for the woman wore a hat with a flowing veil which hid her hair, and her face was hidden by Colfax's bent head; they were clasped in each other's arms, cheek to cheek, a passionate embrace. Marie stood aghast an instant too long, for Colfax lifted his head suddenly and the woman turned and looked, revealing not Mrs. Smith's rich-hued face, but the flaxen fairness of Bella Dunbarton-Kent; in the instant before Marie fled, she had the queer impression that Mrs. Smith must have transformed herself into a blonde, bleached lashes and brows and hair, for the long, strong, graceful lines of the body were so very like Mrs. Smith's, and yet the woman was certainly Bella Dunbarton-Kent. Allen Colfax was looking at Marie over Bella's shoulder, brows raised and lips parted in blank amazement which lowered on the instant into a look of rage.

Marie sprang off the porch and ran, into the shrubbery and straight up the path which led to the High Road. She heard Colfax on the porch, knew he was running after her, then heard him call, "Come back here!" She heard him swear and she ran for her life.

But it was impossible to out-distance him. There was a stile giving on the High Road and Marie scrambled over it; Colfax cleared it at a bound. He was within a few feet of her then, and Marie whirled and stood at bay. "I came—only to—get—my dog—" she panted. "If you touch me—I shall scream—I shall scream!" she said wildly. She was holding the spaniel tightly to her heaving breast; her eyes and her voice and her cheeks were afire.

Though he came close, Colfax did not touch her. "Keep quiet! I'm not going to hurt you!" he commanded. He looked at the dog; he was hot, panting and scarlet. "A likely story!" he said angrily.

"It is—quite true. My dog ran away to your house —and I was afraid your dog would kill her. She ran up on your porch—so I went to get her. . . . I could not help seeing in your window."

"How long were you there? You better tell me the truth."

"I wish to speak only the truth. I was there but a moment."

"What did you see?"

"I saw—the woman who was there."

"What woman?"

"I thought at first it was—some one else—but it was not."

"Indeed! Who was it?"

"It was Mademoiselle Bella—Dunbarton-Kent."

"You're mistaken," Colfax said more quietly. "It wasn't Bella, but some one who looks like her."

Marie knew that she was not mistaken. And she felt that he was not telling the truth. If only she could get back safely to Kent House with her dog! She was afraid of Colfax; he was a big reckless-looking creature; he was as broad-shouldered as Breck, but he did not have Breck's clean look. On that first day when she had gone to his house by mistake and he had frightened her, he was drunk, he had been scarcely able to keep his feet. He seemed to be sober now, but flushed and very angry. One of his eyes was blackened—Marie remembered his fight with Breck—and it made him look ugly, "tough."

Marie was frightened, but she tried to be tactful. "It does not matter to me who the lady was, Monsieur. I am sorry, I did not mean to see into your house. It was accidental. All I wish is to take my dog back now to Kent House, so I say good-by." And she backed away from him.

"No you don't!" Colfax said roughly. "They call you 'the little detective' at Kent House. I haven't believed it, you look like a little innocent to me, but blamed if I don't believe it now. You'll not go a step until you've given me a promise you'll keep—that you won't tell Mrs. Dunbarton-Kent or any one else about what you saw to-day."

Marie flamed first into anger. "I am not a tattle-tale! I would never run to Mrs. Dunbarton-Kent with stories of her niece!" Then stung by the thought that when Breck had named the spaniel he was making fun of her, she flared almost into tears. "I do not understand why I am insulted! Why am I called a detective? I do my work and am honest! Why 'a little detective'?"

Colfax's expression changed; he looked anxious rather than angry. "You won't carry this to the old lady then?"

"I would certainly not tell Mrs. Dunbarton-Kent that I saw you and her niece embracing," Marie retorted hotly. "Of what business of mine is it? If you wish that promise, I give it."

Colfax looked so relieved, he showed so plainly how desperately anxious he had been, that Marie was not so afraid of him. It occurred to her suddenly that she could make him tell her why she was called a detective. Then it rushed over her, her great opportunity! "But I ask something in return," she added promptly. "I wish to know what is the trouble in this Dunbarton-Kent family that makes them all so strange. Why do they treat Mr. Breck Dunbarton-Kent as they do, and also why does he act so strangely?"

Colfax looked nonplussed. Then he collected himself. "Oh, it's just an abominable mess. . . . I tell you, Marie Angouleme, I really haven't a bit of hard feeling because you used your fists on me that first day. I was drunk—I'm a fool when I'm drunk. When I get worried, I drink and then I do fool things. You're not a little detective or any of the rest of it— I take that back. I know you are not spying on us. I think you're a nice little thing, that's why, when I heard you scream the other night, I went for Breck—

there was no telling what he was up to. So I'm giving
you good advice: there's going to be a worse state of
things at Kent House, it's sure to come, and the less
you know about it the better. Don't get mixed up in
it—just quietly clear out."

Marie eyed him for a moment. He did not look
angry, but he had a dissipated, reckless appearance.
He was quite the kind who, when drinking, would not
care what wild thing he did, an irresponsible man, as
Mrs. Dunbarton-Kent had said. Evidently he and
Bella were lovers—a very secret affair—for when
driving Mrs. Dunbarton-Kent and Bella they had
passed him often, and Bella had looked over his head
always, just as Mrs. Dunbarton-Kent did; they were
deceiving Mrs. Dunbarton-Kent.

Marie distrusted Colfax utterly; he was trying to be
pleasant simply because he was afraid she would tell
Mrs. Dunbarton-Kent about his secret affair with Bella
and, naturally, he would want her to leave Kent House
as soon as possible. But it was strange that he should
say to her almost exactly what Breck had said. Breck
had refused to explain, but this man would have to tell
her what he meant by such advice; she would make
him do it. Besides, he also spoke ill of Breck.

Marie's little face was set hard. "I have no intention
of leaving this Kent House unless Mrs. Dunbarton-
Kent should tell me to go," she said. "I like this family
—there are those who have been kind to me. But there
is a thing I am determined to know: why is it that
even you speak ill of Mr. Breck Dunbarton-Kent?"

Colfax looked down. His hung head reminded Marie painfully of Breck's; he looked so very like Breck, all but his slight mustache and the dissipated lines in his face. "Confound it!" he muttered. Then he shrugged. " 'Curiosity killed a cat—it never killed a woman.' I bet it's killed many a man, though. . . . Look here, it's dangerous for me to tell you. I'd rather not tell you, Marie Angouleme. Hang it! My mother was a Dunbarton-Kent!" He looked thoroughly disturbed.

But Marie was immovable. "I will tell no one," she promised firmly. "Of it and of your secret I will say nothing to anybody. I promise you and I keep a promise."

For a moment Colfax looked at her as keenly as Breck might have. "You will, I guess," he said finally. "Perhaps Breck's the one you like. But you're making a big mistake. West's a gentleman—he's straight. He's been courted all his life, but it hasn't spoiled him. He loves artistic and unusual things—he's very clever. He has his own fortune too, he doesn't have to wait for his third of the Dunbarton-Kent money. West won't quarrel with any one—he's always treated me like a cousin—I like West. Everybody likes West. West and Breck and Bella, the Dunbarton-Kent money is to go to them, Mrs. Dunbarton-Kent has only the income from it during her life. But there's a provision in Mr. Dunbarton-Kent's will, that, if either of his heirs should commit a crime, come under the law, he, or she, will lose his portion. It's a queer thing—not that you're

not a fascinating girl and good enough for anybody—
but West has fallen in love with you. If you're wise,
you'll leave Kent House and let West court you somewhere else and marry you and keep you away from all
this family trouble. That's my well-meant advice, so
don't ask me any more—just take it."

"It is not advice for which I asked," Marie flung at
him. "I am not in love with anybody and least of all
with any person's money. More than ever I wish you
to tell me the thing I asked."

"Well, hear it then!" Colfax said in exasperation.
"You have me in a corner, I can't afford not to tell
you. . . . Breck was born and reared a thief. Before
he was twelve years old he was a skilful pickpocket.
When he was fourteen, he took to porch-climbing. He
spent his fifteenth year in a reformatory. Then an old
New England preacher took him into his family. He
stole a roll of bills from under the old man's pillow
while he was asleep and started out west with it and
was caught, and that time Breck went to prison—"

He was interrupted by Marie's gasp; she was dead
white and staring. Her arms had grown lax and the
spaniel slid to the ground. "It's true, every word of
it," Colfax said. "It happened away up in Maine, but
Haslett, Mr. Dunbarton-Kent's lawyer, heard of it, for
there was a trial and Breck gave his right name,
Breckenridge Dunbarton-Kent; the police had always
known him as Ken Smith. Then Mr. Dunbarton-Kent
went to Breck's rescue. He did all he could to get
Breck a short sentence—they gave him two years. . . .

Mr. Dunbarton-Kent was an awfully good sort, a good business man too. He'd made a lot of money and he'd helped West's father to make money. Bella's father was no account and when he died Mr. Dunbarton-Kent took Bella into his family. When West's father died, he gave West a home and looked after West's money.

"That was the kind of man Mr. Dunbarton-Kent was. He had faith in Breck, for there was something to be said for Breck: Breck's father had been the black sheep of the family, crooked as he could be— the Dunbarton-Kents had lost track of him years before—Mr. Dunbarton-Kent hadn't even known that his brother had a son. Breck's father was about as low-down the scale as a man could get when he died and left Breck to shift for himself. Stealing came easy to him, he'd been reared among crooks, you couldn't blame him so much.

"Mr. Dunbarton-Kent believed in the reformation of criminals. He used to go to see Breck while he was in prison and when Breck was released he sent him to school and then to college. He had so much faith in Breck that he made him his heir equally with West and Bella. It was Mr. Haslett who persuaded Mr. Dunbarton-Kent to put that proviso in his will. Mrs. Dunbarton-Kent wanted it there too. She adored her husband and she was willing that his nephews and niece should inherit the money, for she had no children, but she hadn't her husband's faith in Breck. If he turned out well, all right; if he didn't, he had no right to the Dunbarton-Kent money—that's the way she argued.

"Mind you, no one but Mr. Dunbarton-Kent and Mrs. Dunbarton-Kent and Haslett knew Breck's history. All we knew was that Mr. Dunbarton-Kent had hunted up his brother's son and was doing by him as he was by West and Bella. We none of us saw Breck until his first year in college—then he came to Kent House for a visit. I used to be at Kent House all the time, those days, and Breck seemed to me just a silent sort of boy, an awfully handsome fellow though.

"Mr. Dunbarton-Kent and my father died in the same year. West and I and Breck were off at different colleges. West and I came in for our money then." Colfax shrugged ruefully. "West has a lot of sense— he kept straight—but I got tangled up, got worried and drank—gambled too, lord! Then Mrs. Dunbarton-Kent shut down on me, wouldn't let me come to the house any more. As long as Mr. Dunbarton-Kent lived, so far as we know, Breck kept straight, but his third year in college he got into trouble: at a college party, a girl had a valuable diamond pendant stolen. Breck had been with her all evening. Someway or other, the college authorities had got hold of Breck's history and his belongings were searched and they found the pendant. Breck said that some one must have put it among his things. Mrs. Dunbarton-Kent was notified and she and West and Haslett quieted the thing, but Breck had to leave college. It was then Breck's history leaked to other members of the family.

"That was the first year of the war and Breck went to France and enlisted with the French. The Germans

took him prisoner and kept him till the end of the war
—he served out a pretty hard term with them, I guess.
If only he'd stayed in Europe then, but he came back
to Kent House. He was heir to several millions, for,
strictly speaking, he hadn't forfeited his right, it hadn't
been *proved* that he took that pendant. He asked Mrs.
Dunbarton-Kent to give him a chance—that he'd run
Kent House farm for her. Haslett advised against
taking him in, but Mrs. Dunbarton-Kent said she was
going to do what she thought her husband would have
done under the same circumstances, so Breck stayed.
Nobody about here knew his history, only the family.

"It was all right enough for eight months—Breck
was understood to be too much broken up by his war
experience to see anything of society, and he seemed to
want to keep away from people. Then there was the
devil to pay. I had a hand in it: I was broke and, too,
I wanted to get even with Mrs. Dunbarton-Kent, so
first I sold that strip to an agent who sold it to Mrs.
Smith and she stuck a house up on a terrace against
Kent House cottage. I didn't know the agent was buying it for Mrs. Smith. Mrs. Dunbarton-Kent raged
over it, so I told her next that I was going to sell the
Colfax share of the sound view to any one who'd buy
it and, if she didn't want Kent House ruined, she'd
have to buy my share and my price was just one hundred thousand dollars. She had to come through, but
she said such things to me that to spite her I told her
I wouldn't trust her check—she'd have to hand me the
cash when I handed her the deed."

Colfax had warmed to a certain rueful enjoyment of his revenge, but he looked grave enough when he continued. "Now, I'm telling you what's the trouble in Kent House: nobody but the family knew that Mrs. Dunbarton-Kent got the money from her bank in the afternoon. That night she put it under her pillow— I was to give her the deed in the morning. It was stolen from under her head while she was asleep. And worse, a box of jewels, thousands of dollars' worth, were taken that same night from the safe at the head of Mrs. Brant-Olwin's bed and she asleep within an arm's length of the safe. At the Brant-Olwin house there were signs of some daring porch-climbing, but not at Kent House. Every window and door in Kent House is burglar alarmed. The family were all in that night and, when Mrs. Dunbarton-Kent went to bed, the alarm was set and it was in working order the next morning. Not a window or door had been disturbed, there was not a foot-print or a finger-print, not a clue of any kind.

"But it would have been easy enough for some one *in* the house to do what was done. Mrs. Dunbarton-Kent never locks her bedroom door—any one in the house, if he were skilful, could have stolen that package of bills from under her pillow, and have gone to the Brant-Olwin house and have done that stunt too, for every one in Kent House knows how to turn the burglar alarm on and off. Whoever robbed Mrs. Dunbarton-Kent could have turned off the alarm and have gone to the Brant-Olwin house and have come back and let himself into Kent House, then have turned on the alarm again. Or any one in Kent House could have let a thief in who did the job. It might have been a one-man job, but it could have been done more easily by two people, the money and the jewels passed on to a confederate who would take care of the money and dispose of the jewels.

"The Brant-Olwin theft made a great stir, but, except for the questioning to which Mrs. Dunbarton-Kent and Haslett subjected every one in Kent House, the Kent House theft has been kept dead quiet: the family couldn't afford to advertise the thing, and the servants were frightened stiff for fear they might get mixed up in it. It's been an abominable situation: the family certain of who had committed the thefts, and at the same time detectives hired to protect Breck, to protect the family name, and the servants with no idea of who did it, but in deadly terror that they may be accused. Mrs. Brant-Olwin has detectives searching for her jewels, and Mrs. Dunbarton-Kent is doing her best to keep suspicion from being directed to Breck. She's afraid to send him away from Kent House for fear he may bring suspicion upon himself, and at the same time she loathes the sight of him—she's not the kind who enjoys shielding a criminal. Only a clever thief would plan for just such a situation, to rob his family and at the same time be protected by them. Only a patient man could wait quietly until the thing blows over and he can leave Kent House with nothing proved against him and a sum of money laid by to tide him over until he can lay claim to several millions. Breck's both clever and patient. Mrs. Dunbarton-Kent accused Breck of having stolen her hundred thousand, and he denied it as cool as could be. She and Haslett talked to him again when the Brant-Olwin theft was known and he took it calmly, denied it in the same way. Nobody else in Kent House has said a word to him about it, even West left the matter to Mrs. Dunbarton-Kent and Haslett.

"But the whole family feel as if they were on the edge of a precipice: expecting any minute that Breck will do something which will bring suspicion on himself; that he will be arrested for the Brant-Olwin theft; that the theft of the hundred thousand will leak; that their shielding a criminal will come out. Your coming to Kent House gave them a scare. Mrs. Dunbarton-Kent was afraid not to keep you, for they were certain that Mrs. Brant-Olwin or some detective of hers had sent you. Haslett had two theories: first that you might be an innocent-looking detective in Mrs. Brant-Olwin's employ, or that you might be connected in some way with Breck, certainly that you were mixed up in the thing in some way. Haslett had you looked up and, meantime, there wasn't a minute when you weren't watched by the detectives she has about the place. They gave Breck opportunities to talk to you, and he wouldn't take them. Mrs. Dunbarton-Kent stuck to it that you were just what you said you were, and so did West. West insisted that some one who looks like Mrs. Brant-Olwin, some friend of Mrs. Dunbarton-Kent's was tickled at the idea of your proposing to drive a huge thing like Mrs. Dunbarton-Kent about, and sent you to her as a joke. But Haslett looked you up thoroughly and, since the Smith incident, he grants that he was overly suspicious. West believed in you from the first. He's fallen in love with you as well, and Mrs. Dunbarton-Kent, whether she likes West's wanting to marry you or not, likes you, so it's come out well for you.

"But you've been a detective unawares. They are certain you've found Breck's confederate for them. They're finding out all they can about Mrs. Smith. They think Breck knew her from back in the days when stealing was his profession. The whole thing, her building that house just before Breck came back to Kent House, her sudden comings and goings and the fact that nobody knows just who she is or where she gets the money to gamble with—she's been gambling like a fury for the last two months—is suspicious. They think that Breck was watching you that night you were looking into Mrs. Smith's windows, and they know for certain that Breck went to her house the minute he got Willetts out of the way. They think Breck warned Mrs. Smith to clear out, for that's what she did, instantly. Clever thieves will go to any amount of trouble to secure such a haul as the Brant-Olwin jewels. Building a house, as she did, would be a small item, and, as it happened, there was the lucky chance for Mrs. Dunbarton-Kent's hundred thousand too. There's one suspicious thing and pretty convincing: that woman calls herself Mrs. Kendall Smith, and that was the name by which Breck was known to the police, 'Ken' Smith. Breck was around New York for a time, both before he went to France and after he came back, and most likely he's married to the woman. Haslett is trying quietly to find out all he can about the woman and Mrs. Dunbarton-Kent is praying that the Brant-Olwin detectives won't get on her trail. What Mrs. Dunbarton-Kent wants is by some means to get back the Brant-Olwin jewels and return them secretly, then force Breck to leave America.

"That's the whole history, and that's the way things stand at Kent House, Marie Angouleme. You would have the story, and it's better to tell you everything than to give you a fragment. It isn't just your promise that makes me think you'll keep quiet. I can't abide Mrs. Dunbarton-Kent, but I've kept quiet about all this because there are one or two people at Kent House I'd hate to hurt—West is one of them. I know it's the same with you—you have your favorites. Besides it's dangerous to talk, and you have the sense to realize it." Colfax looked at her curiously. "I'd like to know though, whether you're so set on staying at Kent House now? It's been a shock to you, all right."

Marie had listened to him without word or movement, eyes wide and blank and face white. She had listened so absorbedly that when he had finished she looked as if still listening, as if what he had said was being repeated by a voice in her brain. She was gazing at Colfax still, yet did not appear to see him; did not seem to be conscious that he had stopped talking.

He studied her blank silence. "I didn't know you cared so much for Breck," he remarked finally.

Marie turned away, as if trying vaguely to escape him, and stumbled over the spaniel. The sun had gone and it was cold; the little dog had nestled herself against Marie's feet. Mechanically Marie bent and lifted her, then started down the road.

Colfax followed her. "I'll go as far as the farm-house with you," he offered. "You look ill."

"It is not necessary, Monsieur," she returned dully. "Thank you that you have explained so fully to me," she added with an effort.

"What are you going to do? Not stay at Kent House?" he asked urgently. "You'll go, won't you?"

"What I shall do—I do not know at all," Marie answered lifelessly. "I say good-by now, Monsieur." And she moved off.

Colfax watched her go slowly along, and saw her turn in to the Kent House road. She went on past the farm-house, walking very slowly and with head bent, holding the dog in her arms. Presently the trees of Kent House park blotted out her small figure.

CHAPTER XVII

HER return to Kent House after her talk with Colfax was to Marie a complete blank; she had been unconscious of objects about her, of the way by which she had returned, unconscious even of the little spaniel in her arms. She was back again in her room, it was growing dark, she was lying prone on her bed and on the floor the spaniel was whining: those were the first outward things of which Marie was conscious. Her first thought unconnected with the history Colfax had given her was the realization that the little dog must be fed; it is usually some immediate necessity which steadies an excited brain.

Marie lifted the spaniel. "Poor little dog," she said, and began to wonder what she would do with her; then it occurred to her that she must not tell any one that she was a present from Breck. Then she began to think of the future: she could not stay at Kent House; how could she endure the misery of it? But where could she go? She would be homeless.

Marie felt that Colfax had told her the truth. When he told her of the Kent House theft, she had said to herself, "No, no, some one else must have done it—it is possible for a thief to reform." But when he told her about Mrs. Smith, her belief died in agony. That

153

evil woman! She was secret and dangerous and wicked, Marie was convinced of it. And beautiful, the kind of woman to tempt a man into evil. She lived in that house so that she might see Breck often. Such a woman would urge a man to steal that she might deck herself in shining garments and valuable sables.

Marie felt a scorching hate of the woman. There was a steady pain tearing at her: she had never owned it to herself until now, but Breck had been the man of her dreams. And he had been a thief from the time he was a little child. What one learns in childhood persists. It was only natural that when a great temptation offered, that child grown into a man should steal again, and for the woman he loved, who was almost certainly either his mistress or secretly his wife.

It was the telephone ringing sharply in the garage that disturbed her—it must be Gibbs telling her to come to dinner. She went down and the spaniel came whining after her. The little creature rolled down several steps of the stairway and Marie took her into her arms again.

It was Mrs. Dunbarton-Kent. "Angouleme, I want to see you," she said. "I've told Gibbs to bring you up to my room."

"Yes—Madame—" Marie managed to answer.

Mrs. Dunbarton-Kent rang off, and Marie was gripped by fright: Colfax had said that there were detectives watching her, perhaps they had seen her talking with Breck and afterward with Colfax, and Mrs. Dunbarton-Kent meant to question her. But she would tell her nothing—not a word. She had promised, besides it would kill her to have to talk about Breck. . . . It would be best not to explain at all, simply say that she wished to leave Kent House.

Then Marie remembered the spaniel and carried her up to her room and shut her in. After seeing Mrs. Dunbarton-Kent, she would bring the dog something to eat; she thought desolately that she would like to take the little animal with her when she left Kent House.

She went down into the garage, and the spaniel began to yelp and whine with all the misery of a lonely puppy. Then Willetts startled her: he came out from behind one of the cars and, instantly, Marie was certain that he was one of the detectives, not merely a night-watchman. Very likely he knew that she had talked with Breck that afternoon. "It is my little dog," she said confusedly. "She is hungry, yet Mrs. Dunbarton-Kent has sent for me and I must go."

"I was looking at that car," Willetts explained in his turn. He smiled at Marie. "So some one wished the dog on you, did he? I thought you were going to lie down this afternoon?"

He did know then. Marie was frightened, yet determined not to tell what either Breck or Colfax had said to her. "I lay down until I was tired, Monsieur, then I walked. The dog is hungry, so she cries."

She looked like an ill and distressed child, very wide-eyed and white and her black curls loose and tumbled about her face. "Don't you be scared about Colfax,"

Willetts said soothingly. "I was looking about for you, afraid you might have got into some more trouble. I saw Colfax talking to you on the High Road and I saw you bring the dog away with you. Colfax is mischievous—he'd like to have you get into trouble with Mrs. Dunbarton-Kent over the dog. I guess he wished some of his troubles on you as well, didn't he? Told you he was broke and ill-treated by Mrs. Dunbarton-Kent?"

It was evident to Marie that Willetts did not know about her meeting with Breck, and that was a relief. And she could answer his question without breaking her promise to Colfax. "Yes," she confessed.

"I thought so. There's not a Dunbarton-Kent will speak to Colfax. They have no use for him. He doesn't know anything about their affairs, but he's curious. I suppose he worried you sick, trying to quiz you about the family?"

Marie was not too frightened to use her wits: evidently Willetts knew nothing about Colfax's affair with Bella; evidently he did not guess that Colfax knew all about the state of affairs at Kent House. It was Bella, of course, who had told Colfax about the theft of the hundred thousand dollars and just what Mrs. Dunbarton-Kent was doing and what she wanted to do.

"I would not answer such questions, Monsieur," Marie declared. "Besides I myself like Mrs. Dunbarton-Kent too well to be affected by anything Monsieur Colfax might say against her. He seems to me a reck-

less man. I did not wish to talk with him, but it happened so that I could not help it."

"I don't doubt that," Willetts said kindly. "He's
always nosing around Kent House, and he's a good
person to avoid. He had no business frightening you
with his talk. You look pretty sick—does your head
hurt you?" Willetts had come completely to Mrs.
Dunbarton-Kent's view of Marie, plus a very natural
appreciation of velvety eyes and a soft voice: the little
thing hadn't a particle of harm in her; she was not the
wily kind either; she was as honest as the day.

Did her head hurt her? Both Marie's head and her
heart ached. And she wanted desperately to escape.
"I am troubled about the little dog—I wish she did not
cry. And also my head hurts so I feel almost that I
must cry too. But I must go immediately to Mrs. Dunbarton-Kent, for she waits for me." Like most women,
Marie could be wily when it was necessary; it was
quite evident that Willetts admired her.

"I'll look after the dog—you go on to the house.
Tell Mrs. Dunbarton-Kent your head hurts and get her
to do something for it. I haven't told her about Colfax
waylaying you, so you needn't be afraid she'll scold.
Don't worry about it, and, if anything else comes up to
bother you, tell me and I'll help you the best I can."

"Thank you, Monsieur—I will remember," Marie
promised. She felt additionally wretched at having
misled Willetts, but it could not be helped. The important thing was to keep her secret and get away from
Kent House as soon as she could.

Gibbs, with his downcast eyes and bow, was waiting for her at the entrance to the back hall. Marie remembered how hopefully she had followed Breck through the hall that first day. She had never been farther than the servants' dining-room since, but she remembered very well the wide front hall into which Gibbs now preceded her. They passed the library, and Marie felt poignantly ashamed when she saw West sitting before the fire and reading. She had not thought of him once since Colfax had talked to her; she had thought of Breck, only Breck. She wanted to hurry away from Kent House because she could not bear to see Breck again, and she had not thought once of the man who in an open and manly way had told her that he loved her and that he meant to make her love him.

"I have been thinking and acting wildly," Marie said to herself. She was ashamed; she walked quickly past the library door. West had been so honest with her and perversely she had wanted to win the man who had never shown her a particle of kindness; even the little dog he had given her, he had called "The Little Detective," coolly making fun of her ignorance. Marie's white cheeks grew hot.

Then, when they reached the upper hall, Marie felt a clutch at her heart, for, in the room which they passed, sitting at the writing-desk and with her back to the open door, was Bella, gowned in something clinging and shimmering, her splendid shoulders, slim waist and long lines so exact a reminder of Mrs. Smith as she had sat at her piano that Marie experienced much the same shock which had caused her to stand and stare through Colfax's window that afternoon. And with much the same feeling of gazing at an unreality, Marie noticed Bella's halo of flaxen-yellow hair.

Bella turned her head and looked at her, but instantly Marie forgot her, for a door at the end of the hall had opened and Breck, dressed for dinner, came out and toward her. Gibbs had paused to knock on Mrs. Dunbarton-Kent's door, so Marie had to stand still with Breck's eyes fixed steadily on her. She shrank, she could not help it, but though her hands and her forehead grew moist, she could not look away from his intent gaze. She felt that he saw in her eyes the feeling of sickness she could not control.

He passed her without speaking and she was incapable of speech. Then, in a dazed way, she heard Gibbs say, "She is here, Madame." He was holding Mrs. Dunbarton-Kent's door open and was waiting for Marie to go in.

Mrs. Dunbarton-Kent had been walking about; now she stood in the center of the room, an energetic bulk. "I'll be down in twenty minutes," she said to Gibbs, and to Marie, "Come in. You weren't at the garage when I called up first?"

Marie courtesied. "I was walking, Madame," she answered huskily.

Then Mrs. Dunbarton-Kent noticed her white face. "What's the matter?" she demanded.

"I am very tired, Madame—and anxious because I must tell you—"

"You spent the afternoon walking and worrying, of course," Mrs. Dunbarton-Kent interrupted. "Have a headache and all the rest of it, and all because of a man. A man who's in love and thinks he's not going to have things all his own way is harder to handle than a porcupine. He's enough to make even a hippopotamus nervous." And Mrs. Dunbarton-Kent seated herself as heavily as might the animal she mentioned. "You've been picking out the porcupine quills all afternoon, of course, and, as you're not a hippo, you've made yourself sick over it. . . . Put the pillows behind you on the couch there—I want to talk to you."

Marie obeyed her. Evidently Mrs. Dunbarton-Kent was going to talk about West. She was annoyed with him, but she did not seem to be angry with her. Better to hear what Mrs. Dunbarton-Kent had to say, then tell her that she could not love West and that she must leave Kent House. Leaving Mrs. Dunbarton-Kent would be like parting from a dear friend, and leaving Kent House like leaving one's home never to return. Marie's throat ached from the tears she was trying to restrain.

What Mrs. Dunbarton-Kent said was utterly unexpected. "Marie Angouleme, what sort of a life do you think I have here at Kent House with three people who don't love me or one another?"

Marie was so surprised that she did not answer.

Mrs. Dunbarton-Kent answered her own question and forcibly. "A lonely anxious existence! There's something in the nature of these three Dunbarton-

Kents that mixes with my nature about as successfully as oil does with water. I had a wonderful husband, child—I loved every inch of him and every word he uttered, but I haven't him any more. I've had an empty heart ever since he left me," her small usually snapping eyes filled, "and evidently I didn't deserve a child—I prayed every day of my married life for a child—but I haven't any." She paused and steadied her voice to its usual abruptness. "You're a lonely child—I like you. I'm not often mistaken in such things—I know you like me. I'm a lonely old woman —I want you to come into Kent House and be my companion. Not a servant, mind you! Just a bit of sunshine to offset the gloom."

For one moment Marie stared into a desolate, homeless space, a vista unobstructed by kindness or interest; then her face began to quiver, "Oh—Madame—!" Then she burst into tears.

"Come over here to me, child," Mrs. Dunbarton-Kent said in an astonishingly soft voice, and Marie went gropingly to her and Mrs. Dunbarton-Kent drew her down until Marie knelt beside her. She put her huge arm about Marie's neck and Marie buried her face in Mrs. Dunbarton-Kent's ample lap.

She stroked Marie's hair. "You be my little friend," she said in the same soft way. "You shall have a home with me."

"It is such—kindness—" Marie sobbed, "and I was about to tell you—to tell you that I must leave Kent House."

"Why, child?"

"Because—because I was so unhappy. My heart felt broken."

"You didn't want to leave Kent House, but you thought it was going to be pretty hard for you here, eh?"

"Yes, Madame."

"Every girl should have her chance to at least guess at the nature of the man who wants her—give him his chance too, I say. More often than not, marriage is two guesses gone wrong—but let them have their chance. There may be a good deal of the worse about it—this is not a joyous household—but you'll dwell in Kent House—for better or for worse—will you, Marie Angouleme?"

Marie turned her face and kissed Mrs. Dunbarton-Kent's hand. "To have a home and you for a very dear friend—I could not have thought of anything more wonderful. I shall try very hard to be deserving, Madame."

"I believe you," Mrs. Dunbarton-Kent said decidedly. Then with grim amusement: "It'll be a surprise to some people, but why not get a little fun out of life? . . . Do you know why I wanted that dress of yours, Marie?"

It seemed to Marie that a year had passed since the forgotten incident. "No, Madame."

"I took it to a woman who makes pretty things in two days' time. You're going to have an evening gown."

"Madame!" Though the tears hung on Marie's lashes, her lips trembled into a smile. Then she said with quick independence, "But for that I must pay—I will care for the cars and drive you."

"Care for the cars nothing!" Mrs. Dunbarton-Kent returned positively. "Didn't I tell you, you were to turn into a girl? You can drive me and make lace the rest of the time if you want to, but you're going to have the room next to mine and go down with me to breakfast, lunch and dinner. I'll see that you have pin-money and plenty over, and you'll earn it—you'll have your troubles."

Marie had not grasped at all what Mrs. Dunbarton-Kent's offer of a home really meant: sitting at the same table with Breck, with Bella and with West, to become one of the family. Mrs. Dunbarton-Kent meant that she and West were to judge of each other. It would be terribly difficult: seeing Breck every day, knowing the family secret and hiding the knowledge; West would be a difficulty. Then Marie gathered resolution: "Only by will can I do it," she said to herself.

Mrs. Dunbarton-Kent had watched Marie's expression. "Well?" she asked.

"I was thinking that I had not understood fully all your kindness. I was afraid that I might not prove worthy to be taken into your family. But, Madame, I can try."

"Let us hope the family will prove worthy of you!" Mrs. Dunbarton-Kent said involuntarily. "We shall see." She heaved herself up. "You go over to the garage and go to bed—Gibbs'll bring you your dinner. Get your things together to-morrow and we'll move them over in the afternoon. And, mind you, not a word of this to any one, Marie."

CHAPTER XVIII

IT was her last night in her garage home, and Marie had been certain that she would not sleep. She had wanted to think, for the day seemed a jumble of occurrences with the one fact outstanding: the painful history Colfax had given her. She had wanted to think clearly of this future Mrs. Dunbarton-Kent had sprung upon her.

But sleep came before she began to think; in brain and body she was exhausted. She slept heavily and waked early to a feeling of lassitude; all that had happened the day before seemed unreal, and the future a maze of difficulties. The thing to which she clung with a sort of weary gratitude was Mrs. Dunbarton-Kent's friendship and her offer of a home. She thought of West in the same way; she owed a great deal to them both, and she was very grateful to them. How it would be with West, she could not tell; that was one of the difficulties which she must solve as best she could.

Hope or expectancy lifts one buoyantly from one's bed; love is a great vivifier, and duty a mere prod to determination. Marie dragged herself out of bed and prepared for her bath. Then she paused to listen to steps on the stairs; her nerves were awry, for she

jumped when some one knocked on her door. "Who—
is it?" she asked with a caught breath.

"Willetts. I'm sorry to disturb you, but are you all
right?" he asked. There was anxiety in his question,
though he had pitched his voice to a cheerful note.

"Yes, Monsieur—but why—?"

"Is that puppy with you?" he interrupted.

"No. . . . Is she not in the garage still?" When
she had come into the garage the night before, after
her talk with Mrs. Dunbarton-Kent, Willetts had
shown her the dog replete with supper and curled up in
a basket.

"She's disappeared," Willetts said. "It gets me—
the garage was locked up tight."

Marie had thought swiftly. She slipped on her
kimono and gathered up her hair, then opened the door.
"If the little dog has escaped, we can not help it,
Monsieur. I think I would not trouble about it," she
said quietly.

Willetts hulked large in the passageway. He smiled
at Marie but his eyes were keen. "Even if the animal
made an astral body of itself, it's of no great importance," he declared pleasantly. "I wanted to make sure
she wasn't up here, that's all—I didn't like for you to
lose your pet. . . . Did you sleep all right last night?
How are you feeling this morning?"

"I slept well, only I feel a little tired."

It was Breck who had taken the spaniel away; Marie
felt certain of it.

Willetts looked at the little figure swathed in a kimono; there were circles about Marie's eyes and she was colorless. "You look as if you hadn't slept much," he persisted. "Did anything frighten you in the night?"

Marie turned a shade whiter: perhaps Breck had done more than merely steal back the dog; perhaps he had done something dreadful again. "No. What has happened?" she asked.

"Nothing—nothing at all," Willetts declared reassuringly. "You look sick, that's the reason I asked. You want to take good care of yourself, and don't you worry about the dog—she's got out some way and made for Colfax Hall, she's all right enough. . . . I oughtn't to have bothered you and I won't keep you talking," he added pleasantly and retreated down the stairs.

But as soon as he was out of Marie's sight, he frowned angrily: the only way that puppy could have been removed was through the narrow windows up near the ceiling of the garage. It was a slick and swift and noiseless climber who could reach those windows and he, Willetts, circling about the garage all night. The person who took that dog must have used a rope-ladder or something like it to let himself down into the garage. Breck was capable of the feat, but the puzzling thing was that he had seen Breck's silhouette against the window-shade of his room, an outline seated at the desk, until morning came. Who then had got into the garage in that slick way—and swiped the puppy, of all things? Willetts pondered.

In her room, Marie went on nervously with her bathing and dressing. Why had Breck taken the dog away? It was dreadful, a whole family kept in terror by him. How could a man bear to live with every action of his watched, knowing that he was suspected, loathed and feared by his family and knowing that at any moment discovery might come from without!

Then Marie noticed it for the first time: lying on her pile of hair-pins was a pistol, a small but effective-looking weapon, which a woman could easily carry and handle, and, tied to it was a note. . . . Marie stared at the pistol for some minutes, then untied the note with trembling fingers, but not because she was afraid of the pistol, she was accustomed to firearms, she had often used her father's gun and had cleaned and loaded his pistols for him.

The note was a single line, neatly printed: "CARRY THIS WHEREVER YOU GO—YOU MAY NEED IT."

Marie did not touch the pistol; she went to her bed and sat down: some one had been in her room while she slept and had put the pistol there. It must have been Breck.

Gradually Marie thought it out: "Because you are in danger," he had said when he had begged her to leave Kent House. "There are those who do not mean well by you." Breck would not harm her, she was determined to believe that, but if there were others, like that fearful woman, who were implicated in the Brant-Olwin and the Kent House thefts, if, after the commotion in the park, Mrs. Smith suspected that she,

Marie, was the girl whom she had so nearly killed on
the train and that Marie had recognized her and would
tell of her experience, then, certainly she was in danger,
for that woman was capable of anything.

Breck had wanted her to leave Kent House so she
would not be harmed, there was that much good in
him. Why he had given her the spaniel and then had
taken it away, she could not imagine, but evidently he
thought now that she was going to stay at Kent House
and he had given her the pistol secretly that she might
protect herself. It was strange, yet it was quite true
that a man may know a woman to be wicked and at the
same time be enthralled by her. Mrs. Smith was such
a woman—a brilliant snake!

Marie wanted to believe that good struggled with
evil in Breck Dunbarton-Kent, it brought her a certain
comfort; but thinking of Mrs. Smith, her brilliancy
and beauty, turned Marie fiery hot. It might very
well be that by entering her room and leaving the pistol
with that warning message he meant to frighten her
away from Kent House, most likely a plan suggested
by Mrs. Smith. Because of that woman she was being
urged and frightened into leaving, was she? She
loathed the woman as she would a reptile, but she was
not afraid of her. Not one step would she go from
Kent House! If that was a plan between them, they
would see! The interests of the Dunbarton-Kents
were her interests now, even to protecting Breck, but
just let that woman try to harm her! She was not one
whit afraid of the abominable creature!

Marie had grown tense and flushed. She took the pistol and examined it resolutely: it was loaded, a dangerous weapon. No one must see it; she would take it under her coat when they moved her things into Kent House! it would not be safe to pack it in her trunk.

When Gibbs appeared with her breakfast, Marie was packing busily. She did not feel dull and tired any longer; she felt as one does who has lost some one who has been very dear, and yet has been left with a determined purpose. She followed her small belongings into Kent House and observed very quietly the cream and pink and mahogany of her new room.

Mrs. Dunbarton-Kent was there, looking grimly pleased. "Like it?" she asked.

"It is very beautiful," Marie returned quietly. "But it matters still more to me to be so generously taken into your family. Your interests now become mine, Madame—it is of that I am thinking."

"You're a conscientious child," Mrs. Dunbarton-Kent said, grave in her turn. "I've done what I thought was best. We'll see how it turns out."

CHAPTER XIX

IT was Mrs. Dunbarton-Kent's maid, Margaret, the
same girl who had run from Marie's friendly ad-
vances some three weeks before, who assisted Marie
that evening into a cloud of red chiffon, red silk stockings and red satin slippers, with Mrs. Dunbarton-Kent
seated near by, observing the proceeding.

Mrs. Dunbarton-Kent wore her grimly pleased expression, but Margaret's face was, as nearly as she
could make it, a blank, for the significance of Marie's
removal from the garage into Kent House had been
whisperingly discussed in the servants' hall, and Gibbs
had delivered his solemn verdict. "There's a deep purpose in this move—that girl's one of the cleverest born,
as I've often told you," Gibbs declared. "She's taken
in Mrs. D. K., and now she's leading Mr. West around
by the nose, and all the time she's laying for—you
know what. It'll lead to a tragic climax, mark me!
'Be blind, deaf and dumb—it's the only way to keep
out of trouble,' that's what I've said from the beginning. I, for one, intend to know *nothing about anything*." Margaret looked as if she knew nothing about
anything but hooks and eyes.

Mrs. Dunbarton-Kent was pleased by Marie's poise.
It was surprising, and yet it might have been expected

of the little thing, for she had not shown a particle of elation over being courted by a Dunbarton-Kent. It was enough to excite any girl, this being taken suddenly into the family and being given her chance, but Marie seemed simply to have gained gravity; she appeared to be taking her change of fortune too conscientiously to feel elated. When she and her maid invaded Marie's room, Marie had courtesied, just as usual, her unpacking had been accomplished, her room was in perfect order. Her eyes had widened when Mrs. Dunbarton-Kent had bidden Margaret hold up the red gown for inspection, but Marie had gone into no ecstasies, she had touched the dress lightly, "How very beautiful," she had said softly. "Thank you, Madame."

"I made a wild guess at the slippers—put them on first. You'll have to get out of that dress," Mrs. Dunbarton-Kent had commanded.

Marie had disrobed to her lace-edged chemise and had drawn on the red silk stockings with an entire lack of self-consciousness that had amused Mrs. Dunbarton-Kent. She smothered a chuckle when Marie sat down on the floor like any child and tried on the slippers, declining Margaret's help with a polite, "Thank you, Mademoiselle, but it is best I try on for myself." Then she had stood up and had wriggled her toes in the loose slippers, her face intensely grave. "They are, I think, only a little too large," she announced judicially. "Some paper laid within the soles will be helpful."

Margaret "laid" some paper "within the soles," and the ceremony of dressing had proceeded. At its conclusion, Margaret twisted a bit of red tulle and had banded Marie's hair with it and Marie surveyed herself in the mirror. Mrs. Dunbarton-Kent wondered whether the girl would continue to view herself with the same unbroken gravity; she was so really beautiful in the little gown, flame-red made her brunette skin whiter, emphasized the black of brows and hair and eyes; she looked seductive, an exquisite little body partly revealed.

Marie surveyed herself gravely enough, turned this way and that, without any brightening of countenance. Then, suddenly, her mouth lifted at the corners and she broke into a smile. "It is a costume more becoming than trousers," she said with conviction. "It does not displease you, Madame?"

"You'll do," Mrs. Dunbarton-Kent returned with pleased brevity. "Clear out now, Margaret, and tell Gibbs to announce dinner—we'll be down in a minute. The extra plate must be between Mr. West and Miss Bella. You can come up and tidy things here afterward."

At the mention of the ordeal of which she had been thinking all afternoon, Marie's face grew grave. "Please, Madame, may I be permitted to put my own room in order?" she begged. "It is necessary only that I hang up my clothes. Mademoiselle need not trouble herself then." She smiled at Margaret with an entire forgiveness of the slight which, at the time, had hurt

Marie so deeply. Poor servants! It was very difficult
for them, feeling frightened all the time, not knowing
what would happen and thinking of her as a detective
who might try to fix guilt upon them. "I do not wish
to give trouble to any one," Marie added, and Margaret
flushed uncomfortably.

"Very well—just my room then, Margaret," Mrs.
Dunbarton-Kent said, and Margaret hurried off to
confide her impressions to Gibbs in the pantry.

"She seems awful sweet," she whispered in an awed
way. "My, what a dress Mrs. D. K.'s given her!"

"Them high-class detective girls are good actresses,"
Gibbs returned darkly, and stationed himself in the
dining-room where he could, while looking at his
Roman nose, see to the best advantage the entrance of
the family.

West came in from the library and Bella from the
drawing-room, then Breck from up-stairs. They met
in silence and waited in silence, standing about the
table during the extra moment or two consumed by
Mrs. Dunbarton-Kent's ponderous descent from above.
Certainly there was no air of expectancy about them.

Mrs. Dunbarton-Kent came in through the hall followed so closely by Marie that, except to one who was
on the watch as Gibbs was, her presence was not apparent until Mrs. Dunbarton-Kent had reached the
table; her nephews and niece had not looked at their
aunt, they were simply waiting for her to be seated.
Gibbs moved forward to Bella's chair—even the in-
tensest interest would not cause Gibbs to depart from

routine—and West started toward Mrs. Dunbarton-
Kent; when he was at Kent House, West always seated
his aunt and Gibbs seated Bella. It was then West saw
Marie and caught his breath, and Bella turned and
stood petrified. Breck looked up and at West then,
but without the slightest change of countenance; if a
stolen glance had revealed Marie's small form following in his aunt's wake and he was prepared for Marie's
entrance, Breck could not have shown a more complete
lack of surprise; he looked very steadily at West, then
at Bella, and lastly at Marie.

Mrs. Dunbarton-Kent put her hand on the back of
her chair and drew it back with an air of decision, for
West had stopped dead on a forward step; unlike most
fair-skinned men he did not flush easily, but at that
moment he was crimson. "Take that chair next to
Bella, Marie Angouleme—seat her, West," she commanded in her deepest baritone. "We are ready now,
Gibbs."

West spring to Marie's chair and held it for her;
Bella, grown very pale and with head held high, allowed Gibbs to seat her, and Mrs. Dunbarton-Kent
seated herself with an air of the utmost satisfaction.
In the general movement, Breck seated himself without
haste, his shadowed observant eyes on Marie's white
face and downcast eyes; the only change in his face
was the twitching of the muscles in his cheeks, as if
his teeth were clamped tight on some emotion.

Marie had visioned how it would be and had braced
herself for the ordeal, but she had not guessed how

acutely she would suffer in those few minutes during which she walked to her chair.   Though she had looked only once, then had kept her eyes down, she had a vivid impression of two staring faces, West's and Bella's, one crimson and the other white, and, most vivid of all, Breck's utterly unchanged expression, neither surprise nor anger, just the usual shadowed watchfulness. Marie felt that he had known that she was coming.

She felt ill rather than confused; the table-cloth glared white and wavering.   It was West's pleasant voice that steadied her.   "Aunt Bulah, I took a look at the boats to-day.   *Amy Bell* will go to pieces if she's not repaired."

"I don't see the use of keeping them," Mrs. Dunbarton-Kent returned, "no one uses them."   Her voice was quite as usual.

So was Bella's, cool and steady.   "Why don't **you** get a motor-boat, West?"

"I've thought of it."

Marie realized that to the Dunbarton-Kent type poise is a thing carefully cultivated.   Mrs. Dunbarton-Kent had astounded West and Bella, but, after a moment of stupefaction, they spoke quite in their usual manner. At every step of the way into the dining-room, Marie had kept saying to herself, "No matter what I feel, I must be collected."   She lifted her soup-spoon and swallowed a little of the soup, by main will holding herself steady.

There was further talk of motor-boats and the Yacht Club, a conversation carried on by West, Bella and

Mrs. Dunbarton-Kent, for Marie did not hear Breck's voice once. Then West asked pleasantly, "Which do you like best, Marie—a motor-boat or something with sails?"

Marie felt that she must be quite as much at ease as he. "To arrive quickly, I should choose an engine, I think, Monsieur, but for pleasure a sailing-boat. Sails make one think of—wings." There was the slightest quiver in her voice.

West was smiling at her; his eyes seemed to be lighted by an inward glow. "Have you done much sailing?"

"Never, Monsieur. I have been in steamers only."

"May I have the *Amy Bell* put in shape, Aunt Bulah?" West asked. "She used to be a lively little boat."

"My uncle used to say that, if one wanted to drown one's enemy, the *Amy Bell* would be a good boat to choose," Breck remarked. "There was some mistake made when she was built."

Marie could not help looking at him, his voice was so deep and even, as cold as deep frozen water. And she noticed West's face; the glow left his eyes; he looked at Breck as he had looked at him that evening in the garage, calmly and gravely, and Breck returned his look, a flash of the eye, like the glint of steel.

It was Mrs. Dunbarton-Kent who spoke, restrained anger in every word. "You have a habit of quoting your uncle—it's a little out of place."

"My uncle was right about most things," Breck

returned in the same even way. He did not look at
Mrs. Dunbarton-Kent as he had looked at West; he
looked at his plate.

Mrs. Dunbarton-Kent said nothing; an expression of
pain crossed her face. Until Breck spoke she had
looked pleased: she had accomplished an entire surprise, and Marie had borne herself so well. For the
first time, Marie glanced at Bella; a faint smile had
disturbed Bella's regular profile; then she looked as
statuesque as ever. It seemed to Marie an utterly
unreal occurrence, the passionate embrace she had wit-
nessed the day before and the flushed face Bella had
lifted from Colfax's shoulder. Evidently there were
unguessed depths of passion in Bella; undoubtedly
Breck's immobility covered as secret and as passionate
a nature. Marie felt a shrinking dislike for Bella;
Bella's affair with Colfax was none of her business,
Marie considered that she had no right to judge her,
but Bella's long body, gracefully carried head and
haughty profile reminded her of Mrs. Smith; she
seemed to her the same type of woman, secret and outwardly cold, but brilliantly beautiful if she chose to
make herself so; and passionate to a degree, for the
face Bella had lifted from Colfax's shoulder had been
a revelation.

"I wasn't thinking of painful things," West said
gently, his eyes on Marie. "I was thinking that 'sails
make one think of wings.' Some way or other we'll
manage a boat with 'wings,' Marie."

Mrs. Dunbarton-Kent was looking at Marie also.

"Are you chilly, child?" she asked as if looking at her and speaking to her to soothe her feelings. "I forgot to tell you to bring a scarf."

Marie smiled at her gratefully. "No, Madame, not at all. There is a beautiful warmth in this room scented with roses."

"It's a relief to sit down to dinner with beautiful thoughts and not with suggestions of horrors," Mrs. Dunbarton-Kent remarked grimly.

"It is indeed!" West said half to himself. He drew a rose from the vase in the center of the table, dried the stem, removed the thorns and offered it to Marie. He said nothing, only looked at her in an appealing way that made her drop her eyes. She held the rose, not looking at it: it was going to be very difficult for her with West doing such things while Breck looked on with that menacing glint in his eyes; he seemed to hate West. The way in which he looked at West frightened her, and yet, when Mrs. Dunbarton-Kent had spoken so sharply to Breck, she had glanced at him and his face had made her feel like crying; it was so carven and still, so terribly unhappy, as if he realized fully the aversion his family felt for him, and steeled himself against it, enduring it with a certain cold defiance.

Marie was very glad when they rose from the table. "We have coffee in the library," Mrs. Dunbarton-Kent said to Marie. "You can go to your room afterward, if you want to, child—you've had a hard day." She took Marie's hand and drew it within her arm and led

the way into the library; the girl looked so very white.
It would be a stupider person than Marie who would
not sense the family discord and be troubled by it;
besides, West did not seem to be able to control his
feelings, an embarrassing thing to a girl who was not
in love and not in the least dazzled.

"Find a corner there on the divan," she said reassuringly, and with a note of warning, "West, the
divan's not for you—you can enjoy your cachou in a
chair just as well."

"Very well," West answered quietly.

But before he retreated to the chair and took out
his little gold cachou-case, he placed the cushions for
Marie and turned his chair so that he could look at
her. Bella went to a distant lamp and took out her
knitting, and Breck stood backed against the end of
the mantel-shelf, facing them all. It was exactly as it
had been on that first day, yet how entirely different,
Marie thought; she did not feel like the same girl at
all; that time seemed a hundred years ago; now she
felt a painful interest in the three seated there.

Marie only pretended to drink her coffee, and West
took the cup from her. Then, in spite of Mrs. Dunbarton-Kent's warning, he sat down beside Marie. "I am
going over to Huntington in the morning," he said.
"Will you go with me? It'll make the ride a pleasure."

Marie's answer was involuntary. "Oh, no, Mon-
sieur! . . . It is most kind," she added quickly.
"Another day I shall like to go, but to-morrow I think
Mrs. Dunbarton-Kent will wish me to drive her."

There was an appeal to Mrs. Dunbarton-Kent in the refusal.

Mrs. Dunbarton-Kent smiled to herself. Then every one stiffened at Breck's abrupt remark: "Look the roadster over well before you ride in it, Marie Angouleme." He leveled a gleaming look at West, then, with an even, "Good night," he turned and left the room. Marie saw him go up the stairs.

Bella watched his going, her knitting suspended; Mrs. Dunbarton-Kent crimsoned with anger, and Marie sat breathing quickly, terribly startled. Breck had spoken as if he meant to frighten her, and he had looked defiance at West. West seemed to be thinking more of Marie's distress than of his own annoyance, though he looked stern enough. "Don't let yourself be disturbed by Breck's speeches," he said to Marie. "He's queer and we can't help it. The best we can do is not to notice the things he says and does. I'm sorry for him at times, in spite of everything, for he makes his own hell, Breck does—he's a mystery to me." He rose from Marie's side and replenished the fire, muttering an impatient sigh. "Lord!"

Mrs. Dunbarton-Kent was restraining herself with difficulty. "Depravity is a form of insanity, I suppose," she said bitterly.

West had straightened and a smile chased the gloom from his face. "Never mind," he said. "You've managed to introduce a bit of sunshine into the situation." He looked at Marie appealingly. "If you won't ride, will you walk with me to-morrow, Miss Marie?"

He was very persistent, Marie thought. If only she did not feel so wretched and worried, she would like him very much. He had done everything he could to help her through the evening, but he showed too plainly that he cared for her a great deal and it made her heart ache the worse. He looked very handsome standing there by the fire with the color in his cheeks and his eyes bright, such a contrast to Breck's grim immobility. Breck had frightened her; there was something altogether wrong with Breck's mind, and that might explain everything. She wanted to go to her room and think about it. She wanted to be nice to West too, appreciative and friendly. She was much too distressed and excited to be in the least coquettish or elusive; Marie felt as if she would never laugh again.

"If your aunt permits that I should walk with you, Monsieur, I shall be glad to go," she said with rather a wan smile. It seemed a propitious moment for escape, and Marie rose. "And now, Madame, I think I shall go to my room, so I say good night to every one." And she courtesied to the three, even to Bella in her distant corner.

It was a quaint "good night," an old-fashioned dignity clothed in modern firefly garments and surmounted by a gravely troubled little face; she was so utterly without self-consciousness and so anxious to please. Mrs. Dunbarton-Kent lost her angry flush. "Don't worry about anything, child," she said kindly. "Go to bed and sleep and wake up pretty. We'll arrange about to-morrow when to-morrow comes."

West's eyes dwelt on Marie and when she moved toward the hall, he started forward impulsively. Mrs. Dunbarton-Kent's warning halted him: "West!"

"Oh—I know," he muttered, but he watched Marie consumedly, the last flicker of her red gown on the stairs. Then, with an impatient glance in Bella's direction, he attacked the fire instead of speaking.

Possibly to give him the opportunity, Bella gathered up her knitting and with a quiet "Good night," followed Marie up-stairs, knitting as she went. Mrs. Dunbarton-Kent sat on, watching in a satisfied way West's aimless thrusts at the fire: it was a rare thing for West to lose his composure; she had upset him pretty thoroughly. He would not speak to her until he was, outwardly at least, calm; they were all alike in that, these three Dunbarton-Kents.

West straightened finally and faced her. "So you've changed your mind, Aunt Bulah?" he asked quietly.

Her eyes twinkled. "No. I've been of the same mind from the beginning. I was dumfounded at first —I didn't know you had so little worldliness and so much sense. Then all I wanted to know was that you were sufficiently in earnest. You've convinced me of that. I've taken her in and I intend that everybody shall recognize her. I may be a fat old woman, but I can put anything that's half-way decent on its social feet—you know that—so, as far as society's concerned, your way's clear."

"I don't know how to thank you," West said gratefully.

He bent impulsively to kiss her hand, but Mrs. Dun-barton-Kent drew it away. "Don't! Keep your gallantry for some one else! You don't love me a bit better than I love you. You are secretive, you three Dunbarton-Kents, and I'm brutally outspoken—you get on my nerves, every one of you, and I on yours. By nature we're antagonistic—you none of you have the quality that made your uncle and me one." Her deep voice deepened. "I will say though that of the three my dear husband left in my charge, you have shown the best sense and the most consideration for the family name. Doubtless you've had your escapades, but you've never let them loose on the public like the sons of many of my friends. I appreciate it, West. I'm glad to do anything I can to help you win a sweet and honest girl. I like that child—she suits me. I think she'll make you a deal more satisfactory wife than any of the girls who have tried to get you. I can help you to a certain extent, but, West, *it's she who'll do the deciding*. You know best whether she cares for you or not. I don't think she does—so far—and I think you'll have to walk pretty carefully if you mean to win out. Too much urging won't do—there's an independent streak in that child. She's not a whit dazzled or elated—she's more troubled and conscientious over her change of fortune than anything else. Remember, I've warned you."

West smiled at her and his smile was a very pleasant one. "Thank you, Aunt Bulah. There is a good deal of truth in what you say about us—we're not exactly a congenial family. Nevertheless, I'm a good deal fonder of you than you think—one may be born secretive and yet have a big respect for the outspoken sort."

"A respectful amusement would describe it better," Mrs. Dunbarton-Kent said bluntly. "A half-respectful, half-irritated amusement. Breck's secretive to the point of perversion—I don't want to talk about him,—but you and Bella, the things you think about are the things you don't talk about. It's always been so. You have a frank manner and Bella's an oyster, yet, fundamentally, you're both the same—the thing you think is the thing you don't say. Bella spends half her time in town and I hear she's with this friend and that, but not a word about what her interests are, never a detail. She goes and comes and *knits*. I detest knitting in silence. . . . What I'm meaning to say, West, is, that I'm determined that Marie shall have her chance to know you, not just the surface of you, but the inner man. I wouldn't want you for a husband—you'd drive me mad—but perhaps a mysterious reserve is the very thing which would make Marie happy. Anyway, she's going to have the chance to discover what you are under the surface."

West eyed her for a moment, and his expression might be accurately described as "half-irritated and half-amused." Then he looked down at the fire thoughtfully. "Marie said to me yesterday, 'I'm most unsudden, Monsieur.' I told her I liked the quality, and I do. I'm fastidious—I'd feel a distaste for a girl who'd be flustered over what you've done for her or be

elated over my subjection. She was exquisite to-night.
. . . I'm willing enough to have her discover all there
is in me to be discovered—but it's going to be hard
for me to control myself—I want her." He hesitated,
frowning. "I wish I had more 'mysterious reserve' in
my inner man than you say I have, for that's the thing
that has captured her imagination."

"What are you talking about?" Mrs. Dunbarton-
Kent demanded.

West turned and looked at her, distress in every line
of his face. "What's the good of keeping it from you.
You're observant, it'll be plain to you in a day or two—
if she's not in love with Breck, it's something very near
it."

"*What!*" It lifted Mrs. Dunbarton-Kent from her
chair.

"I think so, Aunt Bulah."

"*Think!* You're jealous! Most men in love are
fools!"

"I'll grant it," he said quietly, "but I think I'm not
mistaken. She pities him—he's taken hold on her
imagination. Can't you see how it would be? She
doesn't know, and to one who doesn't he would appear
pitiful—I can't help pitying him myself sometimes.
And he's dangerously handsome."

Mrs. Dunbarton-Kent said something under her
breath; she had grown white.

"Yes, 'more trouble,'" West said wearily. "I wish
I had told you before, but, as you said, I'm apt to keep
things to myself. I didn't feel certain of it until I

talked to her yesterday. I had begged you not to send her away, but since yesterday I've hoped you would. I'd have followed her, nothing will make me give her up, but even your turning your back on her would be better for her than staying where he is. . . . I haven't had a happy twenty-four hours—then the surprise to-night!"

Mrs. Dunbarton-Kent stood massive and motionless. "And he?" she asked.

West flung up his hands. "Set me another riddle! . . . I think he's tied to Mrs. Smith in more ways than one, yet he has designs of some sort—against Marie. I can't make it out exactly, only I know that it's since I've been devoted to her that he has looked as if he'd like to knife me. You saw how he looked and spoke this evening."

Mrs. Dunbarton-Kent whirled about. "We'll see!" she said with grim determination, and made for the hall.

West sprang after her and caught her arm. "Aunt Bulah! You're not going to make her unhappy?" he begged. "Don't do it! I couldn't bear it! You can't tell her the truth about him, we none of us dare do that—let things be!"

Mrs. Dunbarton-Kent shook him off. "I'm not likely to haul out the family skeleton, but I'll get at the bottom of this, or I'll know the reason why!" And she mounted the stairs with forcible decision.

CHAPTER XX

MARIE had undressed and had carefully disposed of her red gown, pondering meanwhile an entirely new idea: perhaps Breck was a little insane? West seemed to think that he was. That would explain many things: Breck's brooding withdrawn look and the strange things he said and did. Probably from the time he was a child he had not been altogether right in his mind. Think of the life he had lived, a neglected criminal boy, locked up in prison where he must have brooded. His uncle must have had a good influence on him, but that had not been for long. Then there had been no one to care for him and he had begun to steal again. Then those fearful years in a German prison! Perfectly sane men had lost their minds under such privations and sufferings. Men came out of prisons with faces carven and still like Breck's, and minds quite changed.

And those who were unbalanced had strange hatreds: Breck seemed to hate West; whenever he looked at West his eyes were like a knife. It was terrifying, the way in which he had looked when he said, "If one wanted to drown one's enemy—" And the warning way in which he said, "Look the roadster over well before you ride in it, Marie Angouleme." He wanted

to frighten West and he wanted to frighten her. He
had given her the pistol in a secret and terrifying way.
He was trying to frighten her away from Kent House,
and instigating him was Mrs. Smith. She would use
a man who was not quite sane; she was capable of
anything.

Hot and at the same time shivering, Marie locked
her door securely, then got into bed and gathered the
covers about her. With knees embraced, she sat thinking: it was a horrible state of things in Kent House;
she had not fully realized until that evening. Was
every meal like this one? Every one on a strain:
Breck looking hatred at West across the table, Bella
deceiving her aunt and endangering her family by telling everything to Colfax, and Mrs. Dunbarton-Kent
oscillating between anger and terrible anxiety, ignorant, in spite of her detectives, of much that went on.

Marie's heated brain evolved question after question.
Why did Bella's height and long lines remind her constantly of Mrs. Smith? She had not noticed Bella
particularly that first day when Gibbs had brought her
into the library, Bella had been seated at a distance,
and ever since she had seen Bella only when she was
wearing her veil and her long fur coat. But the moment she saw Bella in Colfax House without her coat
she had reminded her so vividly of Mrs. Smith that she
had been certain it was Mrs. Smith. It was very
strange, that hateful woman's resemblance to Bella and
Breck, light eyes with black lashes, like Breck's, **and a**
body like Bella's, long and strong and graceful.

Then came the tormenting thought: Breck must meet Mrs. Smith very often and very secretly. Doubtless he loved her passionately, as Bella loved Colfax. Most likely Mrs. Smith had not really gone away, but was hidden in her house. Certainly Breck had been going to meet her that night when she was playing the piano; she was going out to meet him, that was why she was putting on her furs.

Then Marie indulged in despairing thoughts: Mrs. Brant-Olwin had much money with which to search for the thieves; Mrs. Smith was gambling recklessly with the money she and Breck had stolen, she would be caught and imprisoned, as she deserved to be; Breck would be caught—that splendid strength of his would waste away in prison, he would go altogether insane— he, a Dunbarton-Kent! And his family would hang their heads in shame; perhaps in court they themselves would be held responsible? It would be terrible for Mrs. Dunbarton-Kent and it would drive West into a country where he would not be known. He wanted to leave Kent House; it was because he knew that disgrace to his family was certain. Breck's fate hung on a thread; if Colfax should drink a little too much and tell what he knew; if one of the detectives should be bribed; if one of the servants should prove disloyal. Discovery was a certainty; it was horrible!

Marie was so tense and excited that when some one knocked on her door her heart leapt into her throat and she could neither speak nor move. She found her voice only when the knock was repeated. "Who is it?"

"Have you gone to bed?" It was Mrs. Dunbarton-Kent's voice.

Marie hurried to let her in, and Mrs. Dunbarton-Kent closed the door, then looked Marie over, her flushed face and wide eyes and her little figure in its night-dress. "I suppose you were asleep? But it's early, and I want to talk to you," she said. "Get back into bed, child—I'll sit beside you."

Mrs. Dunbarton-Kent had not rushed up to Marie's room as West had thought; she had gone to her own room and had walked the floor: if West's suspicions were correct, she had done an utterly foolish thing in bringing Marie into the house, just the blundering sort of thing she was apt to do; they were keen-sighted, those Dunbarton-Kent children, and she was not; West was particularly accurate in his judgments, he was rarely mistaken. But, if Marie did care for Breck—and certainly when the girl first came, owing to Haslett's advice, Breck had been given every opportunity to talk to her—there was no reason why Marie should not tell her the truth about it. The girl was honest—Mrs. Dunbarton-Kent was as certain of it as that she was walking her room in doubt and anxiety. The thing she must settle in her own mind was what disposal to make of Marie, if West proved to be in the right; just what to say to her without giving her an inkling of the truth.

Mrs. Dunbarton-Kent had thought the matter out before she came to Marie's door, and her manner was quite as usual. She was not in the least angry with

Marie; if the girl had fallen in love with Breck it was
largely her own fault for having yielded to Haslett's
advice; she would always be ashamed of herself for
having done it, kept the child who came to her in perfect honesty and then set spies on her, used her as a
lure, in a way. When Marie had been hurt in the park
and had made her confession, Mrs. Dunbarton-Kent
had felt deeply ashamed and distressed; between them
all the child had been abominably treated. If Breck
had taken advantage of Marie's simple honesty and
tender-heartedness, she, Mrs. Dunbarton-Kent, was
wholly to blame.

When she knocked on Marie's door, Mrs. Dunbarton-Kent was fully prepared for "more trouble." She
must meet it as best she could. When she saw Marie,
looking like a child startled out of sleep, she felt im-
measurably distressed; she was a motherless girl, and
yet, because of mere suspicion, she had done nothing to
guard her from such a man as Breck. If Marie had
fixed her affections on him, there was a bitter heart-
ache in store for her.

"I'll sit here beside you," she repeated. "I simply
wanted to ask you something."

Mrs. Dunbarton-Kent's coming was a relief from
wretched terrifying thoughts, and Marie lay as close
as possible to the chair Mrs. Dunbarton-Kent drew up
to the bed. "I am most glad you have come, Madame,"
she said with sincerity.

Mrs. Dunbarton-Kent put her hand on Marie's
shoulder and looked into her eyes. "Marie," she said

gravely, "you know, don't you, that I am very fond of you and would stand by you in any trouble? And, too, that I would never pry into your heart out of mere curiosity?"

Marie braced herself instantly to answer questions and yet keep her secret; Willetts must have told Mrs. Dunbarton-Kent that she had talked with Colfax, also about the spaniel; Mrs. Dunbarton-Kent's manner was affectionate, but so purposeful. "I am certain of it, Madame," she said gravely.

"I want you to tell me then, child, truthfully and honestly—do you love my nephew, Breck?"

That question was utterly unexpected. Marie flamed scarlet, but also she shrank and shivered and her answer was instant, "No, Madame!" She met Mrs. Dunbarton-Kent's keen look with flushed directness.

"Has he ever made love to you, child?"

"Never, Madame. I am certain that he does not even like me—he has always avoided me."

Mrs. Dunbarton-Kent drew a breath of relief; the shiver that had run through Marie's body was as convincing as the shudder that had shaken her when she had told of her experience with Mrs. Smith. But there was flushed misery in Marie's eyes as well and Mrs. Dunbarton-Kent persisted. "How do you feel toward him, child? What do you think of him?"

Marie tried to explain very carefully and yet truthfully. "At first, Madame, I thought Mr. Breck a strange but a lovable man, and I felt great pity for

what seemed his loneliness. But now that I know him
better, I shrink from him. He is too strange. As this
evening at dinner, things he says are frightening to me.
And at the same time, as Mr. West also feels, I have
pity for him that he should be as he is. Please excuse
me that I speak so of any one in your family, but of my
feelings to him I am telling exactly the truth—I think
of him as an unfortunate man." Marie felt that she
was telling the very truth; she had covered the face
of her love and had buried it—alive, perhaps, but she
did not realize that.

"It's the best way to think of him," Mrs. Dunbarton-
Kent said.

She was tremendously relieved. West had been
right to some extent, Breck had appealed to the girl's
imagination. But there was no mistaking Marie's
shiver; she had sensed in Breck the things she did not
know and had been repelled. She could rely on Marie's
instinct; she could keep her at Kent House. More than
half of Mrs. Dunbarton-Kent's consternation had been
because she would lose Marie's companionship; as she
had told Marie, she had carried about with her an
empty heart.

With a sudden stir of affection, she slipped her big
arm under Marie's shoulders and drew her close, and,
with a caught breath of surprise and joy, Marie flung
her arms about her neck. Mrs. Dunbarton-Kent kissed
her, and Marie kissed her again and again, on both
cheeks.

"You're sweet, child," Mrs. Dunbarton-Kent whispered, and Marie returned, "Oh, Madame, it is all love for you in my heart. I wish to do only what will make you happy."

"Be kind to West then, child. He has his faults, but at bottom he's a fine sort and he loves you. Outwardly West is lively and care-free, but he's not a happy man —there's a restless craving something about him which I have never been able to understand—that and an intense reserve. Love will make a fine man of West, I think. I should like to see one member of this family happy." And she sighed.

"I will remember, Madame," Marie said softly. "To make you happy, I would do almost anything. I have great respect for Mr. West and much gratitude, and I think that by and by I shall feel more happy with him. My interest is now entirely centered upon this family, quite as if it were my own, and to you I have absolute devotion."

Mrs. Dunbarton-Kent patted her shoulder. "Now go to sleep," she advised. "I'm glad we've had this talk—it's brought us closer together. I did want to know just how you felt toward Breck who is an anxiety to us all. Owing to circumstances, when you first came here, and for which I'm sorry enough now, you saw more of Breck than of any one else. I got into a panic after dinner, thinking that perhaps the reason you didn't respond to West was because you might have taken a fancy to his cousin. I might have known better—your instinct is pretty true. I'm a plain-spoken old woman, I don't know how to be anything else, so out I came with my question." She patted Marie's shoulder again. "But it's all right now."

Marie wished that she could tell her everything. She laid her hot cheek against Mrs. Dunbarton-Kent's hand. "There is one person whom I *know* I love," she said tensely, "and that is yourself."

Mrs. Dunbarton-Kent patted her cheek then and smoothed her hair. "Good night, child, good night."

CHAPTER XXI

WHEN Mrs. Dunbarton-Kent returned to the library, West was pacing the floor; it was a perturbed face he turned on her when she entered. In all her experience with West, and he had been part of her household since he was twenty, Mrs. Dunbarton-Kent had never seen him look as he did now. Since Marie had taken hold on him, he had shown more genuine feeling than she had observed in him in all the years she had known him. He was so evidently suffering that she felt a stir of affection for him.

She closed the door behind her. "It's all right, West," she said reassuringly. "The honest little soul told me the truth, as I knew she would," and she related exactly what Marie had said. "She shivered when she talked of Breck, and it was more convincing even than what she said. She'll avoid him, you have nothing to fear, so quiet down."

West had quieted. He drew a long breath. "It's a relief! . . . Thank Heaven you didn't rage at her."

"I had no intention of raging at her," Mrs. Dunbarton-Kent said with feeling. "If there was anything between them, I was to blame—I let Haslett have his way. I didn't forget that for a moment. I've liked the child from the beginning—I loved her to-night. I've

197

had little enough affection bestowed on me these last few years. I've felt a desolate old woman, since your uncle died. . . . You shall have your chance, West; if she grows to care for you, well and good, marry her and be happy—I shall rejoice over it. But, if you don't succeed, the child shall have a home with me. When the time comes, as it will, when we can't hold up our heads here on the North Shore, she shall go with me— if she wants to."

West smiled at her. "You have a big heart, Aunt Bulah."

"And a big body," Mrs. Dunbarton-Kent supplemented a little dryly. "I hurt your artistic sense a thousand times a day. But that's neither here nor there—Marie's quaint enough to satisfy your liking for the unusual, so go ahead and win her, then make a home somewhere for yourselves."

"I will," he said firmly. "That's exactly what I want to do. . . . But, Aunt Bulah, I'm still desperately anxious." They had spoken in low tones, now he dropped his voice to a whisper. "Breck has some object in talking and acting as he did to-night. I've been trying to think it out, and I've decided that he is afraid of Marie—he wants her out of the way. He must know that she recognized Mrs. Smith that night in the park. Certainly the woman must have told him about her experience on the train, and they are both of them keen enough to have made the connection. They are afraid of her, and I'm afraid for her. Breck was trying to terrify her to-night—I think she's in actual danger."

The look of grim distress returned to Mrs. Dunbar-ton-Kent's face; when she left Marie, she had looked happy. "They wouldn't dare to hurt her," he said.

"Their kind will dare almost anything—to remove an obstacle. That incident on the train would be a telling bit of evidence against Mrs. Smith. I believe, as Haslett does, that either she had Mrs. Brant-Olwin's jewels with her on the train, or she had made some journey connected with them."

"If only we could get the jewels into our hands!" Mrs. Dunbarton-Kent said longingly.

"Yes, I know. But, Aunt Bulah, I'm thinking of Marie," he urged. "Don't keep her here. I don't want harm to come to her. I don't want her to be mixed up in any exposé there may be. I love her, Aunt Bulah —can't you understand?" He was tensely earnest.

"I know, West," she said distressedly, "but where could she go where she would be as safe as she is here? I talked that over with Haslett, the morning after she was hurt, and it was his advice to keep her here with me. I was considering you too, here you can be in the same house with her."

"Send her to Canada—I'll follow her there. Send her anywhere that's a distance from here—clear away from all this mess!"

"You talk as if she were a bale of goods!" Mrs. Dunbarton-Kent retorted with sudden exasperation. "I've offered her a home with me, I tell you. The child has a mind of her own and a will of her own—I can't pack her off, hither and yon, at my pleasure! She wouldn't accept even her traveling expenses—she's independent. She wouldn't stay here, if she didn't think that she's earning her keep. If I showed her that I didn't want her here, she'd go into town and work, and that's the worst possible thing she could do. You see, West," she said more calmly, "I went over the whole situation with Haslett. He thinks it would be a great mistake to let her leave Kent House. Of course he takes a lawyer's view: he says that to let her fall by any chance into the hands of Mrs. Brant-Olwin's people would be fatal; that she could give them the very clue they want. He advised me to keep her here and to attach her to me, make her our friend in every possible way. God knows, I haven't acted out of mere self-interest in offering her a home, I love the child; nevertheless I realized that Haslett was talking sense. And, West, Breck's a crook, like his father, but I won't believe for a moment that he'd do a bodily harm to that child. He wouldn't do it. That woman might, if she were in terror of capture, as she was on the train, but I don't believe she'd do it deliberately—there'd be too much danger in it for herself. I'm sorry you're worried, but Marie is going to stay here—if between us we can't protect her, we're a poor lot." She ended with a decision that dismissed appeal.

"Perhaps you're right, you and Haslett," West said doubtfully, "but I shall be anxious about her—I can't help it—he looked ugly this evening."

"Keep watch over her, West. And make her care for you—that's the important thing."

West was studying the fire. "If only there was some way out of this trouble! Those damned jewels! . . . Aunt Bulah, I haven't meddled with suggestions or advice, Haslett is much more capable of advising than I am, but I've thought for some time that there might be a way out."

"What way?" she asked quickly.

"Ransom the jewels. . . . It makes me *sick*—it's putting a premium on crime—but isn't it the only way out for us? I believe it's what they're playing for— their deep game. Hasn't Haslett ever suggested it?"

Mrs. Dunbarton-Kent hesitated. "Haslett has more than suggested it, West," she said finally.

"What do you mean?"

"He made Breck the offer—after we talked, the morning after Marie was hurt."

"No!"

"Yes, he did. He went to the farm and took Breck aside and made him the offer—four hundred thousand, the full value of the jewels. . . . I gave my consent to his doing it—it was his advice."

"What did Breck say?" West asked scarcely above his breath.

"Haslett said that Breck looked at him without any expression at all, except that the muscles in his face twitched. Then Breck turned his back on him and walked away—not one word."

West had flushed hotly. "God! Think of it's being possible to offer such an insult to a Dunbarton-Kent!"

"It made me feel ill," Mrs. Dunbarton-Kent said in a

thick whisper. "Haslett looked ill when he came back to me. 'After all, he's a Dunbarton-Kent,' he said to me. . . . The proposal was: that Breck was to *find* the jewels for me and turn them over to me in any safe way he could devise and receive the *reward* I offered. In return, he must bind himself to go to Europe and stay there—and keep *straight*." Mrs. Dunbarton-Kent's big body shook with disgust and anger. "Breck would still be his uncle's heir, between us all we would be evading the law in shielding a criminal, but anything, *anything* rather than the thing that's coming now, public disgrace, our good old name soiled as it will be, the misery to you and Bella, and Kent House a—byword!" The tears had gathered in her eyes. "Right or wrong, I consented, West—and Breck turned the proposal down. . . . Haslett is in search of Mrs. Smith, he says he hasn't given up hope of some solution, but I'm simply waiting for the inevitable." She drew a huge quivering sigh. "Giving Marie a home, such as it is, has been a pleasure—I've been sick for a bit of sunshine."

West patted her hand sympathetically, his face very grave. "Don't give up like that, Aunt Bulah." He looked thoughtfully at the fire and there was silence for some moments. Then he said with conviction, "It's sickening to think of, but Haslett's proposal was a move in the right direction, only he didn't approach the right person."

"What do you mean, West?"

"He should have made his offer to Mrs. Smith."

Mrs. Dunbarton-Kent stared at him. "How could he? It would be fearfully dangerous! We have only suspicions to go on."

"Nevertheless, she is the one to bargain with. They know they are in imminent danger, they're just as anxious to turn those jewels into money as you are to receive them intact and return them secretly to Mrs. Brant-Olwin. Don't you see, Breck isn't going to risk losing his inheritance—he'll be careful to maintain his innocence. Of course he turned down your proposal. But Mrs. Smith won't. They've counted on your making some such offer—they're clever crooks. She'll demand a stiff sum, but with it divided between them, or shared, Breck will cease to trouble us. He'll go."

"Perhaps Haslett had something of the kind in mind when he said that the next thing was to find Mrs. Smith?" Mrs. Dunbarton-Kent asked quickly.

"Of course he did. . . . Think of being rid of this incubus! Aunt Bulah, if it can be settled in that way, I'll contribute something toward the ransom—tell Haslett so."

"Go see him—talk to him yourself, West."

"I have kept out of it so far, but I will," West said with decision.

"I suppose we can find a safe way of returning the jewels—if we're fortunate enough to get them," she added with a sigh.

As was characteristic of West, he indulged in at least an outward light-heartedness. "A safe way!

Drop them down her chimney, tie them to her door-knob, let her come out from trying on a thousand dollar gown and find them on the seat of her limousine." Then he said longingly, "Little Marie and I and a clear future—it's too much to hope for. Don't worry, Aunt Bulah. Right is might, after all."

"One might question the 'right' of what we're doing," Mrs. Dunbarton-Kent returned grimly. "Mrs. Brant-Olwin would probably have a different opinion."

"She loves her pearls," West said succinctly. Then, "I didn't tell you, I was afraid you'd worry, but she's back—she telephoned me just before dinner."

Mrs. Dunbarton-Kent looked anxious. "I did hope she would stay away. I'll have to call on her and I'm a poor dissembler."

"I'd be as friendly to her as possible," West advised. "She feels that you've never really given her your social countenance. It may help us in the future. I've always liked the little woman."

Mrs. Dunbarton-Kent sat thinking for a time. Then she announced abruptly, "The thing I ought to do—it would make a friend of her—is to give her a party. The right sort, West—a dinner-dance with all the people included who have held off from her. I'd make them come and be charming to her. It would be a triumph for her—she'd forgive our family a good deal, if ever I have to ask a favor of her."

West considered a moment. "Well—why not?" he decided. "Do it. I'll get some men out from town—men she'd like to meet."

"I'll have Haslett—have her meet him. It's just as well she should meet him and like him."

"Surely."

"A week from Friday, that's—" Mrs. Dunbarton-Kent began, then paused to listen. "Some one knocked, West?"

"I'll go," he said. "It sounds like Gibbs' circumspect tap." And he rose and went to the door.

CHAPTER XXII

WEST was right; it was Gibbs whose gentle knock had interrupted their conference. "The night-watchman is asking to see Mrs. Dunbarton-Kent, sir," he announced, and West saw Willetts looming behind Gibbs' portly body.

"It's Willetts, Aunt Bulah," West said.

"Tell him to come in," she answered apprehensively. "More trouble, I suppose!"

Gibbs gave way to Willetts and vanished in the direction of the pantry. West stepped out into the hall, looked up the stairway and into the adjoining rooms, then returned to the library, closing the door behind him.

"Nobody's about out there, Aunt Bulah. I'll leave you two to talk."

"No, stay," Mrs. Dunbarton-Kent said anxiously. "Willetts has something important to tell us."

"It's more a suspicion of mine than anything," Willetts explained. "Just that I'm pretty certain that many a night when we thought Breck safe in his room, he's been out, very likely in town or at the Smith house or anywhere else he chose to go."

Mrs. Dunbarton-Kent looked startled, and West asked gravely, "What makes you think so?"

"Well, there was something happened last night—
or yesterday rather—the little girl brought a spaniel
pup into the garage. She'd been out walking and up on
the High Road and Colfax waylaid her and gave her
the dog. When we came back from my driving you
to the dressmaker's, Mrs. Dunbarton-Kent, I missed
her from the garage and was out looking for her and
saw Colfax talking to her and saw her bring away the
dog. . . . It was all right enough," Willetts added
quickly, for Mrs. Dunbarton-Kent's brow had darkened. "I was there and saw it all, Colfax just nosing
about as usual and of course wanting to get her into
trouble with you over his having given her the dog.
Besides, she told me about it, that she didn't want to
talk to him and wouldn't answer his questions and
didn't want to listen to his grievances. The little girl's
all right," Willetts said positively, "the baby spaniel
appealed to her, that's all—she's been pretty lonesome.
She told me about it, she's all right. This morning
when the pup was gone, she thought it had got out of
the garage someway and gone back to Colfax Hall."

West had been eying him keenly; it was so evident
that Willetts was still another friend Marie had made.
"Certainly she's all right, though you didn't always
think so," he said. "We don't need to discuss that,
just go on with your story."

Willetts did not like West's tone. All Kent House
knew that West was vastly taken with Marie Angouleme, and Willetts had expended some irritated
thoughts on the subject: the kind of man the little girl

ought to marry was the plain sort like himself. It was
all right enough for Mrs. Dunbarton-Kent to be kind
to the little girl, but to take her out of her station and
foist her into another, marry her to her nephew and
things like that, was rank foolishness; there was quite
an active jealousy stirring in Willetts. Possibly it was
jealousy sensing jealousy that made West eye Willetts
so coolly.

Willetts addressed himself pointedly to Mrs. Dunbarton-Kent. "The little girl was worrying about the
pup's being hungry, so while she was with you last
evening I got some supper into it and put it to bed in
the garage. When the little girl came back and went
to her room, I locked up the garage and I took the
house and garage watch and set Jones about something
else. Well, when I unlocked in the morning, the pup
was gone. I circled that garage a dozen times last
night, there was only one way that pup could have
been swiped and that was by some one's climbing the
store-house roof and letting himself down into the
garage through the ventilator windows, then going by
the way he came. I'll grant that Breck could have done
it, but I won't grant it to any one else about the place,"
Willetts said with decision, "and I'll grant it to him
only when I happen to be off my guard, for I saw
what I thought was his shadow on his window-shade
until early this morning. . . . Now, what I've come to
say is, that I'm convinced he's been fooling us this long
time—that it's a dummy he sets up in his chair whenever he wants to take a midnight stroll."

"But we've searched his room a dozen times!" Mrs. Dunbarton-Kent exclaimed. "You know how we have searched it for the jewels, or some clue to where they might be."

"Sure. And I searched it again to-night while you were all at dinner," Willetts returned dryly. "There's a big pot-bellied, long-necked water-pitcher in his bathroom and a walking-stick in his cupboard and a measuring stick just about as long as his shoulders are wide lying on his desk and a roll of cotton in one of his desk drawers. With plenty of soap out of which to manufacture a nose and chin to stick on the inverted water-pitcher and cotton laid on for hair, with bath-towels and his dressing-gown draped on the cross-sticks made out of his cane and the measuring-stick, a stupider man than Breck could manufacture a dummy that would throw quite a respectable studious shadow. I may be wrong about the soap face and the cotton hair, Breck may carry a mask and wig about with him in his breast pocket which he uses on the water-pitcher, but I venture that some three nights a week, ever since this trouble began, Breck has been at large. The other nights he's there, either with his shades up or down. If you want to deceive the public, even a detective, establish a habit—I take my hat off to him."

Mrs. Dunbarton-Kent's lips had dropped apart and West's face had grown expressionless. It was West who asked the practical question: "How does he get out of the house and in again?"

"How did he get into the garage and out again?"

Willetts retorted. "Jones and I can't be on all sides of the house at once! There are two oaks growing close to Miss Bella Dunbarton-Kent's bedroom windows, and she's away half the time. I've watched those trees pretty carefully. But while I was watching them and Jones was doing his best on the other side of the house, Breck may have been maneuvering the roof and sliding down the front porch pillars. Or the low roof of the servants' quarters would serve him nicely—or any down-pipe that came handy. . . . Don't ask me—I know I've done my best."

Mrs. Dunbarton-Kent had regained her usual harassed expression. "You have, Willetts—you have been a great comfort to me," she assured him. "Go on doing the best you can. I've hoped and hoped that by keeping as close a watch on him as we could that we might find the jewels. And, too, I've wanted the place guarded—if Mrs. Brant-Olwin's detectives were about, I wanted to know it. But I don't want any more men knowing a secret that's hard to keep. I have perfect confidence in you and Jones, and all any of us can do is our best. . . . But, Willetts, why should Breck want that puppy? I don't understand it."

"Just a bit of defiance," West cut in. "The same object he had in taking the tires and tools. . . . Sometimes I can explain him only by thinking that he's cunningly insane."

"Insane, nothing!" Willetts burst out. "His head's in just as good condition as his eyes and his feet—he can see in the dark and he can walk as light as a cat.

He's a clever man, Breck, or he'd have cleared out long
ago with the loot—he knows there's more to be gained
by staying—you'd give him more for those jewels than
any one else would."

Mrs. Dunbarton-Kent and West looked at each
other, but said nothing. Willetts saw the exchanged
glance and, as often before, he felt a sincere pity for
Mrs. Dunbarton-Kent. She was a big-hearted honest
woman; it was a great pity she was so bent upon protecting the family name. It was partly because she
adored her husband's memory. Frequently, when considering the situation, Willetts said to himself:
"Damned if I'd be worked by the slick crook! I'd give
him over to the law and brave the scandal." Nevertheless, Willetts respected her for the struggle she was
making; though she had no great affection for those
two, Bella and West, she was considering their future
and the future of Kent House.

He broke the silence. "Well, I wish we could come
at the goods—that's what Jones and I are here for, of
course. I hope they may materialize through that
Smith woman, Mrs. Dunbarton-Kent. Mr. Haslett's
working for that, I guess. . . . I'll be off, now I've
told you what I'm certain of, about the dummy. But
there's nothing to be done about it, except not to let
him or any one else know that we suspect. That's important, for, slick though he is, we may be able to trail
him some night and get a clue to the jewels." Willetts was anxious to save Marie a possible scolding, so
he added, "It might be best not to set the little girl

wondering about the way her dog disappeared, so the less said about it to her the better, I should think."

Mrs. Dunbarton-Kent nodded. "Yes, I'd like some one in this wretched household to be happy—I could even endure the presence of a puppy from Colfax Hall. . . . Good night, Willetts."

As soon as the door closed on him, West said thoughtfully, "I suppose that is the way he has managed his meetings with the Smith woman. I've wondered. But where? Hardly at her house—he'd not risk that—not after the night Marie recognized her." He looked at his aunt's troubled face. "Don't worry so, Aunt Bulah," he begged. "What Willetts has told us doesn't alter anything—what we want is the jewels. Their being able to see each other and confer is a help to us rather than otherwise, they'll arrive at a plan so much the sooner. They want to be rid of the jewels. Let Haslett try to get in touch with her, and you go right on with your party for Mrs. Brant-Olwin. And *don't worry so much.*"

"He has my hundred thousand dollars and he's likely to extort a small fortune from me in addition, why exert himself to steal tires and puppies!" Mrs. Dunbarton-Kent said bitterly.

"To accomplish exactly what he has accomplished— keep you worried sick and in dread of him. The more he can worry us—he certainly worried me to-night by his looks and what he said—the more we will pay to be rid of him. That's an easy sum in crook arithmetic."

"I haven't looked at him once, not in the eye, since

the day I begged him to confess like a man and I'd forgive him, for my husband's sake. I begged him to
give up the jewels and go away and keep straight—
that I would provide for him—and he looked me
coolly in the eye and refused. And since, for all these
weeks, he's sat three meals a day within an arm's
length of me, neither of us looking at the other." She
laughed shortly. "What a situation! It would be
comic, if it wasn't so horrible!"

"Try to forget it," West urged. "You'll get the
jewels and he'll go—I'm convinced of it. . . . Try to
think about your party—certainly we owe Mrs. Brant-
Olwin anything we can do for her. Go to bed now,
Aunt Bulah, do—try to sleep."

Mrs. Dunbarton-Kent rose with a heavy sigh. "I
envy that child up-stairs—she can sleep. My bed's
been a place of torment—for weeks."

CHAPTER XXIII

M RS. DUNBARTON-KENT was mistaken; Marie had not slept; she had been unable to sleep. Before midnight, the house had settled into perfect quiet, except for the big clock in the hall below which tolled the hours and the half-hours. When she could lie still no longer, Marie had sat up in bed with a blanket wrapped about her shoulders and had looked out through her windows at the black gulf dotted by occasional lights which indicated the sound. It was a very dark night, no moon and no stars; she sat in pitchy darkness. She was afraid to turn on the light, afraid even to get up and move about her room, for she might startle a nervous household; Willetts or some other detective might see the light, or her movements be heard and they would think that something was wrong. It was horrible to live like this.

She was wretched: she had deceived Mrs. Dunbarton-Kent; she had told her half-truths, for it would have been impossible to explain and not break her promise to Colfax. Marie felt a passionate affection for the big woman who had kissed her as one would a daughter. "I ought to tell her *everything*—it is most dangerous to her interests, such a man as Colfax knowing everything that goes on here and all her plans, yet it is *impossible* for me to speak. If I should break my promise, Colfax in his anger might do something that would be harmful to the entire family. It is a *miserable* position for me."

Marie had stared into the darkness and had tormented herself into a state of dazed distress. She had flashes of thought, but mostly she simply suffered: it was adominable what Bella was doing, deceiving her aunt, giving herself to such a man as Colfax. If ever a woman was possessed by a man, that woman was Bella—it was written on the face she had lifted from his shoulder. Undoubtedly when she was absent from Kent House for days at a time and Mrs. Dunbarton-Kent thought she was with friends in the city, she was with Colfax; she was another such woman as Mrs. Smith, secret and dangerous. . . . There *must* be times when Breck was wretched over what he had done. Perhaps by some means Mrs. Smith had compelled him to do it? . . . Though she ached for a home and kindness, she should not have accepted Mrs. Dunbarton-Kent's offer. She should have left Kent House. But if she had gone, she would have lived in still greater anxiety, wondering all the time what was happening at Kent House. She was between two fires. . . . And what was she going to do about West? She had promised Mrs. Dunbarton-Kent that she would try to love him.

The darkness melted slowly into gray before Marie's thoughts arranged themselves in any sort of order, and then it was more a weary falling back upon her previous resolution to do the best she could under the circumstances: be faithful to the family that had taken her in, guard their interests in every possible way. Mrs. Dunbarton-Kent longed for affection and devotion, and that she could give in full measure.

Daylight is almost always a comfort to frayed nerves; complexities are better defined, so more easily grasped, and the fear that lurks in darkness, pressing upon a distressed spirit, withdraws its oppressive hand. Marie brought a white face and a fairly resolute spirit with her to the breakfast table. They were all gathered there, Mrs. Dunbarton-Kent looking tired and grim; West grave until Marie appeared, then his face brightened by a smiling "good morning" to her; Bella looking as impenetrable as usual and with her knitting in her lap, and Breck wearing his usual stony expression.

It was a silent meal. West ate little, but looked assiduously after Marie's comfort. Mrs. Dunbarton-Kent's face softened when she saw her. "Well! I thought you were still asleep or I'd have brought you down with me. There wasn't a sound in your room, and I meant to let you sleep."

Marie did not say that she had not slept at all and that for the last two hours she had been sitting dressed and waiting for the soft notes of the Chinese gong which had brought the others down to breakfast. "I have been awake some time, thank you, Madame—I sat and looked at the pretty room and then at the passing boats upon the water."

Mrs. Dunbarton-Kent buttered a hot roll. "Take

that with your coffee, child," she said affectionately.
She eyed Marie's white face and heavy eyes anxiously.
"After breakfast walk a little in the park and later on
take a nap. I never sleep well myself in new surround-
ings."

Marie thanked her, then bent upon giving pleasure
to the two people who were trying to make her happy,
she said to West, "From my window I saw you walking in the park this morning, but if you are not tired
perhaps you will walk again—with me?"

It cost Marie an effort which made the color come
in her cheeks, and then she grew white again, for
Breck lifted his eyes and looked at her in a way that
made her want to weep, haggard eyes in a set and
stony face. Then, swiftly, he looked at West, the
steady narrowed look of the man who would knife
his rival. West met his eyes as steadily, but without
antagonism, merely a calm observance of Breck.

They all saw it. Marie grew pallid and Mrs. Dunbarton-Kent looked apoplectic under the restraint she
put upon herself. But West said with quick pleasure,
"Will I walk with you? Rather! It's kind of you,
little Marie. . . . The jonquils are coming up in the
lawn border—I ordered some for you from the florist
yesterday. Do you like a garden? To fuss among
flowers?"

"My aunt at St. Felix had a most lovely garden—I
worked in it often. At the convent I studied flowers
also." Marie knew only that she was making some
sort of an answer, for it had occurred to her suddenly

that a jealous man would look as Breck had looked, appealingly at her, then threateningly at his rival. Marie felt a sudden elation.

West was talking lightly, "You had a *Botany Book,* I suppose, and, under a plain little pressed daisy, wrote, *Chrysanthemum Leucanthemum,* and things like that?" There was laughter in his voice, but his eyes were very bright and keen.

"Of all the long names, I remember but one, Monsieur, and not because I have an erudite mind. It was the little hornwort in the disagreeable pond in the convent meadow. It was very grandly called, *Ceratophyllum demersum.* One of the pupils by the name of Sarah, when sent upon a botanical walk, in trying to seize the weed, fell into the pond and I said to the others, 'Sarah toppled-in-um demersum.' I was most proud of my English at the time and meant no harm to Sarah, but ever afterward she was called by that name."

It was a burst of light-heartedness and broke the tension: Mrs. Dunbarton-Kent chuckled abruptly, West laughed out, and Bella gave Marie an icy side-glance. Breck did not look up; there was no change in his expression. Then he rose. "Excuse me, please," he murmured and left the room. He moved with extraordinary lightness and opened and closed the door in a noiseless way that suggested vividly the midnight prowler.

Marie lost all animation; the weight returned to her chest. For a moment she had forgotten completely; forgotten Mrs. Smith, everything. She had talked smartly, flushed by the thought that Breck hated his cousin because of her, but the light-footed way in which Breck had left the room made her feel ill; she felt a sickening self-disgust. She was glad that Mrs. Dunbarton-Kent was speaking. Then she was startled by what she heard.

"I am going to give a dinner-dance for Mrs. Brant-Olwin, so don't make any engagement for the twenty-first," she was saying to Bella. "I want you to take charge of the decorating, you're good at that."

A ripple of expression disturbed Bella's regular features; Marie thought that she looked taken aback. But she said quietly enough, "Very well, Aunt Bulah." Then after a pause, "I was going to Philadelphia on the night of the twenty-first—you wouldn't mind if I left before the party was over?"

"No, do as you like," Mrs. Dunbarton-Kent said with a touch of irritation, "only don't appear to slight Mrs. Brant-Olwin. I want you to go this afternoon to call on her—with me."

Again there was a slight pause. "Of course I'll go, if you think it's best. You've called on her once before, but I never have and she doesn't love me. Perhaps it would be better for me to make friends with her at the party—it would appear a little less as if the entire family were suddenly laying itself at her feet."

Mrs. Dunbarton-Kent considered a moment. "You're right," she decided. "Besides,"—there was ill-suppressed irritation in her voice—"you've doubtless made plans of your own for to-day."

"I was going into town this morning to meet the
Brests, I was going for a week's trip south with them,"
Bella returned imperturbably, "but I can go this eve-
ning just as well, and I can come back on the twentieth
instead of the morning of the twenty-first as I intended.
One day will give time enough for the decorating."

Mrs. Dunbarton-Kent looked as she felt, that her
husband's brothers' children were a sore trial to her.
Bella had made her own friends, most of the people
she visited were strangers to Mrs. Dunbarton-Kent,
she did not know even their names or where they lived.
Bella seemed to occupy her time pleasurably to herself
and, as she had always impressed Mrs. Dunbarton-
Kent as too cold-natured and self-contained and
haughty to be drawn into entanglements of any sort,
and was punctilious always in her attentions to the
Dunbarton-Kent family friends, Mrs. Dunbarton-Kent
had no complaint to make—except the painful one that
hers was a divided and unhappy household. With her
husband's death all semblance of unity had disappeared; they were all waiting for a fat old woman to
die, that they might claim their millions.

"Go this morning, by all means, I don't want to interfere with your pleasure," she said with dreary grim-
ness. "All I ask is your help with the decorations.
You must be friendly to Mrs. Brant-Olwin—that I
demand."

"I shall be, of course, Aunt Bulah," Bella answered
in her deep-voiced, clearly spoken way. She reminded
Marie of a gracefully built man, both supple and

strong. Marie was repelled by Bella's superb body, she made her feel little and frail.

Marie saw and understood Mrs. Dunbarton-Kent's grimly forlorn expression, and when Mrs. Dunbarton-Kent turned to her she smiled her affection. "Better go for your walk now," Mrs. Dunbarton-Kent said. "Then get a nap before lunch."

Marie had guessed the reason for the dinner-dance given for Mrs. Brant-Olwin: It was best for the family to make her their friend. In case of exposure, she might be more lenient. Mrs. Dunbarton-Kent was acting wisely. "I was thinking, Madame, that if you wished invitations to be written for your party, I might be able to help?" Marie offered. "They took much trouble with my handwriting at the convent, perhaps it may please you."

Bella's sidelong glance held full as much distaste for Marie's purple-pansy, slender-stemmed beauty as Marie felt for Bella's Junoesque proportions. Marie sensed the glance and smiled the more brightly at Mrs. Dunbarton-Kent. She was determined never to look at Bella if she could help it, for she might look all the antagonism she felt.

Mrs. Dunbarton-Kent smiled in return. "Did they, child? Well, I need a sunshiny secretary. We'll see about it. West is waiting, so run along now, and I'll be in my room when you get back. Wrap up well, for it's windy."

Marie hurried up-stairs, and Bella departed in her leisurely way, knitting as usual; Mrs. Dunbarton-Kent

and West were left alone. West had been dallying
with his breakfast, looking at Marie mostly, studying
her face, his own expressionless. Mrs. Dunbarton-
Kent sighed. "She's doing her best, but the gloom of
this house is affecting her—it would get on the nerves
even of a crocodile. Be careful what you say to her
to-day, West."

"I intend to be," West said gravely. "I thought it
out last night: the thing for me to do is to clear out for
a few days. I can't stay here and not show my feelings,
and she's not ready to listen to me. Besides, Breck
frightens her. He glares at me and it upsets her—
he does it purposely to upset her. Bella will be away,
I'll be gone, and you'll have a good excuse to breakfast in your room with Marie, and you can have some
one in to lunch and dinner with you, so Breck can be
served in his room. I won't worry so much about her
if you'll promise to keep her out of his way. I'll go
before noon, drive into town. I can have a talk with
Haslett then, and call you up after you've seen Mrs.
Brant-Olwin. You can tell me then what men I had
better ask out. Of course I'll come back for the party,
earlier if there is anything you want me to do. . . .
What do you think of it?"

"It's the thing to do," Mrs. Dunbarton-Kent said
decidedly. "Many more meals like this one, and I'll
go wild. I can't talk to Breck, I dread even the sound
of his voice. But I can keep Marie away from his
neighborhood, and I'd get a little peace. I believe too,
West, that your going would help you with Marie."

"It cost her something to ask me to walk with her," West said heavily.

"Nonsense! You've never paid serious court to a girl who's heart-free, or you'd know that when she says a thing like that she means to listen to you. It's just like a man to get discouraged when things begin to look promising. Don't say much to her to-day and then clear out—I hope you'll have the sense to stay away until the day of the party. . . . And, West, urge Haslett to make every effort to find Mrs. Smith. See if between you you can't evolve some plan."

"I believe Mrs. Smith will allow herself to be found as soon as they think fit, Aunt Bulah. The thing for us to do is to be ready with our offer. Don't worry— since you told me of Haslett's offer to Breck and the way he took it, I've glimpsed daylight."

"I wish I glimpsed it!" she said deeply.

West lifted a warning hand. "Hush!" he said. "I think I hear Marie coming."

CHAPTER XXIV

WHEN Marie started down-stairs to meet West, she encountered Bella. She appeared to have stopped on the stairs to correct a dropped stitch in her knitting and she was so intent upon it that Marie hoped to pass her without speaking. But Bella blocked her way; she stood on the lower step, so they were face to face, and she looked Marie directly in the eye.

"Don't you think you're playing a dangerous game a little too long?" she asked coolly. "I'd persuade Breck to turn over the jewels, if I were you—he may hold them a little too long. Get him to take the sum Aunt Bulah will give for them, then clear out—you and Breck."

To Marie it was like a fist thrust into her face; there was the moment of dazed bewilderment, an amazement so complete that she swayed. Then she passed from red to a white heat. It was the involuntary gathering together of a medley of impressions and an instant welding them into a weapon with which to strike. It was aimed with vivid contempt and a passionate championship of Breck.

"Indeed, Mademoiselle! With black upon your lashes and paint upon your cheeks and a beautiful black wig upon your head you would make an excellent Mrs. Smith. You have her body and her cruel strong fin-

224

gers—I have reason to remember them. You 'visit' in Philadelphia and elsewhere, but where you are at those times is close to your lover. He is in need of money, perhaps to him you are furnishing it. And, Mademoiselle, to one who has once done wrong, suspicion is easily directed—in my heart I have sympathy for such a man, so never dare to speak ill of him to me—you who sneak to the house of your lover and betray the confidence of the family to which you belong! . . . Move out of my way that I may go down!"

Bella's knitting hung lax in her hand; Marie saw her grow very white and her eyes grow blank. "I'm no more Mrs. Smith than you are," she said through stiff lips. "What are you talking about?"

"Talk for talk, Mademoiselle. I have quite so capable a tongue as yourself. Go visit with your lover, but be very careful of how you endeavor to frighten me with false suspicions. . . . I intend to remain in this house, so move out of my way upon these stairs."

They looked for a full minute into each other's eyes, Marie at white heat, Bella blanched and blue-lipped but very steady-eyed now. "What you think you know doesn't trouble me," she retorted cuttingly. "You can't prove it. And you don't dare to talk, for you're sailing under false colors. I repeat my advice: persuade Breck to take what Aunt Bulah is offering for the jewels, then fade away, you and he. I think Mrs. Smith will fade then too. . . . It's just a bit of advice —take it or leave it."

There are those who can not control anger, they lose
all capacity to think. Marie's was not a blind rage;
she was thinking now, intently, but her thoughts
brought her to a locked·door only, because her reason
would not justify the involuntary accusation she had
made. She had seized upon a set of impressions and
had flung them at her antagonist, regardless of
whether or not she believed what she was saying. She
had wanted simply to strike a telling blow at the
hatred which looked at her out of Bella's eyes. And
her championship of Breck had been utterly involuntary; it had lifted in her as naturally as one springs to
the rescue of a hurt child. Now that she was thinking
as well as feeling, she was astounded at what she had
said; it had been a sudden flight of imagination. Bella
was not Mrs. Smith—that was impossible. And, in
spite of her pity for Breck which was constantly reviv-
ing and setting her reason at naught, her reason told
her that he was guilty.

Marie writhed under the feeling that Bella had the
better of her. It was true that she dared not talk;
aside from her solemn promise to Colfax was the painful fact that she was concealing things from Mrs. Dunbarton-Kent; Mrs. Dunbarton-Kent would not keep
her in the house for a moment if she knew about her
championship of Breck; without pausing to consider,
she had given Bella that advantage over her.

With the vivid determination to hurt Bella in any
way possible, Marie caught up another weapon: a
woman in love can always be hurt through her lover.

"It is unfortunate, Mademoiselle, that your jealousy
should lead you into such groundless suspicions,"
Marie said loftily. "I understand perfectly both
your insulting suggestions and your eagerness to have
me 'fade away.' But Monsieur Colfax thinks quite differently of me. He is friendly to me. He has, I think,
entirely forgiven me for striking at him that first day
because he wished to kiss me. It is a mistake for me to
be angry at anything *you* may say—a jealous person is
laughable." And Marie laughed softly with a very
good assumption of amusement.

Her shaft went straight through Bella's scornful
armor. "You keep away from Allen or I'll kill you!"
she said furiously. "You contemptible little schemer!"
She had flamed into scarlet, face and eyes ablaze, and,
for the short moment while she stood quivering and
hands clenched, Marie felt the burning sensation in her
throat that recalled her struggle for breath when Mrs.
Smith had throttled her. There was the wish to do her
a bodily harm in Bella's queerly light eyes and yet in
utter recklessness Marie pricked her again:

"You seem not to have much confidence in your
lover, Mademoiselle."

Bella lifted her hands, Marie expected to feel them
at her throat and braced herself to fight tooth and nail;
they eyed each other, both quivering and glaring.
Then, suddenly, Bella turned and swept down the
stairs. Marie was certain that she was going to denounce her to Mrs. Dunbarton-Kent and West, and
Marie started to follow her, ready to carry the fight

into their presence, ready for anything, utterly reckless.

But Bella did not go into the dining-room; she went
on swiftly through the hall and out to the porte-
cochère. She closed the door behind her, Marie could
not see what became of her. Then, suddenly, Marie
felt weak and dizzy, as if she had run a long way. She
sat down on the stairs and stared at the knitting Bella
had dropped, her chest heaving and a sensation of sickness in the pit of her stomach. Her head and her
throat ached. . . . She had said hateful things—it was
hateful to hate. But she had been attacked; Bella had
sneered at Breck, and words had sprung to her lips.
Instantly she had woven a story and had flung it at
Bella and then had taunted her cruelly. Fire leapt up
in Marie again. "It is not *proved* that Breck has
stolen! Then to say that he, that we together, should
extort money from Mrs. Dunbarton-Kent! Oh!"

Marie took her head in her hands and swayed as she
sat. "I do not believe it! I will not! It is more possible of belief, the wild thing I said to her, that she
herself is Mrs. Smith and that she has robbed for the
sake of Colfax."

Marie sat still then and tried to think. . . . It was
very strange, like something revealed in a dream—the
accusation she had flung at Bella. Was it possible,
could it be *possible* that Bella was Mrs. Smith? Would
it be possible for Bella to play such a part and her
family not discover it? She and Colfax plotting for
money? . . . But he had seemed to speak so earnestly

and honestly, a reckless man, but not a scoundrel. Yet
how was it possible to tell? He might have had a purpose? Why would it not be possible for Bella to disguise herself so she could be near her lover, even to
build that pretty house on Colfax's land in which they
could meet during her absences from Kent House?
They would want the blame of the theft to fall upon
some one else than themselves and the person least
able to refute it would be Breck: "Once a thief, always
a thief." . . . But perhaps much of what Colfax had
told her about Breck was not true, all that past history?
Perhaps there had been no wrong reason for Breck's
going to Mrs. Smith's house that night?

Marie grew vividly alive. If only it were so! If
only she had without intention hit upon the truth!
If only Breck were innocent, merely the victim of
others' plotting! . . . It was utterly unaccountable,
why Bella should have told her that Mrs. Dunbarton-
Kent was offering money for the jewels—there were
so many things she could not explain at all. But if
she could really believe that Breck was innocent, she
would be happy. Marie clasped her hands; if she could
help to prove him innocent! *Mon Dieu!*

Then she returned to earth again: all she could do
was to watch and wait, take note of every circumstance
and try to find out the truth without any one's suspecting. Bella would tell no one but Colfax of their
quarrel; whether she was Mrs. Smith or not, she had
every reason for keeping quiet. . . . It was a great
mistake to have put Bella on her guard, but that could

not be helped now. She must take time to consider what was best to do. . . . But West and Mrs. Dunbarton-Kent must be wondering what was keeping her.

Marie was decidedly an amateur detective, for it did not occur to her to glance along the upper hall and observe which door stood ajar; a man might have stood full in the hall and she not have noticed it. She rose alertly and hurried down to the dining-room, her cheeks so flushed and her eyes so bright that both Mrs. Dunbarton-Kent and West exclaimed. "What has come over you, child?" Mrs. Dunbarton-Kent asked, and West said, "What sort of an elixir have you been taking, little Marie?"

"I ran down the stairs," Marie said. "I felt that I had kept you waiting."

"And you're ready now?" West was studying her intently.

"Quite ready, Monsieur," Marie answered more quietly. But there was no hiding the color in her cheeks and the brightness in her eyes—she was a different being.

Mrs. Dunbarton-Kent looked at her with both pleasure and curiosity. Girls were queer things. It would seem that reluctance and doubt had fled. It boded well for West. "Be off with you," she said. "Come to my room when you get back."

CHAPTER XXV

THEY went out together into the gusty April day. The wind clutched at Marie's hat and twisted her skirt about her knees. West pulled his cap down over his eyes and gave Marie a helping hand across the lawn. "I didn't realize that it was blowing so hard," he said.

"Upon such a day I wish for my chauffeur's uniform," Marie returned.

"I like you much better as you are. . . . But look there! What's the matter with my statuesque cousin?"

Marie brushed the hair out of her eyes and looked: fully in the open, half-way between the slope of lawn and the sound, stood Bella, her back toward them, apparently staring at the ruffled water. The wind billowed her light morning gown and had loosened her hair, setting it swirling about her head. She presented an extraordinary appearance, altogether out of keeping with her usual severe dignity. Though the wind was cold, she seemed oblivious of it; she suggested an upheaval, the elemental broken loose. Marie looked, then looked away. She said nothing, but her lips tightened.

West scrutinized Marie, but he said nothing until they had struggled into the park. Then he asked

lightly, "Poor old Bella! Something's wrong with her
—what is it, Marie?"

"Maybe the wind can tell you, Monsieur," Marie returned as lightly. "To great dignity a storm is sometimes disturbing."

"I think you could be a whirlwind on occasion,
Marie." He eyed her amusedly yet keenly.

"I have never whirled upon you, Monsieur."

It was easy to bandy words now. She felt excited;
she could laugh again and the will to fight was tingling
in her blood. Since her talk with Colfax, there had
seemed nothing to fight for, only the stubborn determination not to be driven from Kent House and a bitter
detestation of Mrs. Smith.

"Whirled on me! The Lord forbid!" West said
fervently. "I'm being careful—I'm not going to make
a nuisance of myself to-day. . . . Let's take hands and
run away from the wind? Come!"

They sped down the slope of the park, literally racing
with the wind, and came to a stop at the park wall,
laughing and breathless, Marie's hair loose on her
shoulders. "*Mon—Dieu—*" she gasped, "I must look
worse than Sarah when rescued from the hornwort
pond."

"You look—" West said and stopped. His blond
face was aglow. He was going to help her arrange
her hair, but she backed from him. "My hat, Monsieur
—please hold my hat—until I become respectable."

"Oh—very well," he said lightly, but his face darkened. He watched her twist up her hair, a consuming

gaze that enveloped her, her daintiness, the vivid color in her cheeks and her parted lips and softly rounded throat. He looked frowningly over his shoulder at the Smith house. "Fancy any one's marring that," he said through his teeth.

"What?" Marie asked, startled by his tone.

"I was thinking of what happened to you on the train —to your throat."

"I think such a thing will not happen again," Marie said firmly. "So Mrs. Dunbarton-Kent told you?"

"About that experience? Yes. . . . But I'm not so sure that it will not happen again. It's one of my greatest anxieties."

"I am not afraid," she said resolutely.

"And I am sick with fear over you. That woman—" he stopped, Marie felt certain because he remembered that he must not speak of the family trouble and Mrs. Smith's connection with it. "I believe she's a dangerous criminal," he added.

Marie said nothing. Happily another gust of wind flung her fur tippet in her face. "Ugh! . . . This wind is terrible!" she exclaimed. "I will not again ask a gentleman to walk with me until I have carefully considered the weather. I think we must go back."

"Oh, not yet!" West objected instantly. "It's been a happy walk for me—you're more like yourself. You've seemed so unhappy ever since you came into Kent House. I want you to come to the cottage with me—I want to show you my workshop. We'll be out of the wind there."

Marie hesitated. She was longing to get back to her room and think.

"Do come," he begged and he added firmly, "I promised not to make a nuisance of myself. I want to tell you some things, not about myself, about other people."

Marie yielded; it was a small thing to do for one who had been as kind to her as he had been. Her mind and her heart were full of Breck; she felt excited and hopeful—and very sorry for West. It was hard to love and not be loved in return.

They struggled along to the cottage door and West took a key from his pocket and unlocked it, ushering Marie into a large room. There was only the one room with a beautifully beamed chapel-like ceiling of dark wood and book-shelves built into the walls. In one side of the room was a wide and deep fireplace with paneling on either side. There were casement windows above the book-shelves, but the large windows above the paneling on either side of the fireplace were designed to furnish most of the light for the room, and Marie saw at once why Mrs. Smith's house had ruined the cottage, for the foundation wall of the Smith house must have almost entirely shut out the light. The windows were boarded up now; the only light in the room was from the casement windows which were on the park side of the cottage. The Smith house stood on a terrace which was almost on a level with the Kent House park wall; before the house had been built, there had been a restful view of the sound glimpsed through the huge trees of Colfax Hall. On a sun-clear morning like this, the cottage was sufficiently lighted, for the casement windows looked eastward, but even on a sunny afternoon the place must be gloomy. It was a despicable thing to ruin a neighbor's house in that way, Marie thought; no wonder Mrs. Dunbarton-Kent was angry over it.

Marie felt oppressed; Mrs. Smith's baleful presence seemed to hover over the place. The room had been so beautiful, its woodwork chosen evidently because of its exquisite grain. The floor was also of lovely dark polished wood and the furniture of the same wood, carved and richly upholstered. It had been the retiring place of a studious and artistically inclined man; an escape from the big house to perfect quiet. But now there were the melancholy suggestions of an abandoned dwelling: the book-shelves were empty; there had been paintings above the book-shelves and they were gone, and so were the rugs. There was a huge divan before the fireplace, but no cushions; in the corner, on the fireplace side of the room, was a wide and heavy and elaborately carved secretary, very old-fashioned in its bulk and height, a sort of desk and cupboard combined, and its companion piece was the massive table in the center of the room. But the carving of both was thick with dust; the doors of the secretary hung ajar, and the splendid table was covered with common white oilcloth. The place had been stripped of everything but the furniture, and the hangings at the windows had been replaced by ordinary window-shades.

It was not right to use it as a workshop, Marie thought. On the oil-cloth cover of the table were dried lumps of sculptor's clay, some rusty sculptor's tools, soiled water-cups, and a box of paints and brushes thick with dust. At the right of the fireplace, against the rich paneling, was a rough pine table on which were coils of tiny wire, insulators, bits of copper, piles of little disks that looked like miniature talking-machine records, a litter of all sorts of things an electrician might use. There were several nude dolls on the table, from which the body stuffing had been removed, grotesque objects that would seem to have no connection with the electrical apparatus to which wires were attached. The wires were evidently let into the wall from the outside, just under the window which was boarded up, and were attached to the paneling behind the table, then to the apparatus on the table. To Marie it seemed a desecration, using this chapel-like place for a workshop; and the contrivance of an evil mind, shutting out the light from those splendid windows. The gusts of wind struck against the house, as if angry at such a deed.

While Marie looked about her, West went to the fireplace and set a match to the fire which was laid there. Then he came back to her. "What do you think of it?" he asked.

"It seems to me wicked!" she said indignantly, pointing to the boarded windows. "Mrs. Dunbarton-Kent told me of it."

"It was wicked," he returned decidedly. "Little

good may it bring to those who did it! . . . But come over to the fire, it's as cold as a vault in here."

Marie followed him. "See," he said, "this is my work-table. It looks as if I spent my time dissecting dolls, doesn't it?"

Marie was more interested in the havoc Mrs. Smith had wrought; Bella would be quite capable of doing a thing like this. "I do not see how you can work here," she said, still indignant. "To me this is like a destroyed church—it is pitiful."

"I know, but I wanted quiet, dear. Who could work in Kent House? Breck used the place first, he used to sleep here and do his studying here, then Bella did some clay-modeling here, that's her litter on the table, and when she gave it up I took to working here in the mornings. It's the only time the light is any good. Then, too, it was the only place where I could have my electric wires strung around without inconvenience to any one—up at the house, Aunt Bulah would be in terror of my setting things afire." He took one of the disks from the table. "Sit down and I'll tell you what I've been trying to do—my model's in Washington, so I can't show it to you. . . . I have been working over an electric contrivance to put into the body of a doll. I want to manufacture a life-like, talking doll, controlled by electricity. The speeches for the doll are on these little records. There's no reason why it can't be done, and think what a wonder and delight it would be to a child! Think of a dinner-party of dolls and their conversation carried on just by turning on a switch. It would make a fascinating entertainment for children, wouldn't it?"

Marie looked at him wide-eyed, thoroughly interested now. "It is a most unusual idea, Monsieur."

"A good educator too!" West said with enthusiasm. "Think of what might be taught children by means of these records. And the stories the child's toys could tell: the Teddy-bear or the Uncle Remus rabbit would be wonderful things, instead of mere cotton stuffing made interesting only because of the child's imagination."

"It is most wonderful!" Marie agreed. "It would be like becoming a God to a world of children—teaching them through their toys good thoughts and how to live well." She looked at West with respect and admiration. "Such a work as yours must absorb every moment of your time. Had I such an idea, I would work ceaselessly."

"It's what I ought to do—it's what I want to do— but Kent House and its troubles drive me wild!" He tossed the record on the table and flung more wood on the fire. "Perhaps there'll be an end to it before long," he said through his teeth, "then I can work in peace." He turned and looked at Marie and broke into a smile. "Tell me, small person, what did you say to my cousin Bella that sent her flying out into the wind? You're potential, you know, in spite of being so tiny."

Marie did not know what to say. He was an unusual man; what he had said about his work interested her. She had thought him kindly and very charming, but

of course worried by his family's troubles. It seemed
that he possessed originality. Certainly he was observant; it was he who had first suspected that she cared
for Breck, and now he suspected her interest in Bella.
She wished that she could confide in him, but that was
impossible.

She decided to say, "I suppose, Monsieur, she went
into the wind because she wished to do so."

"A sphinx couldn't do better!" He sat down beside
her, his face grown grave. "Bella is one of the people
I want to talk about. Don't quarrel with her, Marie.
I think Bella has her very serious troubles, though I
don't know what they are, exactly. I do know that
under that cold surface of hers she's seething, and that
she doesn't love you. I know what Aunt Bulah seems
never to have discovered, that under all her calm, Bella
is a violent woman. She can be wildly jealous and
revengeful, and that kind of woman is dangerous;
don't give her an opportunity to hurt you. . . . Let me
explain a little: the night Breck and Colfax fought
and you were hurt, while all that was going on here
below Mrs. Smith's window Bella and I were sitting
in the library up at Kent House. We knew nothing
about it until Gibbs came in and asked Bella for some
lint and stuff which was in Bella's closet. Though
Gibbs never knows anything about anything that goes
on and always knows more about it than any one else,
he declared that he didn't know what had happened,
some trouble with Colfax, he thought. Bella jumped
to the conclusion that Colfax was hurt. She went

wild: 'Allen's hurt! Allen's hurt!' she kept repeating, and she quieted down only when I went out and found just what had happened and came back and told her. Then she flew out at you: 'She went down there to meet Allen!' she kept insisting. It was a revelation to me—evidently she cares for Colfax, a thing she has kept from everybody. If it's true, I'm sorry for Bella. Any woman who persists in clinging to a man in spite of every warning and in spite of her own knowledge of him is simply committing suicide!" Then he added more quietly. "But not for anything would I make trouble for Bella by talking about what I suspect. I felt I must tell you, though, for it's not Mrs. Smith only that I am afraid may do you a harm, Bella's a danger too."

In the beginning, Marie had listened with interest, but now she was not thinking of what he was saying: her little card house of hope had fallen about her ears, for, if Bella was sitting in the library during that evening when she, Marie, was gazing over the wall at Mrs. Smith, Bella was not Mrs. Smith. She was back again just where she was before she built her house of cards, only she understood Bella somewhat better.

She felt utterly depressed, lifeless. "Thank you, that you have told me," she said tonelessly, "and it is kind of you to feel anxiety over me. I think, however, that there is no reason to be fearful."

"*Kind!*" he said with sudden passion. "I love you— I'm worried to death over you—in more ways than one! I'm tempted to tell you everything! If anything

happens to you, it would kill me!" He breathed
quickly and ran a nervous hand through his hair. "But
—I can't tell you—I don't know that it would do any
good anyway—some women will love a man—in spite
of everything—as Bella's doing!"

Then he spoke more quietly. "Listen, Marie, I want
to tell you some things about Mrs. Smith: They say
she is a foreigner of some sort, probably a Russian—
nobody seems to know where she originated, or where
she gets the money with which she gambles. She is a
confirmed gambler, and always plays for large sums.
She disappears then appears again, a mysterious
woman and with no apparent connections. Such a
woman comes in contact with crooks and thieves—
she may well be at the head of some gang of criminals,
the most dangerous kind of a woman. If she is in fear
of the law—and, from your experience with her on the
train and from the way she disappeared after you
recognized her in the park, I think it's very likely—if
she is afraid of you, she would not hesitate to put you
out of the way. . . . You see, dear, for a number of
reasons, I'm desperately anxious about you. I told you
once that I wanted you to stay at Kent House, but that
was before I realized the danger you were in here.
Aunt Bulah doesn't realize it, she doesn't know to what
desperate lengths crooks and thieves will go when they
are hard pressed, but I do. She wants you here, but, if
she felt it was for your good, I know she would make
a home for you somewhere else, help you in any way
she can. So would I. It's because I love you unself-

ishly, that I'm begging you to go away from Kent
House for a time—only a little time, Marie—until we
are certain that that woman,"—he pointed to Mrs.
Smith's house—"will not come back, and until there
is a happier state of things in Kent House itself. Marie,
I beg you to go—for your sake I beg you to go!" He
ended in passionate pleading.

Marie made no answer. She understood so much
better than he thought she did, why he urged her to go
"for a time"; if they ransomed the jewels, Mrs. Smith
would go, and so would Breck, and Kent House would
be at peace. . . . Perhaps it would be best for her to
go, she thought despairingly; "against hope, she had
believed in hope."

She ran her fingers absently over the upholstery on
the arm of the divan, thinking of the future: how
would she be able to endure it? . . . Then her forefinger touched something, a hair clung to its moisture,
giving her a queer thrill, a hair from the pelt of some
animal. Marie lifted her hand and looked at the hair,
then looked at it more closely. A wave of heat passed
over her and she sat upright, staring at her hand.

"What is it?" West asked surprised, and Marie answered involuntarily.

"It is a hair from the tail of a sable." She was seeing distinctly the row of tails on Mrs. Smith's sable
stole—the light above their berths had made the hairs
glisten; they were unusually long and beautiful, those
hairs, like this one.

West took her hand and looked at the hair; then

looked into her startled eyes. "You're certain?" he asked.

"Yes." She was thinking, "How did it get here?"

"So this is where they—!" He caught himself up. "It's a hair from some dog," he declared. "When anybody says 'sable' in my presence I have visions of Mrs. Smith. Ugh! I've worried about you until my nerves are on edge." He sprang up, shaking his shoulders. "Let's get out of here, dear—where the air's more wholesome."

Marie was thinking of Mrs. Smith and of another who must have been beside her on the divan; many times she had wondered where it was they met. She looked up at West with wide hurt eyes. "Do others than yourself have the key to this place?"

"Yes, there are several keys. . . . But do rub that thing off your finger, then forget it." He held out his hand to help her to rise.

Marie started to rise, but she held the hair tightly between her thumb and forefinger. Then she lost her feet, for they were startled by a thunderous bang and a rush of wind into the room which swept up the ashes in the fireplace and scattered them about and blew the smaller objects off West's work-table and made the paneling beside the fireplace rattle. The whole place seemed in a commotion.

But until Marie got to her feet she could not see what had caused it all. She was astounded when she turned and saw Breck in the room. He looked disheveled by the wind, but his face was even more set than usual. West had seen him first, for he had been standing and facing the door. The two were looking at each other, Breck in the narrow threatening way in which he seemed always to look at his cousin and West with a blaze of anger that turned him scarlet.

"Will you close the door?" he said thickly.

Marie saw his hands clench and unclench.

"I'm sorry," Breck returned in a tone so level that it was an insult. "The wind is responsible for the banging of the door. And why close it when you are about to go?"

West made no answer. He had grown perfectly calm, an exhibition of great self-control. He was a little stiff-lipped, that was all. "Come, Marie," he said gently.

Marie did not know why she did it, only that the thing sprang up in her; jealousy is accountable for many strange deeds. She went swiftly to Breck and instantly he looked from West to her. She still held the hair between her fingers; she parted them and showed him what she held. "It is a hair from a woman's sable cape, Monsieur. . . . I found it upon the divan. . . . Perhaps you can tell to whom it belongs?" She was white and quivering, and her eyes were ablaze.

Breck looked, then he looked at her, a long look, grave and steady and observant. Then he took the hair from her outstretched finger and looked at it closely, his face utterly expressionless, except that the muscles in his cheeks twitched. Then he looked at her again in his shadowed distant way. "I see," he said so

softly that his voice was caressingly sarcastic, "but why
should such a *little* thing hurt you so much?"

Marie could not help it, the tears sprang into her
eyes. Then shame and anger swept her. She looked
neither at him nor at West, but went out through the
open door; if the wind had permitted it, she would
have run.

But though she hurried, she caught what the two
men said to each other, West's voice raised but very
steady, and Breck's so coldly triumphant that it was
stinging:

"You're cruel to the one being who has had faith in
you."

"Who has faith still, you mean, and always will.
Walk carefully, my fine cousin."

Marie knew then that West was following her, but
when he reached her she was beyond speech, choked by
shame and misery and smothered by the wind. Driven
by jealousy, she had bared her heart; Breck had seen
with cruel keenness and had smiled to himself, then had
taunted the other man. And, because he loved her,
West pitied her.

Marie struggled on. West said nothing, only took
her arm and helped her along. He led her into Kent
House hall and there he took off her hat and her fur.
Then he put back her hair and looked at her white
face. His eyes were very bright. "Marie, will you
marry me—will you go with me to-day—let me take
you away from all this? . . . You can try to love me
afterward—I'll ask nothing but that."

She knew only that she could not do it. "Monsieur, I can not."

"You know that he must belong to that woman—that is one of the things about him that worries us."

"Yes, I think it must be so."

He looked at her for a long moment. Then, "I can wait," he said evenly. "I'll go away for a little while. You're not the sort to give yourself to a man who—" He stopped, then went on. "I love you too much to stay—I want you too much to stay. I would only distress you. Will you promise me to keep close to Aunt Bulah? Not let him come near you or speak to you?"

"I do not need to promise that—I will never speak to him again—I could not. I can not stay in this place."

West's face brightened. He drew her to him impulsively. "Marie, I love you so dearly! . . . Kiss me—please?"

But she bent her head and he kissed only her hair. Then he let her go. "You know what he is now—I can wait," he said more quietly. "I know that you'll leave Kent House as soon as you can. I shall say nothing to Aunt Bulah about what happened to-day, she's worried enough over him as it is. You'll say what you think best and arrange as you think best, but I know that she'll help you to do anything you insist upon, for she really loves you. I'm not going farther away than into town—I shall be near you and help you if you need me. I think he will leave us before long, Marie, then you can come back to those who love you."

To Marie the future was as miserable a blank as the present. "I do not know," she answered dully.

"I know that you'll come back, and that you'll let Aunt Bulah find a home for you until you do. To Aunt Bulah you're the daughter she never had and to me you're everything. She'll understand if you tell her simply that Breck frightens you. He frightens us all."

"I must think what to do," Marie answered wearily, and turned away. She went slowly up the stairs; then she looked back. West was still standing in the hall, looking after her.

She went to her bed and lay prone, her face buried in the pillow. For a time she simply suffered; then she began to cry.

CHAPTER XXVI

MARIE did not wake until twilight. It was Margaret who, when Marie began to hurry about her room, distressed because she was late for dinner, brought her Mrs. Dunbarton-Kent's message: Mrs. Dunbaron-Kent was glad that she had slept so long and she hoped that Marie would not try to come down, but would have dinner in her room. "Mr. West and Miss Bella are not here and Mrs. Dunbarton-Kent has a guest for dinner," Margaret added.

Marie was glad that she did not have to go down. She wanted only a bowl of soup. Gibbs brought it to her and though, even to a close observer, Gibbs' eyes never wandered from the tray he carried, he verified Margaret's statement: "She's as white as a sheet and her eyes swollen up—something's gone wrong."

Gibbs had just gathered some astounding information in the dining-room and had passed it on to Margaret and the cook. "Mrs. D. K.'s going to give a dinner-dance to Mrs. Brant-Olwin—to Mrs. *Brant-Olwin!*"

The cook and Margaret had stared at him. "What's going to happen?" both asked with caught breath.

"Things is drawing to a head—mark me!" Gibbs said solemnly.

"It's something that worries *her*," Margaret said,

248

pointing upward. "That's the reason she's been crying."

Then the cook asked a question. "You took his dinner up to *him*—how does he look?"

Gibbs turned on her. "Not one word of *that!*" he said with mingled sternness and horror. "Haven't I told you all along that being made out accomplices is our danger? Lord, woman!"

"My nerves has gone to pieces," the cook said in plaintive extenuation. "It's awful being tied here—afraid to give notice or anything. I was only wondering—that's why I asked."

"Curiosity is responsible for half the trouble in the world—it's woman's besetting sin," Gibbs returned scathingly. "I've done my best to keep you girls out of trouble, but I wash my hands of you, if you begin that 'wondering' business. 'Wonder*lust*,' it is—nothing more nor less. 'Wonder not' had ought to have been put into the Bible and enforced on women! Don't wonder about anything and what you don't know you can't tell. Nerves! There'll be those, when the climax comes, who'll know just what day you spoiled the soup and me spilled it on the tray carrying it up. It's little acts like that a smooth detective builds on. Nerves! You couldn't choose a worse time to have *nerves!*" And Gibbs bore the immaculate tray up to Marie.

And later he stood a butleresque statue while Mrs. Dunbarton-Kent told Mrs. Granveston—a stiff-necked social autocrat of the North Shore who was as remarkably attenuated as Mrs. Dunbarton-Kent was bulky—

of how attached she had become to Marie Angouleme.
Related by Mrs. Dunbarton-Kent, Marie's history made
an interesting story, a splendid brave little girl, one of
the best ambulance drivers in all France. Her service
papers were good reading and, in addition, Mr. Haslett
had communicated with Marie's Canadian connections
who had nothing but good to say about her. "She has
the most lovable disposition and is the most companion-
able person I have ever known," Mrs. Dunbarton-
Kent declared. "I have grown to love the child. I've
taken her into my family—as one of us."

Mrs. Granveston was profoundly interested. So
was Gibbs. Mrs. Dunbarton-Kent had aroused the
"wonderlust" of her guest, and Gibbs was also actively
breaking the thirteenth commandment which he had
so strongly advocated. Both were wondering whether
Mrs. Dunbarton-Kent would add that she had legally
adopted Marie Angouleme. Mrs. Granveston knew
Mrs. Dunbarton-Kent too well to venture the question,
one did not ask Bulah Dunbarton-Kent questions like
that, but she judged that it was exactly what Mrs.
Dunbarton-Kent had done. She was that kind of
woman, flinging a gauntlet at convention every now
and then—like this queer freak of taking up that Brant-
Olwin woman—risky things didn't frighten Bulah. Of
course every one knew that the three Dunbarton-Kent
children inherited, but Mrs. Dunbarton-Kent had quite
a nice little fortune of her own besides the huge income
from the Dunbarton-Kent money. Marie Angouleme,
adopted, would be a person of consequence.

"Where is she to-night?" she asked. "I'd like to see her."

"Up-stairs with a headache," Mrs. Dunbarton-Kent answered, and proceeded to angle for an invitation to tea.

Urged by curiosity, Mrs. Granveston said finally, "If you're out driving to-morrow afternoon, stop in for tea, both of you." Then she added with caution, "There'll be just the three of us." Mrs. Granveston did not take people up except after due consideration.

Then Mrs. Granveston—and Gibbs—heard more about Mrs. Dunbarton-Kent's call upon Mrs. Brant-Olwin. Mrs. Granveston had received with such frigid silence Mrs. Dunbarton-Kent's announcement that she intended to give a dinner-dance for Mrs. Brant-Olwin, that Mrs. Dunbarton-Kent had turned to the subject of Marie Angouleme. That matter satisfactorily settled, she took up Mrs. Brant-Olwin again.

"I like her," she said decidedly. "I haven't entertained her before simply because I'd never troubled to discover what a good sort she is. You know that most of the younger set like her and go to her house."

"They'll go almost anywhere they're given a good time, but that's not the way you and I were reared," Mrs. Granveston retorted severely. "I've never had any desire to know Mrs. Brant-Olwin."

Mrs. Dunbarton-Kent proceeded. "Well, I had a delightful call on her. She told me all about her life at the Nevada mines, and it was interesting. She makes no pretenses, and I like her for it."

"I've never talked to her, but I've heard her talk," Mrs. Granveston said. "Most women of her sort get the roughnesses smoothed off before they attempt society."

"The big-heartedness and honesty taken out of them, you mean, Lucile. Her grammar doesn't disturb me. I haven't given a big party for a long time, Kent House is growing dull, so I'm going to stir things up a bit, a party for young and old, the sort of thing we used to have at Kent House in my dear husband's time. West has always liked the little widow, and he's pleased over it—he telephoned me from town this evening that Mr. Haslett and Ward Wakefield and half a dozen other men are coming. I have Marjorie and Bess Caswell on my list—why don't you have them out for the week-end and some of the fun that's sure to follow the party?"

This was bringing pressure to bear upon Mrs. Granveston, for Marjorie and Bess were granddaughters; Mrs. Granveston's daughter had married a Caswell who afterward lost his money, and the two girls had few opportunities of meeting eligible men. Then, too, Mrs. Granveston was intrigued by the possibility that there might be something between West and Mrs. Brant-Olwin—that would be a good reason for Mrs. Dunbarton-Kent's giving the party. West was regarded as non-capturable, but Mrs. Dunbarton-Kent was a healthy sixty and, though very well off, West might not object to the Brant-Olwin millions as a stopgap. When he came into his fortune, the combination of fortunes would be stupendous. Engaged to a Dunbarton-Kent, there was not a North Shoreite who would not pay court to Mrs. Brant-Olwin. . . .

Later on, seated beside Marie's bed, Mrs. Dunbarton-Kent told her about it and chuckled. "I'll make them swallow her whole. Mrs. Brant-Olwin is a good sort, Marie—she has that big house near the Country Club, you know. She's not our kind, but she's genuine and I want her for·a friend. I think you'll like her and I know she'll like you."

Marie was glad that the room was dimly lighted. She was saturated with self-disgust, depression and sick-resignation: she had been weak and without self-control; she deserved to suffer for having believed in a man like Breck and for allowing herself to be jealous of such a woman as Mrs. Smith. Either the law would seize upon those two and prove their guilt, or they would sell the jewels they had stolen to Mrs. Dunbarton-Kent, by that act confessing themselves guilty. Breck had laughed at her and had taunted West. . . . But there was no use in being angry or hurt or writhing with shame. Breck was guilty and she must endure the knowledge as best she could.

Marie slipped her hand into Mrs. Dunbarton-Kent's and clung to it. "I have not seen Mrs. Brant-Olwin, but if you like her, Madame, I know that I shall also," she said softly.

Mrs. Dunbarton-Kent did not tell Marie that when she had told Mrs. Brant-Olwin that afternoon about Marie—the same history which she had imparted to

Mrs. Granveston—that Mrs. Brant-Olwin had shown
no telltale self-consciousness, not even when Mrs. Dunbarton-Kent had said, "Some woman she met casually
in Burton Haslett's office building told her that I
wanted a chauffeur, but wouldn't give her name, so
Marie's as ignorant as I am of who did us a kindness.
I suppose it was meant as a joke, but it has turned out
a blessing."

Mrs. Brant-Olwin had listened interestedly, but all
she had said was, "She sounds good to me. I call her
a lucky kid."

"I'm going to have them all here, the little set that's
held out against Mrs. Brant-Olwin," Mrs. Dunbarton-
Kent told Marie. "They're going to meet you too.
Between us we're going to bring them around."

"I will help you all I can, Madame."

"To-morrow morning we'll have breakfast in my
room, then set to on the invitations," Mrs. Dunbarton-
Kent said vigorously. "We'll have two of the disaffected in for lunch and when they're gone we'll go for
a ride and stop for tea with Mrs. Granveston—she
wants to meet you. I'll have some one for dinner too.
. . . Breck has his meals in his room whenever there's
company, so we won't see much of *him*," she added.

"Yes, Madame," Marie said with as little expression
as possible, though she was immensely relieved.

"West won't be back till the day of the party—it's a
comfort sometimes not to have a man bothering
around."

Mrs. Dunbarton-Kent knew that Marie had had an

unhappy morning. West had not looked cheerful when
he had bidden her a hasty good-by, and when she had
gone into Marie's room afterward and had found her
asleep she had seen that she had been crying. She had
covered Marie up, reflecting as she did so, that, in
matters of the heart, men were "perfect fools!" But
she asked no question. She kissed Marie good night
and told her to go to sleep and sleep soundly.

When she had gone, Marie wrote to West:

"DEAR MONSIEUR WEST:

"I have thought, and I must tell you that I can not
leave Kent House. Mrs. Dunbarton-Kent I love too
dearly to do it, and this seems my home. I beg you
not to feel frightened about me. I shall be careful and
be only with Mrs. Dunbarton-Kent until you return.
This I promise.

"It is only a short letter I write, but one which is
full of gratitude to you for all your kindness to me.

"Affectionately,

"MARIE ANGOULEME."

She had been thinking about it all evening and had
decided: *she could not leave Kent House.* If she left,
she would go mad with anxiety—that would be worse
than the shame she would feel whenever Breck looked
at her. Danger to herself was nothing; if disgrace
fell upon the family, perhaps she could be of some comfort to them.

CHAPTER XXVII

NOT once during that week of helping to launch Mrs. Brant-Olwin and—quite unconscious of any efforts in her own behalf—of helping to launch herself, not once did Marie see Breck. She did not even hear him pass through the hall, though often she listened intently. He was at Kent House, for every night she saw the line of light beneath his door. But he moved so noiselessly; Marie shivered when she thought of the way in which he went in and out of a door.

In twos or fours Mrs. Dunbarton-Kent's guests came to lunch or dinner and left converted. Marie saw the big woman at a different angle, as an entertaining and skilful hostess and justly a leader in her set. Marie admired her very much. She was so interested in the way in which Mrs. Dunbarton-Kent was making "the disaffected swallow Mrs. Brant-Olwin," that it did not occur to her that she herself was a success. Mrs. Dunbarton-Kent did not need to repeat Marie's history, Mrs. Granveston had done it for her, for, at her cautious tea for three, Mrs. Granveston had taken a fancy to Marie. Attempting conversation in rather bad French was a fad of Mrs. Granveston's. "Speaking with you in French has given me great pleasure, Madame—I hope we may speak together often," Marie had said with such a genuine desire to please that Mrs. Granveston became her advocate.

"She's a wonderfully sweet, pretty girl," Mrs. Granveston declared to her friends. "Such an interesting history too and authentic. I hope Bulah will adopt her, if she hasn't done so already. She needs a devoted companion."

By no means all of Mrs. Dunbarton-Kent's friends took Mrs. Granveston's view of the matter, but those who came to Kent House during that week were first surprised then charmed by Marie's quaint courtesy, soft accent, and her unassuming wish to please. Without Marie's realizing it, Mrs. Dunbarton-Kent drew her out, vivid descriptions of the Hudson Bay country and of ambulance work in France, tender recollections of her childhood in St. Felix and of the good aunt and the dear father who had gone. She was so utterly unaffected and so genuinely deferential. And pretty! With color in her cheeks and her eyes alight, Marie was beautiful. Mrs. Dunbarton-Kent looked at her with pride; her child was a success. Gibbs looked at his nose; when in the pantry, he shook his head.

"She's that deep it's *astounding!*" he confided to the "girls," gloomily. "She takes them all in and, as for Mrs. D. K., she's completely blinded. So is West— flowers out from town every day and him telephoning all the time. Now, mark me! Mrs. Brant-Olwin knew what she was about when she placed *her* here, *that girl could give this family away to-morrow,* there's not much hid from *her*, the great question is, is she going to do it? I've watched her face—she's worrying over something and it's this, 'shall I do my duty by those who sent me here, or shall I play them false, hold my tongue and get myself adopted and marry West?'"

"I should think she'd do the last—I would," said Margaret.

"Doubtless you would, being a woman and not accustomed to weigh chances," Gibbs retorted. "But those high-class detective girls has a man's and a woman's brains as well. There's some grave danger in it for herself, is the way I explain her looks—she's not sure she can carry it through. Mark me! it'll end in total disaster—especially to those who don't keep a close tongue in their heads. It's the warning I've give you girls all along. Just you wait and see! It's the unexpected that happens in these cases!"

It seemed to Marie that they were all waiting. In spite of the quiet mornings spent over lace-making in Mrs. Dunbarton-Kent's room, of the coming and going guests, and the pleasant hours when she drove Mrs. Dunbarton-Kent; in spite of the white cherry bloom and the pink-tinged peach trees in the orchard, spring really smiling on them, each day breathed tense expectancy. Mrs. Dunbarton-Kent chuckled over her successful campaign, but it was always followed by a sigh. When the telephone rang she jumped, and she scanned her letters as if under a life sentence and looking for a reprieve. Several times Gibbs brought Willetts to Mrs. Dunbarton-Kent's room, and Marie knew that they talked earnestly together. Frequently it was

West who telephoned, and then Mrs. Dunbarton-Kent would send for her and the usual questions would follow:

"How are you, little Marie?"

"Very well, thank you, Monsieur—I find myself very busy and happy with Mrs. Dunbarton-Kent."

"That's right. Nothing has happened to frighten you?"

"Oh, no, Monsieur! Please do not be anxious about me."

Marie could hear him sigh. "I think about you night and day. Take very good care of yourself—perhaps better days are coming. I hope so."

"He is waiting also," Marie thought to herself.

Mrs. Dunbarton-Kent had long talks with West over the telephone: "I am consulting constantly with Haslett," was the gist of what he told her. "We're doing everything we can to locate that person. We have agents in all the cities. We have decided on the limit sum we thought you should offer for the property you want—in case we can approach the owner. Haslett is writing you about it. . . . I suppose there are no signs of a return?"

"No. Jones says the servants tell him they have not heard a word from her since she left. But, West, Willetts is certain that *he* is never in his room now, after late at night. Willetts is in and out of the house now at night—I thought it was safer to have him. How *he* makes his exit is a mystery to us."

"I don't know that it matters—even if you find it,

I wouldn't interfere. . . . But about Marie—take care of her for me, Aunt Bulah. If anything should happen to her, I don't want to live."

"I am taking care of her—that's the reason I have Willetts in the house at night."

"That makes me think—Haslett wants you to ask Walter Greene to the party. It's best. He'll make himself useful."

Mrs. Dunbarton-Kent sighed. "Whatever you and Haslett think best."

"Don't be down-hearted, Aunt Bulah—I believe it will come out as we want it. . . . I know I want to see Marie—it's all I can do to keep away. Is it of any use, do you think?"

Mrs. Dunbarton-Kent administered what comfort she could. "She said to me this morning, 'It will be nice when he comes back.'"

"She said that!" West exclaimed. "Bless her heart!"

Mrs. Dunbarton-Kent turned away from the telephone with a sigh. She hoped that Marie was not merely persuading herself into marrying West; that would be a poor foundation to build on. The child looked so grave sometimes. Still, all that was in the future; the present held troubles enough without imagining others. Bella had written from Philadelphia that she would arrive at nine o'clock on Wednesday night, and the announcement had not raised Mrs. Dunbarton-Kent's spirits: it would end the tête-a-tête breakfasts with Marie which she had enjoyed, and Breck would appear again in the dining-room. Then two days of tiring bustle over a party in which she felt only an anxious interest. It was an intolerable state of things; every time she and Marie drove through the park entrance and she glimpsed Mrs. Smith's house, her face burned.

Marie experienced the same discomfort. Her eyes were drawn to the Smith house. She believed that Mrs. Smith was still there, keeping herself hidden; that she and Breck met in the cottage. They passed Colfax Hall entrance daily, but never met Colfax. Marie was certain that somewhere he and Bella were together.

On the afternoon of the day on which Bella was expected, Marie drove Mrs. Dunbarton-Kent to the farm by the road they had taken on the day of Marie's arrival at Kent House. Mrs. Dunbarton-Kent said that she wanted to leave a message at the farm, but Marie suspected that she wanted a closer view of Mrs. Smith's house. Marie was just as eager to see whether she could detect any signs of the woman's being there; in most of us there is the perverse urge to look upon the thing that torments us, though we know that the sight of it will augment the ache. Hitherto, Mrs. Dunbarton-Kent had avoided the road that passed the cottage, but to-day she was particularly depressed: time was passing and nothing had been accomplished; the storm might break at any moment. She was thinking grimly that the party would be a good setting for an exposé—Breck taken from their midst—the staring faces of her guests—quite a drama!

"Drive by the cottage," she said to Marie. "It's the shortest way to the farm."

Marie determined that when they passed the place she would not glance at it, but she did, and at the house that topped it. Mrs. Smith's house presented a smiling appearance, its window-shades up and smoke curling from its chimneys. It was a contrast to the grimly forlorn stone cottage; the shades of its casement windows were down and the windows themselves were streaked and dusty; Marie had a vivid recollection of how the interior looked.

They passed it in silence, but after a moment or two Mrs. Dunbarton-Kent said with suppressed feeling. "Poor little cottage! Many's the evening I've spent there with my dear husband, he reading aloud to me. He had a wonderful voice." Then she added with an indignation that would not be suppressed, "I ought to have torn it down when that woman built her house, but first I let Breck use the place, he slept there all summer, then Bella with her clay—"

She had paused so abruptly that Marie was startled into looking at her. Mrs. Dunbarton-Kent's lips had fallen apart and her eyes stared. They were in the roadster and she leaned out and gazed back at the cottage. Then she sat back, silent and grim. "How convenient—" she muttered.

Marie guessed the suspicion that had flashed into her mind: it had occurred to her for the first time, as it had occurred to West when he saw the hair she had found, that the cottage had been the meeting-place of those two. West had said that he would not tell Mrs. Dunbarton-Kent about it, but she had come upon it herself.

She was silent until Marie was about to drive in at the farm-house gate, then she aroused suddenly. "No, go on," she said. "Talking of the cottage has upset me. I'll send the message over to the farm after I get home."

Marie complied in silence; her heart ached so that she felt ill. They came out on the High Road, and Mrs. Dunbarton-Kent told her to take the first cross-road which would bring them down into the Lower Road. Unconsciously Marie drove fast, but she did not forget to give warning before they reached the Lower Road for they were between high banks which hid them from cars that might be passing along the Lower Road. It was a dangerous spot, marked "Danger" on the sign-post for all autoists to read, but the driver of the car that was exceeding the speed limit along the Lower Road apparently neither heard nor saw. Marie's skill and quickness alone saved them from a crashing impact; instead of jamming on the brakes, which would have made an accident inevitable, she jumped the road and the other car cut across their rear, missing them by a bare six inches. Marie had measured the speed and the distance of the oncoming car, and had noted the shallowness of the ditch across the road and the level space beyond. They cleared the ditch with only a bump and on the bit of level Marie whirled her car about. She brought it back into the road and then she looked at Mrs. Dunbarton-Kent. The speeding car had not stopped, it had disappeared around the curve.

They looked at each other, both very white and trembling, but neither of them exclaimed over their escape. *"Madame!* It was *she!"* Marie said.

And Mrs. Dunbarton-Kent said, "She has come back."

For in those few instants they had seen distinctly: it was a roadster with top down and on the nose of the car was a gold eagle with wings spread, and the driver was Mrs. Smith. A veil wrapped her, its ends fluttering in the breeze, but the regular features, high color, and raven hair of the woman could be glimpsed through the veil. And the way she *sat,* as if her fingers were on the keys of a piano and her body arrogantly tense.

"It was she," Marie repeated.

"Yes," Mrs. Dunbarton-Kent returned thickly, "she's on her way home. . . . Drive on, child. You saved our lives."

CHAPTER XXVIII

"FAR better to gamble on the chance," West said. "Mr. Haslett and I talked it over on the way out."

It was nine o'clock and West and the lawyer were with Mrs. Dunbarton-Kent in the library. As soon as Mrs. Dunbarton-Kent and Marie had come in from their drive, Mrs. Dunbarton-Kent had telephoned to Haslett and he had said that he would come out to Kent House that evening. He and West had dined together in town, then West had brought him out in his roadster.

"I shouldn't call it gambling on a chance," Haslett objected quietly. "It's not merely the fact that it's risky to approach her, Mrs. Dunbarton-Kent, but it is one of my rules in practise not to force my opponent's hand. Nine times out of ten a waiting game is more effective. I knew that Breck would not risk his uncle's millions by accepting our offer, but as soon as I felt certain that he had a confederate, it was good tactics to indicate to them that we were willing to pay. Now I advise sitting still—let them make the first move."

He spoke slowly; in speech and manner Burton Haslett was a deliberate man, a very handsome man of fifty-five with iron-gray hair and deep-set dark eyes.

265

He was a capable office lawyer and an indefatigable worker; for many years, he had been Mr. Dunbarton-Kent's legal adviser. "Haslett works too much by rule and precedent and too little by instinct—he's not a good judge of character," Mr. Dunbarton-Kent sometimes complained. "Haslett couldn't be a criminal lawyer—he lacks imagination and he has too conventional a view-point. But he's a very safe adviser in financial affairs—I know of no one who is a safer guardian of property."

Mrs. Dunbarton-Kent had thought often of her husband's criticism; certainly Haslett had been altogether wrong in Marie's case. Both he and Walter Greene had erred in their judgment of her: Walter Greene had pronounced her, "A girl who thinks she knows it all, but is being used by the Brant-Olwin people just the same. She's their tool and doesn't know it." And Haslett had gone further, "She's an innocent-*looking* girl only. Either she is in their employ, or she is connected with Breck in some way." West had been the only person who had been right about Marie—and she herself; her instinct had told her that Marie was honest and nobody's tool.

So Mrs. Dunbarton-Kent appealed to West. "And you really think, West, that we should do nothing—just wait?"

"I do, and mainly because I think that they are desperately anxious to be safely rid of the jewels. I believe that you will hear from them very soon."

"What do you call 'soon'?" Mrs. Dunbarton-Kent

demanded irritably. "I wish it were over with—no matter what it costs!" She looked ill; the barely averted accident coupled with the return of Mrs. Smith had been a shock.

West looked at Haslett. "I think, as West does, that we will hear from them—perhaps in a few days."

"I hope so!" Mrs. Dunbarton-Kent said tensely. "I shan't be able to endure the sight of that stone image at my table much longer! He has more nerve than she —she must have been having a nightmare of capture as she drove along the Lower Road this afternoon. But for Marie she'd have killed herself and us. . . . And, West, I think they have met at the cottage. It occurred to me to-day that, as soon as Breck came to Kent House, he asked if he might use the cottage. He stopped spending all his time there only after you and Bella began to use the place. But you were never there at night and he has a key—think of the little cottage being used for such a purpose!"

Again West looked at Haslett, but he did not tell his aunt of Marie's discovery. "It's possible," he said soothingly, "Mr. Haslett and I have talked of its being a possible meeting-place, and we think that perhaps it's as well for us that they have had an unsuspected place in which to meet. . . . Aunt Bulah, I beg you not to worry so much. You had a trying experience this afternoon and you have the strain of this party in addition—it would be terrible if you were seriously ill. You have a deal of self-control—do use it."

"West is right, Mrs. Dunbarton-Kent," Haslett supplemented. "So much depends just now on nerve and cool judgment. It would never do for you to have a breakdown. I often think of what your husband used to say of you: 'A highly nervous temperament kept well in hand. My dear wife always rises to an occasion —the sun or the moon might fail us, Bulah would fret a little, but she would stand firm nevertheless.' "

The tears that rushed into Mrs. Dunbarton-Kent's eyes were a relief to her taut nerves. She wiped them away, then said resolutely. "Outline your program— I have no intention of taking to my bed."

They did not answer, for some one knocked on the door. Mrs. Dunbarton-Kent jumped, but West said quickly, "It's only Willetts—Mr. Haslett telephoned him that he was coming out."

It was Willetts. "I wanted to tell you that Jones has brought me some news," he said, "first of all, that Mrs. Smith stayed in her house only about an hour, then drove off again. Her darkies told Jones that she didn't tell them where she was going or when she would come back. And the latest is that Breck has just gone into town—he walked out of the house here quite openly, carrying his satchel and at the station he took a ticket for New York."

"Could they be leaving for good?" Mrs. Dunbarton-Kent asked quickly.

"He may not appear again," Haslett answered, "but I believe we have not seen the last of her."

"Perhaps Mrs. Brant-Olwin's people are on their trail?"

"I hardly think so, Mrs. Dunbarton-Kent. I'm inclined to think that he has gone to some place where they will meet—afterward. I think things are tending—as we would have them."

"His going is the most encouraging thing that has happened yet," West declared.

"There's another bit of news," Willetts said with a touch of amusement. "I've located the puppy. Mrs. Smith's darkies have it. They sleep above the garage, and they told Jones that two o'clock one morning—from the date it was the night the pup disappeared from our garage—they were waked by a puppy's yelping. They went down and found the animal inside their garage. How it got there they couldn't imagine, for the garage doors were locked. Jones says they are crazy over it—they've been afraid some one would come and claim it. They were mightily relieved when Jones told them it didn't belong to Kent House. They said they knew it didn't belong to Colfax Hall, for Colfax had only the mastiff."

"Some stray Allen picked up and gave to Marie, I suppose," West said with a touch of impatience. "Is Allen at Colfax Hall now, Willetts?"

"He's been away for over a week, so the darkies told Jones. We haven't seen him about this last week and the place looks deserted. But it always looks that way—he lives in one room and does his own cooking."

Haslett shook his head. "Unlike old days! You've brought us good news, Willetts," he added in the courteously appreciative way that won him the friendship of his employees. "You have been of great help to us in this trouble."

"I haven't done anything," Willetts protested, but he looked pleased. When West had spoken impatiently, his brow had darkened.

"You've been one of the greatest comforts I have had," Mrs. Dunbarton-Kent declared. "I'm not the sort that forgets honesty and loyalty, Willetts."

"You're the sort that draws those qualities to you, Mrs. Dunbarton-Kent," he returned with genuine gallantry. "I'd like to see an end to this business, for your sake. I've been hoping that it might come through Mrs. Smith—I've an idea that it will and that his going is their first move."

Haslett nodded. "We hope so."

"Are there any particular orders for me, Mr. Haslett?"

"No, Willetts. Greene is coming out to-night. He will sleep in the house so you will be relieved of that watch. You and Jones look after the outside as usual."

"Are you going to have Breck traced?"

"No. He may go wherever he pleases—the farther the better."

"Breck's a man who knows what he's about," Willetts said with reluctant admiration, "as smooth a one as I've ever known. Anderson just brought Miss Bella from the station and he was telling me it looked as if Breck had gone for good, all the farm accounts made out and everything left ship-shape."

"Bella is back then?" Mrs. Dunbarton-Kent asked.

"In her room now."

When he left them, West remarked, "He's not a brilliant man, but he's honest. He's a little long-winded, I get impatient sometimes, but I like him for his loyalty to Aunt Bulah."

"He and Jones and Greene all have clean records," Haslett said in his precise way. "Nothing would induce either one of them to take a bribe. Willetts is particularly valuable to us, for he is one of the best gem experts in New York—no paste pearls will ever pass his inspection. . . . Mrs. Dunbarton-Kent, our wisest course is simply to wait. Go on and give your party as if you had not a care in the world."

"And West will stay here?"

West answered, "Yes, for I'm anxious about Marie."

Haslett looked down. He had his opinion of Marie and of West's infatuation for her. She knew what she was about, that girl. In the end, they might have to buy her off, but, for the present, it was best to let sleeping dogs lie. West seemed to have a fixed idea that harm would come to Marie and he had urged Haslett to send a detective to Kent House especially to watch over her. Haslett had chosen to send Walter Greene. West had agreed with Haslett that a final room to room search of Kent House might not be a bad idea, and Haslett had given Walter Greene a few instructions which he had not confided either to West or to Mrs. Dunbarton-Kent.

But Burton Haslett was a politic man. "How is Miss Marie?" he asked.

Mrs. Dunbarton-Kent knew that it was not belief in Marie but fear of Mrs. Brant-Olwin's detectives which had made him urge her to keep Marie at Kent House. But it didn't matter; when he knew Marie better, he'd change his opinion.

"She was shocked by what happened this afternoon," she replied, "but the way in which she kept her head and managed our car at the crucial moment was marvelous. She can think clearly and act quickly, that child."

West drew an audible breath; he had been terribly shocked when Mrs. Dunbarton-Kent had told them of their afternoon's experience. "I wish we could clear the neighborhood of that woman—whether we get the pearls or not!" he exclaimed. "She'll do Marie a harm yet!"

· Haslett considered him as completely an infatuated a man as he had ever known. "I doubt it," he said a little dryly. "However, let us go back to the important thing: you both insist that, if they demand it, you will pay as high as four hundred and fifty thousand for the jewels. West says that he will contribute fifty thousand of that amount. I've told you that I don't approve of it—that I would not pay those crooks one cent more than the jewels are worth, four hundred thousand, but it is your money and not mine that's to be paid, so I have nothing more to say. . . . Now we must have the sum where we can get it at a few hours' notice—they may give us a very short time."

"I don't need to disturb any investments—I can arrange with the bank to advance me the sum, for steel and oil pay in before the end of the month, Haslett."

"I know—over five hundred thousand, Mrs. Dunbarton-Kent. . . . And you, West?"

"I can give you a check for fifty thousand at any moment."

"We shall be ready for them then," Haslett said. "And now, West, get me to the station."

CHAPTER XXIX

AFTER Haslett and West had gone, Mrs. Dunbarton-Kent went up to Marie's door. "Gone to bed, Marie?" she asked.

Marie opened her door promptly. "No, Madame— I do not sleep *all* the time."

She spoke brightly, but she took sympathetic note of Mrs. Dunbarton-Kent's strained look. Mrs. Dunbarton-Kent had told her that West was bringing a man out to talk over business matters with her, and Marie felt certain that it must be about ransoming the jewels. She had not gone to bed, for she knew that West would want to see her after the business conference was over. She had decided that she wanted to see him. Every day during that long week there had been affectionate messages, the loveliest flowers love could choose and money could buy, expressions of tenderness and longing.

Marie had said to herself in utter self-disgust, "Are you an imbecile, that you think and think of one who is despicable! Turn your back upon it and think of one who really loves you." The sight of Mrs. Smith, with arrogant head high, bearing down upon them, had aroused a vivid anger in Marie: let Breck depart with his woman—the man with the gentleman's heart belonged to her.

"Come to my room," Mrs. Dunbarton-Kent said. "West will be back in a few minutes."

"I hoped that he would," Marie answered in a tone that was significant.

Mrs. Dunbarton-Kent set aside her own troubles and considered her. The girl looked so flushed and determined, not exactly as a girl who was eager to see her lover should look. Involuntarily she said, "Be very sure before you promise, child. I love you too much to have you make a mistake." She put her big arm about Marie's shoulders and drew her toward her room. "We'll talk a little before he comes back."

She was thinking now of Marie's problem and not her own, so she did not notice the square of white which lay on the rug just inside her door. It was Marie who picked up the envelope and saw that it was directed to Mrs. Dunbarton-Kent.

"It is a note for you, Madame," she said. "Some one has put it beneath your door."

"Who in the world from?"

Mrs. Dunbarton-Kent scanned the envelope, it was a handwriting she did not know, but not until she tore it open and saw the first lines did she have the least suspicion of what the contents might be; the long expected and much discussed so often comes as a complete surprise.

There was no address and no date:

"Mrs. Bulah Dunbarton-Kent,
"Kent House, the North Shore,
"Long Island.

"My dear Madam :—
    "I understand that you have made inquiries con-
cerning the property which I have for sale. Said property is intact, unmortgaged, and free of any incum-
brance. My price for same is five hundred thousand
dollars, cash.
    "You need not answer this. If at seven o'clock to-
morrow morning, your flag-pole displays the American flag, I shall conclude that the terms are satisfactory, and I shall communicate with you at the earliest
opportunity and arrange for transfer of the property.
    "Kindly excuse an unsigned note, and believe me,
                    "Yours truly,
                            ————————"

Mrs. Dunbarton-Kent raised a blank face from this
communication. But only for a moment: "Run,
child!" she said breathlessly. "Go see if West and
Haslett have gone—tell them to come here!"

"They have gone, Madame. I heard the car go on
the driveway just before you knocked on my door."

Mrs. Dunbarton-Kent grew as flushed as before she
had been pale. "It's too late!" she said. "I'll have to
wait."

Marie had thought quickly. "No, Madame. If you
wish them brought back, I can go. I can take the
car."

"Thank God for your brains! Get it, child. Run,
and I'll meet you down below—you shan't go alone."

"Madame, do not be so excited and go carefully down the stairs!" Marie begged, for Mrs. Dunbarton-Kent was so dangerously flushed that it frightened her.

Then she ran. In the back hall, down-stairs, she collided with Gibbs and so violently that he lost his footing and sat down with a thud on the waxed floor. Marie cleared his portly form at a bound and tugged at the back door which Gibbs had double-locked—at the stroke of nine, as was his nightly custom. But Marie wasted no time over Gibbs; she ran into the passage leading to the kitchen at a speed that gave the cook a severe shock and gained the outer air by a dash through the servants' entrance.

But on her way to the garage she was brought to an abrupt stop, for, as she rounded the servants' quarters, she was seized by powerful hands and whirled about and a flash-light was thrust into her face. It was Willetts. He dropped the light and his arms went about Marie in a protective rather than a detective fashion:

"Why—it's the little girl!" he said. "What's the matter?"

"It is—Mrs. Dunbarton-Kent—wishes—the car—instantly—" Marie gasped.

"I'll be—*blessed!*" And he loosed his hold and Marie was off like a dart to the garage.

Willetts followed. "I didn't know who it was at first," he apologized confusedly. "Hope I didn't hurt you?"

"No, no!" Marie said, though her arm ached. "Open the doors wider!" And she flew to the big car.

"What's happened?" Willetts demanded.

"Only that Mrs. Dunbarton-Kent must overtake Mr. West and the gentleman with him—before the train takes him."

Willetts pulled out his watch. "You can't make it— the train's due in eight minutes."

Marie had started the engine; her face darkened. Then she smiled; she pointed to the telephone. "I shall try. Meantime, telephone to the station-man a message from Mrs. Dunbarton-Kent, that they tell the gentleman with Mr. West to wait until Mrs. Dunbarton-Kent shall join him." And she shot out of the garage and whirled around the servants' quarters and on then to the porte-cochère.

"That's quick thinking!" Willetts said to himself as he went to the telephone.

And, in the kitchen, Gibbs, while he rubbed surreptitiously that portion of his body which had been bruised by his fall, was saying to the cook, "You quiet down! Nothing's happened except that Mrs. D. K. has got to get a message to Mr. Haslett before he catches the train—she told me so. And that girl'll get her to the station in time, mark me! *She* don't give up to no highsterics! *She's* got brains." Gibbs did not mention his fall; Buckingham Gibbs knew how to maintain his dignity; for fifteen years he had ruled, below-stairs, in Kent House.

Mrs. Dunbarton-Kent sat in grim silence while Marie whirled her along the Lower Road. She was collected now: if they made it, well and good; if they didn't, she would have to consult with West and perhaps follow Haslett into town.

They had covered two-thirds of the distance to the station when the whistle of the train told them that speeding was useless. Marie slowed down and Mrs. Dunbarton-Kent said resignedly, "We did our best, child. We may as well turn around and go home and wait for West to come."

"I think perhaps not, Madame," Marie said hopefully. "While I hurried with the car, I told Mr. Willetts to telephone to the station the message that the gentleman with Mr. West should wait till you came."

"You did! I can't thank you enough, child!"

"Shall we not go on, Madame?"

"Yes—of course."

They were very near the station, when Marie said of the car that rounded the curve, "It is they!"

She was right, it was West who drew up beside them and Haslett who said, "I received your message, Mrs. Dunbarton-Kent."

"Marie's message," she answered. "I hadn't wits enough to think of it. . . . Time's precious and you'll miss the next train, but you'll have to come back to Kent House. I've had a letter about that property."

"If you wish to save time, Madame, I can leave you here while I drive on to where I can turn," Marie suggested. "Then the next train need not to be missed."

West had left his car and had come to them. "Trust little Marie for finding a way! . . . Get into my car, Aunt Bulah, and if you and Mr. Haslett want to talk business, I'll talk to Marie."

"It's the best thing to do. But you stay here with us, West, while Marie drives on."

"Very well. Bring your car back, Marie—don't run away from us," he said brightly.

But as soon as Marie was out of hearing, he asked tensely enough, "Have they written to you?"

"Some one has," she said, as he helped her into his seat. "But is there light enough here for Haslett to read it?"

"I have a flash-light."

West stood beside Haslett and held the light while they both read the note. "It's disguised, but it's Breck's handwriting!" West exclaimed almost at once.

Haslett read the note twice, then he said with profound anger. "Damn them! Five hundred thousand! Where they should be is behind the bars. Even with all the Dunbarton-Kent millions, I'd not let myself be gouged like this—I'd rather turn them over to Mrs. Brant-Olwin!"

"I shall pay it," Mrs. Dunbarton-Kent said deeply. "Keeping my husband's name clean before the world is more to me than all the huge income that I don't begin to use. But, Haslett, *I'll make them understand that it's the last!* Any other attempt, and I shall put him behind the bars!"

"And you'll stand for this?" Haslett asked West.

"I am a Dunbarton-Kent and he is my cousin," West answered succinctly.

"Endow a scoundrel with a fortune!" Haslett muttered.

"I care far more for my family name than I do for money," West returned firmly. "I want to marry and have children. I have enough to support a wife and educate our children and if uncle's millions should never come to me, they will come to my children—why should I worry over a fifty thousand?"

"Yes, Bella will be the only impecunious one—until you leave us, Mrs. Dunbarton-Kent, and may that be a long time off," Haslett said with commingled exasperation, genuine sympathy for the big woman beside him, and hot disgust over the missive which he thrust into its envelope. "It's a huge outrage—they already have a hundred thousand of yours. Six hundred thousand!"

"Listen to me, Haslett!" Mrs. Dunbarton-Kent said forcibly. "How much accrued income do you suppose I have laid by? Well, exactly two millions. I can use that two millions as I like—I had intended that it should go, with the rest of the Dunbarton-Kent money, to the three heirs. Now I tell you what I intend to do: if I get Mrs. Brant-Olwin's pearls—if all goes well— I mean to give Bella five hundred thousand, and West the like amount, and Breck I shall have endowed, as you say. He may cease to steal when he has a fortune. Then Breck will depart from my·roof, Bella can knit elsewhere than in my presence, and West can marry and be happy—*I* want peace in my old age. . . . Keep your fifty thousand, West—you deserve it for what you said about my dear husband's name. . . . So, Haslett, we'll have no more comments."

"I beg your pardon, Mrs. Dunbarton-Kent, for saying what I thought."

"You needn't, Haslett—I like you a deal better when you forget to be a lawyer and are just plain man."

"Thank you, Mrs. Dunbarton-Kent. . . . We await their pleasure then."

Mrs. Dunbarton-Kent drew a long breath. "Will they want a settlement to-morrow, do you suppose? It will take a day to make arrangements at the bank— that was why I hurried after you."

"You'd better come into town in the morning. West will take me back to the station now and I'll get the next train."

"As little Marie said, 'the train need not to be missed,'" West remarked softly. "She's waiting a hundred yards or so behind us, tactful as always. I'll call her. And I'll be at Kent House almost as soon as you are."

CHAPTER XXX

WHEN they returned to Kent House, Mrs. Dunbarton-Kent took Marie to her own room and talked to her about West. "I have grown to care for him," she told Marie among other things. "I suppose it has been mostly my feeling that all my husband's heirs wanted was my early demise, that has raised a barrier between us—yes, and the something in them which makes them so unapproachable, their queer light eyes that look through you while they do their thinking. My dear husband's eyes were light too, but such a kind gray." She paused to sigh, then went on. "I don't want you to act in haste, child. Loving you has brought out what is fine in West—be very certain before you accept him that you will be giving him as real a devotion as he is giving you. Waiting a little won't hurt either of you."

"I have decided what I shall say to him," Marie answered firmly. Then, suddenly, she clung to the big woman. "Madame, it is now I wish a mother!"

"There, there," Mrs. Dunbarton-Kent said tenderly. "You tell West whatever you like, only remember that you have both a mother and a home."

Marie came out of Mrs. Dunbarton-Kent's room with wet eyes, and found West waiting for her in the hall. "I couldn't go to bed without seeing you," he said eagerly. Then with concern, "What is it, Marie?"

Marie dried her eyes. "I hoped you might be here."

"You did!" He wanted to take her into his arms, but Marie held him off. "No, Monsieur—I wish to say something: I promise to give you my answer when I know that you and Mrs. Dunbarton-Kent are not so anxious—when Kent House becomes happier."

"You mean—that when Breck leaves Kent House you will listen to me?"

"Monsieur, I wish to be honest with you. I have loved him and pitied him. But I can not love what seems to be despicable. He belongs to that woman of whom I have reason to think the worst things. I do not love such a man. But my heart is sad, and you urge very much. I wish time in which to love you."

"I think he has left us," West announced abruptly.

Marie shrank like one whose wound has been touched, but she asked very steadily, "Has he gone to her?"

"We don't know, Marie—he left Kent House this evening and took the train for New York. He had his satchel—that is all we know. . . . Now have you an answer for me?"

Marie was thinking hotly, that it was the beginning of the end: when they sold the jewels, Breck and Mrs. Smith would travel together. She saw too the nervous movements of West's hand and the determination to clasp her to him, and she felt a passionate wish to be happy when his arms did clasp her, not as she felt now.

She stood near her door and she reached behind her and opened it a little. "By and by—not to-night, Monsieur," she said softly. With a twist of her lithe little body, she escaped his outstretched arms; his hands touched a closed door.

CHAPTER XXXI

IT was West who, at half past six the next morning, hoisted the big flag which the wind from the sound unfurled and set waving above Kent House. The wind whipped it into action, causing a slapping sound that waked Marie. When she looked from her window, she could see nothing, but when she leaned out she saw the flag directly above her; the hoisting ropes led down the side of the house, not two feet from her window; when the wind whipped the flag, the ropes, though drawn down and securely fastened below, slapped taut against the side of the house, the noise Marie had heard.

"They raise the flag in honor of the party," Marie thought, and she bathed and dressed in a determined way. She felt that she had decided upon the future; that she had put Breck out of her mind. She wondered how many women buried a dream and, in the end, were the happier for having done so.

Marie did not glance at Breck's vacant place at the breakfast-table. She lifted Mrs. Dunbarton-Kent's hand to her cheek, smiled at West who sprang up when she came in, and returned Bella's frigid, "Good morning," with a level look and as stony a greeting.

Bella did not look well, there were shadows about her eyes, but she held herself quite as erectly as usual.

Marie learned the plans for the day: West was going to take Mrs. Dunbarton-Kent into the city directly after breakfast and return with her at noon; Bella would superintend the decorating and the arrangement of the banquet table in the music-room, and the placing of the half a car-load of palms and flowering plants which had been ordered for the big glazed room off the ball-room, once the conservatory, but now a room used only on an occasion such as this. Gibbs had entire charge of the kitchen and of the caterers and their swarm of assistants. To Marie was assigned the list of guests and the box of dinner-cards, bearing the Dunbarton-Kent crest. Marie looked at the crest with interest and, bending over her, West read softly the line in Latin, *"Malo mori quam fœdari. . . .* I would rather die than submit to disgrace," he translated. Marie thought of Breck and her lips tightened.

Bella was talking with Mrs. Dunbarton-Kent. Evidently she was very capable—she did not seem to be in the least daunted by the day's work. "We'll have everything in order by three o'clock," she told Mrs. Dunbarton-Kent, and added, "You remember, Aunt Bulah, that I told you I expected to leave before the party was over—for my southern trip? I packed my trunks last night, and I'll send them to the station this afternoon."

"I'd forgotten," Mrs. Dunbarton-Kent said in a pre-occupied way. She thought for a moment. "Come to my room before I go into town," she said then, "I want to tell you something."

Marie wondered whether Mrs. Dunbarton-Kent was going to tell Bella about the letter she had received. With a parting smile for West, she slipped away to her room, taking the cards with her. Mrs. Dunbarton-Kent came for a moment to bid her good-by and patted her cheek affectionately, and Margaret brought her West's daily offering of flowers, but, without any other interruption, she spent the morning in her room. She wrote each name with great care, in her perfect hand, almost like steel engraving, and tried not to think of the Latin inscription.

Marie took the cards down with her at lunch-time and found that there was to be no regular lunch that day, a snatched lunch in the pantry only; the house was overrun with hurrying workers. Gibbs made her the longest speech he had vouchsafed her since she came to Kent House: "Miss Bella and Mr. West have lunched, and Mr. West is helping Miss Bella in the entertainment wing. Mrs. Dunbarton-Kent returned before lunch, but wished me to tell you that she had been called back to the city and had to go immediately. She asks that you rest this afternoon, and she will see you at dinner this evening."

Marie entrusted the cards to him, and went back to her room. She felt very certain that this hurried going to the city had to do with the ransoming of the jewels; she would never see Breck again. *"Malo mori quam fœdari,"* How could he? *How could he!*

CHAPTER XXXII

A T SEVEN o'clock, Marie came down to the drawing-room and found Mrs. Dunbarton-Kent and Bella and West collected there. Mrs. Dunbarton-Kent was gowned in black, as always, and very simply, without jewels and with her huge shoulders and arms covered. Bella looked regal in her all-jet gown with mere straps over her square shoulders. Her skin was so dazzlingly white and her hair so marvelously fair. Like Mrs. Dunbarton-Kent, she wore no jewels, not even rings. Bella's height and her haughty carriage, her wonderfully regular features and unusual fairness, made her most noticeable; she was the more distinguished because of the absence of gems. She was a magnificently handsome woman and, as always, she made Marie feel slight and frail and of little moment.

But most men would have turned with a sense of relief to Marie's iridescent beauty and have experienced a warmer heart beat; she was so vividly lovely in the little gown that Margaret had brought into her room just as she was preparing to put on her red ensemble, the only evening outfit she possessed. It did not take much material to cover Marie and this little imported gown could have been gathered into a mere handful, an all-sequin and jet-edged thing cunningly devised to

289

emit many colors, but the prevailing color a deep orchid, tipped with red and hinting of gold. And her little slippers were gold. She looked like some vivid butterfly with wings sheathed about its slender body.

When Margaret had brought it to her, there had been a note pinned to it: "I ordered this and West chose it—put it on and be happy, or I shall be unhappy." It was another present from Mrs. Dunbarton-Kent, and Marie went straight to her. "Madame—!" was all she could say, but her little outstretched hands and her eyes spoke for her. All afternoon, Marie had been fighting depression, calling on all the resolution she possessed; she had come down to the family gathering determined to make Mrs. Dunbarton-Kent happy, whatever the cost to herself.

Mrs. Dunbarton-Kent kissed her and patted her shoulder. Her eyes twinkled. "You didn't have to 'lay paper within those soles,' did you?"

The dress was short, as was the fashion, and Marie did not have to lift her skirt for Mrs. Dunbarton-Kent's inspection. "No, Madame, not at all. They fit most perfectly." She looked down anxiously at her rounded legs and tiny ankles. "In my chauffeur's uniform I never thought of it, but this skirt displays very much."

Mrs. Dunbarton-Kent chuckled, West laughed amusedly, and Bella turned away with a contemptuous curl of the lip. Marie saw what escaped Mrs. Dunbarton-Kent's notice and the softly accented words left her lips before she knew it. "However, if I hold up

my head and make my shoulders look like a man's, perhaps no man will even look at my feet. To be unlovable must be my endeavor."

She could bring the blood to Bella's face; Bella
flushed scarlet, so much Marie saw before West took
her away. "I want to show you the rooms before any
one comes," he said; then low and amusedly, "Little
hornet!"

As soon as the words were out, Marie had been
sorry. "I should not have spoken so," she said con-
tritely, "but she curled her lip at me."

"Bella curls her lip at most people and manages to
be unlovable, as you say, but there's nothing gained by
making her angry. . . . Little Marie, you look very
lovely to-night. You've been shut up in your room all
day and I have been afraid to try to pry you out of it,
but to-night is mine," he added determinedly. "I have
something in my breast pocket which I mean to put on
your finger to-night."

Marie crushed the feeling of desolation that assailed
her. She looked resolutely ahead and was acutely conscious of the scent of flowers. But she said nothing;
West saw only her long lashes and the firm set of her
lips. He said no more on that subject.

"These rooms have been closed ever since we went
into the war. Aunt Bulah gave thousands to war chari-
ties and stopped all expensive entertaining."

They had come through the big doors at the end of
the drawing-rooms; Marie had never seen them open.
This was the wing of Kent House that jutted into the

park. First there was the music-room, which was luxuriously furnished and ceiling-lighted. At one end of the room was the pipe-organ, as fine an organ as was possessed by any private home in or near New York. At the other end of the room was the grand piano. Beyond the music room was the banquet-room and beyond that the conservatory. All three rooms gave into the long ballroom, and all were ceiling-lighted, a universal soft glow.

Marie was seeing a new Kent House, and it struck her more forcibly than ever before why Mrs. Dunbarton-Kent was so passionately determined to protect the family name. Here were wealth and grandeur, but more than that, a profound dignity, a position established and respected; no wonder she fought to keep it untarnished before the world. . . . And into this home Mrs. Dunbarton-Kent had taken her. And a Dunbarton-Kent was offering her entire devotion.

Marie's hand sought West's. He took it and held it, but though his hand was burning hot, he lifted hers and kissed it only, then let it go. A stupid man would have broken the spell of tenderness that held her, but West was not a stupid man.

He led her through the rooms. As they passed the piano, Marie asked, "Do you play, Monsieur?" Marie was feeling that she had no accomplishments; that she was not deserving of all this grandeur.

"I love music, but I don't know one note from another, sweetheart. Bella is a good musician, but she never touches the piano any more—I don't know why."

Marie thought of Mrs. Smith; she was a brilliant musician. She had stung Bella a few minutes before because her regal beauty reminded her of Mrs. Smith.

West took her into the banquet-room and Marie exclaimed, "How *beautiful!*"

It was Bella's work, but Marie could not withhold her praise: a long oblong table reaching from corner to corner of the deep room, or, rather, a table constructed about an oblong fountain, three cupids entwined, each with a dimpled arm extended and holding an arrow. From the three arrows poured tiny streams of water into the basin of the fountain which was sunk to a level with the table and in which floated pink and white water-lilies and their broad leaves. Moss clung to the feet of the cupids and to the edges of the basin and a tracery of tiny orchids spread from the basin over the table, even to its farthest ends; the faintly earthy scent of the water-lilies sweetened the air.

"Bella is a genius at this sort of thing," West declared. "Mrs. Brant-Olwin would have stacked that fountain with solid gold apples and sheaves of silver bananas, or something of the kind—I hope she can appreciate this beautiful thing. . . . Look at the conservatory, then we must go—the ballroom is like most ballrooms, a place to dance in and a screen of palms hiding the musicians. We are going to have the organ during dinner—that was my suggestion—I loathe jazz with my meals. Campetti is going to play for us."

The conservatory was delightful, couches and chairs arranged behind groups of palms and flowers. "The card-tables are in the regular dining-room where nothing will disturb the fiends," West said. "I have to play host at dinner, Mrs. Brant-Olwin is at my right, but she will have Ward Wakefield, who is a lion, at *her* right and the very important Countess de Lantinelle, who is being fêted in New York just now and who, they say, wants to marry John van Rouvervant, will be at my left. But, as she will devote herself to John Van on her left, I shall be free to look at you most of the time, for you will sit where the table curves, almost as if you faced me. . . . But, dear, we must go back."

When they reached the drawing-rooms, though Mrs. Dunbarton-Kent and Bella were alone, several guests were descending the stairs, Mrs. Brant-Olwin and Mrs. Granveston in the lead, talking amicably together, and behind them Mr. Granveston, a very tall old man with a peaked beard and bright keen eyes, and John van Rouvervant, a man of perhaps sixty who betrayed over-good living more by his thick speech and slightly watery eyes than by his well-cared-for girth. He was very wealthy and a jovial bachelor. Others were above, and others were arriving, the chatter and laughter had begun.

Even before Gibbs' magnificent voice announced her, Marie recognized Mrs. Brant-Olwin, the little plump woman with the round, attractively humorous face and small, intensely black eyes and blue-black dyed hair who had sent her laughingly on her way to Kent House. She was exceedingly well made up, her skin whitened into a youthful contrast to eyes and hair.

But a mouth is unchangeable; Mrs. Brant-Olwin's mouth turned up naturally at the corners, a little like Marie's, a sweet little smiling mouth. Marie succeeded in concealing her surprise—Mrs. Brant-Olwin might not like to be reminded of their meeting.

Marie was right, Mrs. Brant-Olwin either did not or chose not to remember her; she looked at Marie pleasantly, but without any sign of recognition. Mrs. Granveston set the fashion for the evening; she patted the hand Marie shyly extended to her while she dipped in the courtesy which every woman who had met Marie declared was "simply fascinating—just like a child of ten."

"How are you, my dear—but need I ask! You look like a veritable orchid—an exquisite little gown."

Marie answered her in French, and Mrs. Granveston said mischievously, "You must speak French to Mrs. Brant-Olwin," and passed on, for Mrs. Dunbarton-Kent and that lady had turned toward them. "I'm glad to meet you," Mrs. Brant-Olwin said before Mrs. Dunbarton-Kent had time to introduce her. "Mrs. Dunbarton-Kent was telling me about you the other day, a regular romance. Mrs. Dunbarton-Kent's a dear—I've always thought so—and you're as sweet as you can be." She gave Marie's hand a cordial squeeze and Marie saw that her eyes twinkled; it was as if she had said, "Goodness! Don't give me away! It was all a grand joke." At least that was what Marie made of her expression.

Then Mrs. Dunbarton-Kent presented Mr. Granves-

ton and John van Rouvervant and they all stood
together. West joined them and Mrs. Brant-Olwin
spoke to him as one would to an old acquaintance.

"I feel as shabby as an old squaw to-night—no
pearls."

She looked far from shabby, a gorgeous gown of
black and silver. Her hair was bound by a jet fillet
studded with diamonds and her jet ear-rings had as
pendants two magnificent diamonds and the jet bar-pin
at her breast had a center diamond as large as a pea.

"I should say that you had gone into rather magnificent mourning for your pearls," West said smilingly, and yet with kindly sympathy. "Have you had
no trace of them yet?"

She made a *moue*. "Clues." Then her eyes
flashed. "I'll find the thief, and when I do, he'll have
reason to remember me. Back in Nevada, I've seen a
cotton-wood decorated with the likes of him. Being
it's New York, I'm offering a big reward." Then she
changed to laughter; she wrinkled her small retroussé
nose in a delightful way. "This set I'm wearing belonged originally to a Spanish grandee, but it always
make me think of Mrs. Rudy, who kept a boarding-
house in Virginia City. She had supported three hus-
bands, one at a time, of course, and wrote a book of
poetry. When her last husband died, she wrote:

"'Oh, drape me in black,
He'll never come back.

I'll go on scrapin' toast,
And watchin' the roast,
But he'll never come back,
He'll never come back!' "

They all laughed, though there were several in that
group who felt sick at heart. Then a number of young
people came in and it was evident that they liked Mrs.
Brant-Olwin. They shook hands with Marie and
looked at her interestedly, but none of them paused to
talk to her; they were busy greeting one another.
Marie stood beside Mrs. Brant-Olwin, for Mrs. Dunbarton-Kent had told her to stand there, and Bella was
also in the receiving group and West stood near with
a watchful eye on Marie. He looked very handsome,
Marie thought. She felt very proud of him: after all,
it was her dream come partly true, "a man of worth
and distinction."

It was evident that West liked Mrs. Brant-Olwin;
he made her say amusing things. It was evident that
she was either liked or was going to be liked by almost
everybody; she said something bright or amusing to
every one. Marie was very glad, both for Mrs. Dunbarton-Kent's and Mrs. Brant-Olwin's sake; she liked
Mrs. Brant-Olwin quite as much as she had liked her
when she first met her.

And many people said nice things to Marie. The
women she had met during Mrs. Dunbarton-Kent's
campaign in Mrs. Brant-Olwin's behalf were almost
affectionate, and the men looked at her in a way that
Marie understood instantly: they thought her attrac-

tive. Burton Haslett had been among the first to arrive and, after talking to Mrs. Brant-Olwin, he stood
beside Marie for some time. Marie liked his gravely
courteous manner, but not the intent way in which he
looked at her. She knew now who he was, the "Haslett" Colfax had mentioned, Mrs. Dunbarton-Kent's
lawyer; it was he Mrs. Dunbarton-Kent had wanted to
overtake the night before; it was he who had persuaded
Mr. Dunbarton-Kent to have the proviso put in his
will; he had never had any faith in Breck, and Marie
felt that he was not friendly to her.

But Marie smiled at him from beneath her lashes.
He was speaking to her when Mrs. Brant-Olwin
touched her arm. "Who is that *stunning*-looking man
just coming in? A relation? . . . He must be."

In the entrance to the drawing-room, standing tall
and straight, one white-gloved hand touching the front
of his vest, his head thrown back slightly as he looked
at the gathering, was Breck. He was in evening dress
and it accentuated his natural air of distinction. He
was a strikingly handsome man and unmistakably a
Dunbarton-Kent; Mrs. Brant-Olwin's exclamation was
not surprising.

Marie could not answer. Happily their little group
was looking at Breck and not at Mrs. Dunbarton-Kent,
for she blanched as at the sight of a ghost. A flash of
vivid anger crossed West's face, and Bella stiffened
into ice. Breck could see how they looked at him, they
were not looking at one another.

Yet he came forward, lightness and strength in every

movement, unembarrassed and with a casual glance for all but Mrs. Dunbarton-Kent. When he stood before her, he said as any nephew would speak to an aunt he had surprised by an unexpected appearance. "I met Ward Wakefield in town, you know we were in France together, Aunt Bulah. At the last moment, he was unable to come and asked me to take his place—he sent you this note." And, with his eyes steadily on her, he handed her the bit of white which he had been holding against his vest.

They were quick in an emergency, that family. Even Mrs. Dunbarton-Kent said with only a trifling thickness in her voice, "I'm glad you were able to come, Breck."

And West, who had come to her rescue, introduced Breck with graceful ease. "Mrs. Brant-Olwin, you have never met my cousin Breckenridge. Ward Wakefield was more successful than we've ever been in persuading him to attend a party."

Breck bowed over Mrs. Brant-Olwin's hand, and she said with genuine interest and sympathy, "You've been an invalid since the war, haven't you? I've always wanted to meet you. I'm real glad you're better and beginning to go out."

"So am I, Mrs. Brant-Olwin—particularly as I am going to sit beside you at dinner." It was quietly but distinctly said, and accompanied by his slow smile that impressed Mrs. Brant-Olwin, as it had impressed Marie, as pathetic.

Marie had slipped away, and Breck lifted to meet

Haslett's extended hand. They shook hands, a steady look into each other's eyes. Then Bella's cool voice said at Breck's shoulder, "You must meet some of these people before dinner, Breck. Come over and talk to Mrs. Granveston."

West and Haslett had moved to Mrs. Dunbarton-Kent's side. "What does he mean by this?" she asked scarcely above her breath.

"To cover his tracks," West answered, and Haslett said, "There is no telling. You have the money on you still?"

"In the belt—next to me. They couldn't get it without killing me."

"They would never attempt anything like that," Haslett said decidedly. "Don't be anxious, I shall not leave your side all evening and I'm going with you to-night. I'll tell Greene not to take his eye from him and we must have Willetts close to us. They are not planning a double-cross—I think as West does, that he came in order to *appear* to have no connection with the thing— he's looking to the future. . . . Is the note genuine?"

"It seems so to me." She slipped it into West's hand. "You know his handwriting better than I—I know they were together in France."

West went into the hall for a few minutes, then came back. "Wakefield wrote it—you'll have to give him Wakefield's place. . . . Greene must watch her diamonds."

"Perhaps that's what brought him," Mrs. Dunbarton-Kent said with bitter contempt.

CHAPTER XXXIII

MARIE lived through the dinner in a sort of painful dream set to music, the all-pervading organ. She saw Mrs. Dunbarton-Kent at the far end of the table, somewhat pale, but the usual capable hostess, and Haslett beside her. Every one was talking and Marie was conscious that she herself talked; she did her best to please Mr. Granveston and John van Rouvervant. John van Rouvervant paid her compliments, all she needed to do was to smile at him and occasionally answer brightly, besides, the Countess de Lantinelle was on his other side and she was very vivacious. She talked alternately to West and John van Rouvervant, or to both of them; she seemed to admire West very much.

But to Mr. Granveston, Marie was forced to pay closer attention, for he talked to her of Canada; he had spent his boyhood in Canada. In the early days, his father had made a fortune in the fur-trade. Mrs. Dunbarton-Kent had shown good judgment when she placed Marie between the two elderly gentlemen: John van Rouvervant had a penchant for pretty girls and Mr. Granveston would really appreciate her. Both thought her charming, and Mr. Granveston became really interested, for Marie had much to tell him of the present-day fur-trade.

But it was of the two at West's right of whom Marie was acutely conscious, Breck and Mrs. Brant-Olwin; of Breck's face, grave, except occasionally when he smiled. He did not forget to talk now and then to the girl on his right, Marjorie Caswell, Mrs. Granveston's granddaughter, but it was to Mrs. Brant-Olwin he gave his attention. She spoke to West occasionally, otherwise she seemed to be absorbedly interested in Breck; theirs was a tête-a-tête almost throughout dinner. Marie felt that Mrs. Brant-Olwin was a very independent sort of woman, she would not care in the least whether any one remarked, as John van Rouvervant did, that, "The little widow seems to have fallen head over heels for that handsome young fellow."

Marie heard the remark with commingled feelings, an ache in her throat and a sick apprehension; from the moment Breck had appeared, she had felt wretchedly foreboding. That immobile, inscrutable face of his and his pathetic smile that made one want to weep from pity. She wished that she could hear what he was saying; she felt an aching envy of Mrs. Brant-Olwin, and at the same time a certain sympathy. She noticed the footman who rarely moved far from his position behind the two; his face was familiar to Marie, then she realized that he was Walter Greene, the young man who had tried to question her on the day after her arrival at Kent House—a detective. And behind Mrs. Dunbarton-Kent stood Willetts, Marie had recognized him at once, though he looked strange in a footman's livery. Why were they there? What did they think would happen? . . . And she must sit there and talk and smile like these others who suspected nothing.

Just before they left the table, the organ sank into silence, for a few minutes there was only the sound of voices, then, suddenly, the orchestra in the ballroom invited them to forsake the banquet-room. As they left the table, Mr. Granveston said, "I am going to take a dinner-partner's privilege and claim the first dance. I'm over sixty, but, thank heaven, I still have the use of my feet—I was a great dancer back in the old Quebec days. . . . You dance, of course—a little fairy like you?"

Marie dance! Many a soldier she had delighted. She smiled at him, "I dance a *little*, Monsieur—you shall see." But she was watching Breck and Mrs. Brant-Olwin; they stood together talking, as if loath to part. Breck bent and said something to her and she nodded brightly, then turned to West, who stood waiting. Then Breck offered his arm to Marjorie Caswell —he had brought her in to dinner. When Mr. Granveston took Marie into the ballroom, Breck and his dinner-partner were dancing, and West was dancing with Mrs. Brant-Olwin. But, first, West had whispered to Marie, "The next dance is mine, dear?"

As she circled the room, Marie noted how Breck danced, very steadily, very lightly and easily, his face utterly changeless even when he talked to his partner. Mrs. Brant-Olwin and West seemed to be enjoying their dance, but when they passed Breck, Marie noticed how Mrs. Brant-Olwin looked at him over West's

circling arm, a grave tender smile, and he smiled his
rare smile in return. "She is beginning to love him,"
Marie said to herself.

Then Mr. Granveston took her to the group that
was about Mrs. Granveston. Mrs. Dunbarton-Kent
was there and Haslett with her and Willetts was near
them. Marie spoke to Willetts, a soft "Good evening,"
and he smiled and flushed, then busied himself with
a chair which he offered to Mrs. Dunbarton-Kent.

"No, I'm getting the bridge people together," she
said. "Come along with me—I'll need you." She
patted Marie's cheek affectionately. "Have a good
time, child—West is looking after you." Then she
moved on, Haslett carrying her scarf and fan, and followed by Willetts.

West claimed the next dance, "This dance, sweet-
heart, then I must do my duty," he said, "but after
that—"

He held her as a lover would, the clasp a man longs
to make closer. But he talked very little and Marie
was grateful to him. When she stole a glance upward,
she saw that his eyes were bright and watchful; he had
great self-control, but he was excited; he was appre-
hensive, just as she was. Breck was with Mrs. Brant-
Olwin now, and Marie saw that from behind a group
of people, Walter Greene was watching them; they
were talking while they danced, in the same absorbed
way in which they had talked at dinner, Breck's head
bent to catch what she said, and her face lifted to his.

Gradually the ballroom cleared. Groups moved into

the drawing-rooms, those who did not play cards were talking together. Bella was not dancing; she was with the card-players. West brought partners to Marie, she found herself surrounded by young men, most of them mere boys. She felt at ease with them, the soldiers had been little more than boys; she danced extremely well, most of her partners wanted a second or third dance. She wondered achingly, how much longer she must continue to dance, conscious all the while of those two, Breck and Mrs. Brant-Olwin dancing together.

She allowed herself to be led into the conservatory, but then Breck brought his partner into the conservatory and they stood talking together, Mrs. Brant-Olwin's hand in his, as if he were bidding her a lingering good-by. Then Walter Greene came in and began searching for an imaginary object behind the palms. Marie burned with a sick anger: where was Breck going? To Mrs. Smith? Was he parting with Mrs. Brant-Olwin in this intimate fashion while Mrs. Smith sold Mrs. Brant-Olwin's jewels to Mrs. Dunbarton-Kent? Was all this attention to Mrs. Brant-Olwin simply a cover to the thing that was happening elsewhere?

It had been most noticeable. Mrs. Brant-Olwin had danced with others; she had made flying visits into the drawing-rooms and into the card-room, she had been everywhere at once, not forgetful that she was the guest of honor. But, when the party settled down to cards and dancing, she had danced again and again with Breck. And, save for his duty dance with Marjorie Caswell, Breck had danced with no one else. Not once throughout the entire evening had Marie been able to detect so much as a glance in *her* direction. And now he was going—where? . . . Mrs. Brant-Olwin went with him into the music-room; then Marie saw Mrs. Brant-Olwin talking to Bella in the drawing-room; Breck must have gone. . . . He had gone without a word or a look. Marie's finger-nails dug into the palms of her clenched hands. She smiled at the boy who was telling her of his football achievements and wanted to scream; from the moment she had entered Kent House she had longed and longed to believe in Breck and he had dealt her blow after blow; there was nothing left for her but allegiance to those who had shown her affection, tender consideration.

Then West took her away from her partner. They danced and Marie felt the excitement West was trying to curb. "I love you, little Marie—I love you—" he whispered. His oddly light eyes were shining; Marie knew that he was to be put off no longer.

Before the dance was over, he stopped suddenly and drew her into the conservatory. He took her to a couch behind the palms. "Now, I want my answer," he said. He put his arm about her; for the moment he looked as grim as Breck. "What is it, Marie?"

Marie had determined on her answer, but, suddenly her resolution failed her. "Monsieur—have patience and wait a little, until—"

A wild look crossed his face. "I won't wait!" He

caught her to him, kissed her again and again, pant-
ingly, her head bent back against his circling arm, his
hand beneath her chin holding her lips to his. He held
her in a grip of steel. "Are you his—or mine!" he
panted against her lips. "I *will* have—my answer!"

Marie lay perfectly still. When he lifted his head
and looked down at her, she lay motionless and with
eyes closed. She looked strange; her face looked
pinched and shadows circled her eyes.

He loosed his hold. "Marie!" he said sharply,
"look at me!"

She drew herself up slowly and pressed her hands
to her face, but she said nothing. There were long
moments of perfect silence.

West's flush had faded. "What is it?" he demanded. He looked like a man who had lost everything on a throw of the dice.

Marie drew a long breath, then she straightened.
"It is only that I know now—how greatly a man can
suffer. I wish to be forgiven that I have not understood." The color had risen slowly to her cheeks and
her eyes grew brilliant. "I have put uncertainty away
forever—and the man who is despicable. I feel
happy." She slipped her hand into his, her head bent.
"Monsieur—do you not understand—"

He had not realized until her hand lay in his.
"Marie!" He drew her to him, breathing his relief.
"I thought—I had lost!" He regained his usual self-
control. "If you are happy, I am the happiest man
alive. I know you well, little Marie—if you say you

are happy, that you have put away a man who is—unworthy—you are speaking the truth." He took her hand and kissed it; took the ring from his pocket and slipped it on her finger. "It's a Dunbarton-Kent ring, my father's gift to my mother," he said gravely.

Marie looked at it, a cluster of diamonds in an old-fashioned setting. "I am glad it is of the family," she said softly. She lifted her hand and pressed the ring to her cheek, turned her lips to it and kissed it, then looked at him with shining eyes. "To your family I shall give devotion, and you I shall try to reward as you deserve. . . . And now, Monsieur, I wish so much to go to my room for a little and think of what has happened. Will you excuse me for a little time?"

West laughed softly. "You are a quaint being, my little Marie. But you're very much of a woman: when I let myself go, loosed my hold on the cave-man, I won you; and now you want to dream a little, shut away in your room. But I want to talk of the future. When—?"

He had stopped abruptly. Marie had not noticed, but West had seen through the screen of palms: Walter Greene had come into the conservatory and was looking around him as if in search of some one. "I'll be back in a few moments, dear," West said hurriedly to Marie. "Please don't go till I come back." And he went to Walter Greene.

The detective said something to him, then they left the room together. Marie's hand went to her heart.

"In my happiness, I have forgotten!" she said half aloud.

She sprang up and started to follow them, she had almost reached the banquet-room, when some one caught her by the arm, "Wait a minute, Marie Angouleme."

CHAPTER XXXIV

IT was Bella who had stopped her. "I want to speak to you," she said coolly. She was dressed in street clothes and carried a hand-bag. She looked as if ready for a journey, and Marie remembered that Bella had said that she was leaving that night, before the party was over.

As always, Bella aroused vivid antagonism in Marie; unconsciously she brushed her arm where Bella's cold fingers had rested. "Speak quickly then, Mademoiselle—I wish to go to my room," Marie returned curtly.

There was a mocking gleam in Bella's eyes. "I was going to advise you to go—after I've told you something that will interest you. . . . Come over here behind the palms, where people won't see us."

Marie hesitated, then followed her, and Bella said without preamble. "The jewels are going to be turned over to Aunt Bulah to-night in exchange for five hundred thousand dollars." Then her lip curled in scornful amusement at Marie's suddenly widened eyes. "Mrs. Smith has done pretty well, hasn't she—behind your back? . . . Aunt Bulah got their offer last night and accepted it, and to-day, at noon, she got a note fixing the place of meeting—the cottage, at half past

two to-night. They give her permission to take two
people with her—she's going to take Haslett and a detective. . . . It'll be an interesting meeting—I thought
you'd like to know," Bella added sardonically.

Marie said nothing. She looked at Bella with eyes
that did not see her; she was thinking.

"I knew you would be interested," Bella continued
with cool enjoyment. "I thought you might like to
have this key to the cottage." And she held it out to
Marie in the palm of her hand. "You're not likely to
let her walk off with him—and five hundred thousand
dollars. It's a considerable sum, even when divided by
three."

Marie looked at the key, then she took it, but she did
not utter a word.

Bella turned to leave her, the smile still curving her
lips. "I won't keep you from 'your room' any longer.
Let us hope that somebody cleverer than either one of
you three hasn't double-crossed you. . . . Good by,
Marie Angouleme."

Marie paid no attention to her going; she held the
key tightly in her hand and stood still, thinking, her
little face carven. Five hundred thousand dollars!
And worse, an abominable scheme, theft and extortion
being brought to a successful conclusion! . . . . Had
she not said to West, "To your family I shall give
devotion—?" Marie's lips tightened and her eyes grew
hard.

She watched for a few moments, until there was no
one in the conservatory, and then she stole out and

went quickly through the banquet-room and the music-room and cut across the drawing-room into the hall. No one stopped her; in the ballroom they were dancing the last dance before supper, the waiters were arranging the chairs in the banquet-room. Mrs. Dunbarton-Kent was at the far end of the drawing-room, talking to some people who were leaving. Haslett was not with her, but Willetts stood not far away.

Marie gained the upper hall and her bedroom door, her hand was on the knob, then she paused, startled, for she heard some one speaking in her room. She recognized West's voice, raised in anger: "This is some of his work, I tell you. What is the use of asking why he did such a thing? Why has he done a dozen other unaccountable things? Aunt Bulah will never forgive this last outrage, nor will I. Let him ever dare to show his face at Kent House again!"

Marie did not go in. She stood close to the door and listened. It was Haslett who answered sternly. "The pearls have been here; they have been hidden here. There is the proof of it—look at those pieces of chamois and that ring that was overlooked. The pieces of chamois have the imprints of pearls. On that long piece is the distinct imprint of a string of pearls. The jewel-box that held the collection was bulky—the jewels were wrapped separately so they could be put into this narrow space in her trunk. . . . I'm not accusing anybody—but you can see for yourself where the jewels have been. Greene made the discovery—it was understood when he came out here, that he would make a final search. He reported to you and not to Mrs. Dunbarton-Kent, for she's at the breaking-point as it is."

West's voice was milder. "Yes, of course. But I know Marie had nothing to do with it. And there's nothing we can do—except to wait and see what happens to-night. The important thing is to get the jewels."

"But will we get them? Whoever took them out of this trunk was in a hurry, a thief relieving a thief of his plunder, it seems to me."

"Or Breck taking them from the place where he had put them," West said impatiently. "Doubtless he had his reasons for putting them there and certainly there is a good reason for his having removed them—they have to have them to-night."

It was Walter Greene's voice that cut in. "I went through that trunk when we got it from the boarding-house two months ago. There was no double bottom to it then—I'd take my oath on it. And no pistol in the trunk either. It's an amateur's job anyway, the way that lining's been taken off and put back. Any one could detect it, Miss Angouleme would have, if she ever went to the bottom of her trunk. Perhaps she might throw some light—"

"Mention Marie Angouleme's name again and I'll throw light into you!" West interrupted furiously. "I know what he's capable of—any scheme to discredit her! I've felt from the beginning that they'd do her a harm if they could. Marie has no more idea that

her trunk has been tampered with than—Aunt Bulah
has.   Marie's as honest as the day—any one who in-
timates anything else shall answer to me!"

"There, there," Haslett said.   "No one is intimating
anything.   I want to get the pearls to-night—that is
all that's worrying me.   We can do our investigating
and suspecting afterward.   Greene, put those wrappings back in the false bottom and put back the lining
as nearly as possible as you found it.   Put the ring
back too, and the pistol.   Pack the trunk just as it was
and put it back in the closet where it was.   We'll go
and you can lock the door again.   Keep close watch on
this room and Jones will be watching outside.   Willetts
is going with us to the cottage."

Haslett and West were coming out, for Marie heard
the key turn in the lock.   She sprang away from the
door.   Across the hall, Bella's door stood ajar, offering
her shelter, and Marie reached the room and closed
the door just as Haslett and West came out of her
room.   As on the train, Marie stood braced against
the door; as a farewell, the enemy had dealt her a telling blow; fastened suspicion on her, and suspicion is a
difficult thing to combat; there had been good reason
for Bella's look of triumph.

It was some moments before Marie moved from the
door.   Bella had left her light burning; the room wore
a denuded look; all the little things a woman collects
about her were gone.   Evidently Bella had taken all
her belongings.   In the confusion of preparations for
the party, who would notice how many trunks or boxes

Bella had sent away? Not Mrs. Dunbarton-Kent pre-
occupied as she was. Bella had gone and evidently not
to return.   .

For a few moments, Marie walked the floor, her
clenched hands pressed to her burning temples. She
was angrier than she had ever been in all her life before,
a profound settled rage, a consuming sense of outrage
that demanded reparation. "A double-cross," Bella
had said; well, it would be something more than that!
. . . But she must not stay here—her plan would
succeed only if she was very careful. Walter Greene
would come out of her room in a few minutes and be
on the watch; both he and Haslett suspected her; they
had always suspected her.

Marie put the key Bella had given her in her bosom.
Then she set the door ajar and looked out. The door
of her room was closed still and she saw no one, so
she stole out and went down-stairs. There they were
still at supper and Marie went to the card-room where
refreshments were being served and sat between Mrs.
Dunbarton-Kent and Mrs. Granveston. The latter
said, "My dear, your eyes look like great black saucers
and your cheeks like two flames," and Mrs. Dunbarton-Kent patted her shoulder. "Don't tire yourself
out—go to bed whenever you want to." But for her
own flushed cheeks, Mrs. Dunbarton-Kent would have
looked haggard; her eyes were strained and tired.

Then West searched her out and she danced with
him several times, smiling softly at the things he said
to her. Then, at last, Marie went to her room and

West went with her to her door. It was one o'clock. "I am most sleepy and tired," Marie sighed wearily. "I shall sleep so soundly not even thunder could wake me."

"You've promised to tell Aunt Bulah in the morning, Marie." And he kissed her.

"Yes," she promised again; her eyes were almost closed.

But when alone, with her door securely locked, Marie was wide awake. She turned on the lights and drew down the window-shades. Then, without instituting any apparent search, she made sure that there was no one hidden in her room, in her bathroom or in her clothes-closet. Then, with her closet door half closed, she opened her trunk and took from it her chauffeur's uniform, but she wasted no time in examining the trunk. She took out the pistol, hesitated, then put it back again in the trunk; her chauffeur's uniform she left on the floor of the closet. Going back into her room, she undressed, donned her night-dress, and, going to the windows, raised the shades; any one who was watching without would have a glimpse of her in night-dress and with hair down. Then she turned out the lights and got into bed.

But Marie did not stay there; in less than ten minutes she crept out cautiously and, as many and many a time when a light would have been a target for a shell, she dressed in the dark; she twisted up her hair in a knot and put on her chauffeur's uniform, even her thick leather driving gloves. Then she went to the window, crawling on her hands and knees, and when she reached it she raised her head cautiously above the sill and looked out. It was a partly dark night, some stars but no moon. The guests had not all gone yet, there were several cars collected beyond the porte-cochère.

Marie sat crouched and saw one car after the other circle the driveway and watched their tail-lights vanish in the park. There was only one car left, Mrs. Brant-Olwin's limousine, and her chauffeur was having trouble with it; he could not start it. Mrs. Brant-Olwin stood in the porte-cochère, and West tried to help the chauffeur discover what the trouble was. They both gave it up, finally, and it was arranged that West would take Mrs. Brant-Olwin home in his roadster. He brought it from the garage and Mrs. Brant-Olwin climbed in laughingly beside him; her chauffeur seated himself on the running-board. Then the roadster slipped along the driveway and disappeared in the park. Then some one turned out the light in the porte-cochère; there were darkness and quiet on that side of the house.

Marie crawled over to the door into the hall then and laid her ear to the crack. Presently several people came up-stairs and went into Mrs. Dunbarton-Kent's room; Mrs. Dunbarton-Kent and Haslett, possibly Willetts with them, Marie thought, and they would wait there probably until it was time for them to go to the cottage. It must be half past one. Greene was on watch in the hall probably, and Jones might be stationed where he could watch her windows. But she would have to risk that; she dared not delay any longer.

Marie stole back to the window and cautiously straddled the sill. She reached and laid hold of the ropes attached to the flag-pole which she had noticed in the morning. Gradually she drew herself out until she hung by her arms. There was the moment of smothering terror lest the ropes should break; they gave a little, her body sank suddenly a foot or so lower than the window-sill, a sickening sensation. But she clung to the ropes, then let herself down hand under hand, setting her teeth against the agony in her strained shoulders. The first story of the house was of rough stone, and that helped a little, roughnesses for her feet to rest on and relieve the strain on her arms. But her greatest fear was that when she reached the ground a hand would be laid on her shoulder.

She reached it at last, her feet touched sod, and she sank down in exhaustion; until her arms ached less, she could not move. She lay close pressed against the house, smothering her heavy breathing; dreading that she would be discovered.

But she was not molested. . . . Then she began her crawling progress across the lawn, across the driveway, and into the park. She crawled on hands and knees, lay flat every now and then and listened, then crawled on. Only when well within the park did she stand upright.

CHAPTER XXXV

A T exactly half past two, Mrs. Dunbarton-Kent
and Haslett and Willetts paused at the door of
the cottage. It had been arranged that Haslett should
be spokesman; the money which Mrs. Dunbarton-Kent
had carried about with her all evening was now in
Haslett's breast pocket.

Neither Haslett nor West had told Mrs. Dunbarton-
Kent about Walter Greene's discovery. Given his way,
Greene would have subjected Marie to questioning, but
West had been fiery in his objection, and Haslett had
said, in the few moments he and the detective had had
for consultation, "No, let things be. Either we get the
jewels to-night or we don't get them. If they have
been double-crossed, there is nothing we can do *to-
night*." He had emphasized the last word; in any case,
he meant that Marie should be given a bad half-hour;
she should not marry a Dunbarton-Kent, if he could
prevent it.

"I believe it's crook putting it over crook," Greene
had urged, "and that girl has played her part. I believe it's a plot—somebody took the distributor-brush
out of Mrs. Brant-Olwin's car, a neat little trick, and
it wasn't her chauffeur either, I know him, yet that
infatuated fool, West, takes Mrs. Brant-Olwin home

319

with all those diamonds on her, running the risk of a hold-up. I tried to tell him, but he wouldn't listen."

"I talked with him," Haslett had returned. "He's armed—he told me so—and he has the chauffeur with him. Either he had to take Mrs. Brant-Olwin home, or she would have to spend the night here, and I agreed with him that of the two dangers taking her home was the lesser. And we dare not tell Mrs. Dunbarton-Kent anything about it to-night—if she gets through without a collapse, we'll be fortunate." Then Haslett had sent for Jones and Willetts and had told them of Greene's discovery. "Keep a close watch on her windows, Jones, and you, Greene, keep watch up-stairs here— don't allow her to leave her room to-night."

Possibly it was those few moments during which Haslett had talked to the detectives that had given Marie the chance to escape from her room. At any rate, Mrs. Dunbarton-Kent had gone to the cottage with two men who were convinced that Mrs. Brant-Olwin's jewels would not be ransomed that night. Willetts was very certain that Marie knew nothing about the use to which her trunk had been put, yet he did not agree with West's explanation. He was puzzled. He had no hope of getting the jewels that night, however.

It was a very still night, no moon to lend shadows which would suggest life, only silence and gloom; the cottage might have been the home of the dead. "There's no light in the place," Mrs. Dunbarton-Kent whispered anxiously. "Perhaps she'll not keep the appointment?"

Haslett was desperately afraid of the effect disappointment would have upon her. "If she doesn't, we'll hear from her," he said reassuringly. "We will get the jewels eventually." He glanced over his shoulder to make certain that Willetts was directly behind him, then he tried the door. It was locked and he took the key from Mrs. Dunbarton-Kent and unlocked it and they entered. And not into darkness; there was a light there, though a dim one, and Mrs. Smith was there, a figure distinguishable even in the dimness.

It was a tremendous relief. It was apparent that the woman had prepared for their coming; the divan had been thrust aside and the big desk-table had been cleared and drawn near the fireplace and crosswise of the room, forming a barrier behind which she stood, facing them, her back to the high paneling at one side of the fireplace. On the other side of the fireplace was West's work-table and hung low above it was a green-shaded electric bulb which cast a brilliant light on the work-table, but which left the rest of the room dimly lighted. At her right, behind her, in the corner, was the huge old secretary.

They paused for the moment of inspection, Haslett and Willetts keen to discover whether there were possible hidden occupants of the room, but evidently the woman was alone, there was no furniture in the room behind which any one could hide, only the secretary and that stood flush with the walls, as it had always stood. Mrs. Dunbarton-Kent looked only at the woman, trying to decipher her in the dim light.

Mrs. Smith spoke first. "Will you kindly lock the door again and come forward—you, Madame, and the gentlemen?" There was sarcasm in the words: "Since this is a business transaction, let us consider this table a counter. . . . If you will come forward and be seated? This matter should not take long."

Her voice was thick and low, as if obstructed by her decided accent and an uncontrollable lisp, and yet it was a carrying voice, for it was so deep. As they approached her, Mrs. Dunbarton-Kent eyed her with intense interest. Her face and figure were more distinct now: she was a tall woman, superbly formed and expensively and strikingly gowned, swathed in richly embroiderd black satin. Her face was shaded by a wide-brimmed hat, its crown formed of two paradise plumes, and her nose, mouth and chin were obscured by a close-drawn veil with a silken tracery of leaves and flowers. Nevertheless, her rich tinting was apparent and the glint of light eyes between black lashes. Around her throat and shoulders was wound the magnificent sable stole which had made such a deep impression on Marie. A length of it rested on the table against which she stood.

She was a regal-looking woman, and Mrs. Dunbarton-Kent understood instantly why Marie had seen a likeness to Breck; it lay in the eyes, their ice-blue lightness shadowed by extraordinarily thick black lashes. But above them were brows that belonged to no Dunbarton-Kent, heavy black brows that almost met across the nose, marring the face, as did the mouth that was

too large and too vividly red. And yet the woman did
not look made up; her rich tinting looked natural.
She was a conspicuously handsome creature, undeniably
foreign, the vampire type par excellence, Mrs. Dunbarton-Kent thought. She looked capable of dominat-
ing any man.

When they reached the table and faced her, Haslett
spoke. "Have you the jewels here, Madame?"

"*Ici.*" Her lisp made the word a hiss. She drew
aside the length of sable stole which lay on the table,
revealing a long silver box chased with gold and on its
lid the monogram "B. O." outlined in sapphires.
"Within are the pearls—lacking a single ring which I
promise to send to you. It has not been sold, it was
merely an oversight, left behind by mistake."

"We must examine them, of course?" Haslett took
the money from his breast pocket and laid it on the
table. "Here is the money—we simply want to be assured that the pearls are genuine. . . . Will you allow
this gentleman to take them to the light over there?"

"Most certainly."

She shoved the jewel-case toward Willetts, a sweep-
ing gesture, then stood impassive, as if ennuied by the
proceeding. Her manner throughout had been faintly
scornful. Haslett motioned Mrs. Dunbarton-Kent to
a chair which she took. He stood very erect on his
side of the table, one hand in his coat pocket, touching
his pistol, his eyes now on Willetts, now on Mrs.
Smith, and occasionally he glanced about him. Mrs.
Smith's left hand hung straight at her side, she had

used her left hand when she had uncovered the jewel-case, he could not see her right arm, the sable stole covered it, but he felt very certain that her right hand held a pistol, as did his. Mrs. Dunbarton-Kent looked at Willetts; so much depended on his decision. She was crimson and tense with excitement.

Willetts was doing his work thoroughly. He examined through his glass each pearl of the magnificent rope which was the pièce de résistance of the collection, then the ear-rings, rings, and the very beautiful but shorter strings of pearls which were designed for a head ornament. In the lower tray of the jewel-case was a yellowed paper, giving in French the history of the collection and, appended to it, the receipted bill of sale and the listing of the French firm from whom Mrs. Brant-Olwin had purchased the pearls. Willetts counted them, all were there save the single pearl ring which they had discovered in Marie's trunk. Then he placed them on their cream satin couch where they gleamed faintly blue, palely lovely. No wonder Mrs. Brant-Olwin prized her pearls.

Haslett caught Willetts' nod. "Correct?" he asked.

"Yes, sir—lacking the one ring." And he brought the jewel-case to the desk-table.

"Give it to Madame," Mrs. Smith said. "I promise you the mislaid ring—for that you must take my word."

Willetts gave the jewel-case to Mrs. Dunbarton-Kent, and her hands shook as she took it; it was the end of a long and painful journey. At the same moment, Haslett shoved across the table the packet of bills. "Count them," he said, "then our transaction is ended."

Mrs. Dunbarton-Kent rose, the jewel-case held to her breast; they all three stood and watched while Mrs. Smith counted swiftly and deftly, using both hands now, her body bent forward and the bird-of-paradise plumes in her hat a-quiver. Five hundred thousand dollars in bills of large denomination, a fortune! Suddenly there was revealed in the woman the excitement of the gambler: her slim pointed fingers curved like talons caressing a victim, her cheeks glowed and the pupils of her eyes contracted; she drew her breath with a hiss. Then, the count correct, with clenched fist on the pile of bills, her body still bent forward, she flung back her head and laughed noiselessly, her features distorted, her red mouth widened repellently.

They stared at her. All three were so absorbed, all *four* were so intent, that they did not see the cupboard door of the big secretary open or see the small figure that crept out of a space barely large enough to hold a child. They did not notice until Marie appeared at Mrs. Smith's side and, with a jerk, tore the bills from beneath her hand and flung them wide. When the woman shot erect, Marie was facing her with pointed finger. "You are—!"

The woman sprang at her. She struck at Marie's mouth before her lips had formed the third word. It was Marie's involuntary swerve that diverted the blow, Mrs. Smith's clenched fist struck her shoulder with a force that flung Marie back against the secretary and crumpled her up on the floor. Then, simultaneously with Mrs. Dunbarton-Kent's shriek and before Willetts could spring across the table or Haslett circle it and reach the woman, she had backed against the paneling, had lifted her arm and fired at Marie who was struggling to rise. When they did clear the table, Mrs. Smith had been borne to the floor by an assailant who had sprung from—they did not know where.

For a moment, to Haslett and Willetts, what had happened was utterly unaccountable: the pistol struck from Mrs. Smith's hand, a shot gone wild, and a man struggling with the woman who fought with the ferocity of a tiger. . . . But Mrs. Dunbarton-Kent had seen: when she had shrieked, the paneling in the wall behind the woman had opened outward suddenly, like a door, and the man who had sprung upon her was Breck; he had reached his confederate an instant before the shot rang out and had struck the pistol upward; then they had grappled.

So much Mrs. Dunbarton-Kent saw before she dropped the jewel-case and went to Marie like a mother to her injured child. She reached Marie before Willetts did. But Marie had struggled to her feet. She put them both aside, "They—will—kill—each other—" she gasped, and staggered to the table, gasping and panting, and clung to it for support, her staring eyes on Breck and the woman. . . . Then she saw how it was and waited.

They all watched and waited, fascinated. A million

lay scattered on the floor, the jewel-case gaped wide and pearls mingled with their ransom, but they had forgotten. Though a struggle of thief with thief, had Breck struck the woman, Mrs. Dunbarton-Kent would have cried out; Haslett and Willetts would have dragged him off. But Breck had grappled with her only and now he was holding her pinioned. She had struck at him again and again, the blood trickled from a wound in his forehead, twice she had flung him off and had had him down, they had rolled over and over; her sable stole was a twisted mass beneath them, her hat had been dragged from her head, pulling away from her face its framing of raven hair, her gown was torn from throat to waist, revealing her chest. Now, when he had her pinioned and they saw the face of the creature whose strength had been almost equal to Breck's, she was strangely metamorphosed; there was a fringe of fair hair on her forehead, one eyebrow was broad and black, the other light, her cheeks were ruddled, her bosom flat and hairy.

For the first time during the struggle, Breck really saw the face of the creature who had fought with the strength of a mad-woman. He loosed his hold and sprang to his feet. *"You!"* he said.

It was not the prostrate man who answered. It was Marie who said clearly, "Yes, Monsieur—it is West Dunbarton-Kent."

CHAPTER XXXVI

ABSOLUTE silence followed their recognition of West. The surprise that held the group was too overwhelming for even an exclamation, for the first few moments too dazing even for connected thought. Breck stood motionless, disheveled, blankly staring with eyes in which vagueness was quickly changing to a glare of fury; Mrs. Dunbarton-Kent had paled until blue about the lips; Haslett had flamed scarlet, and Willetts, with neck craned and eyes bulging, simply leaned forward and stared. Marie alone showed no surprise. There was a curious radiance lighting her face. She clung to the table and looked at Breck.

West was rising from the floor. He stood upright, a strange figure in his tattered feminine finery. He neither cowered nor looked about him for a means of escape; he squared his shoulders and flung back his head. Apparently the displaced wig annoyed him, for he pulled it off and threw it on the floor. With a deft movement, he peeled off the black eyebrows, all that remained of his disguise except the black on his eyelashes and the streaks of paint on his cheeks. He flipped the eyebrow from his fingers, then folded his arms and with head high, he looked at Marie. "You've won," he said with knife-like incisiveness. He ran his

328

eye coolly over the petrified group, he did not quail even under Breck's look of fury. "Well?" he asked.

It broke the spell of stupefaction. Mrs. Dunbarton-Kent reached gropingly for a chair and sank into it, and Haslett went to her and put his hand on her shoulder, patting it. "Keep—calm—" he said thickly. His own face was ablaze, the profound anger and deep distress of an honest man. "He tried to commit murder," he said aloud to himself.

Willetts straightened suddenly. "The little *girl!*" he said. He ran his hand through his hair, half turned on his heel, then came to the right about, his ebullition of horror, amazement and anger supplanted by his detective's training: he looked at the opening in the paneling which gaped black like the entrance to an underground passage, then at the fortune which lay scattered on the floor beyond the table, and at West's pistol which lay near the secretary where Breck's upward blow had sent it. Then he moved closer to Breck, for Breck looked like a man who was ready to kill.

Marie was looking at Breck also, her eyes grown wide and distressed. She leaned over the table. "Monsieur!" she said both pleadingly and warningly, *"Monsieur!"*

Breck turned and looked at her, full into her eyes, and Willetts saw his face change. He sought his handkerchief and wiped the blood from his face, then stood perfectly calm, erect, his face like stone, his eyes, shadowed and watchful, fixed on West, who was speaking.

For, just as the detective had awakened in Willetts, his legal training had asserted itself in Haslett. He was facing West, a judge questioning a criminal: "What have you to say for yourself, West Dunbarton-Kent?" he had asked sternly.

West eyed him coolly. "Very little in extenuation. I had to gamble, even if I hung for it."

"What have you done with your fortune?"

"Mrs. Smith lost it—gambling. When I came into my money, I hit on that disguise. It saved West Dunbarton-Kent from getting into trouble. Besides it was amusing."

Haslett drew a long breath, then went on resolutely, "And finally you took to stealing to provide yourself with money."

"Exactly. I had only a few thousands left when I built Mrs. Smith's house and dug a cellar against the wall of this cottage." With a backward motion of his head he indicated the hole in the paneling. "There's the entrance to it. I could go in as West Dunbarton-Kent and emerge in the house above as Mrs. Smith. I had planned to get Mrs. Brant-Olwin's jewels and other burglaries. *I had to gamble,* I tell you!" He showed a flash of emotion.

"Were robbing your aunt and Mrs. Brant-Olwin the only crimes you have committed?"

"No. When in college, I filched whenever I could do it safely."

"Have you ever had a confederate?"

"Never. No really clever thief ever has."

"Is there any one besides these present who knows of your double life?"

"No one—not to my knowledge." He laughed shortly. "In spite of my good cousin Breck's conviction that I was keeping a dangerous woman called Smith in my pretty house up there, that I was a bad lot as to women, I've never been guilty of that sort of folly. That's one reason I've never been found out—until I ran afoul of Miss Angouleme. How long she has played me, I don't know. I fancy she made the great discovery some time this evening, hence this denouement."

At mention of Marie's name, Mrs. Dunbarton-Kent suddenly heaved herself up from her chair. She was shaking as from palsy and dead white. "West," she said in a voice that filled the room, "as you will answer before God some day—tell me what you have meant by your conduct to this child? You begged her to marry you—and you tried to kill her. You nearly killed her twice. . . . Are you insane? What are you?" Hers was a commingling of horror, anger and a complete inability to understand the man before her.

West remained utterly unmoved, except that he frowned impatiently. "You'll have to have the whole story, I suppose, before we can reach any sort of an agreement. . . . I was beautifully brought up, Aunt Bulah—I never gambled until I went to college. It took hold on me. My allowance wasn't enough—I stole so as to be able to gamble. Then I came into my money. I had an object lesson in Colfax—he went the limit openly. I thought it best to walk around the conventions. I hit upon a disguise to protect me when I went on gambling sprees. When the fever gets you, it's worse than the thirst for drink.

"It took me ten years to use up my fortune. I've never been very lucky—besides it cost me a pretty penny to keep Mrs. Smith in the proper style. She was known on every race track and in every fashionable gambling resort in the country. Then I planned to steal a fortune. I knew Mrs. Brant-Olwin and her house, every house here on the North Shore and numbers of houses in town. As Mrs. Smith, I bought that strip from Colfax's agent and built my house with its opening into the cottage. Mrs. Smith's house was my real home—I loathed the stiff grandeur of Kent House. I had my pictures and my books and my servants.

"Then Breck came home, and you turned the cottage over to him and I had to give up the use of this entrance. It was while he lived here, that he got the impression that I visited Mrs. Smith secretly—Breck can see in the dark. Well, Bella asked for the use of the cottage in the mornings—she wanted to be near Colfax, of course. Then I asked to set up my table here. That drove Breck out of the place—Bella too— Bella was afraid I would discover her affair, and Breck, like all converts to a religion in which they haven't been reared, detected what he called my 'loose living,' he thought I wanted to be near Mrs. Smith. He talked of, 'the danger of such a woman as Mrs. Smith,' and I told him to mind his own business. I knew he was

too much of a Dunbarton-Kent ever to tattle to you
and, as he was clear off the track, it didn't worry me
particularly. We had a thorough detestation of each
other, though. I'd always hated him.

"I didn't lie about my inventing, I've always wanted
to be an inventor, but the gambling fever got me too
often. I had the cottage back then and I did try to
work, but I was down to my last cent. Then came the
chance for your hundred thousand as well as the pearls.
You were all of you determined to think Breck the
thief—with his record, what use was there of his deny-
ing it? I had counted on that, for, you see, it was I
who had relieved Breck's partner, at the college party,
of her pendant. The hue and cry scared me and I put
it in his room, then let the college authorities worm
Breck's history out of me. It was effective—'once a
thief, always a thief.'

"I wanted Breck to clear from Kent House. But he
stuck. You didn't want him to decamp with the jewels,
try to raise money on them and get himself jailed and
the family disgraced, but certainly you made it a hell
for him, with your detectives and your safeguards and
your offers of a competence and forgiveness, if only
he would confess and turn the jewels over to you. He
simply set his face and waited. It annoyed me, but I
wasn't afraid of him, for I knew that he had the outcast's respect for the man who holds an assured position. He might not approve of my morals, but he
could no more conceive of *my* being a burglar than of
your being one.

"What worried me was my need of money. Nearly all of your hundred thousand was gone. I'd never played in such bad luck—I lost and lost. I was actually in need of the small sum I got for the tires and tools in your garage, besides it served my purpose—you would lay the theft to Breck. I had the jewels, but I didn't dare to dispose of them, or attempt another burglary. It was on my return from my last disastrous spree that I encountered Marie Angouleme on the train. For a few minutes I thought a Brant-Olwin detective had me. Then I knew my mistake and cleared from the train as soon as I could.

"Then, by a queer chance, she came to Kent House. I guessed who she was and why she stared at Breck; either she had seen Mrs. Smith on the train, or she had seen her elsewhere. I knew she was no detective, but exactly what she said she was—a decided danger to me, nevertheless. I tried to persuade you to turn her off, but you wouldn't. I went away myself, thinking that she would have enough of Kent House in a day or two and leave of her own accord. But when I came back, she was still there and, after talking with her, I knew that she was staying because she had fallen in love with Breck.

"After that I played against heavy odds. I was in danger, not only because I might remind Marie of Mrs. Smith, but because of Breck. He had acquired the suspicion that Mrs. Smith might have some connection with the thefts. He was watching the cottage and Mrs. Smith's house, doing some detective work of his own. He was very certain that Marie was in Mrs. Brant-Olwin's employ and was afraid that she would try to fix the thefts on him, and as certain that she meant to marry me, so he tried to frighten her away from Kent House in any safe way he could. He decided that the most effective way of scaring her was to act as if he were going to knife me, and also by intimating that my intentions toward her were not of the best, that she was in the utmost danger of some sort.

"That was the way I sized up the situation when I came back and I thought it would be as well for Mrs. Smith to show herself in her house, quite openly, as if afraid of nothing. But I had not calculated on Marie's being abroad that evening. You know what followed: Breck was watching Mrs. Smith, Marie Angouleme was hurt, and you learned of her experience on the train and, of course, deduced that Mrs. Smith was Breck's confederate. So far I was safe, but I had to get Marie Angouleme away from Kent House and by some means that would not injure me. I have never had the least desire to or intention of marrying any woman, least of all Marie Angouleme, a wife would be unendurable. I dumfounded you by my sudden passion for your little chauffeur—I thought that if anything would remove her tactfully from Kent House, a Dunbarton-Kent bent upon a misalliance such as that would do the trick! But I forgot that you sometimes do unexpected things—you deceived me by a pretended opposition, then actually brought Marie Angouleme into Kent House! I had to keep up the deceit."

Again West laughed shortly. "Then I got interested, not in Marie Angouleme, but in the game I was playing—it's the gamester in me, I suppose—I wanted to win out. She was breaking her heart over Breck, knowing that he was ostracised for some very good reason, she didn't know what, yet determined to believe in him. A woman will get a man, if she is determined enough—I meant that she shouldn't get Breck. She began to suspect that Breck was entangled with Mrs. Smith, and that Mrs. Smith was a desperate character and a wholly evil woman was Marie Angouleme's conviction; she was sick with jealousy and disgust and coming inch by inch to me. I even took her to the cottage, here, to prove to her what a convenient meeting-place Breck and Mrs. Smith had had. Her finding a hair from Mrs. Smith's sable stole and presenting it to Breck, who was in the habit of following us around, was not a denouement for which I had planned, however—so greatly do the plans of men and mice go astray! Breck is a cautious man, else he would have given *his* explanation of Marie's find. Instead, he asserted Marie's undying faith in him which served to bring her nearer to me." He shrugged. "Breck cared no more for Marie Angouleme than I did—he wanted her to clear from Kent House, and hurting her was one way of accomplishing his purpose. He thought that 'the little detective' was trying to fasten something on him and he taunted her—he thought he was taunting me as well. Undoubtedly I had set up an establishment for Mrs. Smith, nevertheless I was determined to marry Marie Angouleme, she being a later infatuation—such was Breck's judgment of me."

West's look and tone showed scornful amusement. "The situation had its comic side: you, Aunt Bulah, doing all you could to forward a match; Marie Angouleme hanging fire and altogether at sea about everything and every one and with the best of intentions all around; Bella convinced that Marie Angouleme, Breck and Mrs. Smith were responsible for the thefts and that Marie Angouleme had engaged the sympathy and, she was afraid, the affections of Allen Colfax; Breck certain that Marie Angouleme was a spy acting for Mrs. Brant-Olwin and a vital danger to him and as certain that she was going to marry West Dunbarton-Kent; and all three of us, Breck, Bella and West, bent upon the difficult task of driving Marie Angouleme away from Kent House without danger to ourselves. Funny!"

His lips had twisted in a smile. Then he grew grave. "Meantime, I was desperate for money. It was a big relief to me when I knew that you were headed in the right direction. The pearls ransomed, and I would be safe. Mrs. Smith could disappear forever and some other disguise serve me. Breck could not prove his innocence, you would be absolutely certain that his confederate had double-crossed him and had made off with the money—he would take the sum you would give him and clear from Kent House— he would never jeopardize his heirship by making a public row. And Marie Angouleme would have no hold on me—I could discredit her. I had spent a few hours over her trunk. The cellar of my house is damp and I had had the pearls hidden there for weeks wrapped in chamois-skin and cotton wool. I put the wrappings and one ring into her trunk. You might lay the thing to Breck, but Haslett would not, he never had any faith in Marie Angouleme. With five hundred thousand in my pocket, I too could lose faith in my fiancée. I would be done with Marie Angouleme— I would have won."

Throughout, he had addressed himself to Mrs. Dunbarton-Kent, had looked only at her. Now he turned to Marie, who still clung to the table, silent and motionless as were the others. His bow and his smile were ironical. "As it has turned out—I have lost and you have won, Marie Angouleme. All the detectives and all the thieves in the world, rolled into one, are not the equal of one perfectly well-intentioned and blundering young woman."

CHAPTER XXXVII

THERE was as complete a silence after West's brazen confession as there had been after their recognition of him. His utterly callous, perfectly assured recital was almost as astounding a revelation as the metamorphosis of Mrs. Smith into West Dunbarton-Kent.

West broke the silence. "I have made a clean breast of it, Aunt Bulah," he said easily. "So far as you are concerned, it is simply one nephew taking the place of the other—you'll want to guard the family name just the same. My falling into the clutches of the law would create even a bigger sensation than Breck's arrest would have caused. You'll want to avoid that. You have the pearls and have not had to pay for them —some little gain to you—now what arrangement are you going to make with me? I told you that I am penniless and, from what I have told you of myself, you realize that I will stop at nothing, not even murder, as you have seen. You were willing to pay Breck to go to Europe and cease from troubling his family—what will you pay me for doing the same thing?"

Mrs. Dunbarton-Kent was not given an opportunity to answer. Breck had started forward, but Marie spoke first. She had moved along the table until she

339

was directly opposite West. She brought her little
fist down on the table; her face was drawn and so white
that it looked blue. "*No!*" she said with passionate
intensity. "It is *I* shall decide this matter. Until to-
night, when I would give you no answer and then you
attempted to play the part of the 'cave man,' I was
utterly ignorant of the truth. In the pressure of your
fingers beneath my chin, there was the *feeling* of Mrs.
Smith, but, more certainly than that, *there was upon
your breath that same cachou.* I knew instantly that
you were that same creature of the train! I understood
everything, and from that moment I deceived you. I
accepted you happily—I was so *happy* that at last I
knew the truth. I vowed that I would be revenged
upon you—did I not tell you that I would try to reward you as you deserved? I learned of this meeting
to-night and its purpose. I planned to unmask you as
soon as the jewels would be safely in Mrs. Dunbarton-
Kent's hands. I escaped from my room and secreted
myself here. I saw you enter the cottage as West Dunbarton-Kent and go hastily through that wall which
you closed behind you. Very soon you returned as
Mrs. Smith. You were in great haste—you were late
from taking Mrs. Brant-Olwin to her home, a little
plan of yours to absent yourself from Kent House
without causing suspicion. . . . West Dunbarton-
Kent, by revealing your frightfulness you hope to terrify your family. For such as you, prison is the only
place. I intend that you shall suffer the full penalty of
the law." She shook her clinched fist at him, a white

epitome of hate. "I shall be revenged upon you to the utmost—you *thief and one who would have murdered!*"

They were all looking at her: Willetts' hands came together in noiseless applause; Haslett with full sympathy, but with a clear understanding of what it would mean to the Dunbarton-Kent family should she carry out her threat; Mrs. Dunbarton-Kent with grim bleakness, the full realization of a necessary public as well as a private disgrace. Breck had paused on his forward step; he was looking observantly at Marie, at her clenched left hand and at her right arm which hung helpless.

Of them all, West was the least moved. His brows lowered slightly, that was all. "When you cool down, Marie Angouleme, you'll think differently," he said with perfect assurance. "Your anger is natural enough, but you'd as soon cut off your hand as to advertise Breck's connection with this affair. He's a jail-bird—his history would be public property, I assure you."

Breck did not move or speak; again it was Marie who flared at him. "What is Breck Dunbarton-Kent to me! From you I have had nothing but ugly deceit, and from him persistent scorn. This family—what is it to me! I do not belong to it!" She struck her fist on the table, her voice suddenly ringingly triumphant. "I said, West Dunbarton-Kent, that *I would be revenged upon you to the utmost!* Do you suppose that, before I hid myself here, I would not carefully make

arrangements? That I would not telephone to the
house of Mrs. Brant-Olwin and talk with her detective? That I have not allowed you to consume time in
order that your capture may be the more certain? The
reward offered by Mrs. Brant-Olwin will make me
rich!" She looked across at him, laughing a little in
her triumph, queer laughter coming from so white a
face. "Whether you go, or whether you remain, your
fate is as certain. Very truly I have *won*, Monsieur
West Dunbarton-Kent!"

Marie was right: West had gambled on his last
chance and had lost. Her scorn of Breck had rung so
true, her revenge triumphant was so ringingly clear, so
amusedly certain. West had shrunk: a high-handed,
perfectly assured, nonchalant gamester, a conscience-
less, clever man-of-the-world, an artist and actor of
talent perverted. West Dunbarton-Kent changing,
while they looked on, into the hunted criminal. His
body seemed to shrink and his stature lessen; his
shoulders lifted and rounded, his neck shortened, his
jaw protruded and sharp lines narrowed his forehead;
his eyes, grown furtive and gleaming, peered from a
face that belonged rightfully in a rogue's gallery. The
metamorphosis was more astounding and far more
painful than the superficial change wrought by a disguise removed; that had been a superb woman changed
into an erect, arrogant, well-featured man; this was a
revelation of mental deformity, revolting, sickening.

He was looking from this side to that, swiftly considering. He moved sidewise toward the black open-

ing in the paneling, glancing into the darkness, glancing over his shoulder at the cottage door, listening the while. He looked at none of them, yet observed them with fitful glances. Then he decided: with a crawling leap, he cleared the far end of the table and ran across the room, catching up some of the scattered bills as he went. He climbed the book-shelves as one would a ladder. He opened a casement window and crawled through it. They all turned and watched him; his body disappeared, for a brief moment they saw his hands clinging to the sill—then they disappeared. . . . The breeze from the open casement stirred the bills that lay on the floor, and, long remembered by them all, from without, a cricket began to chirp insistantly; it had been startled into silence, now it rubbed its wings together again, gleefully—its disturber had faded into the darkness.

Then Marie said softly and sweetly, but in a voice they all heard. "It was necessary. He had but one fear—the law." Then, suddenly, she drooped against the table and, before Breck could reach her, she slid to the floor, a huddled heap.

Willetts had sprung toward her, but Breck had leaped to the table and had reached her first. He lifted her up. "She has fainted," he said more to himself than to the others. "I ought not to have let her do it, but it was the only way."

He held her carefully, guarding her oddly twisted, hanging arm; stood upright and, over her head which drooped against his breast, he looked at the three who had crowded close; at Haslett and Willetts, who did not know what to do next, at Mrs. Dunbarton-Kent, who was saying in quivering agitation, "Give her to me, Breck—they may come at any moment. . . . My poor child! And you—" She looked old and broken, her head shook spasmodically.

"No one is coming," Breck said briefly. "She was acting—she beat him at his own game and without any one's help. You're indebted to *her* for your release from that man. I've suspected Mrs. Smith for some time. I've searched her house several times. I've watched it night after night, under difficulties. I searched it again to-night. She was not there and no clue to the jewels. I went a second time to her bedroom and found it locked. There were movements and I knew that she must have come by some secret way. When there was silence again, I knew she had gone, and then it came to me. I got into the room and searched every inch of it and I found it, a concealed stairway down into the cellar. Then I heard voices—there was a gap in the cellar wall and only the paneling between me and the cottage—the paneling was a door which was closed. I opened it in time, thank God!" He had spoken very rapidly; he gave his orders tersely. "Gather up that stuff on the floor, Willetts, and I'll tell you what to do with it. And you, Mr. Haslett, look after my aunt—she's ill. The trouble here is a dislocated shoulder, I think,—I didn't notice till she used her left hand. The sooner we get to the house the better."

CHAPTER XXXVIII

ONE afternoon, three weeks later, Burton Haslett walked briskly along the Lower Road until he neared the entrance to Colfax Hall. Then he walked more slowly, his eyes keenly observant. The old brick pile was being repaired, there was scaffolding across its front and piles of lumber on its unkept lawn.

He went on then to Kent House entrance, stopped there and stood gazing. Mrs. Smith's house had disappeared; where it had stood was a heap of blackened debris; the young leaves on the trees which had stood nearest to the house were seared and shriveled. Burning timbers from the house above had fallen on the cottage roof; there was nothing left of the cottage but its blackened walls.

Haslett walked up the road and inspected the ruins more closely. All the woodwork of the place had been burned away, only stone left, the walls of the cottage and the park wall against which the cottage had been built. In the wall of the cottage where it abutted on the park wall was a gap which had not been caused by the fire. The gap gave into darkness, evidently into the cellar of the house above. The heaped ashes and dead cinders had been swept aside from this opening, evidently people had explored the cellar. . . . Haslett

looked his fill, then went on, up through the park; he
was on his way to Kent House.

Gibbs, looking utterly immune to either tragedy or
comedy, intent on his Roman nose, as usual, received
the Dunbarton-Kent lawyer and relieved him of his hat
and cane. "Mrs. Dunbarton-Kent will receive you in
the library, sir."

"It has been a warm day, Gibbs."

"Yes, sir."

Haslett went on into the library, wondering how
much Buckingham Gibbs knew? Almost as much as
he himself did—perhaps more. But Gibbs' knowledge,
whatever its extent, would never reach the public ear;
he had known Gibbs for some fifteen years.

Mrs. Dunbarton-Kent was seated, from winter habit,
before the fireplace whose only warmth now was its
shining brass. She looked older, her huge cheeks
sagged more and, at times, the jerking of her head, a
relic of shock and prolonged nerve strain, was very
noticeable. "So you chose to walk from the station—
I suppose you wanted to see the ruins again," she said
with her usual abruptness. She eyed him keenly.
"You've had some word from him, of course. I knew
it as soon as you telephoned that you were coming out."

The spasmodic jerking of her head was very marked
now; excitement was a bad thing for Bulah Dunbarton-
Kent; her physician had talked with her lawyer. "It's
good news," Haslett said quickly. "He's out of the
country—he writes from Paris:"

"He wants money, I suppose?" she said grimly.

"Yes—an allowance. He has seen our New York papers and he realizes that Miss Angouleme tricked him."

Mrs. Dunbarton-Kent's red-brown eyes flashed. *"Not one cent!* Notify him that we've turned him over to the police."

"That was Breck's advice, but we wanted your sanction." Haslett took a paper from his pocket. "Breck advises that I send him this letter: 'Your communication received. I am instructed to notify you that the Dunbarton-Kent family have given your present address to the police. Mrs. Smith is charged with theft and arson, and you are implicated with her. Wherever you are, she is supposed to be. Furthermore, competent witnesses have made statements which have been appended to Mr. Richard Dunbarton-Kent's will. So far as your family is concerned, you have ceased to exist.' . . . I agreed with Breck that it is the only way to deal with him."

Mrs. Dunbarton-Kent nodded. "Take all hope away from him. He'll gamble away what money he has with him, then he'll drift—out. It's the end he deserves. . . . I mean to put him out of my mind."

"That's right, Mrs. Dunbarton-Kent. Willetts, Greene and Jones,—all are pleased over what you have done for them. Willetts is the only one who knows the whole truth, Greene and Jones think as the public does, that West was entangled with Mrs. Smith and that he ran away to escape the scandal. Willetts is devoted to you and to Miss Angouleme, and he admires

Breck tremendously—he feels that he wants to make amends for his suspicions of Breck. He will never speak unless the Dunbarton-Kent interests demand it. He's trustworthy."

"Breck says he is, Haslett." She spoke Breck's name with respect and contrition.

There was the same note in Haslett's confession: "I am a poor judge of character, your husband often said so, Mrs. Dunbarton-Kent. I should have judged Breck more correctly. I apologized to him, but he cut me off: 'Forget it,' he said. 'My uncle taught me the wicked folly of being dishonest. I have never had any desire to steal from that day to this. We will not refer to the matter again.'"

"The same thing he said to me, Haslett, when I begged him to forgive me. 'Don't think about it, Aunt Bulah—we'll never speak of it again. Just remember that my uncle was a good judge of character.' He's been wonderful, Haslett, the way he has taken charge of things here, advising me what to do about Bella and Colfax, and other things. I feel like weeping from shame and pity when I look at that carven face of his. He looks like a man who has been tortured to death— whose features have settled into calm after death. If only I could see him smiling and happy, I would feel that I was—forgiven—" Her lips quivered too much for her to go on.

Haslett looked very grave. Mrs. Dunbarton-Kent's future depended so much upon relief from anxiety and strain. And she was not happy, far from it. "He is a

strangely quiet and self-contained man, Mrs. Dunbarton-Kent. And very capable. I have been endlessly
grateful to him for insisting that Mrs. Brant-Olwin's
pearls must be put back at once in the hole in the cellar
where West had had them, and that her detectives
should be allowed to make the discovery. As it turned
out, West's setting fire to his house before he made
off was a most fortunate thing, for it disclosed the entrance to the cellar and brought Mrs. Brant-Olwin's
detectives to the scene. Breck saved the day for us."

"And Marie," Mrs. Dunbarton-Kent said jealously.

"Yes, indeed—Miss Angouleme too," Haslett agreed
promptly. Her love for Marie was Mrs. Dunbarton-
Kent's greatest joy, and Haslett grasped at the safe
subject. "How is she?"

"Her shoulder is well again," she said more brightly.
"You'd gone to the fire, so you didn't hear what she
said to the doctor. She had all her wits about her!
When Jones brought that jabbering idiot over from
Huntington, she saved me and Breck from any explanation. 'Monsieur, Doctor,' she said, 'once before
my head fell upon a stone, now my shoulder fell against
a desk, so again you must mend me.' That little
sycophant was all deference to her this time," Mrs.
Dunbarton-Kent said with grim amusement. " 'The
little adopted daughter,' as he called her. He was
quite right in that—that's what she is, my daughter."
Her voice sank again. "I'd like to see her happy too."

Haslett rarely asked Mrs. Dunbarton-Kent an abrupt
question, but it was a thing he had pondered. If Breck

should marry Marie Angouleme and settle down happily with Mrs. Dunbarton-Kent at Kent House, Mrs. Dunbarton-Kent's way would be smooth; she would have companionship, and Breck would be an efficient manager of the estate. "Does she love Breck?" he asked.

Her face clouded. "I'm not certain. I know she never cared for that—for West. I've told her his history, as we regard it now, an experience that has made a noble man of Breck. But all she said was, 'It is a most sad history, Madame—his face shows how he has suffered.' That was all. She is just the same devoted child to me, sweet, but so grave. She never speaks of Breck, and nothing would induce me to ask her a question or meddle—I've had one severe lesson in matchmaking. She and Breck talk, at meals and so on, but it's plain that they avoid each other. I'd like to believe that she's happy—I know Breck is not—he's wretched, for, Haslett, I'm certain he loves a woman, but it's not my little Marie—it's Mrs. Brant-Olwin."

"Mrs. Brant-Olwin!" Haslett exclaimed.

"Yes. They are devoted to each other—he goes to see her every day. They've been devoted to each other ever since they met—at my dinner. What troubles Breck is that history of his—he will have to tell her and he may lose her."

Haslett had been surprisedly pondering. He said with decision. "She grew up in a rough country, his early history won't matter to her. If she loves him, she will marry him."

"Yes, like Bella. She threw everything to the winds
and married Colfax. Willing to risk life with him in a
Brooklyn flat—do her own work and all that! Bella!
I must say the letter she pinned to my pillow before she
eloped changed my opinion of Bella somewhat—she's a
woman after all. I suppose we're all alike, given the
chance." She was thinking of Marie. She did not
know, but she was very certain that her child loved
Breck as dearly as she had loved Richard Dunbarton-
Kent. Her heart ached over Marie.

"I think Bella and Colfax will come out all right,"
Haslett said hopefully. "I've thought so ever since I
went to see them and took Bella your forgiveness and
your offer to make them comfortable in Colfax Hall
and give them an income *provided* Colfax made good.
I told you how Bella broke down and Colfax vowed
he would make good. Colfax is not a bad sort—what
he needs is some one to keep him straight. He told
me he'd loved Bella ever since she was a little girl and
that he went to pieces because of a quarrel they had.
Evidently she loved him throughout that wild career of
his, for she has married him, finally. It shows that
there is something fine in Bella. When I told them
what Miss Angouleme had done for the family and of
the wrong we'd done Breck, they were terribly upset.
Colfax said, 'I told you, Bell! I knew she was a good
honest little thing. That child an adventuress and trying to inveigle me! You write to her and beg her
pardon.' Bella said she would—did she?"

"Yes, not a bad sort of letter, stiff but evidently

ashamed of herself. I doubt if Marie and Bella will ever enjoy each other, but if Bella will make a man of Allen Colfax, it's all I'll ever ask of her."

"Well, on the whole, things have turned out better than I expected, Mrs. Dunbarton-Kent."

"Yes," she agreed half-heartedly. "I don't mean that I am ungrateful—I'd like to see Breck looking happier, and my little Marie. . . . You had better stay to dinner, Haslett."

"Thank you—no. I must get back to town. . . . And, Mrs. Dunbarton-Kent, remember that Marie Angouleme is really your daughter now, you have legally adopted her—you have that joy. She'll marry happily some day. And, if Breck marries Mrs. Brant-Olwin, he will be near you—you won't be losing him."

"All very true," Mrs. Dunbarton-Kent said grimly. "We all want to juggle with fate, however."

CHAPTER XXXIX

THAT evening, as usual, they took their coffee in the library, Mrs. Dunbarton-Kent, Marie and Breck, Mrs. Dunbarton-Kent seated in her huge chair, Marie in the corner of the divan, Breck backed against the mantel-shelf.

Marie had set her cup down and was idly platting into little folds the red chiffon of her gown, a fold for each thought: only three months ago, she had seen, for the first time, Breck standing like that. Three months? A lifetime! . . . He had grown thinner. He looked so wretched always, when he came back from visiting Mrs. Brant-Olwin. But to-night he looked better, as if he was excited. . . . Evidently the bad days were over for him. Mrs. Brant-Olwin was a real woman—to-day he had told her and she had understood. They were happy. . . . It was very true that one made or marred one's own life. Way down in her own heart, she had never really believed ill of him; she loved him. It was jealousy of Mrs. Smith—a creature who had never existed—that had led her to strange imaginings. Jealousy distorted everything, bred suspicion, destroyed faith. . . . She had tried to atone by helping to clear his name, by serving his family, by driving West out in a way that had saved the

353

family from exposure. . . . But he had turned to
another. It was a bitter punishment.

Marie's hands came together, gripping. Then she
stiffened, for Breck was speaking. He had said
abruptly, "I am going away, Aunt Bulah. . . . Mrs.
Brant-Olwin has an immense tract in Arizona. She
wants me to make salable property of it, irrigate it and
divide it up into ranches. It's work I can do. It will
be just as well for me to live at a distance, there is
always the likelihood of the past's flying up and hitting
you, through me. I have been considering it for the
last two weeks—to-day I decided. Mrs. Brant-Olwin
says that she will come to see you and explain."

There was perfect silence for a moment. In the
days past, had West made such an announcement, Mrs.
Dunbarton-Kent would have said, "And when are you
and Mrs. Brant-Olwin to be married?"

But of Breck she asked no questions: there were few
people whom Mrs. Dunbarton-Kent respected as profoundly as she did Breck, or of whom she stood in
greater awe, or over whom her heart ached more. And
there was her child to be considered—Marie first of
all. Breck and Mrs. Brant-Olwin had decided wisely;
Mrs. Brant-Olwin belonged in the West. They would
go west and be married and live there; Breck would be
happy. And, for her little Marie, it would be far
better. Breck and Mrs. Brant-Olwin in Mrs. Brant-
Olwin's great house, happy, and Marie looking on!
This was the best solution of a wretched situation.

"It is for you to decide, Breck," she said in the af-

fectionate way Marie knew so well. "I have hoped
that you would stay at Kent House,"—there was a
slight quiver in her voice—"find your happiness here
and, in a way, take the place of my dear husband. I
am not in the least afraid of your past—it's made the
finer man of you. All that will ever worry me is that
I misjudged you. . . . But you know best in which
direction your happiness lies. And, Breck, I have
already made arrangements, I want you and Bella to
live in comfort: there are two millions of your uncle's
money that I have saved for you children. I have
settled one million on Bella and with a proviso, Colfax
—the other million is yours, without any proviso.
West doesn't exist."

Breck had flushed to crimson. He held out his hand
to his aunt. "Thank you, Aunt Bulah. I—don't
know how—to thank you enough. . . . It's what
you've said—not the money—" he said jerkily. "Mrs.
Brant-Olwin has been—kind—too. I'll explain—before I go away—I *can't*—now—" And he left the
room. He went outside, for they heard him close the
hall door. The window-shades were up and it was a
white night, no haze and a radiant moon. Marie saw
Breck pass the windows; he was going into the park.

Mrs. Dunbarton-Kent was looking at her child. The
light fell full on Marie's face; she was looking at Breck
through the window. There are times when misery
invites sympathy; there are other times when sympathy
would be an added hurt. Mrs. Dunbarton-Kent rose
and left the room as noiselessly as possible.

Marie did not know how long she sat alone but Gibbs knew. He appeared with his tray. Contrary to all custom, he bore on it the evening paper. He took Marie's coffee cup, but that did not stir her from her frozen attitude. The tinkle of the spoon which Gibbs, also contrary to custom, dropped on the floor did startle her. She looked at him with wide vague eyes.

"I beg pardon, Miss," Gibbs said, "but have you seen the evening paper, Miss?"

For the first time Gibbs had asked her a question. If Marie had been in a condition to notice, she would have been astonished. "No—" she returned vaguely. She looked, without seeing, at the folded paper Gibbs had placed on her knee.

"There is a little notice of yourself there, Miss—of your adoption—just under the paragraph on Mrs. Brant-Olwin," and Gibbs indicated very exactly the "paragraph on Mrs. Brant-Olwin," by pointing at it. "I have been in the service of the family for fifteen years, Miss, and I make free to offer—"

Just what Gibbs was making free to offer, Marie did not hear, for she had read the first lines of the paragraph on Mrs. Brant-Olwin, and, if Gibbs had not drawn hastily to one side, he might have fared as badly as on a previous occasion, a little experience which he had not mentioned in the kitchen. For Marie had risen as if lifted by wings. She passed through the library and then the hall and through the outer door like a winged Mercury. From the window, Gibbs watched her flight into the park and smiled.

CHAPTER XL

M ONSIER—BRECK?" Marie said.
Breck turned with a convulsive start. He
had been looking at the ruins of the cottage. But only
for a few moments, for he had come down slowly
through the park and Marie had flown. He was so
astounded that he said nothing.

Marie came nearer, into the clear moonlight. Her
black curls were loose on her white shoulders, her
cheeks vivid, brows knitted, intent upon a purpose.
"I ran—to ask you—a question—"

"Yes—" Breck said vaguely.

Marie came close. He looked very white, very expressionless. "Why is it that you leave—Kent House,
Monsieur?"

He looked less blank; the color began to darken his
face. "Because—I can't *endure* it here!"

"Because you love Mrs. Brant-Olwin and she is to
marry Monsieur Wakefield?" tensely.

"*I* love *Mrs. Brant-Olwin!* No!"

Marie's whole being relaxed into utter relief. She
breathed words that sounded like a prayer. She bent
her head, her little hands lifted to her breast, palms
together, the attitude of prayer.

Breck looked at her and the muscles in his cheeks began to twitch. Suddenly his hands settled on her shoulders. "Marie! That man was not lying then—just to hurt you? You have faith in me?"

She looked at him with shining eyes. "It is true. I have loved you from that very first day—it was ugly jealousy that made me strange. It was for your sake that I drove him away without exposure to your family."

"*And I have loved you!* I've feared for you and agonized over you—I thought you had turned away from me forever!" His face was a-quiver, like a glassy pool whose stillness has been suddenly broken by a fallen branch. He caught her up, held her as one would a rescued child, clasped close, rejoiced over. He kissed her, eyes and cheeks, lips and throat; there were unguessed depths of emotion and devotion in Breck Dunbarton-Kent, as in Bella, and a world of love and tenderness in little Marie. Her arms about his neck held him strained; for a few moments life ended—then was born again.

Breck put her down lingeringly. "I want my arms about you!" he said. He stripped off his coat and laid it across a gap in the wall of the cottage. He lifted her up and set her on her throne, full in the moonlight; put his arms about her and laid his head in her lap. "I have longed and *longed* for you—ever since the time you said, 'Ah, Monsieur, now I know why you look so sad!' . . . Little one, I was a thief because I didn't know any better than to steal. You understand, don't you—just ignorance, just wrong

training? That reform school! Why, it was only a
place where I was made to feel that I was an outcast.
And the preacher who took me from it and used me
to clean his stable and chop his wood—at prayers each
day he used to ask God to have mercy on the sinner in
their midst and he would as soon have touched a toad
as my hand. But my uncle! He brought love and
understanding. I had no moral sense—I barely knew
how to read and write. He was a big-hearted man and
a courtly gentleman. He told me my mind was good
and he bought me books. He said I had in me every
good quality he possessed, and that he hoped I had
none of his bad ones. He made me laugh and feel
happy. Whenever he came he shook hands with me.
I loved him—I worshiped him. When they let me
out, he took me to the Maine woods with him, to hunt
and fish. Think what that was to me, a gamin grown
into a jail-bird of eighteen! He sent me to a boys'
school—he told me he would send me to college, if I
had it in me. I was older than the other boys—I
worked like mad to catch up—ambition was born in
me. Then he put me in college—how I worked. Then,
my first vacation, he brought me here. He told me
then who I was, his nephew, a Dunbarton-Kent. For
hours, here in the cottage, we talked together, and I
longed and *resolved* to become a worthy Dunbarton-
Kent. I loved Kent House—I was a Dunbarton-Kent,
part of it. . . . Then I lost—him—" He caught his
breath in a sob. "It was—hard. . . . I loved him
so—"

Marie stroked his bent head. "Do not tell me any
more, dear one—I know everything, and I understand."

"I *must!* I've *longed* so to tell you. . . . Aunt
Bulah wrote me to go on in college and try to do well.
She hadn't much faith in me, and I worked the harder
because of it. I stood well in college. But no one
knew my real history. Then West did to me what he
said. Every one shunned me—I went through hell. I
went to France to get away from it. . . . It helped me
though. It got worked into my marrow that Ger-
many's cause was that of the world thief. When they
took me prisoner, I felt that they imprisoned me because I had done *right*. There's a vast difference.
And I lived through it somehow, to come back to Kent
House. It was my dream, to come back to the home
of my family and make myself respected and loved.
Aunt Bulah took me in for my uncle's sake. . . . But
West was here—*that*—!"

"Monsieur! Breck, do not!" Marie begged.

He calmed instantly. "I will not, dear. I should
not denounce, for I know them so well, those who have
allowed an obsession to eat away their souls. And who
knows? When he has reached the depths, perhaps even
he will find his soul. It was my uncle's belief that
there is no depravity that can not be cured, that the
spark of regeneration lies in every criminal, however
great his criminality. My uncle's belief is the right
one—it redeemed me: optimism vivifies life, pessimism
destroys it.

"But, Marie, there are some things I must tell you. West was right in some of his deductions: I did threaten him; I did know that he visited Mrs. Smith's house secretly; I did think her a bad woman, even before I became certain that she was the thief; I did watch her house and search it several times without results. But, Marie, about some things he was *wrong* —he judged me by himself. I loved you throughout, utterly and unselfishly and without hope.

"For your sake, I tried to frighten him, but he held the key to his secret and I did not—he himself was Mrs. Smith. I thought him the kind of man who would mislead you if he could. I did want you to leave Kent House, but for your own sake, not for mine. I *couldn't* tell you what was the trouble at Kent House, I was so *desperately* afraid that if you were friendly to me they would think that you were my confederate. I knew that at first you pitied me, I loved you for coming to ask me what ailed me, you child with a big heart! I forgot caution and gave you the little spaniel, you were so lonely and distressed, and I begged you to leave Kent House. But I couldn't explain—it wasn't safe. I had to behave like a dumb fool, or something worse. Then I was afraid that my gift would get you into trouble and I took the spaniel away. I gave you the pistol both as a protection and a warning.

"Then they took you into Kent House and I knew some one had told you my history, as *they* regarded it, and that you abhorred me. But I went on trying to guard you. I followed you and West about and I made him understand that, if he hurt you, I'd kill him. Just once the misery I was in got the better of me—that morning at the cottage. You were accusing me of meeting Mrs. Smith, his woman, and I felt that no matter what I said, you would not believe me. I flung at him the thing I would have given anything to believe, that you had and always would have faith in me.

"And, Marie, I did make one friend. He knew my history, he knows many things he is supposed not to know—he's an observer and, too, he knew my uncle. Gibbs was my friend. He helped me—he used to let me in and out of Kent House. He played his part well. He kept the servants under his thumb, he even used you to frighten them, making them believe you were a detective sent by Mrs. Brant-Olwin. But Gibbs liked you and watched over you. He did not like West—he used to tell me that he was certain that you did not care for West, but that you loved Aunt Bulah. When I decided to leave Kent House and give all my time to finding the thief, Gibbs promised to watch over you. I went the night before the party; the next afternoon Gibbs telephoned me Mrs. Smith had come back. But for Gibbs, I don't know what I should have done.

"And, Marie, Mrs. Brant-Olwin has been like a sister to me. You see, I knew Ward Wakefield well when we were in France. He is a brilliant young lawyer and I thought that should I be arrested, he would help me, so I went to see him. I told him nothing about my affairs, but he told me, as a great secret, that he was engaged to Mrs. Brant-Olwin and that they meant to surprise society. They are very much in love with each other. While she was in Florida, she used to make stolen visits to New York to see him, and it was on one of those visits to his office that you met her and she sent you to Kent House, and not as a joke. She has told me that you were so young and pretty and she knew that Aunt Bulah would take an interest in you. Little she knew to what she was sending you. . . . Gibbs had telephoned me to come back and, as Ward was not feeling well, I took his place at the dinner. I wanted Mrs. Brant-Olwin to like me—I liked her as soon as I met her, she is wholesome, genuine. I was Ward's friend and I knew their secret, and that made her my friend too, but, Marie, from beginning to end and world without end, you have been my love. I hadn't a hope left, I thought you still abhorred me, you scarcely looked at me or spoke to me, and I couldn't endure it. And though I have my arms about you now, it still seems a miracle! . . . But I have made you cry—I didn't mean to make you cry, dear—"

Marie's thoughts were as disjointed as her words. "It was such suffering for you! . . . I suffered too—my heart ached and was broken—I wished these last three weeks to be dead. . . . Mr. Gibbs is a noble man, so long as I live will I love him. Purposely he sent me to you to-night, by showing to me about Mrs. Brant-Olwin in the paper. I know it now. . . . In the past which will never come back, I was wicked with jealously over a bad woman who did not exist. Never again will I be jealous like that without reason!"

A graver man than Breck would have succumbed to Marie's jumbled English. For the first time in her knowledge of Breck, Marie heard him laugh, clearly and happily. He laughed and held her the closer, and grew grave again. He dried her tears by kissing them away. "And I'll love you with all the love and gratitude there is in me as long as I live. I'll be a true husband to you, Marie."

It was a glimpse into the future, and Marie said softly, "And you wish most of all to live with me here in this beautiful Kent House—as did your uncle?"

"Yes!" he said deeply.

She put her arms about his neck. "Then lift me down from here, please—Breck—and we will go and tell it to Mrs. Dunbarton-Kent at once. I think she suffers alone in her room."

From the library window, Gibbs saw them coming up through the park and into the full moonlight, hand in hand.

THE END